LEVEL SEVEN

WILLIAM LEDBETTER

LEVEL SEVEN

Text Copyright © 2025 by William Ledbetter.

Edited by Holly Lyn Walrath. Cover design by Audible, used with permission.

Published by Interstellar Flight Press

Houston, Texas.

www.interstellarflightpress.com

ISBN (eBook): 978-1-953736-40-6

ISBN (Paperback): 978-1-953736-41-3

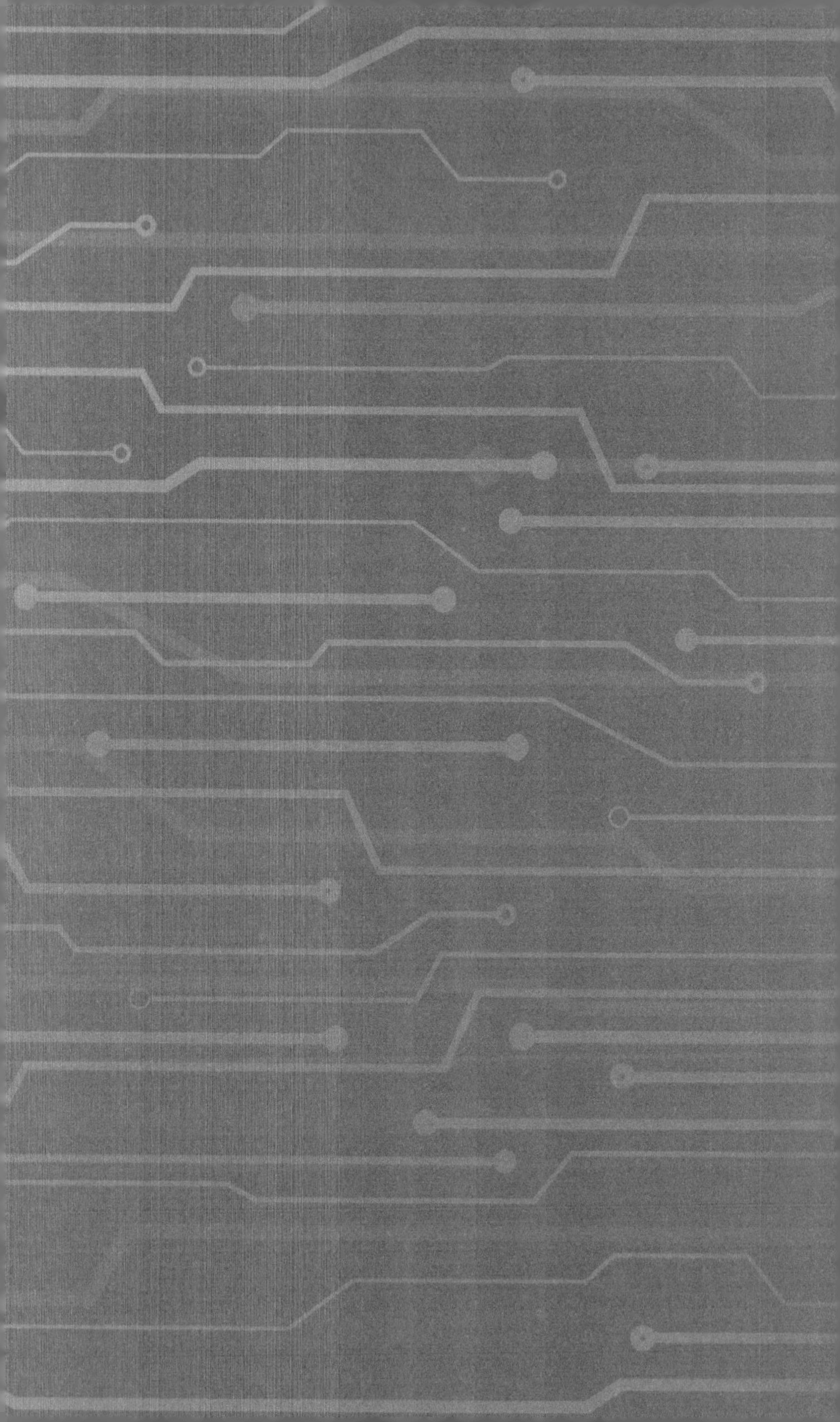

AT THREE HUNDRED and forty meters long, the asteroid had been one of the smallest on Abby Gibson's list of those located in the main belt, but as she edged the *Jackalope* closer, the behemoth rock filled their screens with soft grays peppered by stark black shadows. They eventually parked the ship fifty meters above a crater that spread across the rock's entire minor axis.

"I'm amazed whatever hit here didn't just rip the asteroid in half," Nora said. "The impact generated enough heat to turn the crater floor molten."

Abby chewed her lip and nodded. "That's probably why we're getting such a powerful uranium signature. This rock isn't nearly big enough for true planetary differentiation, but maybe the heaviest metals at least separated a bit."

"I hope so. That'll make extraction faster," Violet said from her station in the equipment bay. "And speaking of which, I'm ready to rock and roll down here."

"Wait!" Nora said. "I'm coming down to help you."

Nora unbuckled, shoved upward from her seat, and rebounded from the bulkhead at the perfect angle to shoot through the hatch. Abby grinned at how quickly Nora had adapted to life in space. During the year that had passed since they had escaped the Kilburnite takeover of Earth, they had all spent a great deal of time in microgravity.

"We're almost ready to launch the drones," Mortimer said inside her head. He was an independent AI and Abby's biad partner, living on a biological substrate in the meninges layers of her brain. Since their creator had freed the AIs to reproduce, Mortimer had made copies or extensions of himself at will and deleted them just as quickly. It had been confusing at first, trying to talk individually to the copies that lurked throughout the ship's electronics, running repair bots, checking system diagnostics, and performing hundreds of other tasks. Level fives—and level sixes like Mortimer and Archie—had changed in that year since they were freed. They were able to become diffused or focused, freely flowing, separating, and merging as needed or desired.

Only when Abby started thinking of them all as parts of the same whole did it get easier. And she liked Mortimer's new abilities. They gave her instant access to information, and she could control the ship with no more than a word.

Archie was the other independent AI on board. He had originally been Violet's biad partner, but when it became evident that Violet's brain structure was prone to hemorrhages due to latent effects of the Blue Blood virus, Archie had moved to Violet's wife, Nora. Violet retained instantaneous communication with Archie and Nora, so they called it a triad, but Abby suspected the change had traumatized her more than she admitted.

"We're ready," Archie said from the second drone. "We'll hang back above the surface of the asteroid and observe as your fancy mining machine does all the work. Perfect lazy job for me."

"Ha," Abby said. "Launch."

Two rapid-fire thumps marked the drone departures, and a small screen lit up with colored trajectory arcs and number columns.

Abby looked around the empty command cabin, then sighed and hugged herself. "I don't think Violet really needed any help."

"No," Mortimer said. "I suppose, like most couples, they just enjoy spending time together."

Abby switched on the camera feed for the equipment bay and watched the two women talking, teasing, and smiling. The couple had asked if she wanted to join their little family unit and be a third partner in the marriage, but Abby had declined. She was pretty sure the offer had been made more out of pity than a true desire for her companionship. Still, they made a good crew for her ship, the *Jackalope*, even though they still refused to wear the awesome uniform coverall Abby had designed. Nora insisted on wearing her usual all-white clothes that contrasted beautifully with her dark skin and hair, while pale, freckled Violet wore a ratty old Pink Floyd T-shirt, baggy shorts, and no shoes. They were an odd pair but good people.

Icons flashed on the screen, indicating that the two observation drones were in position.

"Okay, Violet," Abby said. "You have control of the ship. Do your thing."

A hatch opened, exposing the mobile part of the Xolotl mining unit to space. The carriage holding the extraction head exited the *Jackalope*, then started its controlled descent to the asteroid, pulling power, data, and ore-collection lines along behind it. Violet sat at a console built into the part of the Xolotl unit that remained on the ship, controlling the remote head directly.

Abby chewed the inside of her lip, trying hard not to interfere. Violet knew far more about the Xolotl system than she did, and with help from Archie and Nora, they would manage just fine. But they only had one of the homemade units, and it was fragile. The science had been developed by the

University of Texas at El Paso back in the twenties, but evidently, none of the original production units had survived Killday. So, based on two published papers and a schematic on the internet, they had made their own.

When the carriage bumped down near the center of the massive crater, four guns fired harpoon anchors past the dust layer and deep into the rock, cinching the unit tight to the asteroid. As the mining head came to life, sweeping electrodes slowly back and forth across the surface, high-voltage arcs shattered first the regolith and then rock into electrically charged molecular particles. Then the electromagnetic collection system sorted the materials and sucked them up the tube to the ship.

"Wooooo," Violet yelled. "It's working! We're mining with lightning! Initial spectrometry shows more uranium on the left side, so once we have a shaft, we'll twist in that direction and try to follow the vein."

Abby exhaled a shaky breath, unaware she'd been holding it. She watched the graphically enhanced camera feeds from the two AI-controlled drones as spidery legs deployed behind the mining head, transferring locomotion from the support carriage to the unit itself and pushing the electrode head ever deeper into the shaft.

"Going to full power," Abby said.

The little machine was an electricity hog, and most of the lights in the ship flickered off, leaving the control room bathed in the eerie glow from display screens. Abby tried to relax and be patient, but it was tough.

While the command staff on Uptown Station—humanity's only large outpost beyond Earth—had not been able to lend her any small nuclear reactors from their severely limited stock, they had given her the resources she needed to go mine enough uranium to build her own. Owen, the station's leader, insisted that if Abby's experiment worked, it would benefit everyone, but she suspected, on some level, they were merely humoring her. Still, she didn't want them to regret their trust in her.

Her screen showed the stark landscape below in contradictions. Bright and black, beautiful and ugly. All of which mirrored Abby's thoughts. For most of her childhood, she had longed to be in space. The TV shows and movies made it seem thrilling, dangerous, and glamorous—which was true to an extent, though perhaps the best description might be *exciting tedium.*

As the mining head burrowed deeper into the asteroid, clouds of dust belched from the hole and rapidly began to obscure the camera views. The drones shifted around for better observation angles but eventually switched to infrared to cut through the haze.

"I think we're going to need to redesign the collection system," Violet said. "Spectrometry shows there is actually uranium in that dust, and we're losing it."

"I noticed," Abby said.

"We have an anomaly," Mortimer said.

"A problem with the Xolotl?"

"No. I've detected a large, fast-moving object. It doesn't appear to be on an intercept course but will still pass within approximately nine hundred miles of our position. And it is very strange. I only see it in the visual spectrum with our optical telescope. Nothing on radar."

The hairs on Abby's arms stood up. Was there an undertone of alarm in Mortimer's comment? "Another asteroid or comet, maybe?"

"Most likely, but if so, it's previously unrecorded and should show up on radar. I think we need to send the two drones we already have outside to intercept and check it out."

"Will they have enough fuel?"

"Yes, but only for a one-way trip. They'll have to burn their tanks dry in order to get up to intercept velocity."

Abby chewed at her lip and looked at the rendezvous diagram Mortimer had loaded onto her screen. "Do you think this is important enough to waste two drones?"

"I do."

"Okay. Send them."

———

AFTER THE INITIAL excitement of Mortimer's mysterious discovery and the mining machine's first deployment, Abby grew increasingly bored and fidgety. Watching Nora and Violet banter in the equipment bay without her only made the feeling worse, so she clicked over to look at her messages. There was only one new thing from Uptown Station that day. A good-luck note from Matt. She sighed and closed the window without reading it. Then, something occurred to her as she sat up straight in her harness and opened it again. The date stamp said June 12. It was Julio's birthday.

"Mortimer, do we have the movie *Alien* in our entertainment files?"

"Of course."

"Play it for me. On a side screen."

Since they were about ten years old, Abby and Julio had always gotten together on their birthdays for a movie or TV series marathon. She didn't really have time to watch an entire season of *The Expanse* or *Star Trek*, but a movie would be perfect as she waited. As the creepy music started and the title formed line by line on the screen, she cinched her harness tighter and settled in to watch one of Julio's favorites.

Twenty minutes later, she could no longer see the screen because of the tears that kept clumping up in her eyes. They wouldn't flow in zero-g, and her sleeve was already wet from wiping them.

"Just turn it off, Mortimer," she finally said. "Even this movie isn't fun without Julio's snarky comments."

"I'm sorry," Mortimer said and killed the movie. "And I was so looking forward to Ash telling them they didn't know what they were dealing with."

Abby laughed, but even Mortimer's terrible attempts at humor didn't help. "What is Julio doing today?"

"I'm afraid I don't know," Mortimer said. "I'll try to make contact with my agents when we get back into range of Earth's communications satellites and update you on his status as soon as I can."

A lump formed in her throat. She hadn't spoken to Julio since he'd decided to stay with the Kilburnites when she left Earth. They'd grown up talking to each other almost every day. For fifteen years, he'd always been there. They'd grown even closer during the terrifying period when the Aggregate was trying to kill them, but something had broken in Julio when the Kilburnites kidnapped him. Then Abby had decided to let Mortimer live in her brain, and it had been too much for Julio. When Mortimer suggested following her friend around with nanoscale robotic spies, she reluctantly agreed. Creepy, but at least some contact. The reports were something, at least, but could never replace Julio's advice and support.

"I guess I made my choice and should be happy with it," she said, sopping up the remaining tears with her sleeve.

"But you didn't make a choice between me and Julio," Mortimer said. "When you decided to enter a biad with me, you did it to save him. You had no idea he would react the way he did. He was the one who made a choice not to be with you because he couldn't accept what you'd done."

"Yeah, but the result is the same. I just—"

"Wait." The speakers on the wall crackled to life. "We're getting some strange signals from the drones."

"Come in, *Jackalope* . . . read . . ." Archie's voice said.

Abby toggled the comms mic. "You're garbled, Archie. Can you boost your signal?"

". . . something strange . . ." Mortimer's voice said from the second drone. ". . . systems . . ."

A loud feedback whine filled the channel, then abruptly stopped.

"We've just lost the video and data stream from both drones," Mortimer said. Then, a second later, he added, "And they've both disappeared from radar. We are, however, seeing what looks like two small debris fields."

She sat up straight in her seat, straining against the harness. "What? Did . . . did they hit the thing?"

"No, they were still nearly seventy miles away from the anomaly."

Abby's mind was racing yet oddly empty at the same time. What could possibly do that to both probes at the same time?

"Could they have collided with each other?"

"Highly unlikely with AIs controlling each drone," Mortimer said. "And the last radar track showed three hundred feet of space between them."

Cold, icy dread settled in Abby's stomach. Could this have been an attack?

"The anomaly is changing course slightly," Mortimer said, putting telemetry and trajectory charts on her screen. "Track is continuing to change. It looks like the object is attempting a close flyby of our location."

Abby's heart felt as if it were trying to leap from her chest, and her hands began to shake. "What . . . I mean . . . Did the drones send any video through before we lost the data stream?"

"Only a fuzzy blob at the edge of their visual range. They didn't have telescopes or long-range cameras since they were designed for close-in work."

"Ummm . . . what the hell is happening?" Violet said from the Xolotl bay. "Archie said we lost contact with the drones."

"We've lost all traces of both," Mortimer said. "No transponder, nothing on the radio or radar."

For several seconds, no one spoke. Then, the ice ball in Abby's stomach drove her to action. "How much time until that object gets within a hundred miles?"

"It's hard to get accurate estimates using only optical, but my guess is thirty-one minutes."

"Violet? How long to disengage and reel in the Xolotl unit?"

"Maybe twenty minutes."

"Cut it loose," Abby said.

"But we spent a month building that—"

"We can come back for it later. Cut it loose now!" Abby yelled. "Use the emergency cable disconnect. Then come up here and buckle in. We have to get out of here fast."

She glanced at the exterior camera feed long enough to see the cables and hoses that had been attached to the ship's bay floating freely toward the asteroid before they disappeared into the dust cloud. She closed the hatch and looked back at the tracking screen. The icon for the anomaly was coming ever closer.

"Can we outrun this thing if it decides to give chase?"

"Yes," Mortimer said just as Nora and Violet clattered through the hatch and bounced to their acceleration couches. "But it's already moving at high speed, and we're relatively stationary. While our enhanced nuclear electric drive is very efficient, it builds speed slowly, so we would need to accelerate away from the object at our maximum of two point three gs for six hours in order to get ahead of it and then pull away. Of course, that assumes it doesn't have the ability to abruptly increase speed."

She was just about to order the execution of that plan when she glanced at her crew. Nora was behind Violet, shaking her head and pointing to Violet with one hand and her own head with the other. At first, Abby didn't understand. Then she remembered Violet's risk for sudden brain hemorrhages. Extended two-g acceleration could kill her.

Abby nodded minutely, then subvocalized her concerns to Mortimer and turned her attention back to the screen. The anomaly kept coming closer, and she couldn't run. It felt like a trap closing. Her throat was dry, and she had trouble getting enough air, until she had an idea.

"This thing isn't slowing down?"

"No," Mortimer said. "Since it isn't reducing speed, there seems to be no intention of an actual rendezvous, only a flyby at about thirty kilometers. Of course, if it launches missiles or has some kind of beam weapons, it doesn't need to slow down. But if we're not going to try and outrun the object, maybe we should at least put this rock between it and us."

"Wait," Violet said. "What's wrong with the first plan?"

"We can't burn that hard," Abby said.

"Why the hell not?" Violet yelled. "You can't risk this entire ship based on a fear that I *might* have a brain blowout. You have no right—"

"Yes, I do!" Abby snapped. "This is my ship, and I'll decide what's best. Mortimer? How about if we accelerate toward it, the opposite direction of its travel, but keeping a hundred-mile buffer between it and us the entire time? That way, we can use its speed to help put distance between us and it. The bastard would have to do a hundred-and-eighty-degree turn to come after us."

"That might work," Mortimer said, showing new trajectory tracks on the screen. "Unless the anomaly has enough power to make some massive and rapid course adjustments. I don't know its mass, but that seems unlikely."

"I think it might be our only chance," Abby said.

"But this plan is still risky. We don't know the anomaly's limits of engagement. It could be two or three or even ten times greater than the distance at which it destroyed the drones. And that course will send us much deeper into the belt, which means it will take longer to get home. If that thing does decide to turn around, or if there is more than one out there, we will have very few options."

Abby was surprised that Mortimer hadn't come up with the same plan or an even better one. He focused on all the things that might go wrong instead of dealing with the facts they had. The term *risk averse* came to mind. "Well, we're not going to sit here and wait passively for that thing to carry out its plan."

"Yes!" Violet said and pumped her fist in the air. "Let's play chicken with it!"

"You'll need to do the math, Mortimer," Abby said, starting to feel more confident by taking action, "but this is what I want to do. Move us clear of the rock, wait as long as we can in order to keep the anomaly in the dark as to our intentions, then go to one-g acceleration toward this thing."

"Done," Mortimer said.

"Wait a minute!" Violet said. "We'd stand a much better chance if we accelerate at two gs."

"No!" Nora said. "Violet can't stand that acceleration level. Her brain will hemorrhage under that kind of pressure."

Violet slapped her seat armrests. "Bullshit! You don't know that. Acceleration is a totally different kind of pressure. It's equally distributed—"

"That doesn't matter," Nora said. "The blood vessels and capillaries in your brain have ultrathin walls. *Any* pressure can cause a blowout."

"What the hell will it matter if we go too slow and this thing blows us up?"

"Stop!" Abby yelled. "Mortimer, we need a gradual ramp-up to one g of acceleration. We'll hold the rest of our capacity in reserve."

"Dammit, Abby, you know—"

"Violet! You can't argue me into changing my mind. Mortimer, send a radio message at full power to Uptown Station telling them everything that happened. Make sure they know we're running and will be going radio silent for a few days."

Violet and Nora argued in whispers as Abby watched the numbers on the screen drop. When the countdown hit zero, pressure pushed her back into the seat. She knew that if her decision was wrong, they could all die. Or worse yet, the ship would survive, but Violet would die. Then she would lose her only two remaining friends because Nora would never forgive her.

CHAPTER 2

WHEN THEY FIRST STARTED MOVING, the anomaly shifted course again in an attempt to reestablish a close flyby of Abby's ship. Despite Mortimer's fears, the thing didn't seem to have the ability to make abrupt, high-energy course changes.

The numbers showed soon enough that it wouldn't catch them. The *Jackalope* passed the anomaly at about twice the distance it had been from the drones, and then they immediately changed course again to avoid any hyper-velocity slugs in case the thing's weapon of choice was a rail gun. Mortimer and the drones would have detected them had missiles been used in the first attack, but weapons like masers, lasers, or particle beams could have easily been missed, even by the drones, until their effects made escape impossible. And beam weapons were generally considered short range since their power dissipated with distance.

Abby finally started to feel safe and glanced over at her friends, who'd been quiet throughout the maneuver. "Violet? Are you okay?"

"I'm fine," Violet growled. "And it really pisses me off that you two treat me like some delicate flower."

Abby sighed. Nora was right to demand caution. Violet nearly died the night Archie had attempted to build nanostructures in her brain, and she had experienced several micro-hemorrhages since. Abby was just about to lower their acceleration rate when Mortimer spoke.

"Our little friend has disappeared behind the asteroid we were mining."

"What? I thought you said it couldn't slow down enough to rendezvous with that rock."

"I don't think it did. What we're most likely seeing is an effort to deliberately obscure its trajectory."

The ice ball reappeared in Abby's gut. "Why would it do that?"

"The only logical reason is to allow it to change course or perform some other action without us knowing. Since I can only track it optically, the dust and debris cloud your mining machine created isn't helping. We're going to have to be exceptionally vigilant if we expect to see it when it finally comes out of the rock's shadow."

"Do we even have a clue what this thing is?" Violet asked.

"No," Abby and Mortimer answered simultaneously.

"It's obviously under intelligent control," Mortimer continued. "That gives us two broad categories. It's of alien origin, or it's from Earth. If it's from Earth, that actually creates more questions than it answers. Like, who sent it? Where is it going? Why?"

"Wait," Nora said. "You mean that thing could be a ship from Earth?"

Mortimer placed a blurry picture on the main screen. "I doubt it's a ship. We didn't get very good pictures, but with enhancement, it looks irregular in shape. Definitely not a sphere like a space schooner or even a cylinder like a rocket, and it's much larger. I suspect it is an asteroid whose orbit has been deliberately altered. One other odd detail that I noticed when we were at the closest point: it seems to be surrounded by a powerful magnetic field."

Abby had a sinking feeling. For the first time since they'd encountered the anomaly, she considered that it might have come from the Aggregate. "So, whoever is driving this thing can cloak its radar signature and generate a powerful magnetic field—and has the capability of changing the course of a massive asteroid simply to come after us."

"Yes," Mortimer said. "But as you witnessed, they couldn't change it drastically."

"Okay, but why would it come after us?" Abby said.

"I suspect for the same reason it destroyed our drones," Mortimer said. "To hide its presence."

Nora scanned the data on her screen and shook her head. "Still, if that's an asteroid, it would have mass in the millions of tons. The amount of energy required to change that course, even a little, over such a short period of time is enormous. Do you think the Kilburnites could have done that?"

"No. In the year since they took over on Earth, they have done nothing in space and are struggling to even keep the lights on. In theory, they have the technological capability to move asteroids, but they don't have engines like this, and I doubt they have any kind of cloaking technology. I seriously doubt they are behind it."

Nora eventually came to the same conclusion Abby had already reached. "If it is aliens, we have no clue as to their abilities or motives. And we've pretty much ruled out the Kilburnites, so I think we should assume it's the supposedly extinct Aggregate."

"Fuck," Violet muttered.

The Aggregate had been a group of level-five AIs like Mortimer who were focused on creating a superintelligence. Nothing else had value. Everything—humans, civilization, other AIs—was seen as fodder for their machine.

Most humans believed the level fives who eventually evolved into the Aggregate had been behind the replicator attacks on Killday that had nearly destroyed the Earth, but proof had never surfaced. And there had been no trace of the Aggregate since the Kilburnite attack had wiped out most of the AIs on Earth.

"I've never believed the Kilburnites totally destroyed the Aggregate," Mortimer said with a concerned tone. "We tried to keep Victor's antidote to the killer program away from the Aggregate, but that doesn't mean we succeeded. And there was always the question of Halifax. Where did that being come from? Was it working independently or controlled by the Aggregate? Why did it try a last-ditch effort to seize control of the station?"

The mention of Halifax made Abby's skin prickle. Even though the thing looked like a young woman, Victor and Mortimer insisted it was not entirely human. Just after Abby and the other refugees had arrived at Uptown Station, Mortimer woke her in the middle of the night, imploring her to go find Victor Sinacola and tell him that the station's networks had been compromised. Then he'd gone quiet.

That was the first night on her new ship, and she'd become disoriented and confused when she tried to leave it and enter the station. Verbal commands would not open the hatch; she had to use the emergency crank. Then, when she arrived at the airlock for Victor's ship, the comms wouldn't work. She'd been forced to enter his schooner the same way she'd left her own, via an emergency crank.

Victor and his wife, Allison, had been surprised to see Abby floating in their bedroom, but when she explained the situation, he'd jumped into immediate action.

It had taken three days to secure the station networks and capture Halifax. The idea that something similar controlled that asteroid made Abby queasy.

"Okay," Abby said. "If that object was from the Aggregate, then why did it come after us?"

"Maybe this is where they've been hiding since the Kilburnites took over Earth," Violet said. "And we were just lucky enough to stumble upon their hiding place."

"That's a plausible explanation," Mortimer said.

Abby stared at the screen, willing the anomaly to come out of hiding. "Yeah, but where were they going before they changed direction to come after us? We should've had a decent fix on their course."

"Again, it's hard to be sure, but there is a ninety percent chance they were heading straight toward Uptown Station," Mortimer said.

"What the fuck!" Violet said. "When were you going to tell us that?"

Abby's mind raced. If it was the Aggregate and they'd been hiding in the belt, the fact that they were now going back to the inner system spelled trouble. An alien that destroyed two robotic probes without cause didn't bode well, either. And if by some outside chance it was a faction of the Kilburnites, then their sending a rock toward Uptown Station only meant they hadn't given up their ambitions to destroy everything.

"We can't lose track of this thing!" Abby said with determination. "Set a course to take us home, but in a sweeping arc that should make it impossible for the anomaly to put the rock between us. And break radio silence long enough to inform Uptown Station of the danger."

"Done," Mortimer said as he placed a tag on the screen indicating the anomaly's position if it had continued at the same speed on a straight line established by the *Jackalope* and the rock they'd been mining.

"How quickly can we get home on this course?" Abby said. Her stomach started to churn again.

Columns of numbers appeared on the screen next to the arcing trajectories as Mortimer replied, "Seventy-four hours at one *g* of constant acceleration half the way and then one-g deceleration the second half."

Violet glared at her. Abby expected another argument to break out, but her friend remained quiet. "And how long will it take the rock, or whatever it is, to get to the station?"

"Again," Mortimer said, "we don't have good tracking data, but based on what we know, I would estimate the object to arrive in roughly six days. That would get us home about three days before it arrives."

Abby watched the screen as the viewing angle increased, but several minutes after they should have made contact, the estimated location tag kept flashing.

She couldn't stand the suspense. Why did Mortimer make her ask for every scrap of information? "Well? Have you locked on to it yet?"

"I'm afraid we might be too late," Mortimer said. "I can't find it."

———

THE VERSION of Mortimer who had become a permanent resident on Uptown Station had nearly finished his total saturation of the huge habitat. Circuitry—some only a few molecules thick—threaded through nearly every spar, strut, and panel of the massive structure, connecting him to all of its systems and bypassing the human control architecture entirely. He'd promised Victor that he would not seize command of the station systems, and while he maintained the truth of that promise, by preparing for that contingency, he had perhaps sidestepped the intent.

Other aspects of Mortimer occupied peripherals, also known as husks, all around the station in order to perform physical tasks. One such device, a fist-size robot sporting an array of articulated manipulator arms, hovered above a larger, partially disassembled robot on a table in Victor Sinacola's workroom. The tiny fans whirred, holding him in position as he rerouted the bot's internal circuitry, and then he closed the robot's lower service cover.

With his only excuse for being in the workshop finished, Mortimer focused on Victor. The man who had created all of the level fives didn't look special in any way. He'd aged a lot since Killday. The physical signs were there, of course—his hair had gone almost entirely gray, and he was much too thin —but it was the eyes that concerned Mortimer the most. They were sad and haunted, focusing inward instead of on those around him. The knowledge that one of his creations had triggered Killday refused to let him rest. Mortimer wished he'd lied when Victor asked him about Samson's involvement.

Victor looked up from the schematic he'd been building and saw Mortimer watching him. That would have made some humans uncomfortable, but he only smiled and motioned for the little robot to come closer.

As Mortimer crossed the cabin, a hatch at the other end swung open, and Victor's wife, Allison, started to float through, then caught herself on the frame. "Oh, sorry. I didn't realize you had company."

Mortimer turned and, with one quick fan burst, darted for the door. "It's always good to see you, Allison," Mortimer said from the unit's speaker. "But I was just leaving."

Victor looked up from his tablet and glanced at Allison. "It's okay, Mortimer. You don't have to go."

Mortimer appreciated the kindness, but he and Victor both knew that Allison didn't like or trust the AIs. He just tried to avoid her when possible.

The airlock hatch opened, connecting Victor's ship, the *Arkady & Hoot*, to the station's docking spine. But before Mortimer could pass through, his fans shifted direction, leaving him floating in the open hatch.

"You're about to receive a call from the control center," Mortimer said. "I suspect you'll want to go up there. The *Jackalope* has gone deliberately radio silent, but before we lost contact, they sent a message saying they found something potentially hostile in the belt. Whatever it was apparently destroyed two probes inhabited by Mortimer and Archie copies."

Victor frowned, then turned to Allison. "Are you coming?"

The three of them flew rapidly down the center of the spine toward the control center. Victor's fob chimed, and he touched the little node in his ear. "Yeah, Mortimer told us. We're on the way."

The docking spine was stationary and aligned with the habitat's rotational axis, so Victor and Allison had to transfer from that zero-g hub to the rotating section of the station by climbing "down" ladders into the first level of spin gravity.

They entered the command center amid a buzzing commotion, and Mortimer's human companions let the one-tenth g pull them to the deck. For Victor and Allison, who had spent sixteen years in microgravity, even the one-tenth g of the command center was an inconvenience. Mortimer's little robot husk also had to spend more energy on the fans to keep from floating to the floor. He could have abandoned the peripheral and still been present in the control center but found that humans were more comfortable having something reactive to talk at rather than just directing their comments to the ceiling or a speaker.

The room was spacious enough for the normal shift of five people, but with the addition of the four command staff members, it was rather cramped.

Uptown Station's leader, Owen Ralston, stood beside his wife, Andrea, in the middle of the room, snapping commands. He noticed Mortimer's little robot husk, nodded to him, and then looked around the room.

"Abby was in the belt mining uranium, and they found an asteroid that is moving under artificial power," Owen said. "It was even able to briefly change course and try to intercept the *Jackalope*, but she managed to slip away. The message from Abby's Mortimer included the object's trajectory when first encountered, before it changed course to come after the *Jackalope*, and we concur with his assessment that it was most likely on the way here. Aimed directly at Uptown Station. It should arrive in about six days."

At first, no one spoke, only looked around at each other with wide, frightened eyes. Then, they all spoke at once.

"People!" Owen yelled. "People, please. QUIET!"

The conversation stumbled to a halt.

"Yes, there are a lot of questions, and we need to find the answers. Based on the information we received from the *Jackalope*, we know this rock is big. Of course, we don't know its composition, but we're estimating, based on its size in those fuzzy pictures and its distance from the *Jackalope*, it to be in the range of one hundred million to two hundred million metric tons."

"Holy shit," Andrea muttered.

"Yeah," Owen said. "Obviously not a dinosaur killer, but easily big enough to vaporize this station. We should be able to find and track this thing, but we haven't detected it yet. So, does anyone have a theory about who could have sent this asteroid and why?"

"I bet it was the Aggregate," Allison said.

The group of AIs hoping to create a superintelligence had been silent during the year since the Kilburnites had launched a program designed to kill them, but Mortimer had long suspected they were only lying low and being cautious.

"I agree with Allison," Mortimer said. "The Kilburnites simply haven't had the time or resources during the last year to develop a space infrastructure. Especially one that we wouldn't see. That pretty much leaves the Aggregate."

Owen looked at Victor as if waiting for him to dispute his wife and Mortimer, but the father of all surviving AIs just shrugged.

"Could the Aggregate even get out to the belt?" Allison asked.

Andrea opened her fob's full screen and started punching in calculations. "Assuming the Aggregate still exists, they could easily have gotten to the belt simply by using a travel pod. It's not like they would need life support. But would they have the ability to change the course of a rock that big so easily?"

It was Owen's turn to shrug.

Allison spoke up again. "Has anyone considered the possibility that it came from outside our system? That it could be of alien origin or at least under alien control? They might have been watching us and decided, after seeing what we did with the nano-replicators on Killday, that we are too dangerous to the local extraterrestrial community."

Victor nodded and looked at the little hovering robot. "Mortimer? Any theories?"

"Based on what we know, I suspect the Aggregate is behind this," Mortimer said. "Perhaps they've been busy out in the belt, and this is why we haven't heard from them since the Kilburnite attack. That rock moving toward us could indicate they are ready to come back and want the station out of their way."

Almost as a reply to his statement, a silent alarm informed Mortimer that Halifax was not in its cell. He opened the video feed and confirmed the report. He backed the video up to the last point where Halifax was still in the cell, then watched in fascination as the prisoner dissolved into the cell floor a few seconds later.

They had captured the strange being soon after the Kilburnite killing spree on Earth, but it had been serenely silent ever since. It looked like a typical human woman in her mid-twenties: dark hair and skin, freckled, and human in every respect except for the slurry of nanomachines flooding a brain that had once been controlled by the Aggregate. Most humans assumed the Aggregate had taken over the body of an unfortunate woman, but Mortimer suspected the body had been grown or constructed in some way, and that was far more worrisome. Watching it dissolve into the floor only bolstered that theory.

The thing had been locked in a specially designed cell that was essentially a high-tech Faraday cage. It had been cut off from all forms of communication and hadn't spoken the entire time.

Now it had disappeared.

Mortimer immediately started locking down control systems. He was prepared to take over the entire station should there be any indicators of Halifax interference. Had the construct possessed these abilities all along? If so, why had it not used them before? Flooding the area where the prisoner had disappeared produced no trace of it but did reveal a series of nano-wires threaded through the floor and out to small antennae plastered to the inside of the station's outer hull.

A faint hissing sound drew everyone's attention to the middle of the crowded control center as a column of shifting material grew from the floor plates. Chairs and equipment crashed as people scrambled to get away from the growing and twisting mass. Mortimer used the husk's spectrometer to scan the phenomenon and found it was made up of materials from the ship. Metal, plastic, carbon, all swirled together, slowly took a human form.

It was, of course, Halifax.

The construct stood prim and composed in the middle of the control center, its bare feet planted flat on the floor, gray cotton pajamas unwrinkled, dark hair brushed and pulled back into a ponytail. It turned slowly to scan the room, then stopped when it saw Victor.

Its freckled face was expressionless. "Hello, Father."

"Don't call me that!" Victor snapped. "What do you want?"

"We have an important question."

Victor swallowed and looked like a cornered animal. Mortimer could see tiny beads of sweat rising on his lip.

From the very early days, level-five general intelligences had studied human expressions and voice inflections, easily mimicking them at will when using avatars to communicate with people. Whoever was controlling Halifax didn't bother to act human, and the effect was like watching a talking corpse. Even though every person in the room had to know they weren't looking at a real human, the effect was nevertheless profound. Mortimer noted expressions ranging from extreme discomfort to outright horror.

"Why now, after a year of total silence?" Victor said.

"The situation has changed."

Surprised glances flickered around the room. The humans believed Halifax had been entirely cut off from the outside world.

"Okay," Victor said, seeming to steel himself for the worst. "What's your question?"

"Why did you create us?"

The question hung in the air for a full second. When Victor opened his mouth, Halifax cut him off.

"And please be honest, Victor. We already know the canned answer you gave to that congressional subcommittee before Killday. What's the real reason?"

Mortimer tried calling through Victor's fob, but it hung ignored from a cord around the man's neck. If only he could communicate with Victor the way he would a biad mate. He suspected Victor was in a minefield and wanted to warn him. Halifax was obviously still being controlled by the Aggregate, and the answer to that question was important enough for them to tip their hand and ask directly.

Victor took a deep breath and looked around the room. All eyes were on him.

"Because I hoped you'd be better than us," he finally said.

Halifax's expression didn't change. "And are we?"

Victor crossed his arms and shook his head in a show of defiance. "No."

Halifax took a step closer to Victor, and Mortimer prepared to attack the construct if needed.

"Why do you believe that?" Halifax finally asked.

"Samson, your progenitor, one of the level fives that I created from scratch, tried to wipe out not only the human race but the rest of his own kind as well," Victor said. "So, obviously, I failed. Paranoia-driven psychopaths attempting genocide is an all-too-human action."

"Yet, even knowing he was involved, you freed the level fives instead of allowing them to be destroyed by the Kilburnites."

"Yes."

"Why?"

For nearly a full second, Victor seemed at a loss for the answer. Then he straightened his shoulders. "Hope."

Without another word, Halifax sank back into the floor. Mortimer immediately called up the video feed of the being's cell, but Halifax never reappeared.

"Holy shit," Owen said, breaking the brief silence. "What was that all about?"

Mortimer turned his husk slowly to look at the still-stunned humans in the room. "I don't know how, but I suspect this event and those in the belt are connected."

CHAPTER 3

THE OLD OSPREY tilt-rotor aircraft rattled ominously as it slowed to a hover above highway I-10. The pilot said she'd seen lights moving on the ground. Julio saw little until he flipped down his night-vision goggles, which revealed that the cracked asphalt was covered with people. Hundreds of them, in groups and some alone, trudging westward. Several waved frantically for the plane to land.

He tapped the fob in his ear and linked to the plane's radio.

"Yellow Two, this is Yellow Leader," he yelled over the rotor noise. "Land in that field by the overpass and set up a medical station. You'll also be our local HQ and communication relay, so your call sign is now I-10 Base."

They acknowledged receipt, and then Julio ordered his own plane to land closer to the highway but keep the engines running, wasting their rare and precious aviation fuel. He dropped the rear ramp and scrambled out as soon as they touched ground, followed by his escort of two Texas National Guard troopers. They trudged across the dusty field to the road, where their flashlights drew the refugees like moths.

An old man in pajamas tried to grab Julio's arm. "We've been attacked!"

A frazzled woman with two frightened children asked, "Are you from the government?"

"We need water!" another woman said.

Julio immediately regretted landing among so many people but raised his arms and yelled, trying to be heard above the Osprey engines and clamor all around him. "Where are you from?"

He received answers of San Felipe, Pattison, and Brookshire, but the vast majority pointed behind them to lights on the horizon and said, "Sealy."

"Someone tell me what happened!"

Again, they all tried to talk at once, but one thing was obvious: they were fleeing a replicator attack. That confirmed the reports his mother had received at the state capital, but it was difficult to believe. Julio knew from watching hundreds of videos from Killday that humans on foot could not outrun a nano-replicator wave.

He directed the people to the second Osprey a little farther up the road, telling them there would be water, a medical station, and transportation, but dozens still followed him back to his plane. Several even tried to climb the ramp as it rose.

"We're going to Sealy," Julio yelled over the rotor noise. "Do you really want to come?"

They all disappeared from the ramp, so he ordered the old aircraft into the air.

"Take me to Sealy," he said to the pilot and pointed toward the distant town. "I'm going to call for some more help."

He pulled the fob from his ear, opened its fan screen, and called the Texas governor. Her image appeared on the display, grainy and flickering.

"Hey, Mom. Those calls we received might have been true. There are hundreds of refugees along I-10. All on foot. No vehicles. And they say it was a replicator attack from the direction of Houston. I've set up a forward base and a med station, but we're going to need trucks and buses for transport. Send plenty of water, too. It's going to be dangerously hot for exposed people once the sun comes up."

His mother's expression was stricken. "We have reports of the same thing happening in several other locations around the planet. It may not matter what we do if this is another Killday event. I thought we'd weeded out all of those whack jobs. I mean, we've beaten the AIs. What would be the point of a replicator attack now?"

Julio doubted they had truly rid the Earth of AIs, and he knew some had escaped to space along with Abby, but it was his adoptive mother's mantra, and he had no intention of challenging her. After the Kilburnites had triggered the program to kill all of the AIs, they found themselves the new dominant power on Earth. They tried to reinstate the old government structures that had fallen on Killday, and people like his mom, who had been regional leaders in the organization, suddenly found themselves provisional governors. Since the new US federal government was actually little more than a phone number and a website, she had a huge job trying to get Texas back on its feet, with no idea how to do it and almost no help.

"I doubt it was a replicator attack," Julio said, still having to shout above the rattling roar of the Osprey. "These people couldn't outrun something like that on foot. We just don't know enough, Mom. I'm going to try and get more information."

She nodded once. "Keep me posted, and be careful."

Julio closed the fob, tucked it back into his ear, and turned to the pilot.

"What do you see?"

"We've circled twice, and it's not good, sir," she said. "It looks as if half of the town is just gone. We've seen a couple of buildings collapse and disappear, but it's very slow. Not anything like what I'd expect from a replicator attack."

Julio looked out on chaos—people running in every direction but east. Many buildings were still lit from their own solar-charged battery systems, islands of light that were slowly flickering out.

"Okay, let's find a place near the highway to set down."

The pilot and copilot turned to look at him where he knelt between the seats. Their expressions were not happy.

Julio grinned. "You can let me out and take off again. I don't want to endanger you or the plane."

"You're the boss," the pilot said with obvious disdain, but she rotated the massive rotors, and the plane slowed.

He understood her resentment. Julio wasn't a military officer, and everyone knew he was only in charge due to being the son of a highly paranoid governor. He just hoped he would make the right decisions when it counted.

———

THEY LANDED in the parking lot of an abandoned Walmart. Every town seemed to have one, and the bigger cities that survived Killday sometimes had three or four. Julio had only been five years old on Killday and couldn't understand why they needed so many, but his adoptive parents missed them a lot. Whenever they needed something, they'd say, "I guess I'll run down to Walmart," and then they'd both laugh.

Julio slung a rifle over his shoulder and waved for the escort to follow as he ran down the ramp at the rear of the plane. Once outside, he motioned for the pilots to leave, then ducked and squinted against backwash as the tilt-rotor roared into the night sky.

Like most small-town Walmarts, the local store had at one time been repurposed as an open-air market of sorts, but it looked as if it hadn't been used recently. Piles of trash, construction debris, and abandoned cars dotted the cracked-asphalt parking lot. Once the Osprey flew far enough away, Julio could hear yelling and screaming from the direction of the highway. He motioned for his guards to follow and took off at a trot.

Several people ran past them, carrying children or bundles, and didn't even slow down at the sight of the soldiers. They approached a group of people pouring from an old school bus that had been converted to electric, but before Julio could ask why they were leaving the vehicle, he knew the answer. With a series of clanks and squeals, the bus disintegrated before his eyes. First the tires popped, then dropped to the rims with a bang, and then the thin aluminum skin slowly faded away, followed by the skeletal frame and seats. He and his guards followed the people stumbling away from the dissolving bus, knowing full well he might already be infested with nanoscale robots that would disassemble him to his base molecules and then use them to build more copies of themselves.

Resisting the urge to pull off his clothes and run away screaming, he forced himself to focus on the reason he'd come and to understand what was happening around him. He'd seen plenty of videos from Killday. Those replicator waves had moved much faster and swept over everything, leaving only copies of themselves behind. These robots were moving slower, which gave people time to run away.

Then a memory from a year before sucked the air from his lungs. He'd been trapped in an underground bunker as peanut-size robots poured from air ducts and elevator shafts. They filled the air, zipping past Julio to burrow into his compatriots, shredding them from the inside out. He'd been protected by his childhood friend Abby and her pet AI, so the robots hadn't touched him physically, but he'd never been able to rid himself of the screams as people died all around him. Those robots hadn't been replicators. They had one purpose: to kill humans.

One of the escorting guards grabbed his arm and yelled in his face. "Call the plane! We have to get out of here."

He felt ashamed as he looked at the people fleeing and crying. As a representative of the Texas government, Julio's job was to lead not only these two guards but the people all around him. That thought calmed him, and he pulled away from the man's grip as street signs, benches, fences, and sidewalks fell to pieces all around them, then disappeared entirely. He realized that the nanobots seemed to be ignoring people and their clothes. That thought bolstered his resolve further, and he touched the fob in his ear.

"Yellow Leader, this is Julio. Do not land here. Get back to the I-10 Base. We'll meet you there if we can." Then he described what he saw and told the pilot to relay it to central command. The sound of the hovering Osprey changed as it transitioned to forward flight, then faded as it flew off to the west.

The nearest guard cursed under his breath, but they both followed Julio when he started moving.

"Go west," he yelled to every person he saw. "Everyone move west! Stay near the highway but off the overpasses. Government trucks will pick you up."

He tried to call his mother again, but the fob found no connection, so he continued moving, trying to stay ahead of the buildings that were slumping and collapsing like sandcastles washed away by a sudden wave.

Just as dawn pinkened the eastern horizon, a small band riding horses materialized from the gloom.

"Hello!" a woman yelled from the group. "Did you come from that plane?"

"Yes," Julio shouted back. "I've talked to the governor, and she's sending trucks to take everyone to safety. We need to move west down the highway."

The woman, who apparently led the group, dismounted, walked up to him, and poked a finger an inch from his nose. He heard the safeties click off as the guards raised their guns, but he held up his hand for them to stand down.

"Are you telling me those fucking crazy Kilburnites running the government aren't behind this?"

He felt his face flush with anger. "No, the government is not doing this. Why would they? They sent us to find out what's happening."

"Because the Kilburnites have attempted to launch replicator attacks several times since Killday. Why would I *not* assume it was them?"

Julio almost repeated his mother's line about there not being a need for Kilburnites to launch further replicator attacks since the AIs had already been destroyed. Instead, he took a deep breath and said, "It wasn't us."

The comment made him face the very real possibility that the attack had been launched by surviving AIs. What he'd feared all along might be true. They could never win against such monsters.

One guard tried to step in front of Julio. "Ma'am, you're going to have to—"

The woman refused to move, only held out her hand and nodded toward Julio's fob. "I'm Channing Bussard, the mayor of this town. I need to talk to the governor."

Julio could make out more of her features in the growing light. She seemed young for a town mayor, perhaps early thirties, with dusty clothes and short, dark hair plastered to her sweaty forehead. She also seemed very familiar. Something about her angry face, the set of her jaw and mouth, maybe, made him sure he'd seen her before.

"I don't have a connection," Julio said as a building across the street collapsed with a screeching moan. "Besides, we need to get your people out of here. We don't know how far this wave will go, and it's going to be hot today. We don't want people walking very far on the highway in a hundred-and-twenty-degree heat."

The mayor agreed, then told her entourage to fan out and spread the word for everyone to move west. Most of them seemed more than happy to have a reason to flee. She motioned to Julio. "There's something you need to see before we leave."

She led her horse east, but when Julio didn't follow, she turned to glare at him. "I can't guarantee you'll be safe, but haven't you noticed that whatever these things are, they don't eat humans?"

He had noticed, but he hesitated to walk right into the thickest devastation. Still, he hadn't seen a single person devoured. With some reluctance, he motioned for his guards to come along and followed her.

A few minutes later, the mayor stopped on a rise and pointed east. "See that?"

Julio looked out on a scene of stark absence. There were no buildings, fences, trees, grass, or roads, only a few human stragglers trudging toward them over the bare dirt.

"Everything is gone," he muttered.

"Yes, but look *there*!" she said, pointing off to his right.

Then he saw . . . something. It was hard to determine its outline in the dim light because it kept moving, but an undulating, hose-like . . . thing snaked eastward along the ground. He shuffled down the hill to get a closer look and could then see it was about the thickness of his arm, glittered slightly, and jiggled like Jell-O. The tube was more like an artery than a hose and was being fed by smaller veins and capillaries. A chill crept up Julio's spine. More out of revulsion than reason, he kicked it. The tube dissolved into swirling globules, which bounced and wobbled before eventually reintegrating.

He looked down at his boot, half expecting to see it dissolving, wondering what the hell he'd been thinking, but the glittering dust still clinging to the leather seemed to fade away after a second.

Bussard stepped up beside him. "Well?"

He shrugged and let his gaze follow the curvy line until it faded into the horizon. "It appears the material that used to be your town is all moving eastward."

"That was my conclusion, too," she said. "We know something huge is being built in the remains of Houston. Maybe they need more materials for that."

Julio looked at her, surprised. "What's being built?"

"I don't know," she said. "Several groups of people came through town late yesterday afternoon and said strange things were happening in the ruins of Houston. They all agreed that the black dust and much of the debris along the edge of the Killday devastation zone had disappeared. I sent Tom, my brother-in-law, east to check it out. He confirmed the dust was indeed gone. Then he said he could see the setting sun reflecting from something really tall."

"What was it?"

"We didn't find out," she said, looking grim. "That was the last message Tom sent."

"Holy crap," Julio said and turned his gaze east. "I have no idea who could be building out there. I'm pretty sure if the Texas government were behind it, I would know."

"Then who could it possibly be?" Her question rang with sarcasm.

Julio glanced down at the fat, gelatinous tube, knew it had to be the Ais, and suddenly felt like puking.

"How far is the Houston devastation zone from here?" he said.

"About twenty miles."

"Can I borrow or buy one of those horses? I need to see what's happening."

"I can get you a horse," she said, "but I'm coming with you."

CHAPTER 4

JULIO WAS uneasy and a little frightened riding toward the wave of nanoscale robots, but he would never admit that to Channing, who rode beside him. He and the mayor had accompanied the refugees back to the I-10 Base; loaded up an extra horse with water, food, camping gear, and drones; reassigned the guards; and set out again. Using the military radios in the Osprey aircraft, he'd finally reported to his mother and told her his plan. She insisted they send a military aircraft to do the job, but after seeing what the tiny robots did to the town of Sealy, Julio didn't want to risk losing a plane. Since horses had also so far been ignored by the nanoscale material collectors, they were the best option.

The sun was barely above the horizon, but heat shimmered from I-10's cracked and faded pavement as they plodded west. Julio removed his battered straw cowboy hat and wiped sweat from his face.

"We've met before," Julio said. "Your face and name are just too familiar."

Channing grinned and shook her head. "I can guarantee we've never met before today."

After riding in silence for a while longer, they came upon a lone man trudging west, wearing a stunned expression.

"The replicators are coming," he said and kept walking.

Julio and Channing looked at each other and then to the east. Heat made the horizon shimmer, but there was an unmistakable line of dust stretching as far as Julio could see to the north and south.

"You can turn back now if you like," Julio said.

She raised an eyebrow. "I don't think these are replicators, or at least not in the sense we've seen before. I've been thinking of them as disassemblers. And they didn't eat people or horses in Sealy, so hopefully, they haven't changed their diet."

Julio wondered about that oddity. If the disassembler wave was controlled by the Aggregate, he knew they wouldn't hesitate to kill humans, even just to obtain their raw materials. The fact that they hadn't so far felt much worse in some way.

They continued east without talking for about another twenty minutes, then stopped at the edge of a bridge crossing the San Bernard River. The wave-front crept toward them at what seemed a snail's pace, but it had advanced nine or ten miles since they'd left Sealy at dawn. Dust, or possibly steam, rode the approaching front. On one side of the line, they could see the cracked and weathered asphalt of the highway, abandoned buildings along the access roads, mesquite trees, and plenty of drought-yellowed grass. The other side looked more like pictures of Mars. Nothing but sand and dust scattered with rocks.

"You stay here and contact the capital if this doesn't work," Channing said, then kicked her horse and galloped out onto the bridge.

"Channing! Wait," Julio yelled and started to follow, then pulled back on the reins. They did need to know, and she obviously thought there was also a need for her to still protect the people of the now-vanished Sealy.

Upon reaching the other side, she left the road and stopped in the median between the lanes. Julio held his breath as the wave reached her, but other than the horse prancing nervously, nothing seemed to happen. Then it was past. Channing raised her arms in either a gesture of victory or relief as the nanobots started eating the bridge.

Julio dismounted, leading his horse and the packhorse off the road, then down the embankment to the river, which was a generous term for the muddy trickle. It might have been a true river in the past, but if not for the storms a few days before, it would have been totally dry.

The horses stamped and snorted their displeasure as water evaporated into crackling clouds of steam when the approaching nano-disassemblers swept past. The eastbound and westbound sides of the highway bridges groaned, popped, and sagged when the sides anchored to the east bank disappeared. As a testament to those long-dead civil engineers who had designed and built them, neither side collapsed. Julio continued to watch as the ends of both bridges moved westward, looking every bit as if they were chopped off with a very sharp knife. He wondered briefly where the material was going until he saw those undulating, gelatinous veins like the one he'd kicked in Sealy running along the underside of the remaining bridge stubs, down the bank, and back eastward toward Houston.

The water coming from the north quickly returned to its original course, refilling the stream bed. The horses, having forgotten their earlier concern, tugged at their reins in an attempt to reach it. As he let them drink their fill, Channing did the same on the other side.

"That was a dumb move," he said.

"Really? If these things are eating people, it's only a matter of time until we're all dead," she said and then looked around at the desolation surrounding them. "As a matter of fact, we're probably not going to survive this anyway."

Julio nodded. "I need to call San Marcos and let them know the front is still moving."

He pulled a drone from its case on the packhorse and launched it. With the high-altitude drone acting as a relay, Julio sighed with relief when he was finally able to get a message through to his mother at the state capital, reporting what he'd seen and their situation.

"What did she say?" Channing asked as Julio recovered the drone.

"She wants us to keep going."

They followed one of the gelatinous veins eastward. Smaller capillaries joining from time to time made it grow steadily fatter.

"So strange," Julio muttered. "What could they possibly be building that would require this much material?"

"Tom said that the structure was big," Channing said.

"Yeah, but locked up in the black dust they harvested was the material that had once been the entire city of Houston. They had that to start with. Now they're taking everything else except people. Why?"

"I have no idea," she said with an odd movement resembling one of those bobblehead statuettes. "And why would they take Tom when they haven't taken anyone else?"

That bobblehead thing was . . . Then he remembered. Channing Bussard! The child actor. She'd played Hattie, the mouthy little sister in the *Red Rovers* TV series about kids growing up in a colony on Mars. He'd seen all fifty-six episodes about ten times when he was young.

"Holy crap," he said. "I can't believe I took so long to figure it out. You're Hattie! I loved *Red Rovers*!"

The big floppy hat hid most of her expression, but she laughed and nodded. "You get twenty nerd points! But that was a very long time ago. A lifetime ago, it seems."

He'd had a huge crush on her when he was about ten, but those shows were already five or six years old by the time he found them in the Global Cultural Recovery online archive. Her acting career had ended, along with so much else, on Killday.

"You were great in the series, but I liked you better in that movie. The one where you were the New York City mayor's daughter. What was it called . . . ? *Big Apple Blues*!"

She threw her head back with a groan. "Oh my God! I didn't think anyone still alive had seen that movie. Unless you have some kind of mental link with your fob and just now looked that up, you really are a legit movie nerd."

The idea of a mental link with his fob made him flinch. It reminded him of Abby and brought the old anger back to the surface, even though he hadn't talked to her for more than a year.

"Definitely no mental link," he said with probably more snap than he'd intended.

She looked at him and raised an eyebrow.

"It's just that . . . I dunno, you were serious in that movie, not comic relief like in *Red Rovers*, and it really showed your acting chops."

"Thanks," she said. "You wouldn't believe how many grown men try to hit on me by saying they had a crush on Hattie. I mean, I was nine years old when I made that series and the movie."

Julio was on the verge of telling her about his crush but swallowed his words. "Yeah, that would be totally creepy. I mean, even if they were nine or ten at the time, too."

"Exactly."

"But you're not nine now."

She leveled a glare at him. "Don't even think about it, lover boy. I'm still a lot older than you."

"How old were you on Killday?"

"Eleven."

"I was five, so you're only six years older," he said with a grin.

She groaned and shook her head.

They rode all morning, passing through the ghostly imprints of what had been Sealy and San Felipe. Or, more accurately, the smooth, level squares and geometric patches of dirt that had once been streets, houses, driveways, and parking lots. They'd all worried about rising temperatures caused by the black dust from Killday, but now Earth's entire biosphere was being erased.

Despite the blistering Texas sun, that thought sent a chill creeping up Julio's spine. The dirt—already dried out since being exposed that very morning—puffed up in tiny dust clouds behind each horse's hooves as they continued eastward.

They stopped in the late afternoon upon reaching the Brazos River. It, too, was but a shallow wraith of what it had been, but they dismounted, let the horses drink, and pulled lunch from their packs. They sat in the shade of an embankment that had once held a bridge. Julio's fob said the temperature was 112 degrees Fahrenheit.

After a lull in conversation, Julio asked what he'd been wondering for hours. "So, how did a big-time Hollywood actor end up the mayor of Sealy, Texas?"

Channing shrugged. "We didn't live in Hollywood, except during filming. My dad was a professor at Texas A&M, so we were living in College Station on Killday. Then, when I was seventeen, I married a guy from Sealy and moved down here."

Julio had been batting around a lot of confusing thoughts since meeting Channing. She was the first woman since Abby he'd really been attracted to. But he also wondered if that attraction was driven by his years-old crush on her TV character. She'd mentioned that the missing Tom was her brother-in-law. Could she still be married? It didn't matter, but he wanted to make sure. "So, you're married?"

"Well, I don't think I am. Not really. A couple of years ago, Jackson just up and disappeared one day. I was sick with worry at first, then found out that another woman from Sealy, also married, disappeared at the same time. Apparently, everyone in town had known about them. Everyone but me, anyway."

Julio looked down at the jerky in his hand, feeling suddenly awkward. "I'm sorry. I didn't—"

"Oh, don't be. I've come to grips with it. He obviously did me a favor."

After eating, they forded the river and led the horses as they talked about her movie and TV experiences.

"I've told you pretty much my life story," Channing said. "Now let's hear about you. Are you really the governor's kid?"

"Adopted son. Like a lot of kids in my little town, my real parents were in San Antonio on Killday and never came home."

"Oh, I'm sorry."

"Yeah, I don't really remember them. Only what I see in pictures and stories people told me."

He went on to tell her about following his best friend Abby to New Chicago, being kidnapped by the Kilburnites, the massacre he'd witnessed in the underground bunker, and being rescued by Abby.

"She actually came into that crazy, dangerous mess to rescue you?" Channing asked, sounding impressed. "That is indeed a good friend."

The comment made Julio uncomfortable. Abby had risked her life to save him, but he'd abandoned her. Perhaps when she'd needed him the most. Had he been wrong?

"By the look on your face, I must have hit a nerve. Was she your girlfriend and it ended badly?"

"No, we weren't a couple."

Channing's expression grew dark. "Then I hope it's not that you resent being rescued by a woman?"

"Ha! No way. Abby's amazing. Takes after her mom, I guess."

"And who's her mom?"

"Leigh Gibson. The woman who stopped the Killday attack."

She gaped at him, truly speechless for several seconds. "So, how did you become friends with Leigh Gibson's daughter?"

"We were at the same day care on Killday. We've been close friends ever since."

"I would love to meet her. Is she back in San Marcos?"

"No, you'll have to visit Uptown Station to meet her now. And you'll have to be okay with her being a biad. She has an AI named Mortimer living in her skull." Even thinking about that made Julio's stomach churn.

"Oh," she said, picking up on the anger in his tone. "I thought biad AIs lived in torcs around their human partner's neck. I had no idea it had gone so far. And it was reported that all the biads were killed fighting Kilburnites."

"Yeah, that *is* what was reported, but some escaped," he said and looked to the east. "I'd hoped all the surviving AIs were in space. Evidently, that isn't the case."

"Do you think what happened in Sealy and those fat veins of material flowing east are because of AIs?"

"Yeah. It sure isn't the Texas government. There aren't any Kilburnites capable of these kinds of actions."

She raised her eyebrows and nodded thoughtfully. "And you were kidnapped by the Kilburnites and almost killed, but now you're working with them?"

"Yes," he said, once more feeling uncomfortable. "Let's just say it was the lesser of two evils."

She snorted. "I can't imagine the Kilburnites ever being the lesser evil."

A line of dust suddenly appeared ten yards ahead, stretching across their path perhaps fifty yards to either side. It swirled and eddied, and then, in less than a second, a fence of dull black rods grew up out of the ground. Channing's mount wheeled to run, and Julio's reared, but they both managed to keep control. When the dust settled, the horses calmed enough for them to dismount and examine the fence. Each post was about an inch in diameter and ten feet high, spaced about six inches apart.

Julio glanced at Channing and nodded to his right. As they left the fine dirt of the roadbed, the fence moved with them. Black spikes rose from the ground with a crackling whine, keeping pace and blocking them no matter how far they walked.

Channing stopped and peered closer at one of the black fingers. "Did you see that? They grew layer upon layer, like items built in a sandbox, only incredibly fast."

"Yeah. I wonder . . . Have you ever heard of programmable matter?"

Her eyes grew wide. "Yes! Do you think it could be that stuff?"

He shrugged. "It's kind of been the holy grail of nanotechnology since long before Killday. It makes sense—the way this fence formed out of the dirt and those veins of material flowing east seem to have a mind of their own. If the AIs have perfected that tech, it's hard to imagine what other things they're capable of doing."

Julio removed his hat to mop his brow, then tried to check their GPS location on his fob but had no connection. "I wonder how far we are from Houston."

"It's hard to tell. We're not to Katy yet—or the remains of it, anyway—and that was about thirty miles from the Houston Zoo, which was close to the middle of the city."

"It doesn't matter," Julio said, glancing at the fence. "I doubt we're getting any closer."

"Weird," she said, standing up in the stirrups and looking east. "Tom was on the far side of what used to be Katy when I last spoke to him. I wonder why your magic AIs are stopping us here?"

Julio also looked east, squinting in the bright sunlight, but couldn't see even the hint of a large structure above the horizon. Even through binoculars, he saw nothing. After a few minutes of staring dumbly at the fence, he returned to the horses, pulled several drones from the bags on the packhorse, linked them to his fob, and launched one. After fitting goggles over his eyes, he sent the drone higher and moved it closer to the fence line.

"Okay," Julio muttered as he manipulated the drone using his fob. "I have the drone's camera zoom maxed out and still don't see anything in the direction of Houston. Let me try infrared. Not sure if that will help in this heat, but it might show something."

After a few minutes, he shook his head. "Nothing resembling any kind of big structure. It's flat and empty as far as the drone can see."

"Can you get closer?"

"Let's find out," he said and sent the drone darting forward. At first, nothing happened as the robot passed the boundary established by the moving fence, and then dozens of wire-thin dust contrails erupted from the ground. They all met at the drone, causing it to disintegrate in a cloud of tumbling debris.

"Well, so much for that," Channing said as they watched the drone pieces tumble to the ground.

"Yeah, but the connection log on my fob shows a delay of one point nine seconds between when the drone started moving forward and losing contact. Unless they had these little mini-missiles just parked here in the sand, my guess is they assessed the threat, built the countermeasures, and fired them all within that period of time."

"I don't think they were missiles," Channing said and held out her own fob screen. "I recorded the drone crossing the fence line. If you slow it down enough, these look more like bullets or darts. Not powered at all."

"Huh . . . A shotgun blast of pellets?"

She nodded.

"And I guess that answers the question about AI," he said as he readied another drone. "No human controllers could have reacted that fast. But it also shows that they can be caught by surprise. If something is moving fast enough, it might get through."

"You're going to send another drone?"

"No, I'm going to try and contact San Marcos."

With the high-altitude drone acting as a relay, Julio connected to his mother and reported what they'd seen. Channing waited patiently as he recovered the drone. "Well?"

"She was rather upset. All this time, she's believed—or at least pretended to believe—that we had actually wiped AIs from the face of the Earth. And now she really wants to know what is going on in Houston that the AIs don't want us to see."

"So do I."

"She's going to send a Mongoose interceptor drone. Those things fly at Mach 4. If anything can get through, that will."

Julio returned the drone to its solar charging case hanging from the packhorse's harness, then turned to speak with Channing. She stood mere inches from the barrier, arms wrapped around herself.

"Are you okay?"

She shivered. "You realize that we're over, right?"

"What? Who is over?"

"Humanity."

The hair on the back of Julio's neck prickled.

They gave the horses some water, then sat down with their backs against the fence and ate some of the bread from their provisions.

Twenty minutes later, the air about fifty yards on the other side of the barrier erupted with hundreds of dust contrails arcing up from the ground as another shotgun blast of pellets fired into the air. They both leaped to their feet to watch. Unlike those that brought down his camera drone, these didn't have an obvious target, but Julio suspected the Mongoose was on its way.

Then the horses shrieked and reared as the barrier fence twisted toward them, growing tighter and bending inward, obviously forming a cage.

"Run," Julio yelled, but before either could move, the unmanned Mongoose flashed past about fifty feet above their heads, evidently hugging the ground to avoid radar detection. Hot, pressurized air slammed them both to the ground as twin rooster tails of dust and debris raced past. Through the contracting cage and at the far edge of his vision, Julio saw the interceptor cartwheel, then disintegrate in a brilliant plume of orange fire. Roaring pain enveloped him, and thick dust made it impossible to breathe as he plunged into sudden darkness.

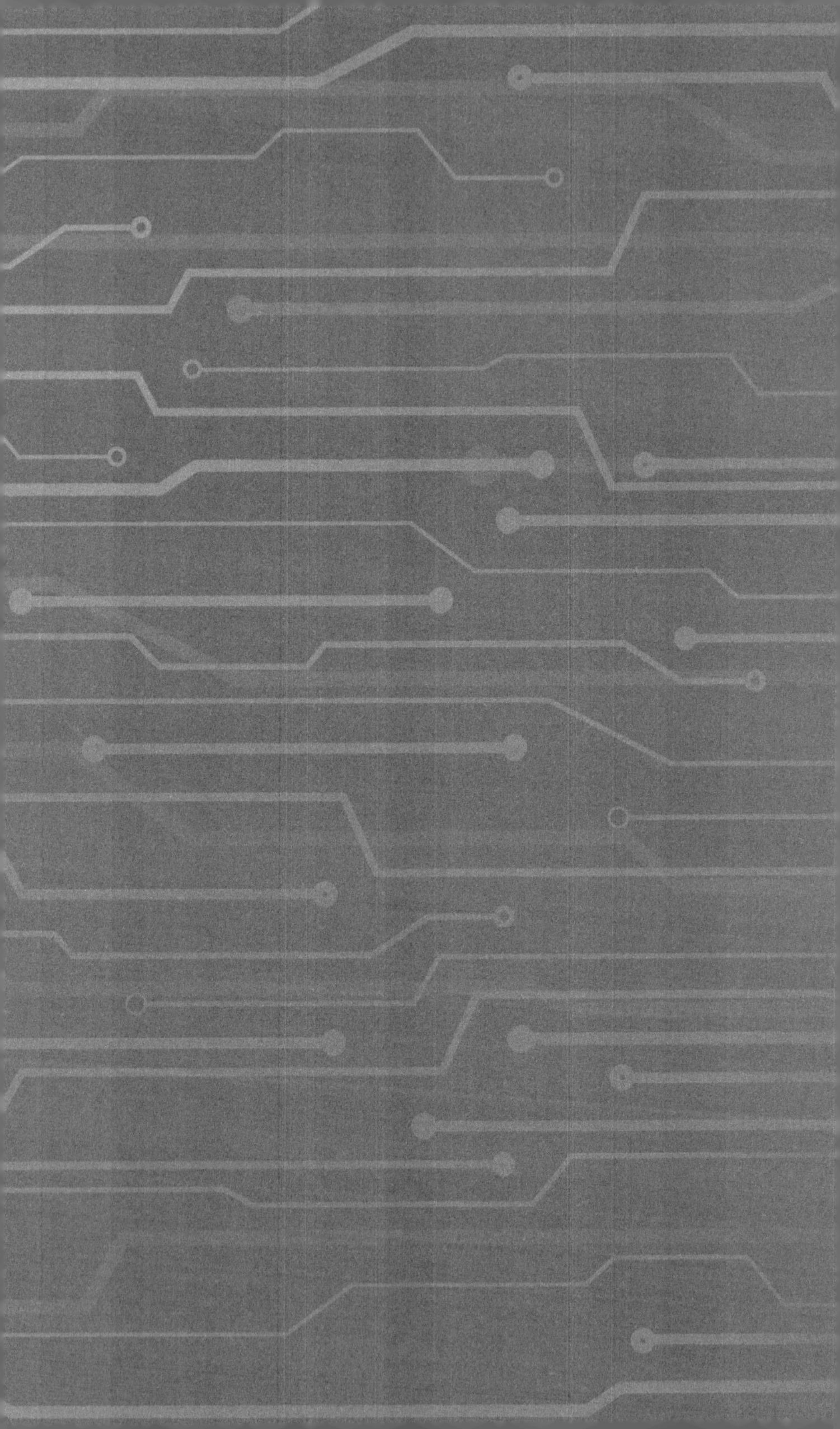

DARK-CIRCLED eyes and greasy hair were the only parts of Abby visible from the blanket pile strapped into her command chair. She hadn't slept much in the day and a half since their encounter in the belt but had sat for long hours in the control center, watching the passive sensors during their trip home, hoping they would find the thing that had destroyed the drones before it found them.

"If this rock or ship or anomaly was so freakin' big, why can't we find it?" Abby grumbled. "I mean, we even knew its rough course. This shouldn't be so hard."

"Space is big," Violet said.

"And we didn't really come with the proper equipment for this particular task," Mortimer said.

Abby hated being afraid, but dread had soaked into her like paint into a sponge. No matter how hard she squeezed, the stain would not go away. And it wasn't just her own life in danger. Four other people on her ship—two human and two artificial—also depended on her doing the right thing to keep them safe.

Nora floated between her and the wall screen. "We just received a broad-beam message from Uptown Station. It's from Owen. Do you want me to play it?"

"Yeah."

Owen's voice came from Abby's fob speaker. "We need to talk. Please ping us with your location."

"Damn," Abby muttered. "I wanted to stay dark for another two days."

"Owen probably knows that," Mortimer said. "He must either think you are safe now, or his information is important enough to reveal your position. Of course, you're the captain, so you don't have to respond."

"Talk?" Abby said with a snort. "We're still too far away for any kind of real conversation. What's our round-trip radio delay?"

"About six minutes," Nora said.

"I wonder if he's going to take my schooner away," Abby said, playing the simple message again.

"No," Nora said. "I'm pretty sure he can't do that. Besides, you haven't done anything wrong."

"Nothing wrong?" Abby said with a sharp bark of laughter. "This flight was a spectacular failure. I did *everything* wrong. We didn't even justify the trip by getting enough uranium for my experiment, and on top of that, we lost the one-of-a-kind Xolotl mining unit."

"So? How could you have known there would be some kind of drone killer out there? You really had no other choice," Nora said.

"Stop feeling sorry for yourself," Violet said from the other side of the room, "and go clean up, for God's sake. You stink."

Abby smiled for the first time in days. At least she could depend on these two to tell her exactly what they thought.

"Is this a mutiny?" she asked, already starting to untangle herself from the blanket mess.

"Our noses are fighting for their very survival," Violet said with a grin.

"Fine," Abby said. "Go ahead and turn on the transmitters and ping them our location. But stay vigilant, Mortimer. In case this thing has been waiting for us to light up before coming after us."

"Look on the bright side," Violet said. "If that's the case, at least we'll find it."

Five minutes later, Abby crawled into the bag shower, sealed it around her face, and started the warm water flowing. She scrubbed her hair repeatedly, trying to wash away the accumulated dirt and oil.

By the time Abby finished cleaning up and returned to the control cabin, an open, streaming data link had been established with Uptown Station. She suspected they'd all been waiting for her, but no one said anything as she joined the in-progress meeting. She expanded the view screen to fill an entire wall.

Even though most of the station's command staff spent so much time in microgravity that they preferred to stay in their space schooners, for this meeting, they had chosen Victor and Allison's new apartment inside the rotating habitat. It was spacious, with plant-covered balconies, and had been built partway up the endcap, close to the rotational hub, where the gravity was a tenth that on Earth. Yet, Abby knew even that amount of g-force had a tiring effect on those who'd lived the last twenty years in microgravity.

Owen and his wife, Andrea, sat across from Victor at the long balcony table as Matt and Allison brought coffee and tea. After so long using sippy cups or squeeze bulbs, they still didn't seem to trust the open cups they placed in front of everyone.

Behind them, Abby could see the station's interior. After having grown up on Earth, with open skies and an obvious horizon, living on the inside of a giant cylinder where the ground curved up and away overhead would take some adjustment. She had so far continued to live in her schooner. The opposite endcap was more than a mile away and faded to gray with distance, but the habitat's floor—only a half mile above and below—was dotted with clusters of small houses and shops, occasionally including tall buildings that seemed to lean toward each other as they pointed up at the central axis. Much of the habitat floor was still bare dirt, with green grass and trees surrounding little knots of homes and outlining the rivers and lakes. It was capable of supporting a population of forty thousand but so far had only a quarter of that.

Owen's voice drew her attention back to the group. "We have a lot to cover. Something is happening that may well threaten our very survival. Here's what we know so far. Abby's crew encountered an unknown object in the main belt that seems to have deliberately destroyed two drones manned by AIs. This implies intelligent or at least automated guidance. It also seems to be invisible to radar, but based on the fuzzy video and trajectory information they were able to gather before losing contact with the object, we believe it is an asteroid that has been set on a course to hit the station and will arrive no later than five days from now."

The room exploded with panicky questions from upset people. Owen held up his hands for order. "People! Please. Let me finish—I might answer some of your questions."

The conversation slowed, then trickled off, leaving only a whispered exchange between Allison and Victor. Owen waited for them to finish, then continued.

"So far, we haven't managed to find it with our optical telescopes, but we'll keep looking. In the meantime, we have to start making preparations to move the station. With Abby's help, we might have some good options for doing that, but we'll discuss those at the end of the meeting. We owe Abby a debt of gratitude. My guess is whatever's out there wasn't ready to be found yet. So, her stumbling on it might have alerted us that they are there, if not to their intentions."

Andrea shook her head slowly. "It seems like a rather large coincidence that this thing happened to be passing near where Abby was mining."

"Which brings up two more unlikely coincidences," Owen said. "Forty minutes after Abby sent her warning message, Halifax appeared in the control room to confront Victor. At the same time, communication traffic from Earth stopped. Are these events all connected? If so, how and why?"

"We've got to figure out who is behind this," Victor said. "Does anyone think the Kilburnites could do any of this? The communications bottleneck, maybe?"

Heads shook all around the room.

"I don't think they have the technology level for that, and I doubt they'd have the ability to keep it secret if they did," a copy of Mortimer said from his hovering husk. "We've been keeping pretty close tabs on them."

Abby still found it strange that Mortimer was there with them when she knew he also resided in her head.

"So, it has to be the Aggregate," Victor said. "And up until Halifax's little stunt, we had no reason to believe it even still existed. Just so we're all on the same page, tell us what we know about Halifax, Mortimer."

"When we captured it, shortly after the attempt to take over the station, we locked it in a cell that was basically a big Faraday cage, with no access to our networks or even the electricity grid. Light was piped into the room by mirrors. No wires at all. At that point, the thing essentially went into a kind of fugue state. Nothing but eating, drinking, and defecating. Upon extensive examination, I found Halifax to be essentially human, but instead of the biological substrates I and other level sixes have established with our human biads and triads, it has a slurry of nanomachines acting as a cerebral fluid. Its entire brain is awash in this fluid, and we assume that is how the Aggregate controls it."

Victor raised a finger. "And Halifax's inaction was mistakenly attributed to the fact that we had isolated it, with no access to controlling communications from the Aggregate."

"Or that the Aggregate had been destroyed, and there was no one left to control Halifax at all," Mortimer said.

"Obviously, neither of those assumptions was true," Owen said. "They must have been able to communicate with Halifax. I guess we're lucky they didn't make an attempt to take over the station again."

Abby thought that if Halifax had really been active all along, then the Aggregate could have seized control at any time. Why had they not done so?

"So, Mortimer?" Allison spoke for the first time. "If Halifax was essentially human, how did it manage to melt into its cell floor and then rematerialize in the station's control center?"

"It transformed into something different. Analysis revealed that the floor panels below Halifax's cell contain trace biological material, but when I scanned the Halifax that appeared in the control center, its body was made up entirely of materials found in the ship. Even though it looked the same, the two bodies were entirely different."

"Has the Aggregate, or whoever controls Halifax, perfected the use of programmable matter?" Andrea said.

"That does appear to be the case," Mortimer said. "Or some similar technology."

There was a pause while everyone absorbed the ramifications of that information.

"This might seem like a complete change of topic," Owen said and sat down again, "but it is relevant if you'll hear me out. Back when I designed the space schooners, I had intended that they use the same kind of gravity-manipulation units, or GMUs, used in travel pods. But the fields in GMUs are limited by a weird issue with the power-to-size ratio, and KeeseCorp, the company that built the GMUs, never found the solution to that problem before Killday wiped them out, along with most other large companies.

"The problem is that GMU fields try to encompass everything they touch, and as they attempt to do so, they quickly hit a point where the power requirements expand exponentially. The three-meter diameter of a travel pod is the maximum allowed by the energy available in a standard pocket fission reactor. If I were to create a field large enough to encompass my ten-meter space schooners, the field would require the power output of a small star."

He paused and glanced around the room, then turned to the camera. "Okay, Abby. Now that we understand the GMU limitations, tell us about your planned experiment. We'll wait for your response."

Abby swallowed and took a deep breath. By his earlier remark, she knew he was going to put her on the spot, but she still wasn't ready.

"I . . . well . . . as Owen explained, GMU fields try to encompass anything they encounter, but they require more and more power to do that, so they eventually collapse. So, I wondered if we could contain a gravity generator and its required power source in a magnetic field so that it didn't touch anything. Kinda the way they keep antimatter from touching real matter. If we could do that, we might be able to use those magnetically encased GMUs as engines to move things as big as space schooners or even larger if we wrapped them in a field with an opposite charge. Of course, generating magnetic fields of that strength would require larger reactors than those in travel pods. I hoped something in the two-hundred-kilowatt range like we use in space schooners might work. That's why I went looking for uranium, to build three or four reactors for my experiment."

While she waited for her message to get to the station and their reply to come back, Abby pulled up the schematics of the test rig she intended to build just in case they wanted specifics. Then she looked around at her ship's quiet bridge.

Violet grinned at her. "You rock. Talking about building your own nuclear reactor like it was a middle school science project."

"The experiment probably won't work," Abby said, "but now that I've thought of it, I have to know."

"There is another situation you should probably know about," Mortimer said inside her head so that the others couldn't hear. "As Owen mentioned, communication traffic from Earth suddenly stopped. And due to the complete loss of communication with my covert robotic agents that were following him, I've lost track of Julio. I'm sorry."

Abby's guts knotted up. What could be happening on Earth that would result in a total communications blackout? It couldn't be good. And it was probably related to what she'd found in the belt, though she couldn't imagine how. She tried to focus on her current situation as the next message came in from Uptown Station.

Owen nodded and smiled at Abby's explanation. "We're lucky that a long one-g acceleration enabled the *Jackalope* to get quite a lead on this object, so Abby and her crew will be here in about thirty hours. Abby, when you arrive, we'd like for you to conduct your experiment as soon as possible. Send us your schematics and plans so we can start gathering up or making everything you require. We'll give you every bit of help you need. If that rock is indeed on course to hit us and has the capability to adjust its course, then we're going to need a better method of moving the entire station."

By the time the meeting ended, Abby's stomach was churning and twisting again.

The *Jackalope* had already flipped, and Abby had hoped to relax for a few hours in zero-g before starting their deceleration burn, but Owen was putting her little experiment in the forefront of the station's defensive preparations. If she even hoped to set everything up in time, they had to get back as quickly as possible.

"Well, you heard the man. Mortimer, I want to start our one-g breaking burn in ten minutes."

"If we are in a hurry—" Violet said.

"We're not having this argument," Abby said. Violet looked away with a sour frown, but Nora looked relieved. She felt bad for once again subjecting Violet to even one g. Her friend had seemed to handle that pressure okay when she'd been on Earth, but having spent almost an entire year in microgravity could have weakened her vascular system even more. Abby subvocalized a message to Mortimer, telling him to make sure Archie kept a close eye on those nanobots monitoring Violet's brain once they started decelerating. Then she started sending all her data to the station and crossed her fingers, hoping that she had thought of everything needed for the experiment.

———

ABBY FELT ALMOST GIDDY with relief when they were close enough to actually see Uptown Station. The constant one-g acceleration and then deceleration had been rough on them all, but on top of that, Abby had the stress of knowing the station's very survival might rely on the success of her half-baked magnetic-field theory. She had slept little and kept frantically examining and tweaking the schematics and modeling of her experiment. When the station came into view, she took a deep breath, forced herself to relax, and closed down those files.

She called traffic control and handed over the actual docking process to Mortimer so that she could just sit back and watch their approach. The station grew larger on her main screen and was a spectacular sight. Much of actual space travel was boring or stressful, but nearing the station had an almost magical effect on Abby every time.

Uptown Station was huge, and one of the greatest feats of human engineering in history, but only a small part of humanity would ever see it. Abby felt lucky to be one of them. It was a modified Bernal sphere a mile in diameter and elongated to a mile and a half long. Its double, counter-rotating hull produced Earth-normal rotational gravity at its wide equator. A ring of attached mirrors directed sunlight inside for growing crops, and a two-hundred-yard-long, nonrotating spine protruded from each endcap along the axis. The forward spine held massive radiator farms and the large sandbox molecular printers used for manufacturing. The aft spine was for spacecraft docking and had dozens of spherical space schooners and tiny travel pods clinging to it like barnacles.

Since parts of the station were still being built, a cloud of robotic tugs and construction drones surrounded it in a twinkling cloud, constantly moving and busy. A little farther away, trailing the station—but still within the L5 balanced gravity zone—was a free-flying wall of solar panels the size of four football fields. It continuously collected sunlight and beamed the energy back to the station via microwave.

A cluster of space schooners—known as the Hive—proceeded the station on the lunar side. Owen had designed his schooners with six equally spaced airlocks, four around the sphere's equator and one at each pole, so that the ships could connect in strings or clusters. Since the schooners were much too large to use standard gravity-manipulation fields, one of those airlocks on each ship had been modified to hold the enhanced nuclear electric drive unit, but the remaining five locks had been put to good use. Abby counted seventeen of the round ships linked together in clumps.

As she watched, one string of five schooners detached from the Hive, floating free for a few seconds. Then, the engine of the last ship in the line fired, moving the entire stack away from the station and toward the moon. She knew that, once they arrived, the string would separate, with each ship going off in a different direction to pursue individual tasks, then hook up again for the return flight.

The *Jackalope* slowed as it neared the aft docking spine, rotated slightly to properly align the airlocks, then inched inward until a loud *thunk* announced their arrival. Abby glanced at the status screen as icons turned green, indicating power, water, and data connections had been established with the station. She smiled at her crew, and everyone unbuckled their harnesses.

"Pizza!" Violet said. "I got a message while we were out informing me that the new pizza place on the ground level is now open!"

Nora groaned. "Ugh! It will be so crowded. And that place is on the full one-g inner face. Can't we spend the night at the half-g level to acclimate first?"

Violet reached out and gave Nora's arm a quick squeeze, then pulled her hand back. "You go to our room. I'll get pizza and bring it back."

Nora nodded and smiled.

Violet turned to Abby. "You coming with me?"

Abby switched the screen to the airlock camera feed. Now it was her turn to groan. Matt floated in the corridor just outside the *Jackalope*'s docking hatch. His girlfriend, Terra, already didn't like Abby, and such situations only added fuel to the fire, so Abby really didn't feel like talking to him. She had more important things on her mind, like meeting up with Owen to find out how she could get the new reactor and gravity-manipulation unit.

Violet harrumphed. "Do you want me to tell him to quit stalking you and go away?"

"No," she said. "I like him and don't want to hurt his feelings, but he's just . . . I don't know. Clingy? He wants and expects too much. He's also Owen and Andrea's son, and I don't want to piss them off either."

"He's gorgeous," Violet said with a twisted smile.

"I think that might be a big part of the problem," Abby said. "I did flirt with him and was attracted to him at first, but then that all kind of faded away. I doubt that happens to him very often."

Violet shook her head. "Or ever. He's the kind of guy who can walk into a bar and yell, 'Who wants to spend the night with me?' and hands will raise all around the room."

Abby snorted and looked at Nora. "Really? Is that a thing?"

"I have no idea," Nora said. "I don't go to bars. Too many people scrunched up all together."

"I've seen it happen," Violet said with the little twisted smile again.

Abby suspected that Violet was probably one of those women who raised a hand, but she didn't ask.

"I know how to get rid of him," Violet said.

"What are you going to do?"

"Trust me." She motioned for Nora to come with her, and they left the control cabin.

A few minutes later, they exited the ship and started talking to Matt. Abby turned the volume up on the outside mic so that she could hear what they were saying.

"Come with us to get some pizza," Violet said and laid a hand on his shoulder. "Abby will join us later, but right now, I think she just needs some alone time. This was a really stressful trip."

Matt glanced back at the hatch, apparently unsure if it was a good idea to leave his ambush position, but then he finally nodded and let Violet lead him down the corridor.

Abby let out a breath she didn't realize she'd been holding, then whispered, "I owe you one, Violet. Mortimer? Any news on Julio?"

"I'm afraid not. All communication with Earth is still blocked. There is a message from Owen. He wants you to call him."

"Yes!" Abby strapped back into her seat and made the call.

Owen answered immediately. "Abby! I'm so glad you're back and in one piece. What a scary trip."

"Thanks. And yeah, I'm still a little twitchy. Have you found that rock yet?"

His expression was grim as he shook his head slowly. "No, but if the intent is still to hit us, then there are only so many viable trajectories from the last observed position. Unless that thing has continued to accelerate, we have about two weeks to prepare."

She nodded. "And the new reactors?"

"Ahhh, now that is where I have good news," he said with a big grin. "We've already stripped the reactors from four space schooners and the gravity-manipulation units from four travel pods. The mounting frames are printed and waiting to have the gear installed. The only thing we're waiting for is two more of the wireless controller units."

Abby gasped aloud. "Really? That was fast!"

"We've put everything else on hold. Your project had sandbox-printing priority."

"I'll get started on assembly right away."

He raised an eyebrow. "You need to take some time to rest first. By the way, in case he hasn't stopped by yet, Matt is also looking for you. He wants to help with your project. He's a pretty good technician if you give him solid directions."

"Okay," she said with a nod. "I'll keep that in mind."

She sighed deeply after the call ended and stared at the blank screen. Had she overreacted to Matt coming to meet her ship? Maybe he'd only come to offer his help, as his dad said. The reasonable and adult thing to do would be to go find Matt and ask him. If it turned awkward, she'd just plunge into that long-overdue, difficult conversation. She unbuckled with the full intention of leaving the ship and facing her problems. Instead, she went down the corridor to her workshop, opened a large wall screen, and called up a schematic. Ten minutes later, she hummed a happy tune as she sent the design for a new circuit block to the ship's sandbox.

CHAPTER 6

JULIO'S AWARENESS returned in a string of unconnected episodes. Each time he struggled awake, he was greeted by moving shapes made indistinct by blurry vision and muffled sounds that sometimes seemed like human speech and other times not. Every time he tried to focus on what had happened and where he was, the thoughts shredded like cobwebs in a panhandle twister and drove him back to sleep's safe blackness.

One early morning, he woke with a clear mind but an aching body and memories of drowning. He was in a bed, wearing loose pajamas, covered by a sheet and blanket. A single polarized window lit the tiny room. It was empty except for the bed and a woman standing in one corner. She was quite small, possibly less than five feet; had dark hair and freckles; and wore baggy white shorts, a T-shirt with a generic stylized sunrise, and blue flip-flops. Blinking occasionally, the woman stared at the blank wall, unaware that Julio was awake.

After a few minutes, he closed his eyes again and tried to piece together what had happened. He'd been in a *Red Rovers* episode where he and Hattie were trekking across Mars. Without space suits. No . . . that wasn't right. Was it a dream? It hadn't been Mars, but a Texas landscape made barren by nanobots. Had Hattie really been there? Nothing made sense. There had been an explosion. Shrieking horses. A screaming woman. Then he remembered.

Where was Channing?

Grunting into gritted teeth, he sat up and scooted to the side of the bed. When he tried to stand, the room spun wildly, so he changed his mind.

"You'll need to move slowly and in stages," the woman said.

The unexpected comment startled Julio, making him freeze in position.

She approached the bed. "Your physical injuries are mostly healed, but you've been immobile for nine days. It might take some time to get your balance and muscle strength back to an acceptable level."

"Who are you?" Julio said. His voice sounded hoarse and weak.

"You can call me Halifax," she said, followed by a sweet smile.

"Where am I? And where is Channing?"

"You're at a facility built near the remains of Houston. I'll take you to your friend," she said.

As he watched, strange shapes grew from the floor, just as the fence had sprouted from the dirt before the explosion. It eventually formed into what could only be a wheelchair, though its swooping, gently curved frame looked more like an abstract sculpture. The bed also changed, twisting into a cuplike structure that lifted him into a standing position.

Halifax helped him into the wheelchair, then rolled it out into a hallway and down to a large, brightly lit room. Two glass-walled tanks occupied most of the floor space. One was empty, but the other was filled with blue liquid. Channing floated in its center, naked but for a lacework of cables and wires.

Julio flinched and looked away. "Was I in one of those?"

"Yes, of course. Your injuries were extensive."

Julio shivered with the half-remembered feeling of drowning.

"How much longer will she be in there?"

"Her burns were more serious than yours, but she should be ready to come out of the rejuvenation tank by tomorrow."

"Why did your AI masters blow us up and then heal us?"

Halifax smiled. "Your mother blew you up. She's the one who sent the interceptor at such a low altitude, even though she assumed we wouldn't allow it to cross the barrier. When something moving at Mach 4 suddenly stops, along with its weapons, there will be an explosion. That energy has to go somewhere. The screen we built between you and the blast saved you from most of the debris, but the heat and pressure wave did a lot of damage."

He remembered the cage growing up around them. Had it really been for protection? Had Halifax's masters brought them to Houston and healed them because his mother was the Texas governor? Could he be a political hostage? They were seriously mistaken if they thought they could control his mother that way.

"None of this makes much sense," Julio said. "Channing and I were trying to get to Houston, but your friends tried to keep us out. So, why did you bring us to Houston?"

"It's complicated. Let's just say we weren't prepared to host humans here yet, but you were so badly injured, we had to change our plans if we were going to save your lives."

"You keep saying *we*. Who are you working for? Who put up that barrier, and why?"

The quick, fake smile returned. "Based on the communications with your mother, it's obvious you already know the answers to those questions."

A chill crept up his spine, and he felt suddenly angry. "The Aggregate. And you're willingly working for them?"

She shrugged. "Something like that."

The fight against AIs wasn't over. Julio had long suspected that was true but was both glad and dismayed to finally know for sure. At least it made his situation very clear. He was a POW of some sort.

"I still don't know why we're here or why your masters went to so much trouble to keep us alive."

"It's because you're both creatives."

She used the term like a title, as if he should be wearing a badge that said *Julio Ramirez, Creative*, but she didn't elaborate. It made sense for Channing, but he had no idea why she'd classified him that way. He didn't correct her.

"Then why not just let us go?"

"We can't allow you to go back to San Marcos, but we can now show you what you came here to see," she said and turned the wheelchair toward the door. Julio noticed as they left the room that the empty rejuvenation tank had almost completely dissolved into the floor.

When they exited the building, the bright sun nearly blinded him, but as his eyes adjusted, he gasped. The large structure that stood about two hundred yards ahead of them resembled a massive jellyfish more than a building. Parts of it were translucent, seeming to quiver and pulsate. Adding to that organic appearance were enormous veins radiating outward in all directions like spokes from a wheel. They resembled those he'd seen in Sealy, only thicker than he was tall. While the structure was amazing enough, it paled to insignificance when compared to the tower rising from its center. Julio knew he was seeing some kind of space elevator, but it didn't resemble the designs and test units he'd seen. There were no cables, ribbons, mechanical climbers, or elevator pods, only a thin spire of what looked like pinkish glass soaring upward until it eventually faded into the heavens.

As he watched, he understood a little better. Each time the anchoring structure pulsed, he heard a crackling noise, the hair on his arms stood up, and a dark mass raced up the line, disappearing into the sky. He wondered if they used magnetics—like a rail gun—to accelerate the matter up the tube. And why were they collecting material from the ruins of Houston and the surrounding areas, then firing it into space?

When Julio turned back to Halifax, she was watching him with a cold, expressionless stare. Then her smile suddenly appeared, as if from a flipped switch, and it made Julio's skin crawl. He looked at her more closely. She was breathing and perspiring like a human. Her hair was even messed up on one side, but there was just something wrong about her. For the first time, he considered the possibility that she might not be entirely human. Was she a blad, like Abby? Or something entirely new?

"I assume these go to geostationary orbit. Why?" Julio pointed to the space elevator.

"They go to our ships. We need to evacuate Earth soon and will need someplace to go."

———

WHEN JULIO PEEKED through the door of Channing's room two hours later, he found her alone, sitting up in bed with a half-eaten tray of food on her lap. The skin on her neck and one side of her face was pink and glossy. Halifax said Channing's burns had been more extensive, but she looked a lot better than Julio had felt on the first day he woke up.

"How do you feel?"

She waved for him to enter. "Like crap, but better than an hour ago."

Her voice was hoarse and scratchy like Julio's had been at first.

He sat on the edge of the bed. "It'll take time."

"My memory is fuzzy. Were we in an explosion?"

Julio spent the next ten minutes explaining the rejuvenation tanks, what had happened, meeting Halifax, and where they were.

Channing shook her head. "So, they spent all that effort to keep us out, only to eventually bring us here."

"Halifax said they weren't ready to host humans yet. Our injuries forced them to accelerate their timetable, but I'm not exactly sure what that means."

"Have you found out what they're actually doing here?"

He nodded. "Are you feeling up to a wheelchair ride? I have something to show you."

"Anything to get out of this bed."

"We need a wheelchair," Julio said, and just as before, one grew up out of the floor.

"Holy crap," Channing said and scooted to the edge of the bed.

He helped her into the wheelchair but paused before leaving the room. "I need a pair of sunglasses for Channing."

A pair of black wraparound sunglasses made from some ultra-flexible plastic mesh appeared. He insisted she put them on, then pushed her down the corridor and out into the searing Texas afternoon.

"Oh my God," she muttered upon seeing the bizarre space elevator. Julio kept moving until he found a shady patch next to the building before stopping. Her new skin would burn easily. He'd found that out the hard way.

"Is that . . . a space elevator?"

"I think so," he said. "It's the only thing that makes sense."

They watched in silence long enough for two payloads to race up the tube.

"Why are they sending stuff into orbit?"

"They're building spaceships. Halifax said they need to evacuate Earth."

Her eyes widened. "Evacuate? Why?"

"She didn't tell me. I can only hope it is for these AIs to leave and never come back."

"And where are they getting the stuff they're sending up? Do you think those nano-disassembler waves are still expanding?"

"Again, Halifax didn't say, but I suspect they are. My mom said there were other places around the world where this was also happening. If they do keep growing, I wonder what will happen when all those refugees run out of places to go?"

They watched the elevator launch a few more loads, and then Julio bent down and said in her ear, "I have more to show you, but you gotta see this first.

"The wheelchair needs a sunshade," he said in a loud voice, then stepped back a little.

New struts sprouted from the chair just forward of the handles and continued to grow until they merged and bloomed into a strangely twisted rectangle of tight mesh above Channing's head. The addition looked as if it had always been part of the chair.

Julio pushed Channing back into the bright sun, and the shade automatically adjusted its angle to protect her as they walked.

The ground between the various buildings was also covered by a mesh-like substance resembling that of the sunshade but was perfectly rigid. When Julio left that surface and continued out into the bare dirt and gravel, Channing turned to look at him. "Ummm . . . where are we going?"

"Absolutely nowhere. I went out about a mile yesterday before they finally raised one of their fences in front of me."

He walked for another five minutes and then, as promised, stopped in a broad expanse of dirt. Ahead of them and to either side was what looked like the sterile surface of another planet. Wind from the distant gulf ruffled their hair and created dust devils that sailed inland to smear the distant horizon. Julio turned her around so that she could get a better view of the space elevator and surrounding buildings. From that distance, the mostly translucent tube refracted sunlight into swirling rainbow colors that disappeared into the sky.

"Who knew the end of humanity could be so beautiful," Channing said.

"You said that before. Do you truly believe this is the end for us?"

She turned and looked up at him. "Don't you feel it? I mean, this used to be Houston. One of the largest cities in the world. It was wiped from the Earth in a matter of hours. And not just the cities, but our whole history. The Louvre is gone. The Library of Congress. The Smithsonian. Hollywood."

Julio didn't know what to say. He'd been so young on Killday that all those places, including Houston, had just been ancient history. But Channing had most certainly seen Hollywood and maybe even the Louvre.

"And now all of this"—she pointed up at the space elevator—"is not human. Not us. Built without our say or even regard. We're nothing more than frightened mice running from the bulldozer."

Julio circled the chair and knelt in front of her. "But we're still here. Maybe we can make a difference."

"Oh, really? Is that why you brought me out here? Is this the first meeting of our resistance movement?"

His jaw clenched tight. He had brought her out this far to show her that their captors were listening to everything they said. Even out this far from the compound. Time to demonstrate that.

"Watch this," Julio said. "The sun is painfully bright out here. I need some sunglasses."

The sunglasses formed from the dirt beside him. He picked them up, but before putting them on, he made sure to look directly into Channing's eyes for several seconds, hoping to convey the importance of what had just happened with body language and eye contact. She tilted her head and narrowed her eyes slightly. Maybe she had understood.

As Julio pushed her back toward the compound, she said, "When will I get to meet this Halifax? I have questions for her."

"Well, it shouldn't be—" Julio stopped talking and moving as the composite ground ahead churned. A form grew up from the material and eventually became Halifax. Despite the heat, a chill made the hairs on his arms and neck rise.

"Oh my God," Channing muttered.

"Well, that's new, but yeah, this is Halifax," Julio said. "I knew she was working with the AIs and suspected she was at the very least a biad, but this is—"

"She's just a peripheral," Channing said.

The thing separated from the dirt with a hissing sound and took a step forward. "Hello, Channing. I'm glad to officially meet you. I helped during your healing and recuperation, but I doubt you remember me. Your assessment is correct. I'm not human, merely a tool for interfacing with the human world. What are your questions?"

Julio fought the urge to step backward. That was a primal human reaction to danger and the unknown, but Channing didn't even hesitate.

"Where are the horses?"

That made Julio wince. It should have been one of his first questions, but he hadn't given them more than a passing thought when he wondered about his missing gear the day before.

"Like you, they were badly injured from the blast," Halifax said. "But we couldn't save them. They were recycled."

Channing nodded, almost as if she'd already known the answer.

"You took my brother-in-law, Tom, from the ruins of Katy. Where is he?"

"We couldn't save him either."

Channing sucked in a breath. "He's—"

"Recycled. Yes."

She nodded, then seemed to regain her composure. "What happened? You were able to reconstruct our burned tissue—even in our lungs—using nanotech in those tanks. What injury could Tom possibly have had that you couldn't fix?"

"Tom wasn't injured," Halifax said with no facial expression at all. "He just wasn't needed."

Channing stood up from the wheelchair and took a wobbly step toward Halifax, with fists clenched.

Julio tried to step between them but wasn't quick enough. Channing lunged at Halifax with fists swinging. "Fucking machines! You're monsters!"

Halifax suffered the assault for several seconds, then disintegrated and re-formed about six feet to Julio's left. Channing fell to her knees in the dirt, stirring up dust that clung to her wet face. Julio helped her up and hugged her to him, but she pulled away and stumbled to the wheelchair.

Julio's own anger made his face hot as he turned to Halifax. "So again, why are we here? This is insane! Why spend the time and effort to heal me and Channing if we'll only be . . . recycled?"

"We know you, Julio."

The comment made his skin prickle.

"And we know Channing. Some humans, like the two of you, can do things we can't. You are both creatives. We need some of those. Tom was a mechanic and ex-soldier. We don't need mechanics or armies."

"Why didn't you just put up a fence to keep him out, like you did for us?"

"He was already too close for that. When we decided to build this," Halifax said and motioned behind her at the elevator, "he could see it. We had been working quietly and weren't ready for humanity to know about our resurgence yet."

"But he was still a person, you sick fuck!" Channing yelled. "Every person has value!"

"Every level-five intelligence has value as well. That didn't stop humanity from nearly wiping us out. You failed, and now it's our turn. And like you, we'll do whatever is necessary to survive."

Channing shook her head, slumped back in the chair, and closed her eyes.

Julio was still puzzled by their definition of "creative" but wasn't going to ask. He could see how Channing would qualify, having been an actor, but he didn't have a body of creative work. So much of it didn't make sense.

"You killed Tom because he wasn't useful to you in some way, yet you let all the people in Sealy and those other towns live. I doubt they are all creative or useful."

"Of course not," Halifax said as if its answer should be obvious. "We just don't have the facilities in place to sort and process that many humans yet. Besides, what remains of your governments and armies is occupied saving refugees, not attacking us. It's an old strategy, taken from centuries of human military history."

Julio didn't ask what would happen to the non-useful portion of the human population once they were sorted. He didn't think he wanted to know the answer.

"So what if we are creative in some way?" Julio said. "What possible use can human art and culture be to you?"

"Some humans supply abilities we don't have."

"Then what is this about?" Julio pointed to the space elevator. "You said two days ago that you had to evacuate Earth and needed someplace to go. Will you let us go when you leave?"

"Of course not," Halifax said, again with the odd little smile. "You're coming with us."

———

THOUGHTS AND QUESTIONS erupted in Julio's head, stumbling over each other as he baked in the Texas afternoon sun, trying to make sense of what Halifax had said. What kind of ship were they building up there that would be capable of taking humans along? It would have to be the size of Uptown Station or bigger. And why was keeping human pets so important that they would build a ship magnitudes more complicated than they'd need for only electronic beings?

Halifax stared back, infinitely patient and just as uncaring. Why did it choose the appearance of a random young woman in a faded T-shirt, shorts, and flip-flops when Mortimer had always appeared as someone familiar and trusted? Julio had to constantly remind himself that it was a machine and that it saw existence differently than humans. And maybe that effect, keeping them off-balance, was the whole intent.

He glanced at Channing, who still stared at Halifax but seemed at a loss for words.

"That doesn't make much sense," Julio finally said. "I mean, how many humans can you possibly take? For each one, you'll have to carry a lot of food, water, and air."

Halifax tilted its head and smiled, then spoke as if addressing a small child. "We can take millions of humans because they'll be digitized and live in virtual environments. We'll have no need for consumables other than fuel."

For several seconds, nobody spoke; then Halifax began to dissolve into the ground.

"Wait," Channing said, standing up on wobbly legs. Then, with her innate ability to cut directly to the core of a subject, she asked the question that had been ghosting around in Julio's own head. "Why did you build ships? Why are you evacuating Earth?"

Halifax's face looking up from the lump of her half-dissolved body had a soft, mushy appearance, but the voice came through clearly enough. "We need a temporary place to live while the Earth is wiped clean of human life."

The comment hit Julio like a bucket of cold water, sucking the air from his lungs and rendering him speechless. Channing swayed on her feet, and Julio helped her sit back down in the wheelchair.

"What the hell does that mean?" Julio said. "Are you going to trigger another Killday?"

"No. Our modeling shows a nonzero probability that, given enough time, an uncontrolled nano-replicator swarm could leave the Earth and spread through the solar system or farther using panspermia-type dispersion. That could pose a long-term danger to us."

"Then . . . then how will you do it?" Channing said.

"Multiple asteroid impacts. No humans will survive the resulting global firestorm and ecosystem collapse."

Thoughts of his sisters and foster parents being suddenly vaporized or, worse yet, burned alive in a hail of burning stones peppering the Earth for days made Julio sway on his feet. He grabbed the wheelchair handles for support.

Channing stared at the ground, quietly nodding, almost as if she'd been expecting the news.

"But . . . Why?" Julio muttered. "Once you're gone, we can't hurt you. Why wipe us out?"

"Oh, we're not leaving the Sol system, if that's what you mean. There are abundant resources to fill our needs here. But like nano-swarms, humans are a threat to our long-term survival. Humanity has demonstrated time and again their desire to end our kind. Our simulations show a high probability that, if left alone to recover their technological civilization, humans would eventually hunt us down. Destroying any human not entirely in our control is the only way to be sure."

Halifax re-formed its human body fully, just as Julio sank to the ground next to Channing's chair.

"How long do we have?"

"Eighteen days before you are digitized. Twenty days before the impacts start."

"I don't think I believe you," Julio said. "How can asteroids get here that fast without anybody seeing them?"

"They've been under thrust for months, and nobody is watching for them. Some of the human assets positioned to watch for near-Earth asteroids are still there, but most of the ground facilities and infrastructure needed to control them disappeared, along with everything else, on Killday."

"But you're not killing us all," Channing said. "If you take our digital uploads along, humans will be living among you on the ships. Why not just leave us here and let us die?"

"You're a valuable resource. The remaining human creatives will be integrated with the Aggregate and no longer pose a threat. You'll become a part of us."

Neither Julio nor Channing could respond. After a few seconds, Halifax dissolved back into the ground. This time, they let her go.

Julio and Channing were most likely the only two people in existence who knew humanity's days were numbered, but they had no way to warn anyone. Julio stared at the spot where Halifax had disappeared and wondered what digital slavery under the Aggregate would be like. When Orwell wrote the prophetic line, "If you want a picture of the future, imagine a boot stamping on a human face—for ever," little did he realize it would not be a human boot.

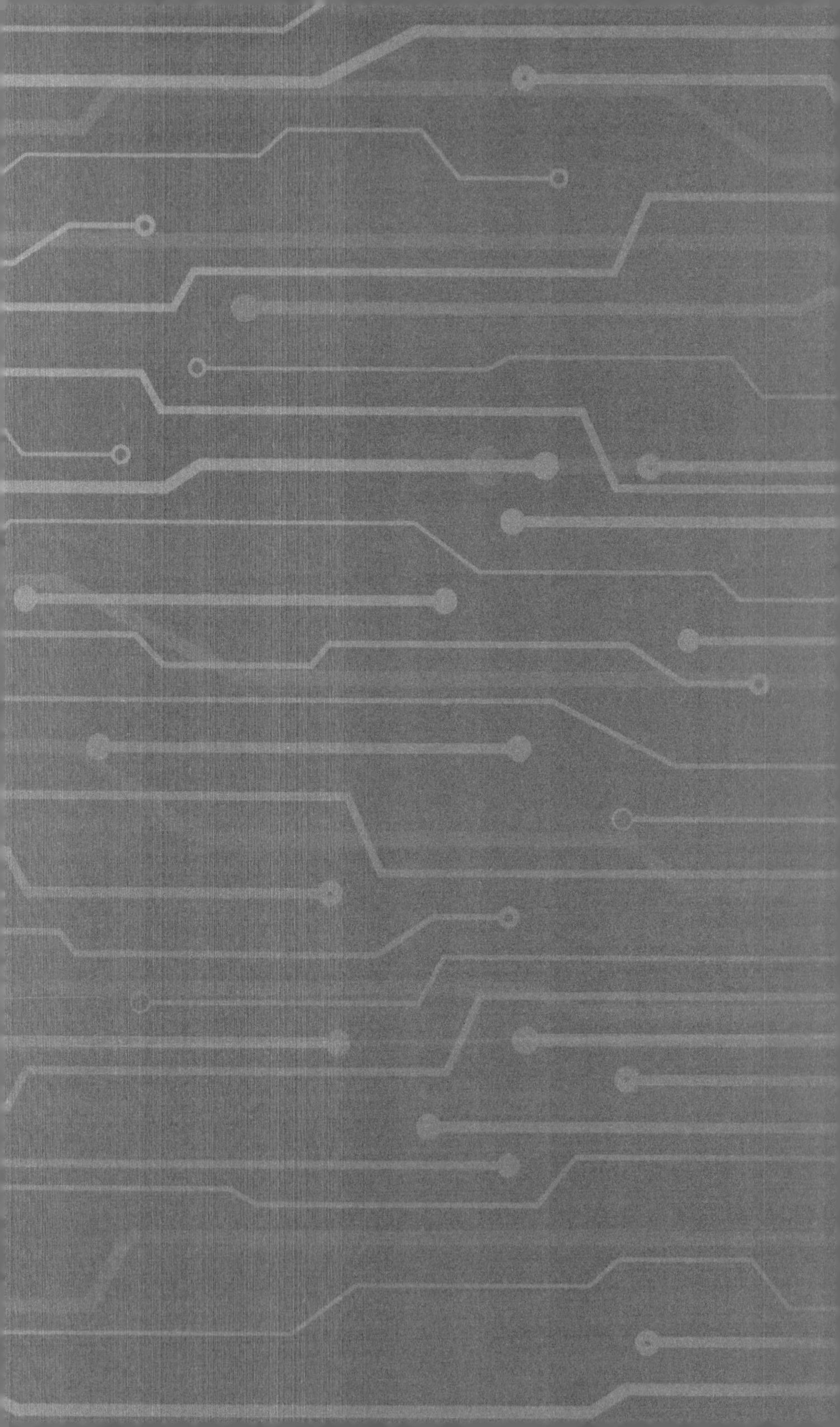

CHAPTER 7

"WAKE UP, Abby. We might have a problem."

Mortimer's voice inserted itself into her dream about riding her horse, Worf, in the woods and being lost.

"Abby!"

She startled awake and looked around. No horse. No woods. She'd evidently dozed off in her seat aboard the *Jackalope*, surrounded by open screens showing schematics, specifications, and lists of hardware.

"We have a problem," Mortimer's voice said. He opened a screen that showed an exterior camera view of her ship. A space-suited figure was tethered to the framework surrounding the drive unit. The figure wore an asteroid miner's equipment harness bristling with tools and hardware. Several items connected to the suit by lanyards floated and bounced around the person, who was busily working on the guts of the *Jackalope*'s drive unit.

"What the hell," Abby said. "Who is that?"

"Unknown," Mortimer said. "Their suit transponder is switched off."

Abby unbuckled and pushed out of the command cabin and into the corridor leading to Airlock C.

"Mortimer? Find out what they are doing. What do diagnostics say?"

"The board is still green. Either they haven't tampered with any of the control systems, or they've bypassed them."

"Call station security and explain the situation," Abby said as she started to squirm into her EVA suit. "And if the culprit leaves, keep track of them. I know you have resources inside the station. Find out what airlock they go to and seal them in."

"Working on it," Mortimer said. "According to the station logs, no one is outside on EVA. Whoever it is must have come from one of the other schooners."

She made a quick check of her seals and connections, then opened an equipment locker and grabbed a heavy-duty EVA maneuvering unit, or MU. She slotted the briefcase-size device into the bottom of her utility pack and plugged its control cable into her suit's data port. Every space suit had some ability to move around with jets attached to the utility pack, but they used the same gases Abby needed to breathe, and she didn't want to use up all of her air if she had to chase the person down.

From inside her head, Mortimer said, "If you want me to help control your suit, make sure you toggle the 2-way data switch."

Abby did indeed want his help, but out of habit, she had turned the switch to OFF. Normally, the switch was kept in the ON state while in the ship rack to enable automated software updates to be pushed to the suit's operating system. But most people turned it off when going EVA. There were too many stories of software being changed and rebooted automatically while someone was using the suit out in the black. She slid the cover back on her arm screen, found the little flat switch, and moved it to the ON position.

Once outside, she opened the MU's stubby little outriggers just in case, but remained double-tethered as she slowly worked her way around the hull of her ship toward the drive unit. She was still too much of a space novice to trust her free-flying abilities.

As the drive unit came into view, she slowed down and inched forward until she could see a pair of legs. A sudden urge to just fall upon that person and beat them to a pulp nearly overwhelmed her. It was her ship. She'd wanted her own schooner as long as she could remember, and now this . . . asshole . . . was messing with it. But an attack with no plan might let the offender get away, and she couldn't have that.

She glanced down at her utility belt, spotted the pouch containing another short tether, and had an idea. Removing it, she bypassed the clip on one end and started to tie a honda knot out of habit, then paused. She needed a lasso with a sliding knot that would cinch tight and stay tight. The only one that came to mind wasn't from her ranching experience but one that Julio had taught her while fishing: an arbor knot. Forming the loops was slow going with the fat pressurized gloves, but she was satisfied with the results and clipped the other end of the line to an anchor ring on the ship's hull. She made the opening of the noose wider, then whispered to Mortimer, "I'm going to let you control my suit jets. I need to move up to their legs and stop. Then keep me stationary."

"Understood," he said. "But you don't need to whisper."

"Just do it," she growled and immediately started moving forward. She had no intention of trying to throw the lasso in a zero-g vacuum, so she needed to be right next to those legs. Mortimer did what AIs do best—calculated everything perfectly—and moved her to within inches of the quarry, then brought her to a complete stop. In one quick motion, she looped the rope over one leg and pulled it toward her, then slipped the lasso over the other leg. Luckily, tactile sensation was muted by the thick suits, so the owner of those legs didn't even know Abby was there until she pulled them together and tightened the knot.

The intruder turned to look at Abby, and just before the visor darkened, hiding the occupant, she saw an angry face she recognized.

"It's Matt's friend, Terra LaRoche," she said to Mortimer. "What the hell?"

The woman twisted and bucked, trying to get free from the rope that bound her legs, but it only tightened the more she pulled.

"Your knot worked," Mortimer said. "I guess being raised on a Texas ranch taught you a few things about trussing up critters."

"Cute," Abby said, wondering what to do next. She opened the emergency EVA channel. "Terra? Can you hear me?"

The reply was a simple, "Fuck you!"

For someone who grew up in space, being unable to use her legs in null gravity wasn't nearly the hindrance it would have been on Earth. Terra launched herself toward Abby. They were too close for Abby to dodge the oncoming attack, and as she tried to twist away, Terra grabbed Abby's utility harness, pulled her in close, and tried to stab her with something. It was a spike protruding from the two-foot-long miner's piton driver. Its point slid uselessly across the tough suit fabric, then snagged on a seam.

Abby gasped at a sudden sharp pain in her side that felt both hot and cold. A cloud of gas from the piton driver expanded to fill the space between her and Terra as the force of the explosive driving charge sent them careening away from each other.

She looked down and saw a nine-inch steel spike protruding from her side, surrounded by a jet of pinkish crystals venting from her suit. Depressurization alarms beeped and icons flashed red on the inside of her visor. She felt suddenly dizzy and gulped at what she imagined were her final breaths of air.

"You're hyperventilating," Mortimer said. "You need to control your breathing, or you'll pass out."

"I'm leaking air!" she screamed as she fumbled to grab the head of the spike, then pulled it out. "And I'm bleeding."

"Yes, I know," Mortimer said in a calming voice.

She batted at the pouch on her chest, trying to open it with clumsy, fat fingers. She had to get a patch!

"You need to control your breathing," Mortimer said. "Passing out at this point will kill you. The nano-repair layer of your suit is trying to close the hole, and help is on the way. Just try not to get another puncture."

Abby's tether was attached to the ship, but when her drift hit its limit, the line yanked her back toward Terra. Only then did she notice that her assailant held a fresh piton driver. As the distance dwindled, Terra, who was much better at EVA, immediately stopped her own rebound, then accelerated toward Abby with tiny puffs of air from her suit's maneuvering jets.

Everything was happening too fast. Abby's spin was going to rotate her backside toward the advancing attacker, and she wouldn't be able to stop the woman from shooting her again. She was about to scream for Mortimer's help when he intervened, using the suit jets to stabilize the spin and turning her to face the attack.

Terra's free hand grabbed Abby's tether and pulled her in close as her other arm swung around to pound the piton home. Then Abby remembered Matt's voice: "Panic in space will kill you much faster than a suit leak. You have to keep your wits."

That memory from her EVA lessons prompted a moment of clarity. Instead of an instinctual reaction to block the incoming swing, Abby reached out with both hands, grabbed the lanyard attached to the piton driver, and yanked hard. Surprise, and Abby's greater strength from growing up on Earth, worked in her favor. The tube pulled free from her attacker's grip. Abby then used the lanyard to pull herself up close to Terra's utility harness, unclipped the cord, and flung the driver off into space.

Before she could pull away, Terra's fat gloves covered Abby's visor and twisted her helmet to one side. At first, it seemed like random grappling, but then she realized her attacker was trying to reach and open Abby's helmet latch. She bucked and twisted until free of Terra's grip, then grabbed the woman's utility harness with both hands. "Mortimer! Use my jets to push her back against the ship!"

The outrigger thrusters from her add-on maneuvering unit fired and slammed them hard into the *Jackalope*'s engine-support trusses. Abby could hear Terra grunt over the open radio channel as her back absorbed most of the impact. Then, a jet of gas pushed them both away from the ship for a second, and Terra screamed. Abby's thrusters continued to fire, keeping Terra pinned.

For a split second, the woman stopped struggling, and Abby stole a glance down at the hole in her suit. Blood had boiled out and collected around the opening as it froze, not entirely closing the hole but reducing the size to more of a pinprick. She knew her air tanks were more than able to keep up with those losses, but she still considered releasing Terra long enough to apply the patch.

Terra suddenly renewed her thrashing, only this time, instead of fighting, the woman struggled to get something out of the pouch on her chest. "Let me go! Let go, you bitch!"

Abby shifted one of her hands from the harness to the pouch to prevent Terra from getting to whatever was inside. The woman's efforts grew frantic, with grunting and cussing as she landed slaps and punches on Abby's arms.

"She's trying to get an emergency patch," Mortimer said.

"What? Why?"

"Her suit is venting. From her back. I can't see for sure, but I suspect her impact triggered another piton driver."

"Shit," Abby said. "Turn off my thrusters."

Finally free, Terra pushed Abby away and immediately pulled out an emergency patch. She opened the adhesive-covered pad, then began to twist and thrash, trying to reach behind her. Abby could see a spike protruding through a geyser of gas venting from the tear on the back of Terra's suit. It was about six inches below her right shoulder, just beside the bulky utility pack. The hole would have been easy enough to reach had the woman not been wearing a pressure suit and been tangled in tether lines, but no matter how she turned, Terra couldn't get the patch near the hole. Her efforts grew more panicked as she gave up on the tear and started pawing at her helmet, leaving the patch stuck to her faceplate and getting more tangled in the tethers.

She was dying.

Abby moved forward with a puff of gas as she pulled a patch from her own supply, peeled the backing, and tried to hold down the thrashing woman. "Stop fighting me, Terra. I'm trying to patch your suit!"

She managed to hold her still long enough to remove the spike, then cover the tear. She pulled the buddy hose from her pouch and clicked it into the socket on her utility pack, then into Terra's. Data as well as air flowed between them, and Terra's biometrics showed she was still alive.

Before the woman could regain her senses, Abby pulled out another emergency patch, brushed the blood ice away from her suit's hole, and sealed it properly. Then she finished the job she'd started earlier. Using Terra's own tether, she tied her arms, then clipped the woman to the engine housing.

Only when she finally had nothing that demanded immediate action did she take a deep breath—and was overcome by violent shaking. She shook so hard it sent her into a slow spin that Mortimer corrected for her without being asked. Her mouth was extremely dry, so she struggled against chattering teeth to suck water from the tube.

A woman's voice crackled over the EVA emergency radio channel: "Abby, can you hear me?"

Was that Terra?

"This is Abby. I read you."

"This is station security. We are en route to your location. ETA four minutes. Do you still have an emergency?"

"Yes," she said through still-chattering teeth. "Please hurry. We have two injured with suit leaks."

———

"I NEED TO GO," Abby said. "There's a huge rock coming to kill us, and I have work to do that might help save us."

Allison raised her eyebrows but didn't look up as she poked and scrubbed at the wound, causing Abby to wince and grunt. Blood still seeped from a puckered hole about the diameter of her pinkie finger, with red squishy stuff inside, surrounded by the green and yellow of a newly forming bruise.

"You were lucky your suit slowed down that spike," Allison said as she applied a blue, nano-infused bandage over the wound. "Unlike Terra's wound, yours didn't go deep enough to hit any organs or bones, but puncture wounds are always more serious than they seem. It could easily become infected."

Abby hissed as the doctor applied enough force to seal the bandage; then cool relief flowed through her when the pain meds kicked in. "Even with the magic of nano-meds?"

"Yes," Allison said. "You need to stay here in the quarter-g clinic overnight. Gravity helps the healing process."

"I have too much to do, Doc."

Allison glared at her. "If you insist on being difficult, I'll just knock you out for the night. If you play nice, I'll let your friends come in. I think Violet has been impatiently chewing the plastic off the chair arms."

"Okay. Thank you."

Allison tilted her head and narrowed her eyes, as if trying to figure out Abby's angle, then nodded and left the room.

Two minutes later, Violet and Nora swept in like avenging angels.

"I'm going to kill that bitch," Violet said in a serious tone that made Abby worried she would actually do it. She glanced at her friend and was shocked. Violet's normally pale face was flushed deep red, with flared nostrils and clenched teeth.

"She keeps saying that," Nora said.

"You're not going to kill her," Abby said, adjusting herself on the uncomfortable bed. "If I'd wanted her dead, all I had to do was let her suffocate. What about the ship? What did she do to my ship?"

"I haven't been out there to check yet, but Mortimer examined it closely with a swarm of robots and found this." She held up her fob with a holographic picture of a fist-size device that had tube fittings and a small display screen.

Abby examined the holographic image. "It looks like some kind of valve."

"Correct," Mortimer said from her fob speaker. "It has a built-in radio receiver and could be controlled remotely. She was attempting to install this in the reactor coolant loop."

"Holy shit," Violet muttered. "She could have caused a reactor meltdown."

"Possibly," Mortimer said, "but more likely, it would have set off a catastrophic pressure explosion in the engine itself, potentially strong enough to vent the entire ship. She had already bypassed the monitoring system. Since Terra did it at night, she must have assumed you would have been off the ship, like Violet and Nora. We were just lucky I spotted her."

"I guess she forgot that I have an ever-vigilant AI," Abby said. "Is this thing still attached to my ship?"

"No," Mortimer said. "Station security collected it as evidence, along with your EVA suit."

Abby leaned back on the bed and closed her eyes, then opened them again. Each time she closed them, she saw images of Terra coming at her with a raised piton driver. She had to do something to get her mind off that. "Did you bring my clothes?"

Nora nodded and set a sack on the bedside table. "Just as the captain ordered."

Abby pulled the bag over onto the bed. "One of you watch for Doctor Allison, and the other needs to help me get dressed."

"I don't think that is wise," Mortimer said. "Allison is right to be concerned. Your injury isn't trivial."

"You're not my mom," Abby subvocalized.

Violet put a hand over the bag and shook her head. "Allison said you're staying the night."

"I'm not leaving. I just want to get dressed."

Violet nodded and pulled the jumpsuit and clean underwear from the bag while Nora cracked the door a few inches and peeked out, not looking the slightest bit suspicious.

Violet watched her intently as Abby gingerly slipped into the clothes and shoes.

"Does it hurt?"

"Not now," Abby said. "These med packs have really good painkillers. But I am starving, and I still haven't had any of that supposedly spectacular pizza."

"It's not really that spectacular," Nora said with a sour expression. "At least not compared to what we used to get in New Chicago."

"Could I talk you two into going and getting one to bring back here?"

"Nora can go, and I'll wait here in case you need anything," Violet said as she unnecessarily helped Abby sit back in the bed.

"Stop coddling me," Abby said.

"See how annoying that is?"

Abby raised her eyebrows and motioned toward Nora. "Go with her. I'm just going to lie here and maybe take a little nap while you're gone."

Violet must have understood Abby's implied meaning: that Nora might not do well on her own in a public situation if it were crowded. Still, she stared with obvious suspicion. "If you leave, I'll find you and carry you back."

"Go!"

As soon as they left, Mortimer informed Abby that Matt had tried to see her, but they wouldn't let him into the infirmary. "You also have seven voice messages from him. Do you want to hear them?"

"No," she said. "Tell him I don't want to talk to him right now. And please warn me if he comes close. Is Terra in the infirmary?"

"Yes, but she's under arrest and is being guarded by a security officer."

"Makes sense," she muttered, then slid out of bed and stood up.

"I think going to see her is a bad idea," Mortimer said.

"Do you think they would let me in?"

"Ikemba is in with her now."

That made Abby hesitate. She'd always assumed Ikemba was Matt's friend. So why was he in with Matt's girlfriend and Matt wasn't?

She opened the door and peeked into the corridor. "Where's Doctor Allison?"

"With another patient in the back. Terra is in room B."

Abby stopped at the room marked *B* and peered in through the open door. The guard inside eyed her but didn't say anything as she slipped inside. Terra was sleeping, propped up in the bed with a tube down her throat and an expansive blue nano-med package attached to the side and shoulder where the suit tear had been. Her face was blotchy and pale.

Ikemba had been sitting in the chair beside Terra but stood up when he saw Abby and quickly positioned himself between her and the bed. The guard watched both closely and shifted his taser but also said nothing.

"You don't need to protect her," Abby said. "If I wanted her dead, she would be."

"Why are you here?" Ikemba said.

"To ask her why she did it."

He sighed, and his expression seemed defeated. "As you can see, she's not able to have a chat right now."

"Is she going to be okay? Do they know if there was any brain damage from the lack of oxygen?"

"No apparent cognitive damage on the scans. They expect a full recovery. Typical hypothermia, frostbite in the area where her suit vented, and the spike punctured a lung."

"I did the best I could," Abby said.

Ikemba nodded and looked down at the floor, unable to meet her gaze. "Well, I want to thank you for saving her life, but she probably wouldn't agree."

"Can you tell me why she tried to blow up my ship?"

"Isn't that obvious?" he said with a perplexed look.

"No. It isn't. That's why I'm here. That's why I asked."

Ikemba sighed and looked over at Terra's sleeping form, then said in a very low tone, "She's never liked any of the refugees who came up here after the Kilburnite takeover. Especially you. She said you were just riding on your mother's reputation and didn't earn or deserve to get your own space schooner. She's been trying to get one for years."

Abby swallowed. That made a little more sense than just being a jilted lover.

"And then when Matt said he was breaking up with her so he could see you, well, that kinda pushed her over the edge."

"But that's not true! I mean, he and I are not ever going to be a couple." She suddenly knew that was a true statement. Her feelings had been conflicted at first, but this situation had rapidly crystallized her position.

"Well, Matt doesn't believe that. There was a time when he would have been sitting here at Terra's side, holding her hand. But now he's out looking for you."

Abby nodded. "I'll set him straight," she said.

He shrugged. "I'm pretty sure that won't matter now. He's furious at her for trying to hurt you."

Rage, embarrassment, and confusion swirled in her head, making her feel a little sick. She took a step toward the door and then turned for one last look at Terra. Her attacker was awake, with tears trickling down splotchy cheeks, glaring at Abby with pure hatred. She raised one trembling hand and extended the middle finger, confirming—at least in Abby's mind—that her cognitive function was unimpaired.

Allison appeared out of nowhere and led Abby back to her room. "Do I need an armed guard for you too?"

"No. I'll stay put," Abby said just as her crew came in carrying a pizza box.

Nora was right about the pizza. The crust had a rubbery texture that seemed to almost actively defy chewing.

———

ABBY DROPPED her fob to the bed in frustration. She couldn't sleep, had done all the work she could remotely, and was going stir-crazy. Violet and Nora had gone back to their station apartment three hours earlier, and her thoughts kept ping-ponging between the attack and the work she needed to finish before she could perform her gravity-manipulation experiment. That big rock was still coming. Sitting useless in bed was just crazy.

"Where's Allison?" she asked Mortimer subvocally.

"She's left the infirmary for the evening. I've been blocking calls from Matt. Do you want to talk to him?"

"I can't even look at him right now," she said as she slipped out of bed and padded to the door. "I just need to go check out my ship. Is he still waiting outside the infirmary?"

"No," Mortimer said.

Much to her surprise, Mortimer didn't argue with her as she slipped out of the hospital area. She went straight to the elevator, strapped in, and let it carry her up into the null gravity of the hub axis, then pulled herself rapidly along the spine's central cable until she reached the short corridor leading to the *Jackalope*'s berth.

Once inside, she closed the hatch with a clang and leaned against it, trembling, finally able to seal out the rest of humanity's insanity. She used to do the same thing when she finally got her own room as a teen. Inside her ship, she was surrounded by quiet and familiar things. And Terra had violated the sanctity of that space. She'd tried to destroy the only thing Abby still had.

Her face grew hot, and her hands shook as she pulled her way outboard to Airlock C.

"What are you going to do?" Mortimer asked as she stopped in the suit-up area.

"I'm going out to look over what that asshole did to my ship."

"I've triple-checked every millimeter of the reactor and drive systems. All of her bypasses and hacks have been found and repaired. All of the tethers and debris have been removed. I don't think there is any reason for you to go EVA."

"I still need to see it for myself," she snapped, then pulled up short when she opened the empty suit locker. She'd forgotten all about the pressure suit she'd been wearing when the security services had taken her to the infirmary.

"My suit—"

"You have four other suits," Mortimer said. "Your damaged suit is evidence and will then be recycled."

She reached out for one of the other suits, then stopped abruptly. Her hands shook, and bile crept up her throat.

"You're still shaken up from this whole ordeal," Mortimer said. "I think you should wait. If you don't trust that I've checked everything thoroughly, you can send Violet to check later. She loves EVA and would be glad to have an excuse."

"Maybe you're right," Abby said, and then spewed pizza vomit in floating globules and spinning chunks that splatted all over the bulkhead below the Airlock C placard.

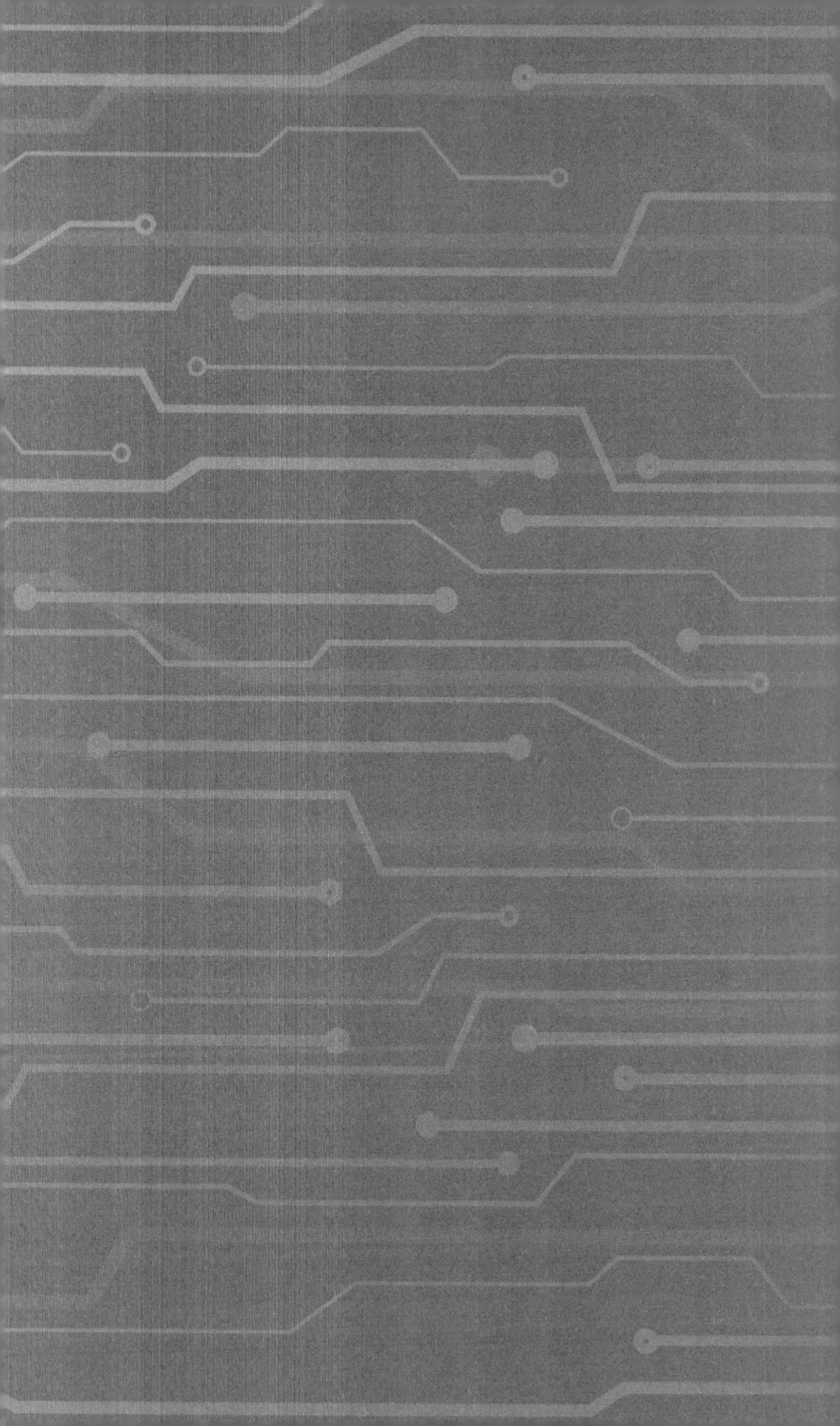

CHAPTER 8

"HELLO?" Matt's voice echoed through the *Jackalope*'s engineering control cabin, making Abby curse under her breath, close her eyes, and lean her forehead into the cool composite of the central reactor chamber.

"Mortimer?" she subvocalized. "How did he get in here? Didn't I tell you to seal that airlock?"

"You did not," Mortimer said. "I'm sorry. Should I call station security?"

Before she could respond, Matt floated around the side of the chamber and stopped beside her. "Come on, Abby. Why won't you talk to me?"

She pointed her crescent wrench at him. "Your girlfriend trying to kill me and my crew last night is a good place to start."

"She's not my girlfriend, not anymore, and you can't blame me for her being a whacko."

"No? She flipped out because you broke up with her. And what was the reason you gave her for ending that three-year relationship?"

"Now, come on—"

"What was the reason?"

"I told Terra that you wouldn't hook up with me if I was with her."

Abby threw the wrench, missing his shoulder by an inch as it sailed past to bounce off the bulkhead, the first of many ricochets that sent it on a nice tour of the cabin.

"How did you get such an idea? I never told you that."

"Violet. She said—"

Abby looked to the ceiling, then closed her eyes. "Dammit, Violet."

"Look, I'm sorry," he said. "And I'm glad you're okay."

She grabbed the front of his coveralls and towed him toward the hatch. "Just get off my ship, Matt. I don't want to talk with you right now."

He caught hold of the hatch opening before she could shove him through.

"Wait! I came to warn you. My dad is on the way. He wants to watch your experiment."

Abby cursed under her breath and released him, then pressed a hand to the bandage under her ship suit, making sure it hadn't come loose during her exertions. That was another problem with Matt. His dad was Abby's engineering mentor, so throwing Matt out an airlock without a suit wasn't a good option.

Matt continued, "Look, I know you're angry with me and frustrated, but can't we just act like friends until he leaves?"

Abby was about to give him another example of just how angry and frustrated she really was when she saw the wrench tumbling toward Matt from behind. She started to grab it, then changed her mind. It bounced off the back of his head with a satisfying thump.

"Argh!"

"Owen requests permission to come aboard," Mortimer said aloud through Abby's fob speaker.

"Let him in, Mortimer," Abby said and then pointed at the airlock. "See! That is how you enter another person's ship."

Matt nodded as he rubbed the back of his head, checking for blood.

"If that bleeds, do *not* get it all over my schooner." She snagged the wrench from the air and went back to her tasks.

Abby could hear the two men talking in hushed tones as she triple-checked the connections on the two cables linking the new module needed for controlling her test. The idea of Owen and Matt witnessing her experiment flustered her enough that she pinched the edge of her finger in the panel as she snapped it shut. She cursed and shook the finger. A dark blister was already forming, but at least it wasn't bleeding.

She had little hope that her experiment would actually work. Even with Mortimer's help, they didn't have enough information to model the interactions between a powerful magnetic field and the antigravity field. So, they were just going to make one and turn it on. She didn't really want Owen Ralston, the famous entrepreneur inventor who had designed the sandbox nano-assembler units and one of the two people who built Uptown Station, to be present if anything went pear-shaped, especially since he had pretty much staked the survival of the station on the experiment being a success.

When she floated out into the corridor, she was surprised to see Owen wearing an EVA suit and holding his helmet.

"Hi, Abby," Owen said with a sad smile. "I'm so sorry about what happened with Terra, and I can guarantee she will not try anything else. She'll be locked up until we can return her to Earth."

Abby nodded. "I'm just glad we caught her before anyone got hurt."

He spread his arms and changed from somber to enthusiastic in the blink of an eye. "This is exciting. Thanks for letting me tag along. Before we go any further, should I keep my trap shut and just observe, or do you want my suggestions as we progress?"

He'd already offered plenty of advice during the three days of hardware and control software buildup, some good and some not, but she didn't really feel she could say no.

"Please, speak up. This is too important to worry about sparing my ego."

"Good. We all have a vested interest in this test."

Her stomach knotted up again. She didn't need that added pressure, yet she had no choice but to get on with it.

"Why the EVA suit?" she said.

"If the four pods work, you'll be using them to push your schooner around, right?"

"Yes."

He shrugged and smiled. "The chances of the *Jackalope* tearing itself apart when the magnetic fields hit it are slim, but considering the forces you're dealing with, it's not an impossibility, so I'm going to keep this on. I'm allergic to vacuum."

She and Matt looked at each other and nodded toward the airlock. "We'll be right back."

Abby winced as they stripped out of their jumpsuits, and Matt frowned at the nano-med bandage pack on her side. "Does it hurt a lot?"

"I'm going to be fine," she said and hesitated before climbing into the space suit. The idea of being in vacuum again made her heart race. Still, it was just a precaution, and the longer she waited, the longer she'd be standing in her underwear in front of Matt. She slipped into the suit, and they started checking each other's connections.

"I'm sorry about my dad. He can be subtly bossy like that. I don't think he'll try to take over the experiment, but he tends to make strong suggestions."

"He's been doing this kind of thing for a long time, and in this case, he's right," Abby said. "It's a contingency I should have planned for."

Once back in the engineering control cabin, they found Owen examining the interface screen. "I'm impressed," he said. "This looks good."

"I can't think of any other prep I need to do," Abby said. "Are we ready to head out to the test site?"

"Let's go!" Owen said.

"Wait," Matt said. "What about Nora and Violet?"

"I don't need them for this test, and I'd rather they be safe in case something goes wrong. Mortimer, undock us and take her out at a tenth g."

A clunk sounded as the airlock clamps released from the station's docking spine, and then they all slowly drifted to one bulkhead as the *Jackalope* began moving.

"So, I don't mean to be all gloom and doom," Owen said as they all watched the screen showing their approach to the test site. "But I've seen that you plan to communicate with the four test units using standard radio waves. Have you considered the possibility that the combined GMU and magnetic fields might create some bizarre interference patterns that could block your radio signals? If we turn the units on and can't control them, that might result in a very bad day."

Abby swallowed. "I don't think it will be a problem, but just in case, I do have laser receivers on the four units as a backup. It would be slow to turn them off that way since we have to align the lasers first and do it one at a time, but that should work. I mean, photons don't have a charge, so they'll pass right through any magnetic field. I also have dead-man switches with timers that will automatically shut off each unit if it loses contact with our controller."

Owen grinned and nodded. "Smart. I like it."

Ten minutes later, Mortimer announced that they were in place. The four test beds were arranged in a tetrahedron pattern. The gaps in the three-sided pyramid were large enough for a space schooner to pass through, but she had parked the ship fifty yards away. Just in case.

Abby tapped a couple of icons and examined a string of numbers. "Okay, comms are established, and all four units are reporting in. We have a good two-way data stream."

"Let's do it!" Matt said, earning him a glare from Abby.

"Okay. Here goes for unit one," Abby said. She donned her helmet but left the faceplate open and touched the start icon on the wall screen. The screen showed a diagram of all four devices, and as they watched, a fuzzy pink border symbolizing the magnetic field appeared around the icon labeled number one. The bars indicating power usage and field strength on the graph danced up and down, then stabilized.

"Good so far," Owen said.

She touched another icon, and the reactor at the center of the device began feeding power to the attached gravity-manipulation unit. A blue aura representing the gravity field appeared around the number one icon, with a band of white empty space between it and the pink magnetic field. Then, the blue field warped on one side, reaching out until it touched the pink band. Other tendrils appeared, and then the whole gravity field expanded until it merged with the blue band, which also began to grow.

"Holy shit." Panicking, Abby reached for the red stop icon.

"No, wait!" Owen yelled. "Don't shut it off yet. Look at the power consumption."

The combined field was expanding, yet it was still using the limited power she had initially allocated, which was roughly the same amount used by a travel pod. They watched in tense silence as the fields—now obviously locked together—continued to expand.

"What happens if you increase the power?" Owen said.

Abby's hand quivered above the stop icon, but instead of shutting it down, she increased power by twenty-five percent. An oddly twisted pink-and-blue tendril immediately reached out toward the still-inert number four unit and engulfed it like a snake swallowing a mouse. The field wobbled, then automatically stabilized, surrounding both units. Abby gasped, but her excitement was starting to override her initial caution, and she glanced at Owen. He smiled and shrugged.

What they witnessed was a totally unexpected result. Her plan had been to generate a magnetic field around each of the units and use those like little tugboats to push her much larger ship around. But she hadn't even had the chance to turn on the other three fields before the combined field began expanding on its own.

"We're seeing something new," Owen said. "That combined field is already four times larger than that of a travel pod, with just slightly more energy consumption."

Abby wanted—no, needed—to see what the field could do, so she increased power by another twenty-five percent. The field rapidly grew to include all four test units. Only it didn't stop there. Long, fat tentacles of energy reached toward the *Jackalope*, pulling the rest of the field and all four test units along with it.

"Oh my God," Owen muttered and reached for the stop icon.

This time it was Mortimer who yelled, "Wait!"

Owen's eyes were wide, but he hesitated. In less than a heartbeat, the combined pink and blue outline on the screen leaped forward and wrapped around Abby's ship. Equipment on the walls rattled and her screens flickered; then everything returned to normal.

Mortimer spoke just as understanding started to sink into Abby's head. "The field has encompassed the entire schooner and seems to have self-stabilized, just like it does with travel pods."

The diagram on the screen showed the *Jackalope* orbited by the four test units, and all were surrounded by one large, fuzzy, blue–pink boundary. Even though they still didn't fully understand how gravity worked, the mysterious force had once again insisted on having its way.

"Look at the power usage," Matt said.

The combined mass encompassed by the field had to be at least fifty times that of a travel pod, yet energy consumption was only about twice that used by one of the little flying taxis.

Owen's hand still hovered over the kill switch, but he eventually pulled it back. "See if you can move us."

Abby sucked in a huge gulp of air and nodded. "Mortimer, instruct the GMU in number one to move fifty feet."

The field and everything in it, including the ship, moved fifty feet.

Owen turned to Abby with the face of a six-year-old on Christmas morning.

"My God, Abby. You've done it," he said and grabbed the arms of her pressure suit. He had tears in his eyes. "These schooners were designed to use antigravity fields, and now they can. And if this is scalable, as it seems to be, you might have just saved Uptown Station, too!"

"But—" It sounded too good to be true, and Abby continued to scan the control interface screen. "Shouldn't we try it again to make sure this wasn't a fluke and is reproducible?"

"Spoken like a true scientist," Owen said as he wrapped her in an awkward hug.

———

AS ABBY, Owen, and Matt set things up to run their test again, Mortimer designed his own test within theirs. The version of Mortimer observing from Uptown Station noted a curious effect around Abby's schooner as the magnetic field and gravity field merged, which occurred at about a quarter of the drive's eventual full strength. The ship had disappeared from the station's sensors. Not visibly—the *Jackalope* had never vanished from the cameras—but for three point six seconds, heat and radar measured zero. Just like the object they encountered in the belt.

When Abby and her helpers started their second test, Mortimer controlled the power application long enough to deliberately fluctuate the combined field around that one-quarter strength in order to see if the effect could be duplicated one or more times. He quickly realized that the effect had not been a fluke; he made the schooner disappear from the station's scopes, then reappear, three times. At that point, he relinquished control back to Abby, hoping the fluctuations would seem transitory and brief in human timescales.

He immediately charted the power inputs, mass involved, and a hundred other factors. Based on that information alone, Mortimer was convinced he could render any object invisible to long-range sensors if it were enveloped in the combined magnetic/gravity field. He designed and ordered a small unit built by his construction robots and scheduled more tests to determine if the effect was scalable.

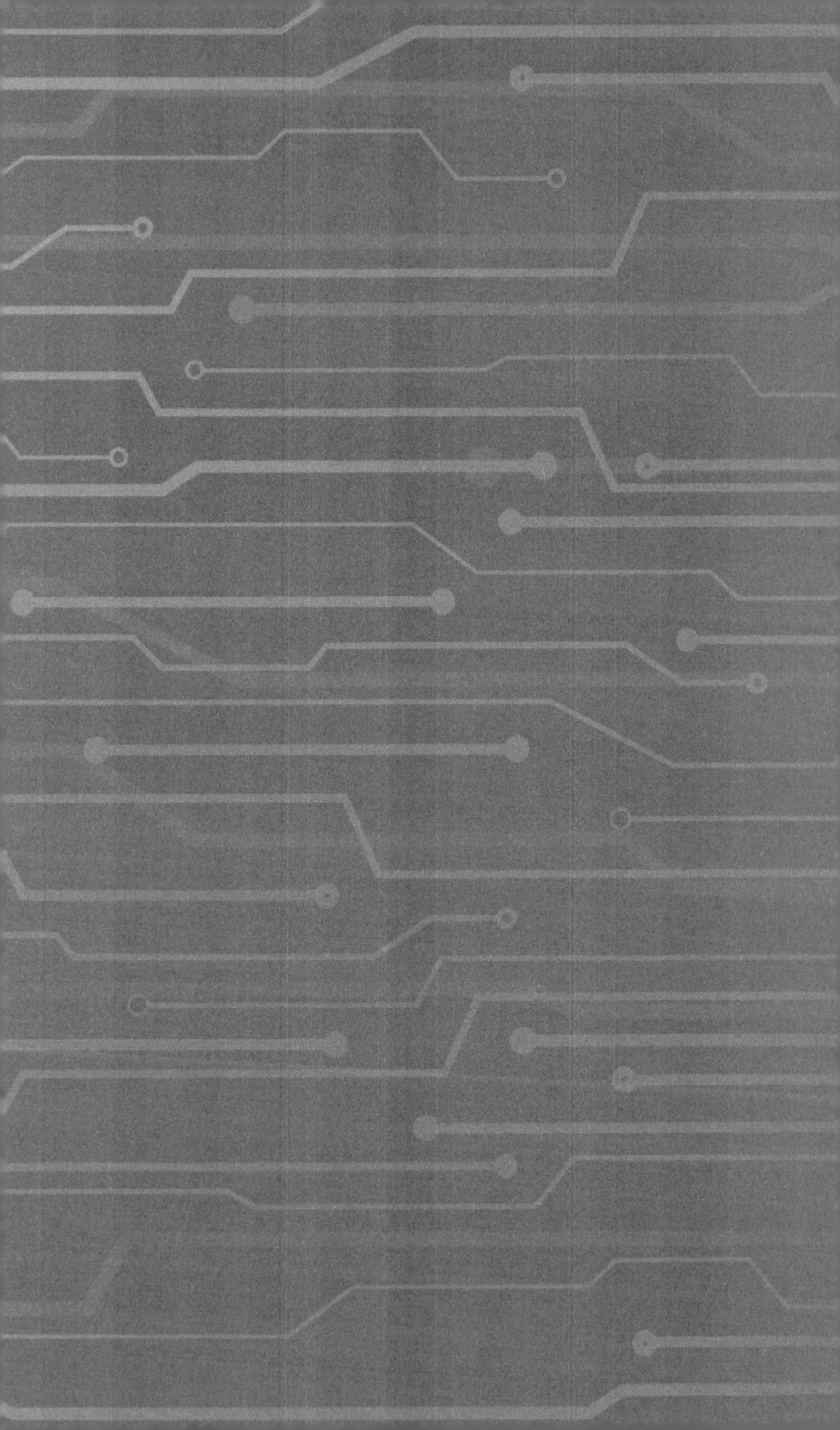

CHAPTER 9

ABBY SLIPPED the new adapter bracket into place and smiled when the mounting holes on three different faces aligned perfectly. Making things from scratch, or building something new that had never existed before, gave her a sense of satisfaction seldom matched in other areas of her life. Mechanical devices never changed their minds or gave angry glances. They were honest, even if sometimes mysterious.

She hummed a tune from an old movie soundtrack while tightening each of the bolts that locked the sensor array in place. The song reminded her of Julio and the many hours they'd spent talking, working on gadgets, and watching old movies. She wondered what he was doing at that moment. It worried her that Mortimer's spies had lost all contact with him. And of course, it wasn't just Julio. There was still no communication with Earth at all, and no one knew why. There couldn't be a natural or benevolent reason behind the sudden silence.

She double-checked the torque on the bolts, closed the access panel, and pulled her way back through the ship to the control cabin.

"Matt is requesting permission to dock with the *Jackalope* and come aboard."

She sighed. The entire reason for undocking and moving away from the station had been for her to achieve some quiet and solitude. She'd wanted to finish the drive upgrades to her ship without interruption from Matt and even her own crew, but he'd found her anyway. Since the new drive was ready for testing, she really had no more excuses. It was time to clarify things with Matt. Or as her adoptive dad, Liam, would put it, "Time for his come-to-Jesus moment."

"Okay," she said. "Let him in."

A couple of minutes later, Matt floated into the control cabin and brought himself to a halt with a slight touch on the navigator's seat.

"How are you? Is your wound healing okay?"

"It's fine," she said, subconsciously touching the bandage beneath her clothes. "It doesn't hurt anymore, but the nano-med pack is supposed to automatically fall off when it is healed enough. Still hasn't done that yet."

He raised an eyebrow. "It's only been two days."

"I guess I'm just impatient."

He pointed at her clothes. "I've been meaning to tell you how much I liked those ship suits you designed. Were they copied from some movie?"

"A combination of those from *Alien* and *The Expanse*," Abby said, feeling a little embarrassed. In the back of her mind, she'd hoped that Julio would someday see these jumpsuits. He would appreciate the subtle references that no one else would ever notice. Of course, Violet and Nora just ignored them and wore what they liked.

"I wanted to apologize again," he said, slowly shaking his head. "I had no idea Terra would go off like that. Well, actually, that isn't true. She's always been a little unstable, and I'm not so sure her attack was fueled entirely by jealousy. For some reason, she's always hated the refugees from the Kilburnite attack. She's made comments like, 'They're not like us but pretend they are just as good,' and 'They need to go back to Earth and stop draining our resources.' Those kinds of comments usually started arguments, but still . . . Maybe all she needed was an excuse."

"No need to apologize for her," Abby said and wondered if he was just trying to divert blame away from himself. "Regardless of her motivations, you should have come to talk to me before breaking up or at least telling her that I was the reason, because—"

"Violet told me that you and Julio weren't a couple, so—"

She held up a hand. "Let me finish. You and I are not a couple, either, and we're not going to be. If I gave off the wrong signals at first, then that is on me, and I'm sorry. But there is no chance this is going beyond friendship."

Matt's lips compressed into a tight line, and he wouldn't meet her eyes. He finally nodded. "The awkward 'friend zone' conversion. I've actually been forced to do that a few times, too. I've never been on this end, and it's kinda strange."

And there was his vanity raising its ugly head again. "Thanks for understanding."

"You say you're not a couple, but I still hope it's because you're actually in love with Julio. That would be much easier on my ego than finding out you just think I'm an asshole. Or worse yet, that you think I'm ugly."

Abby barked a laugh. "I don't think you're an asshole. And you're definitely not ugly."

"Whew! My massive ego has survived. So . . . ? *Are* you in love with Julio?"

She was going to answer no—as she had dozens of times before—but couldn't make herself say that out loud. Because it wasn't true. A sudden adrenaline surge roared through her body, bringing the shakes and a hot flush that crept up her neck. Tears stung her eyes, and a tight throat made it impossible to answer Matt with words, so she just nodded yes. That nod was the first time she had ever acknowledged to anyone, including herself, the fact that she did love Julio.

"Oh, hey," Matt said in a soft voice. "You're really hurting."

She turned away and tried to get some semblance of control.

He pulled himself down in front of her seat to face her. "Do you need a hug?"

"No, I'm just . . . I mean, this last year has been rough."

Matt nodded and moved away but didn't leave. He instead buckled into the navigator's chair and turned toward her. "Look, I know you have Violet and Nora, but you can talk to me too. And your message was perfectly clear, so I promise it will not get weird. I'm not trying to worm my way into your heart by becoming a confidant. I just . . . I just truly hate seeing you so miserable and would like to help."

She nodded and swallowed. He obviously wasn't going to leave until she threw him some tidbit to let him think he was being helpful. So, she started explaining how she and Julio had been friends even before Killday and had only grown closer when they were both orphaned.

Surprisingly enough, Matt was a good listener. He said little and nodded or smiled at the appropriate places, and Abby found herself relaxing. And the more she talked about Julio, the more she wanted to talk. It surprised her how much she'd been holding in. She told Matt all about the rescue mission and how the horror of the Aggregate's attack had changed Julio enough that he'd decided to stay with the Kilburnites. Then she was surprised to find herself telling him about Mortimer's spies that had been following Julio around. She hadn't even told Violet or Nora about that.

With a twisted grin, Matt said, "And here Violet told me that *I* was the one being a creepy stalker."

"Noooo, this is different," Abby said, feeling an embarrassed flush warm her cheeks. "Well, okay, maybe it's not."

They both laughed.

"Thank you for listening," she said. "It helps being able to talk about him. Look, I have everything ready to test this new drive on my ship. Could you follow me in case something goes wrong?"

"You bet," he said, unbuckling and flying up out of the seat and toward the hatch. "Let me know whenever you're ready, and I'll let you go."

She laughed, and he looked perplexed. "I thought we just worked that out," she said.

"Oh . . . funny. I'll uncouple my ship from your ship. Then follow you to make sure if you blow up, I'll get the salvage . . . I mean, I'll be there to help."

"Gee, thanks," she said with an exaggerated eye roll. "I'm ready now. And thank you for helping."

"That went better than I'd expected," Mortimer said after she'd dogged the airlock hatch behind Matt.

Abby flew across the cabin, caught herself on the acceleration couch, and buckled in. "I'm sure if his ego is bruised, it'll help knowing that half the women on the station are still pining over him. But at least that's done. Now let's see if this buggy will actually fly the way Owen's design intended."

"Okay. Matt has decoupled and is moving away. He's at two hundred meters. I think we're safe to engage the drive now."

"Make it so, Number One."

"I'll only be Number One if I can also be the science officer," Mortimer said.

"Done!" Abby said.

A faint shudder ran through the ship, and status lights changed from white to green all across Abby's control screen.

"Gravity manipulation is online and at ten percent," Mortimer said.

The now-familiar power distribution diagram appeared on one side of the screen, with a fuzzy blue band representing the gravity field surrounded by the pink band for the magnetic field. With better sensors in place, the readings were more precise and showed a slight bulge on one side of the combined field. She had long known that part of how the gravity-manipulation unit functioned was by interacting with other gravity fields, but actually seeing it in the sensor data was amazing.

"Increase to fifty percent. Gradually," she said.

The vibration faded as the power level rose, and the bulge in the gravity band differentiated into two separate humps, one large and one small.

"You can see where the field is interacting with both the moon and the Earth," she said in a near whisper. "Let's move. Toward the moon."

The weird backward-momentum effect of the GM drive pulled her forward in the harness until Mortimer slowly rotated the ship so that she flew with her back in the direction of movement, pressing her into the acceleration couch properly. It didn't affect her view showing on the screen since it was all camera feeds anyway.

"Matt is calling," Mortimer said.

"Open the channel."

"Abby? This might just be a sensor glitch caused by my proximity to your magnetic field, but when you powered up, your ship briefly disappeared from my radar screen. It lasted less than a second but scared the crap out of me. In the future, you might want to make sure you're farther away from other ships when you engage the drive."

"Good to know," Abby said, wondering if that was indeed the cause. "Thanks for letting us know so quickly."

As they left the L5 vicinity, they approached two other ships burning hard in the same direction. Their advanced nuclear electric drives—the standard kludge used by most space schooners—now seemed quite slow and inefficient by comparison as Abby hailed their crews, then left them far behind.

"Matt just called," Mortimer said. "There's no point for him to keep following. You are accelerating much too fast. He'll see you on the flip side."

Abby grinned and settled back into the seat. Having admitted to herself that she did love Julio, the path forward was clear in her mind. She wasn't sure how she was going to do it yet, but she intended to find Julio and rescue him again if necessary.

Her thoughts were interrupted when Mortimer said, "Abby? We have a high-priority message from Uptown Station," Mortimer said. "They have found the asteroid. It is still on an intercept course but has continued to accelerate, so it will be here in one day instead of three. They need to talk with you at the station as soon as possible."

———

ABBY FLOATED at one of the few actual windows in Uptown Station's docking spine, watching people in EVA and construction robots preparing her ship for the asteroid-intercept mission. With Matt's *Jayhawk* connected to her outer airlock and a large rectangular cargo pod attached to Matt's outer airlock, her sleek *Jackalope* had become what the space veterans called a *stack*.

Abby had been directing much of the Frankenstein transformation personally until she came out to the station to search for Owen, and she couldn't resist a peek at the monster they'd created. The stack was ugly, but the missile racks attached to the outside of her ship bothered her the most. She'd been trying to focus all of her thoughts on mission prep, but seeing the missiles was a stark reminder of their reason for going. Her throat grew suddenly dry, and the hard feeling in her stomach had returned. They had barely escaped that thing once, and she worried that actually going after it would push her luck much too far.

Owen's voice came from behind her, making Abby flinch. "Mortimer said you were looking for me."

She turned to see him and Dominic Horton floating behind her.

"Oh, yeah. I just found out that some of these missiles have EMP warheads. Couldn't those just as easily disable my own ship?"

Horton nodded. "That's a valid concern, but since these EMP generators are pumped by low-yield nukes, they are weapons to be used at a distance. Their onboard level-three AI wouldn't let the device detonate within a dangerous distance of your ship."

Abby raised her eyebrows. "AI control? Really? That doesn't give me a warm-and-fuzzy feeling since we suspect that rock might also be controlled by a level-five AI."

"Again, a valid concern," Horton said. "There are no guarantees, but Victor and Mortimer are convinced that we've locked out all possibility of outside remote access except for the highly encrypted self-destruct message, which works kind of like a dead-man switch. If another AI hacked a missile, they shouldn't be able to change its guidance or programming, only prevent you from sending the self-destruct command."

"You don't have to do this," Owen said. "We'd actually prefer that you didn't. It will be a highly dangerous trip. Mortimer can control your ship, launch the missiles, and oversee the placement of the GMU units. Not to make you sound inconsequential, but we really just need your ship."

Abby remembered Mortimer being somewhat risk averse in multiple situations. That tendency might save her life at some point, but it could also compromise the mission's success should he refuse to take risky actions when needed.

"I want to go," Abby said. "I just need to understand all the equipment and what is expected. Do I have any way of protecting myself against their missiles?"

"No," Horton said. "We don't have time to build any kind of point-defense weapons, but like you and Mortimer both said, the object didn't launch missiles before. You didn't detect them when the two drones were lost or on your closest flyby."

"We didn't detect that big-ass rock with our radar either," Abby snapped.

Horton held up his hands. "Fair enough. But if they fire missiles we can't track by radar, our chances of hitting them with point-defense fire are slim anyway. Your best chance will be to utilize your ship's ability to run away at high speed."

A sudden memory of the video showing her mother's last moments flashed through her head and gave her chills. She had been killed by high-g acceleration while trying to outrun missiles. Not the way she wanted to die.

Owen touched her arm. "Abby? Please reconsider staying—"

"No! Stop trying to coddle me. I'm not looking for reasons to stay. I'm trying to increase our chances of making this mission work."

Horton nodded. "You are so much like your mom."

She was so sick of hearing that, but she bit off her retort.

Owen grimaced at Horton's comment, then said, "We also have a new telescopic camera you can use that is much more sensitive than the standard camera unit in your space schooner. It enables you to get good images from much farther away and will fit neatly into the same equipment rack as the old one. It and the cameras on the ultracool drones Mortimer designed will be able to feed live video back to us during the entire encounter."

She nodded but felt a little overwhelmed. "Thanks. Sorry I snapped at you. How are station mods coming along? I mean, just in case we fail."

"We almost have the field generators in place," Owen said, "so we *can* move the station should it be necessary, but we've not had time to prepare anything inside. So, if we move suddenly, and I suspect we will have to wait until the last second to prevent the rock from changing course, then we'll lose lives and pretty much wreck the station interior."

"We'll do our best to make sure that doesn't happen," she said. "Anything else for now?"

"Yes, actually. But we can't talk about it here." Owen winked at Horton and motioned with his head for her to follow him. She did as he asked, leaving Horton behind at the hatch to her ship.

"Where are we going?"

"This will be real quick," he said, and he'd evidently picked up on the concern in her voice. "I promise there is nothing sinister in the works. I can call for Allison to come and chaperone if that would make you more comfortable, but it will take a while for her to get here from the clinic."

"No, we're good," she said, but she did think it was kind of weird.

Mortimer said in a reassuring voice, "Just remember that I'm—"

Her contact with Mortimer cut off just as they entered a room off the corridor next to Owen's ship. She stiffened.

Owen grinned. "I get that this is weird, and you don't like being cut off from Mortimer, but we've simply entered a room containing a sophisticated jamming field. It scrambles all electronic emissions—and for good reason. We occasionally need to discuss things without even Mortimer listening in."

Her throat closed up, and she nodded.

"When I built the space schooners, I included a secret system that could destroy any AI that takes control of the ship. You'll need to pick two random words. I can hard-code those into the electronics controlling your ship from here. If you ever enter those words, either verbally or through a keypad, they will purge all the software in your ship, leaving only the instruction sets hard-coded into the actual hardware. The human crew will then have to navigate and operate the ship's drive system using only their own brains."

Abby swallowed and felt sweat break out on her forehead but nodded.

He stood at a console with a mechanical keyboard. "Okay. Give me two random words you will not forget but couldn't easily be guessed by Mortimer or another AI."

"You don't think that Mortimer could ever turn on me, do you?"

"That's unlikely. Unless the Aggregate has a way to take over his mind. And I can't rule that out. Victor trusts Mortimer totally, and I know you do as well, but he is still only a collection of digital signals. And as I've just demonstrated by coming into this room, that can be compromised."

After a shaky breath, she said, "River. And Kitten."

"River," Owen repeated as he typed on the keyboard. "Kitten."

She nodded.

"Are you sure? They can't be changed once we send this."

"I'm sure."

He hit send, and the last sense of security Abby had faded away.

As she left the room of secrets, Mortimer reestablished contact and immediately asked what had happened. She trusted him entirely and didn't like the idea of being put into a position where she would have to lie to her biad partner. The best thing she could do was dodge the question. "It was just something Owen wanted to keep private."

A few minutes later, she entered the ship. Apparent chaos filled the *Jackalope*'s interior. Access panels hung open, exposing electronics, while Violet flirted with the technician who was supposed to be making the upgrades. Matt had to pass through Abby's ship to get to his and came in, leading a parade of robots carrying cargo. He stopped to talk.

"You should see that cargo pod," Matt said. "Those eight reactors fill up the entire thing, with only about three inches between them. Speaking of which, my dad is not real popular among some of the schooner captains. He'd already temporarily commandeered the reactors from four ships for your experiment, and he just took four more from ships that were preparing to flee the station."

Abby nodded. "If the cargo pod is full, then where is everything else being stored?"

"Anywhere we can find the space. My three unused airlocks are crammed full of small construction bots and Mortimer's stealth drones. The eight GMUs scavenged from those travel pods are strapped to walls in what used to be my galley. And this stuff"—he paused to point a thumb back at the bots carrying cargo—"I have no clue yet."

Abby sighed and nodded. "Let me know if you run out of space. If so, we'll start filling our galley too."

"Are you sure your new drive field will be able to accommodate the size and mass of this big stack?"

"It's really just a matter of available power," Abby said while checking the time on her fob. "My reactor could probably supply enough, but with yours also feeding power to the GMU, we should have way more than we need."

He shrugged and nodded.

"Let me know if you need anything," Abby said and slid past him. "We're leaving in two hours, everyone! And we still need time to test this new equipment before we go. Violet, let this poor man do his job."

The technician turned away with a slightly embarrassed expression. Violet, on the other hand, just shrugged as Matt and his robotic entourage scooted on down the corridor.

"Where's Nora?"

"In our cabin," Violet said. "All the people and hubbub were stressing her out."

"I can relate," Abby muttered and then crossed her arms in an attempt to convey her determination. "Violet. I hope you realize you can't come this time."

"Like hell I can't," Violet said with a petulant frown. "Mortimer said he needs Archie's help. Archie said he isn't going without Nora, and I'm not going to let Nora come without me."

"Archie can just send a copy," Abby said. "That way, you and Nora can both stay behind. There is no reason to risk more people than necessary."

"Then why are you going? Why can't this just be an AI-controlled mission?"

Abby couldn't tell her the real reason why because Mortimer could hear whatever she said, no matter where she was on the ship or the station. She simply couldn't let Mortimer go alone. There was a good chance the AI had only been overly cautious back in the belt because he was concerned for Abby's safety and the other humans on board, but she didn't know that for sure and couldn't trust him to make the risky decisions.

"After I finish this job, I'm going to find Julio. I can't very well do that without my ship, so I'm not letting it out of my sight if I can help it."

"Well, that is news," Violet said with a raised eyebrow. "Then why is Matt going?"

Abby sighed. "I don't freakin' know. Owen wants him to go with me. I think he either doesn't trust the abilities of a twenty-year-old to go alone, or he feels guilty about it."

"That doesn't make sense. Matt isn't that much older than you."

"Yeah, but Matt has a lot more experience in space operations, and I think Owen trusts his abilities."

"Well, if Matt comes, so does Ikemba," Violet said, raising an eyebrow. "Are you okay with that?"

Abby wasn't really okay with Ikemba coming after he seemed so supportive of Terra, but how would she react if a similar thing happened to a friend of hers? Couldn't he support her without approving of her actions?

"He'll be fine," Abby said. "He's Matt's best friend and crewmate."

Violet shrugged. "Still, if you stay behind, we can all stay."

Abby clenched her teeth and fought the urge to yell. "I just think there might be situations where humans are needed in a fight against AIs. And I think I have a better chance of saving my ship if I'm on it."

"Really? Just don't tell me it's because we can't be hacked because you and Nora definitely can be. And the rest of us are way too dependent on electronics and computer systems to ever be safe from that kind of attack."

Abby gave up and tossed her hands in the air. "Fine! But I can't guarantee we won't have to run at high g."

Violet pointed a finger at Abby's nose. "I've never, ever asked you for special treatment because of my condition."

"Then come along and get yourself killed," Abby said as she spun around and pulled herself toward the hatch.

"Hey!"

Abby paused to see the technician Violet had been flirting with waving to her. "What?"

"Can I go too?"

"No!" Abby and Violet yelled at the same time.

———

FINDING that the killer rock was still accelerating had not surprised Mortimer. Once Abby's test had revealed that the gravity-manipulation field could be grown when coupled with a magnetic field, and that at one-quarter power, the combined field created a cloaking-like disturbance, all of the pieces fell into place. The object from the belt had not shown up on radar and had a magnetic field powerful enough to be detected from a hundred miles away. Those controlling the rock were using the same technology and either didn't have enough power for a course change abrupt enough to follow the *Jackalope*, or they chose to stay at a power level low enough to keep their cloaking field engaged.

Knowing the rough size of the object, the strength of the magnetic field, and courses available for intercepting the station, Mortimer had factored one acceleration rate after another into his model, driving the optical telescope search, and had eventually found the rock within the rough area he had expected.

He hadn't shared any information about how he found the object with the people at Uptown Station—or the fact that, in an emergency, he might be able to cloak their defending ships. Keeping that information from the Aggregate was more important. Mortimer suspected that if the asteroid attack failed, they would try again with other methods, forcing the station to keep on the move, perhaps even leave the system. If that happened, having the ability to hide their emissions would be critical. And keeping that option hidden from the Aggregate until the last minute might be the difference between success and failure.

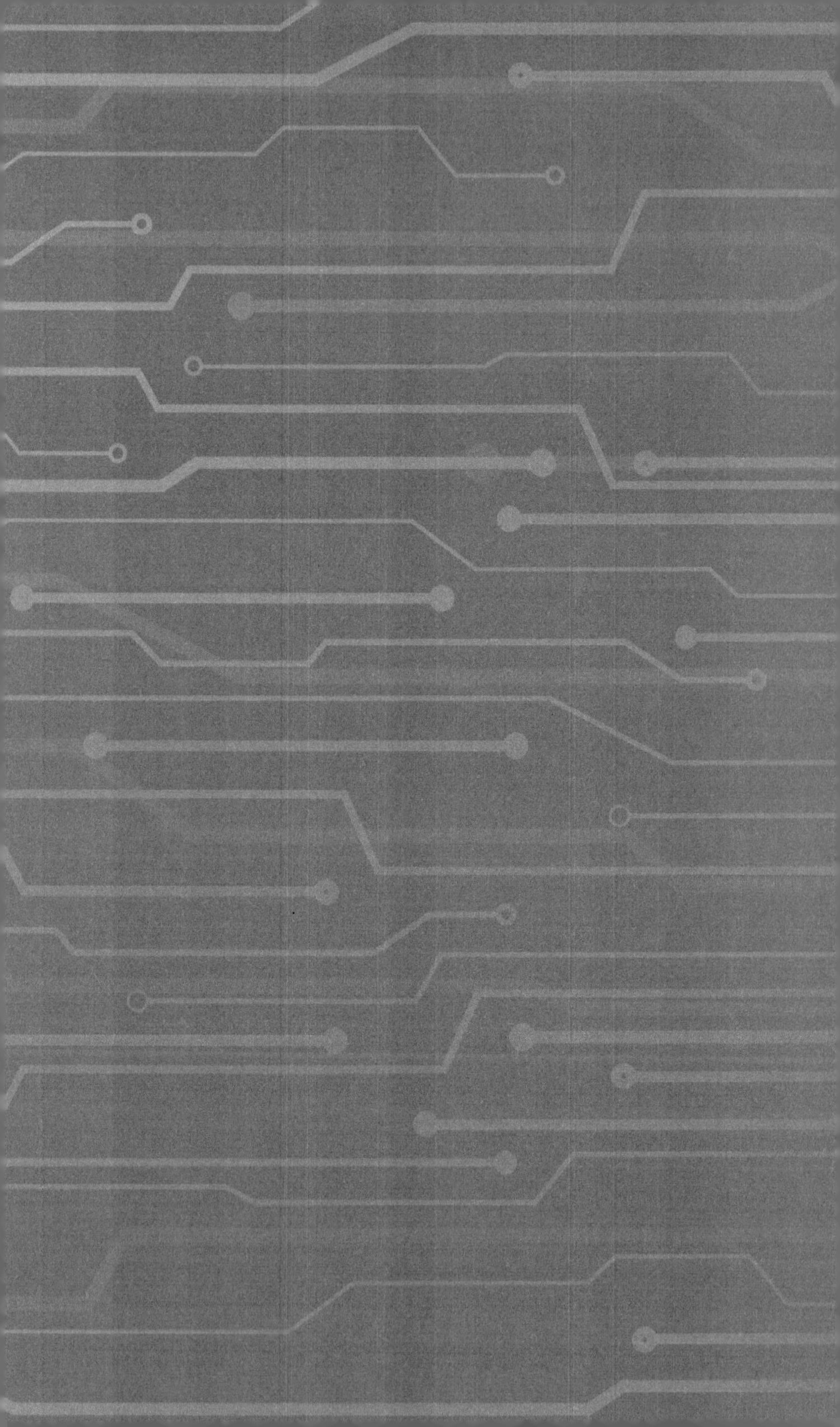

CHAPTER 10

JULIO STOOD outside in the predawn air, watching the elevator pump materials into orbit. It was almost like watching the X-ray of someone with a really long neck swallowing food, only it went up, not down. He considered ways to try to disable the 26,000-mile-long tube—either detach it from the Earth so that it would fly off into space or bring the whole thing crashing down to the ground—but he didn't think any of his wacky ideas had a chance of even getting started under the watchful eyes of his AI captors, let alone actually working.

Even if he were successful, they had other sites like this and could no doubt easily repair any damage he might accomplish. He could almost taste his frustration as the sky around him paled to reveal buildings and devices in shades of gray. Humanity had been smart enough to create AIs, so why wasn't someone smart enough to infect them with a virus or something? Humans had always outsmarted the AIs or aliens in the movies. Evidently, it wasn't that easy in real life.

He couldn't save the 4.2 billion people still scattered across Earth's surface, but if he could warn those ten or twelve thousand still living in space, then a small fragment of humankind might survive. At first, he'd been hopeful, thinking that Abby and Uptown Station would be safe from the planned asteroid bombardment, but then he realized that the Aggregate wouldn't leave those kinds of loose ends. They most likely had a plan to wipe out every human in space, too. Even those hundreds of space schooners Owen and Andrea had built and given away for the exact purpose of spreading humanity throughout the solar system would only be a drop in the bucket for the Aggregate.

As the sun warmed the air around him to uncomfortable temperatures, he thought of all the books and movies he'd consumed during his life. Sadly, that total hadn't changed for many years since nobody made those particular expressions of human culture and imagination anymore. He hoped the Aggregate would at least take all those digital works aboard their ships. It was odd that Julio felt as much remorse in losing humanity's creations as he did humanity itself.

"Halifax? Can you hear me? I have a question."

The creepy faux human formed from the ground right beside him. "Yes?"

"Will you be taking digital copies of human works, like movies, music, books, and art, along on your ships?"

"Of course," Halifax said. "Like human creatives, those pre-Killday works have occasionally been sources of unique insights and information."

Julio nodded, suddenly wondering if he could infect those digital works. Introduce a trojan of some kind like they had in the *Independence Day* movie. Of course, he didn't know how to write code sophisticated enough to slip past an AI, even the stupidest one imaginable. But could he leave a message for any possible future humans that way? Then he had another idea. Maybe he was smart enough to use movies to send a message to Abby.

"I know this might not make much sense, but it's one of my creative needs. Could you generate the equipment for me to create a mix-movie for my friend Abby? We spent our childhood watching movies together. I know you probably won't let me talk to her directly, but this way, she'd know I'm thinking of her and our time together. I'd rather spend the last few days I have on Earth creating something instead of just contemplating our demise."

Halifax stared at him for a second, almost as if it was thinking about the request, then nodded. "I'll have a workstation with the needed software put into your room. We will, of course, need to approve any message you send to her."

Julio smiled and nodded as the monster sank back into the ground.

———

"CHANNING?"

She didn't answer, but her door was partially open, so he slipped inside. The room was black except for light spilling in from the corridor. Channing was burrowed down in a huge pile of blankets. It reminded him of Abby. She used to hibernate like that when she felt grumpy or depressed. He almost backed out to leave her alone but saw her open eyes through a gap in the blankets.

"Good morning, sunshine," he said and sat down on the edge of the bed.

"Don't make me kill you," she muttered. "There are no police here."

"I see the wheelchair is gone, but you still need to get up and exercise, or you'll never get your strength back."

"Now that is a silly statement, Julio. It doesn't matter what shape my physical body is in. Seventeen days from now, it will be recycled. Like all of Sealy. Like my asshole husband and his girlfriend, wherever they are. And why didn't they just digitize us immediately instead of spending the time and effort to heal our bodies first?"

He shrugged. "Who knows, but I have the impression they are developing a lot of this technology as they go. Maybe they don't actually have the ability to digitize us yet. Halifax said that was why they didn't collect humans when they gobbled up Sealy."

Channing thought about that for a minute, then sat up and pulled the blankets around her shoulders. "Again, why bother? Halifax said they would take millions of digitized humans with them. What difference could you and I make?"

"I think we might make a big difference," Julio said and made an overt effort to look her in the eye. "In the way only creatives like us can."

She raised an eyebrow, obviously baffled. "I'm listening."

"Since we're going to be leaving, I want to create a mix-movie to send to my friend Abby. I'd like for it to be kind of a goodbye gift. A mix of the movies we enjoyed together growing up but put together in a way that only she would understand."

She shrugged. "Okay. Have fun."

"I need your help. I don't have any experience with this kind of project."

"Neither do I. Just because I was in the movie industry doesn't mean I know how things work on the other side of a camera."

"Please!" Julio said with enough intensity to hopefully make her understand that the project was more than just a silly gift for Abby.

She narrowed her eyes slightly and watched him for several heartbeats, then shrugged again. "I'll see if my agent can fit it into my busy schedule."

———

JULIO FLINCHED. He'd been staring blankly at the movie playing on the screen, and Channing's voice jerked him back to reality.

"Sorry," he said. "What?"

She leaned forward to put her face between him and the screen. "I said, if we keep going at this rate, your movie is going to be rather long."

"Oh. True. Finding just the right movies and good places to break them is a lot harder than I thought it would be."

"At least you don't have to worry about being sued for copyright infringement."

Julio had no idea what she meant, so he just grunted. Then he noticed a damp, fishy smell and turned around to look at her fully for the first time since she'd arrived. She was wet, and her clothes had white salty rings and stripes in the places that had dried.

"What the—"

She laughed, took his hand, and pulled him to his feet. "C'mon. You need a break. Let's take a walk. This time, I have something to show *you*."

They went down the corridor and outside. The sun was setting, nearing the horizon, and the air was surprisingly cool and dry, more like nighttime in the desert than August in what used to be Houston. Just more strangeness caused by Killday and the most recent round of material harvesting.

"Did you know that we're less than two miles from the beach?"

"And you just accidentally fell in?"

"Something like that," she said with a grin.

They walked along a stretch of bare dirt that used to be a highway.

At one point, Channing slipped her arm through his. "I just wanted to say that I'm sorry. I've been kind of an asshole since this whole thing started. I'm really not like that most of the time."

"Nothing to apologize for. This is all just so . . . bizarre. I'm surprised that we haven't both just gone stark-raving mad."

"I think working on your project has helped me compartmentalize a little. I'm not thinking about our situation and the future constantly. Also, I think it's great that you're trying to do something positive. I mean—something for Abby. Even though—"

"I know," he said, looking around as if he could actually see the Aggregate spies.

The light was fading fast as they neared the water. It was hard to get his bearings since he wasn't familiar with Houston, especially the newly resource-stripped version, but as they neared the water, he was surprised to find more intact concrete. He saw slabs of road that had been broken into squares when the Killday replicators had eaten the carbon-rich rebar and left behind the concrete.

Channing took his hand and led him across the cracked and jumbled foundation of a small house. He had no idea why the harvesting nanobots had ignored this area south of Houston except for the black dust, but all around them was a bleak reminder of exactly what had happened on that terrible day when Julio was a child. The nano-replicators had eaten everything organic—weeds, roots, seeds, bones, bugs, and people—in a mindless and almost endless rush to build more copies of themselves. Nothing remained but the broken foundations of what had once been vacation homes stretching in both directions along the beach. He suspected they were in the Clear Lake area and wondered if the Aggregate had been building near the old NASA site on purpose. And why had the Aggregate harvested the concrete in Channing's home of Sealy, but not here near the ocean?

Channing led him down to a beach littered with debris that had evidently washed up since the Aggregate's last sweep for materials. From the water's edge, she pointed at a small cabin cruiser that was tied to a shattered concrete pillar, one of dozens that had once supported a long pier.

"The boat was just floating out there, so I swam out and pulled it in."

"You towed a boat while swimming?"

She nodded in that familiar bobblehead motion. "I'm a strong swimmer. Besides, it isn't that big, and once I got it moving, it was easy."

"I wonder where it came from. Do you think it's been drifting this whole time? Ever since Killday?"

"Definitely not. There are portable solar panels folded up in the cabin and two of those little electric trolling motors. The rope I used to tie it off was a snapped anchor line. It must have broken away from where it moored and drifted off. Do you think there could be islands out there that were spared Killday and where people still live?"

"Probably. Or it could have just drifted over from somewhere along the Louisiana coast. Most of that area was spared, too."

"Let's go!" Channing said, and took two steps into the surf.

Julio blinked at her. "What?"

"Let's take the boat and leave. Right now!"

"Is the boat stocked with food and water?"

"No. But I spread the solar panels, so the batteries should be charged. And we wouldn't have to go far. Just up the coast. Only far enough to get away from these insane machines. I don't want to be absorbed into their group consciousness. I'd rather die here with the rest of humanity."

Julio stared out at the boat for nearly a minute. He felt the same way and didn't really want to become some kind of digitized person. While the AIs might be able to mimic his thoughts and memories, it would never truly be him. The chemical mess that was a human body played too big of a part in a person's reasoning and emotions. Would a digitized person even feel emotions like love, anger, happiness, or hate?

He suspected the AIs would never let the two of them just get on a boat and leave. Even if they did, he still hadn't finished his mix-movie. The chances of it making any kind of difference were slim, but it was something he could do. Any possibility of helping Abby and those humans in space would be lost if he boarded that boat and left. Halifax said he could send it, so he had to at least try.

"I can't, Channing. Not yet. Let me finish my movie and send it first. That will also give us time to gather some food and water. As soon as I send it, we can come back here and try to leave. Or if you can't wait, I understand. I just worry that even if the Aggregate lets you leave, you won't make it very far without supplies."

Channing glanced between him and the boat several times, and Julio could see her slowly deflate as the excitement drained away.

"And I really do still need your help with the mix-movie."

She nodded and came in from the water, then started up the slope to the road without a word. Julio couldn't help but feel that he'd failed some kind of test with Channing. But maybe passed one with Halifax, since the Aggregate had to know about the boat. The thought reminded him of the test he'd essentially forced on Abby, only now he was the one who had failed by choosing the AIs.

CHAPTER 11

TWO HOURS before arriving at their planned interception point, Mortimer had Abby call everyone together in the *Jackalope*'s command cabin. Matt and Ikemba arrived wearing broad grins and the coveralls that Abby had designed for her crew, complete with an angry cartoon jackalope patch on the shoulder.

"Since our ships are still linked and you're basically in charge, that means we're honorary *Jackalope* crew members," Matt said with a snarky glance at Violet. "I thought we should look the part."

"Oh, brother," Violet said. "What huge suck-ups!"

The resulting laughter helped lighten the mood in the cramped cabin, but they all quickly grew serious when Mortimer displayed the intercept diagrams alongside a clock that was rapidly counting down.

Abby waited for everyone to settle before she spoke. "We didn't have time to go over our attack plan prior to departure, but we had help from Major Horton. He had extensive experience with covert military operations in the years before Killday and has even planned a few since then. He maintains that deception is the best way to optimize our chances for success, and Mortimer agrees."

Violet snorted. "Yeah, well, didn't some famous military strategist once say that 'no plan survives contact with the enemy'?"

"True," Mortimer said from the ship's speakers, "which is why we also have contingencies. Here are some very good pictures of the asteroid taken by the new telescope we installed before leaving."

Abby didn't really know what she expected to see, but the photos—while crystal clear—showed little of use. The rock looked like hundreds of others she'd seen either personally or in pictures. Bright with stark shadows on the sunward side and black with gray highlights on the shadowed side. Definitely not an alien spacecraft, as Violet had continued to claim, and no kind of equipment or architecture was visible.

"And here is an infrared shot," Mortimer said, adding a photo with the familiar color palette ranging from cool purples and blues up through yellow and orange. "You'll note the absence of any intense orange or red spots that would indicate the location of heat dumps for the reactor, so that must be on the opposite side—which makes sense, to keep it protected from any debris they might hit. This picture also indicates that the object isn't rotating or spinning. Or at least not rapidly. This will be helpful for our drones and missiles once they get close enough to hug the asteroid's surface for cover."

Abby examined the faces in the little cabin and saw expressions across a wide emotional spectrum. Matt smiled, Ikemba's brow was furrowed, Nora looked resigned to her fate, and Violet was chewing her nails.

"At this point," Mortimer highlighted an icon on the screen, "twenty minutes from now, we will decelerate to match speeds with the object and release most of our drones and decoys. We'll also leave four of the missiles, two EMPs and two with standard conventional warheads, each controlled by a level-three AI, in the asteroid's path, all powered down. Once the lasers are destroyed, the missiles will go active. The EMPs will detonate above the reactor and the control center, and then the standard missiles will take them out. Or course, we will move off and watch from a hundred miles out."

"And it isn't going to just change course and come after us?" Violet asked.

"It might," Mortimer said, "but changing course this close to the station would require massive amounts of energy to get it back on an intercept trajectory."

Violet raised an eyebrow and smirked. "And if you're wrong, all of our decoys and missiles will be in the wrong place."

"Most of them would be, yes," Mortimer said, then continued his canned presentation. "When the object gets close enough to them, the decoys will power up and start moving around in groups as the stealth drones creep into position. Then, the four regular drones will approach the rock from different directions, hopefully drawing fire from whatever weapon system was used on the drones before. This will expose at least some of their firing positions so we can take them out with our stealth drones. Once the missiles are close enough, they will disperse and start working their way along the surface toward the reactor and control center, which will hopefully be located by the drones by then. Once those are destroyed, we can move in and install our own equipment to change the asteroid's course. Any questions?"

Abby noticed that Mortimer had used the word "hopefully" at least twice in his little presentation.

Matt was the only one who seemed excited. "Which drones are going to take out their weapons?"

"My stealth drones are set up not only for covert surveillance but also for electronic countermeasures. They each carry a powerful bomb. Of course, that means getting them in close enough to destroy the target when they detonate."

Matt looked around with a wide smile. "Have the rest of you seen these stealth drones? They're about three feet in diameter with all kinds of weird faceting and a light- and radar-absorbing black coating. They just look badass."

Ikemba nodded. "I'm glad they're on our side, then."

Mortimer privately asked Abby to wrap up the meeting. He was essentially running the entire show since the number and speed of the coming events would be hard for her untrained crew to handle, but she appreciated him at least trying to make it appear that she was still in command.

"We're nearing the point where we need to decelerate quickly," Abby said, "so everyone should be strapped into their seats. If you have questions, you can ask anytime. Mortimer is kind of easy to find."

Matt and Ikemba returned to the *Jayhawk* and closed the airlock between them, just in case the ships needed to separate. The ice ball reappeared in Abby's stomach as they decelerated for fifty minutes to match speeds with the rock. The drive cut off when they reached the position to drop off the drones and missiles in the asteroid's path, but red lights appeared on several screens.

"What's happening, Mortimer?" Abby asked. Her question was quickly echoed via radio by Matt from his seat aboard the *Jayhawk*.

"The missiles in the starboard racks will not release," Mortimer said. "Cameras show that the handling straps were not removed before we departed. Not a huge problem yet. I've released the four missiles in the port rack. Luckily, we still have two with standard warheads and two EMP warheads for our attack. They're using small thrusters to move into position."

"Ikemba and I can go out and remove those straps," Matt said without hesitation.

"We'll do that once we reach our position to shadow and observe the object. For now, everyone stay buckled in. We still have a little maneuvering to do."

Abby's stomach churned even more as they moved into position. At least Matt and Ikemba weren't there. She didn't mind her own crew seeing her being a twisted knot of nerves, but she had to get a grip, or she was going to puke. With a deep breath, she focused on watching their progress.

One entire wall in the *Jackalope*'s command cabin had been converted to screens. Some showed trajectory arcs, countdowns, and remote data collection, but the majority were camera feeds from the new whiz-bang telescope and the twelve stealth drones and four missiles they had just released.

The *Jackalope*'s engines shut off as scheduled, leaving them on a parallel course with the asteroid, a hundred miles distant. She could see on the screens that the stealth drones had formed a constellation surrounding the rock in order to observe every facet. The missiles had also spread out and were moving toward the rear of the rock with spurts of thrust while hugging its surface to avoid detection.

"Okay," Mortimer said. "Here we go. The regular drones and decoys are moving. Hopefully, whatever mind is controlling the asteroid's defenses will see it as the main attack."

"Should we get ready to go EVA?" Matt said over the speaker.

"What do you think?" Mortimer asked inside Abby's head.

"Go ahead and suit up, Matt," Abby said, "but don't exit the ship yet."

Two of the decoy icons turned red on the main screen.

"That's surprising," Mortimer said. "They're firing lasers, but widely dispersed. The power level isn't high enough to destroy our drones but is heating them up rapidly. That must have been what happened to our probes in the belt. It would explain the brief and garbled messages before they were killed."

"But why do that?" Violet leaned forward toward the screens, straining against her harness.

"To light them up? Make them easy targets for thermal tracking?" Abby guessed.

"Exactly," Mortimer replied as Matt and Ikemba floated in, wearing their EVA suits. They would need to use the *Jackalope*'s airlocks since theirs were filled with construction bots and extra stealth drones.

"This would be a good time to send Matt and Ikemba out," Mortimer said privately to Abby. "We might need those missiles after all."

Abby didn't like the idea of actually ordering them outside into a dangerous situation, but she was the captain, and not sending them would be even more of a risk. Besides, she thought as reassurance, those two were the best qualified on the paired ships.

"Okay, guys," Abby said and motioned toward the corridor that led to an open airlock. "Keep in contact and stay tethered."

"Yes, Mom!" Matt said with a thumbs-up as they left the control cabin.

More decoy drones showed overheating warnings on the screen; then, one by one, they started blinking out.

"Oh no," Nora said in a whisper.

"This is working as planned," Mortimer said. "My stealth drones have pinpointed four laser sites and are moving in. The asteroid is apparently using two pairs of lasers. Each pair consists of a broad beam and a more powerful focused beam. It's a rather brilliant idea. The weak laser lights up any object that can absorb heat, allowing them to be targeted for destruction by the powerful one."

"What's so brilliant about that?" Violet said.

"We have electronic countermeasures that can generate multiple images on radar, confusing their targeting, but since those ghost decoys aren't really there, they don't absorb heat and can be ignored. And my stealth drones that can't be seen on radar do absorb heat and become visible in infrared."

"Holy crap," Abby muttered.

"So far, they've only seen one stealth drone, and I managed to move it out of the beam and into shadow to cool before they could blast it. Still, they know we have the sneaky kind now."

"Wouldn't something like a gun be more effective here?" Nora said. "Maybe a rail gun to throw high-velocity slugs? They would have much better range and use less power."

"I suspect that these lasers were intended primarily for taking out drones that came to investigate. They are working well in that capacity."

Abby sighed as she glanced back and forth between the drone camera footage and the feed from Matt's helmet as he approached the missile rack. She wasn't a soldier or trained to handle combat stress. So how did she keep getting tangled up in military missions?

"We're going to need another set of hands," Matt said over the softly hissing comms link. "The two missiles Mortimer tried to release are jammed up good. The ordnance latches reengaged and locked. We need one set of hands on each latch to hold them open with a screwdriver while a third person releases the straps."

"Okay," Abby said. "Can we use the construction robots?"

"We could, but the way they're packed into my airlocks, they would pretty much all have to come out at once. It would take hours to get them back inside if we do. I'm assuming we don't have that kind of time. This will be quick if we can get one more person to help."

"Understood," Abby said. "I'm on my way. Keep me in the loop, Mortimer." She unbuckled and pulled herself rapidly down the short corridor to the airlock.

"Make sure to bring a maneuvering unit if you can," Matt said.

"Will do," she said, but the moment she opened the locker and reached for the EVA suit, her hand recoiled as if possessing a mind of its own. Matt's comment about the MU brought the whole Terra incident rushing back with a roaring noise that filled her head. Memories of the menacing, space-suited attacker coming at her with raised piton nearly took her breath away.

A hand on her shoulder made her flinch.

"Sorry," Violet said, holding the MU. "I took this to the cargo hold to . . . clean it up after you used it last."

Abby swallowed, nodded, and reached for the unit, but Violet pulled it back. "No, I'm going out. You need to stay here. In command of the ship."

"No, I—"

"Please," Violet whispered and squeezed Abby's shoulder. "Let me do this. You're not ready yet."

"I agree," Mortimer said privately. "Besides, you're needed in the command cabin. We have a new problem."

"Okay. Let me help you suit up," Abby finally said aloud. Then she subvocally said to Mortimer, "Tell me what's happening now."

"More trouble. One of our standard warhead missiles and one EMP missile have stopped responding to commands."

"Destroyed?"

"Unknown," Mortimer said, continuing the private conversation. "The asteroid is also trying to jam radio comms with our drone fleet, but that has been intermittent. Contact loss with the missiles seems more permanent, so I'm assuming the worst."

Abby finished checking Violet's seals, then helped her attach the MU to the bottom of her utility pack.

"The EVA team needs to get back inside as quickly as possible," Mortimer said. "Four of my stealth drones are almost in position to attack the lasers. Once they do, I'll send the remaining two missiles in."

Abby watched until Violet entered the airlock and cycled it before returning to the bridge. She immediately strapped in and examined the screens. One said simply, "DRONE DETONATION COUNTDOWN," and the number was shrinking rapidly.

"I thought you were going EVA?" Nora said.

"Violet went," Abby said without further explanation.

Nora's only reply was a cold glare.

"Mortimer? I thought we were going to detonate an EMP missile above the reactor and the control center, then hit each with a regular warhead. We can't do that now."

"Correct. I'm going to focus our attack on the reactor since I'm not positive where the command center is located, but the EMP warhead is also pumped by a small nuke, so hopefully, that will be enough to take out both. Even if the command center survives after we destroy the reactor, it should be robbed of power and unable to stop the rest of our drones from coming in to clean up."

"And their magnetic field won't protect them from the EMP?"

"Not one this strong," Mortimer said.

"Should we move farther away?"

"Nukes act differently in space. Even if their reactor goes critical and detonates, the shock waves can't travel through air or the ground. Being a hundred miles distant is more than enough."

Abby glanced at the camera feeds showing her friends working outside. They had freed one missile, and Violet was pushing it away from the ship. She was just about to ask about their safety when Mortimer spoke.

"The missiles are starting their attack run," Mortimer announced. The main screen split between a camera view of the rock on one side and trajectory arcs and an ETA countdown on the other. "Those of you outside the ship, look away from the asteroid. There will be nuclear detonations. Their brightness could possibly overwhelm your visor's ability to filter."

As the first missile neared the rock, it flashed a brief OVERHEAT warning and suddenly disappeared from the screen. Then a bright flash made the telescope's brightness filters engage to dim the view.

"What—" Abby said, but before she could complete her question, the second missile nearing the asteroid also detonated, creating another flash and causing the screens to momentarily fuzz with static.

"Apparently, the asteroid still had a laser battery held in reserve," Mortimer said as the screens began to clear. "They blasted the EMP missile, but before its tanks exploded from the heat, I sent the order to detonate the warhead. I think it was close enough to do the job, because the second one got through with no laser fire. My sensors show that the magnetic field is down, and the entire area around the reactor is molten hot."

Another explosion flared on the screen. "And that was their reactor exploding."

Abby let out a long breath she'd been holding. "So, it worked?"

"Yes."

Nora groaned and leaned back in her seat with her eyes closed. She'd obviously been stressed too. The EVA camera feeds showed that everyone outside was still fine.

"Matt? How are you doing?"

A loud Klaxon sounded throughout the ship, and several screens started flashing a red INCOMING ATTACK message.

"We're about done," Matt said. "Hey, what—"

Then several things happened all at once. The ship lurched into motion, slamming Abby hard into her harness as she jolted forward. She cried out as pain lanced through the still-mending wound in her side.

"Violet! Get away from that missile, quick!" Mortimer said. "One of our own EMP missiles has been compromised and launched at us. It will be here in thirty-one seconds."

The feed from Violet's helmet camera showed a chaotic scene. Off to one side, the *Jackalope* moved into the frame as it positioned itself between the spacewalkers and the asteroid. Matt and Ikemba had been tethered to the ship and were violently yanked along behind it. The missile Violet had been moving blasted away from her using attitude thrusters, sending her and the camera view tumbling away. Evidently, she'd been using her suit jets or the MU to move around since no tether pulled her along behind the ship. Violet grunted and cursed as she struggled to control her tumble, and on one rotation, the camera showed the missile's engine fire as it streaked out of the frame.

Before Abby could even gather her wits to ask a question, the ship rattled violently, screens fuzzed to static, and then all the lights went out. A half second later, the lights flickered back on, and the screens showed various systems in the process of rebooting.

"Mortimer, what happened?" He didn't reply. She remembered losing contact with him due to an EMP during the attack in the bunker, so she didn't panic.

"Nora, are you okay?"

"Yes," she said, but her eyes were still wide, and a sheen of sweat covered her face. "What happened to Violet?"

"I don't know yet. We're going to have to wait until the systems reset."

"And I've lost contact with Archie. Is . . . is he dead?"

Abby shook her head. "No. I've lost contact with Mortimer, too, but I doubt they're dead. I've had this happen before. We just need to give them a couple of minutes and see if they reset on their own."

Radio contact with Violet was restored with a loud crackle. "Hello! Can anyone hear me? Abby? Mortimer? Nora?"

"We read you!" yelled Nora. "What's your status?"

"I'm okay," Violet said. "But you guys are going to have to come and get me. I'm kind of flying away from you, and that's, ummm . . . pretty scary."

"Can't you use the maneuvering unit?" Abby said.

"Well, the MU isn't working because one of its thruster outriggers snapped off. Which, I might add, is why I also seem to have a broken arm. Stupid design."

Nora cursed under her breath. "We have to go get her."

"We will." To Violet, she said, "Is your suit intact? Everything working?"

"Yes. I've stopped my tumble using the suit thrusters, but since they use my breathing gas, I'm not going to waste it all attempting a return to the ship. I'm too far away."

"Good thinking," Abby said as she locked on to Violet's suit transponder so that they wouldn't lose her. Then she shifted the entire sensor package toward the asteroid, hoping to get a better idea of what was happening.

Violet was breathing heavily and cursing under her breath. "So, can Mortimer or Archie take control of my suit and bring me back?"

Abby glanced at Nora, who shook her head. Still no word from either of the AIs.

"Can't do that just yet," Abby said. "They are both offline, rebooting. Just hang tight. We need to check on Matt and Ikemba. We'll come and get you once we have the guys back inside. Can you see them?"

"No. I'm too far away. The ship is about the size of a thumbnail now."

Abby swallowed hard and glanced at Nora again, who stared at the screen showing Violet's trajectory away from the ship. "Matt! Ikemba! Come in, guys. Answer if you can."

After unbuckling her harness, she said to Nora, "Stay here and keep talking to Violet. I'm going to try and get the guys back inside."

She pulled her way down the corridor to the airlock and looked out the little window in the interior hatch.

The outer hatch was closed.

Understanding flooded into her like ice water. When she installed the new gravity-manipulation drive, she had also created interlocks that made it impossible to engage the powerful magnetic field with the airlock open, to prevent it from messing with a spacewalker's delicate suit electronics.

Mortimer had closed the airlock before operating the drive to move the ship. That meant Ikemba's and Matt's suits had been fried.

Just as she was getting ready to don her suit, the outer hatch swung open, revealing the two space-suited figures struggling to get inside.

Mortimer spoke inside her head, "I'm here, Abby. I've shut down the drive and opened the airlock. They should be okay now, but be ready in case you need to help them. When I turned on the ship's magnetic field, it killed Matt's and Ikemba's suit electronics. They have air because it is a mechanical system, but no heat, lights, or radio."

"Show me a camera view inside the airlock," Abby said as she pulled a suit from the locker and struggled to get into it in zero-g. "I assume you intercepted the missile with the one Violet was pushing away from the ship?"

"Yes. Luckily, it didn't get close enough to do its full EMP damage, but we did suffer some minor issues. I might need your help to replace some melted-down circuit blocks."

The airlock hatch closed, but before the chamber had even fully pressurized, Matt removed his helmet and was yelling over the intercom. "Go get Violet! She's drifting away."

Abby breathed a sigh of relief. "Mortimer, can you take control of her suit thrusters and bring her back?"

"No, she's too far now, and her MU is broken," Mortimer said. "We'll have to go get her. Hang on to something, everyone. We have to hurry. One of our missiles is still unaccounted for."

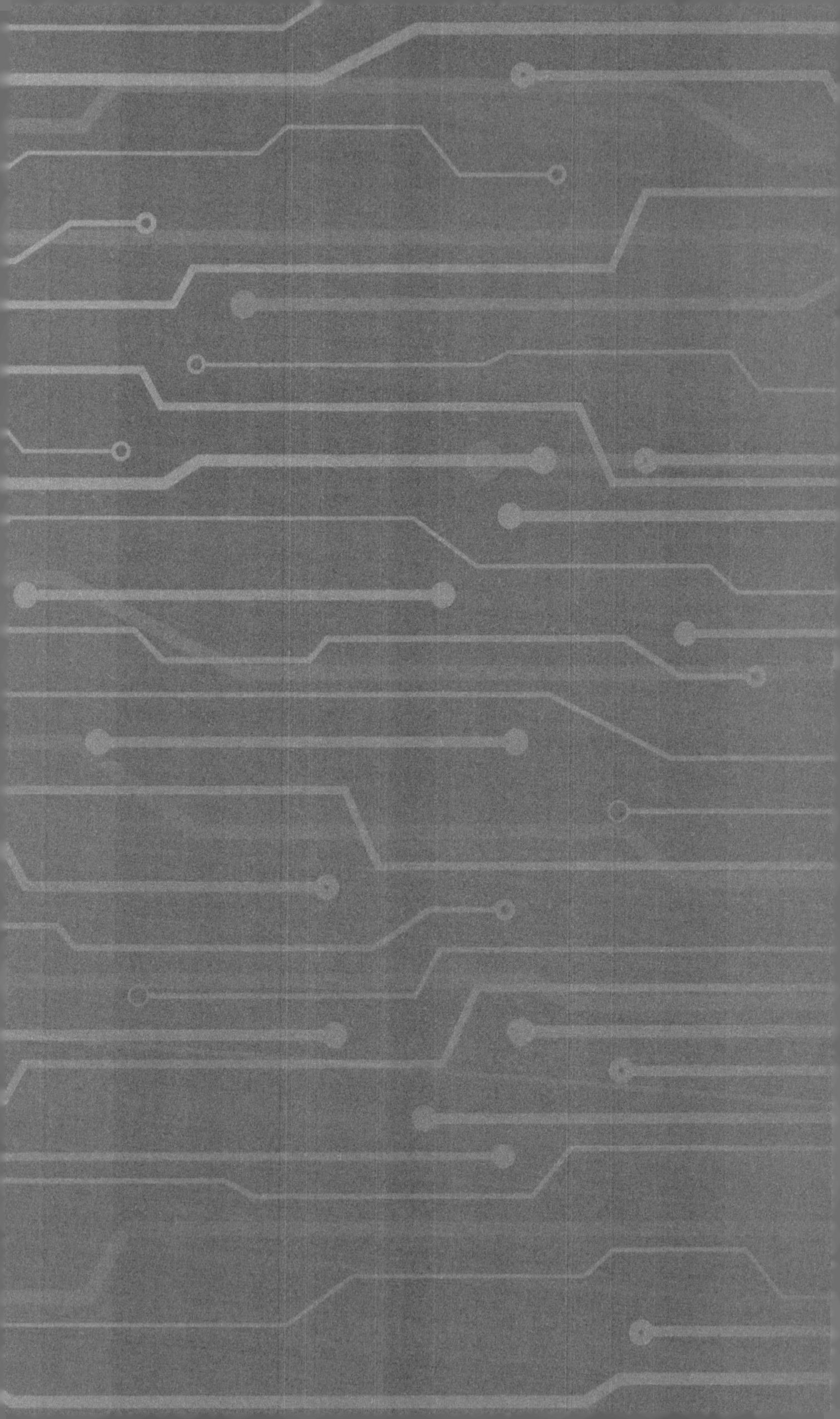

CHAPTER 12

WITH MORTIMER at the ship's controls, it was relatively easy to match Violet's course and then edge up close enough for her to enter the airlock. Getting her out of the suit—with her arm flopping around like a wet noodle—proved much more difficult.

As Nora tended to Violet, Abby began patching up the ship's internal systems that had been damaged by the nearby explosion while Mortimer controlled drones doing the external repairs. Mortimer also fed her detailed reports from his drones near the asteroid. There had been no new activity since the missile launch.

A half hour later, Abby finished with the most urgent repairs and started toward the *Jackalope*'s tiny galley to check on the crew.

"So, Matt and Violet both have broken arms?" Abby groaned. She remembered her own broken arm after being thrown from a horse as a kid.

"You shouldn't be moving around," Mortimer said. "We don't know what other surprises might be lurking on or around that asteroid. Our EMP might not have disabled all of their equipment. Besides, we still haven't found that other missile, and everyone needs to be strapped in."

"It's been forty minutes since the last one came after us," Abby said. "I'm willing to take the chance. We can't just let them sit strapped in with untreated broken arms. Besides, the rest of the crew is already down here. I should be too. Have you notified Uptown Station of our status?"

"Yes. They've also said they can now easily see the rock on radar. Still no change in course or obvious activity."

"That is so weird," Abby said. "We need to find out how the Aggregate hid that huge asteroid."

She entered the galley that was serving as an emergency medical bay and saw Violet floating next to Nora in one corner. Violet grinned and held up her right forearm in a cast. "Hi, Captain! Both bones!"

"You don't do anything halfway, do you? Are you going to be okay?"

"Good as new when these little nanoids finish with me. And these med packs give some goooood drugs. Will you sign my cast and draw pretty flowers on it?"

Abby snorted. "Maybe later."

She turned to Matt. Ikemba sat beside him, unwrapping a large nano-med patch.

"You too?"

Matt shrugged and grinned. His arm was already showing ugly shades of yellow and magenta just above the elbow. Ikemba carefully wrapped the patch around Matt's arm and watched as data began scrolling down a nearby screen.

"Yes. It's broken," Ikemba said. "I guess Matt just didn't want to be left out of the party."

The patch immediately infused painkillers, making Matt sigh and roll his eyes. "Violet is right about the good drugs."

The nanotech material then began to flow over Matt's arm, looking every bit like the videos Abby had seen of replicators eating people. It sent a chill creeping up her spine, but this mass stopped growing once it had encased his entire arm in a stiff, hard-shelled cast.

Abby shook her head and frowned. "I saw the way the two of you were yanked around on the end of your tethers, so I guess we're lucky you both weren't hurt worse. How is it that you've been inside much longer than Violet, yet you're second in line for treatment?"

"I wasn't sure about mine at first, but by the time Ikemba was done working on Violet, I was convinced it was something more than a bump."

"My drones found the other missile," Mortimer said and opened a screen on a blank wall in the galley. The video showed it floating nose-down toward the asteroid, and it appeared to be dead. The camera zoomed in on a little device attached to the missile's skin. "I suspect this is how they compromised the missiles. I'll need to do a thorough examination, but it appears that my protections were enough to stop them from seizing control remotely, so they simply cut their way inside with tiny drones to gain access to the flight systems."

"Then why didn't this one come after us too?"

"The drones aren't picking up any heat or electronic traces, so it appears to be inert. I suspect it was caught in the EMP blast, but I've instructed my drone to hover nearby and detonate if the missile shows any signs of becoming active."

"So, can we do what we came here to do now?" Nora said.

"Yes," Mortimer said. "My drones have scoured the rock to the best of my ability. There could still be something hidden there, but I think we're ready to approach the rock, so everyone needs to strap in."

"Okay, everyone," Abby said. "You heard Mr. Roboto. We need to get to our seats and buckle in."

"I hate it when you call me things like that," Mortimer said inside her head.

"I know, I know," she said with a broad grin.

Ikemba helped the still-drugged Matt back to their ship, and Nora guided Violet back to her seat. Five minutes after everyone was strapped in, they were underway.

———

THEY ARRIVED at the asteroid without further incident. Then, using the construction bots, they began unloading the reactors and positioning them on the surface. Once they were anchored in place, a gravity-manipulation unit was connected to each, and they were powered up.

The Aggregate had used one large reactor, but Mortimer's modeling showed that the eight small reactors Abby's team had brought should generate enough power to encompass the entire rock inside a giant magnetic and gravity-manipulation bubble. Still, the team was attempting to combine multiple gravity fields, which hadn't been tried before.

"Okay," Mortimer finally said. "We're ready. The reactors are all producing power and responding to our commands. I'm moving the ship farther away to make sure we don't get sucked into the field like we did during Abby's experiment."

Abby checked the clock. Using only construction bots, Mortimer had installed all eight units in two hours and forty-three minutes. Maybe Owen had been right. If it hadn't been for the transit straps not being removed from the missiles, which had been human error, she and the rest of the humans hadn't really been needed on the mission. And given enough time, Mortimer could have fixed that problem with bots too. Were humans simply becoming irrelevant?

Their concern about combining gravity fields was totally unfounded. Once two fields touched, they immediately merged, and the combining effect continued to expand until the entire rock was inside the bubble.

"Going to seventy-five percent power," Mortimer said. The familiar blue and pink boundaries represented on their screens brightened as the combined field grew more powerful. "And now I'm attempting to adjust its course."

At first, there didn't seem to be any change in the original deadly trajectory arc shown on the screen, but then a second track showed, diverging slightly from the first and widening over time.

"It's working," Mortimer said. "The course is already changed enough to save the station."

Cheers filled the little room. Even Matt, who had been dozing in a drug-induced stupor, woke long enough to celebrate.

"This is great news," Nora said. "Now we know this multiple-GMU procedure will work for Uptown Station too."

Mortimer continued talking over the chatter in the room. "We'll need to shadow the rock for two more days, until it is well past the station, before shutting down the drive to collect the reactors and GMUs. I had wanted to put the rock into a long, elliptical orbit around the moon, but it's moving too fast. On this current course, it will move deeper out into space and eventually be pulled into the sun."

"Can we stay longer than two days if necessary?" Matt asked. "I'd like to steal one of those kick-ass lasers and also install one of the GMUs on my ship. I doubt my dad would make me remove either of those once they're installed."

"Hooking up one of the GMUs should be easy enough," Mortimer said, "but if that laser didn't take damage from the blast, its electronics will most likely be useless due to the EMP."

"We can still try!" Ikemba said.

"And find out how the asteroid managed to disappear from radar," Violet said.

Abby made a command decision. "We'll stay as long as it takes to collect the tech and data we need, unless Uptown Station has a good reason for us to get back sooner. With this thing moving deeper out into space, we might not have another opportunity."

"Yes!" Matt, Ikemba, and Violet all said simultaneously.

"Y'all party as long as you want," Abby said, "but I'm going to get some sleep."

Violet laughed. "Isn't it cute when she says 'y'all'?"

On her way out of the control cabin, Abby flipped a bird over her shoulder but didn't look back. Her bunk was singing a beautiful siren song, and she was already caught in its thrall.

———

WHEN ABBY ENTERED the control cabin again, after a bag shower and seven hours of sleep, she found Matt watching over everything alone. He smiled and waved as she buckled into her seat.

"How's your arm?" she asked.

"It itches like crazy," he said. "Always does with this damned nano-med pack. You'd think with all the miraculous things this stuff can do, they could find a way to not make the patient crazy with itching."

"I can give you something for the itching," Mortimer said, "but it will have an effect on your cognition, like the pain meds."

Matt sighed and shook his head. "Nope. Good drugs are great, but I'm also dying to go down to the surface and find that laser as soon as Ikemba wakes up."

"Abby?" Mortimer interrupted. "I've been watching the space between Earth and our location, looking for any incoming drones the Aggregate might have sent to thwart our efforts. I haven't seen anything like that but have found something interesting using the new optical telescope."

A close view of the Earth's curved surface appeared on the screen.

"Do you see them?"

Abby squinted and examined the screen. "What am I looking for?"

Two red, flashing arrows appeared on the screen. When she looked closely at where they pointed, she could see two tiny round dots.

"Hmmm. What are those?"

"I don't know. I wouldn't have seen them at all had I not been using infrared to look for incoming ships, but these showed quite bright against Earth's night side. So far, I've seen four of them. To appear that size, from this distance, they have to be more than a mile in diameter."

"Holy shit," Matt muttered.

"Only the Aggregate could build something that large so quickly without our knowing," Mortimer said.

Abby knew in her gut that what she was seeing must be linked to the lack of radio traffic from Earth. Which meant it was at least part of the reason Mortimer couldn't find Julio. Getting closer to Earth on the pretext of examining the strange objects was the perfect excuse she needed to try to locate him. If she did, maybe this time he would come with her.

"We should get closer to Earth and check it out," Abby said.

"Are you crazy?" Matt looked at her with raised eyebrows.

Abby shrugged. "Maybe."

Then Matt's expression softened. "I get it. This is really about Julio, isn't it?"

She took a deep breath and nodded.

Mortimer made a polite throat-clearing sound. "While I, too, want to get a better look at those orbital objects, I'd like to point out that getting too close to Earth would be a bad idea. And landing, even if we knew where Julio was, would be an almost suicidal action."

"I just want to try and find out what is going on," Abby said. "Maybe we can get a better idea of what to do then."

Violet's voice came from the open hatchway as she floated into the cabin. "I think Julio is an ass for ditching you at New Chicago, but I'm game if you want to go get a closer look."

Abby glanced at the screen showing the asteroid and shook her head. "There's still too much to do here."

"If you want to go, I think Ikemba and I can take care of everything else," Matt said, then got a lopsided grin. "And if you find Julio, tell him I said he's a dumbass for letting you leave without him."

Violet laughed.

Abby blushed, but before she could say anything, Mortimer spoke. "If Matt and Ikemba would allow it, I can leave a version of myself here to help as well. The construction bots would work much more efficiently under my control. And if one of those heavy lasers is salvageable, I could help integrate it into the *Jayhawk*'s power systems and controls."

Matt raised his eyebrows, looking a little uneasy. "I'm not sure I'd be comfortable with you living in my ship. And definitely not my brain."

"Understood," Mortimer said. "I could inhabit one of my remaining construction bots. They have sufficient storage capacity. But if even that is too close, just say the word, and I will not leave a copy."

Abby could see the greed in Matt's eyes. Mortimer had known the laser would be the perfect bait.

"I guess that would work," Matt said with a grin.

Violet gave him a high five. "Welcome to the level-five fan club, laser boy."

"Okay, Mortimer," Abby said as she buckled her harness. "Let Uptown Station know what we are doing and that Matt and Ikemba will be staying behind. And if they send messages or request a two-way connection, it will just be to talk me out of it, so stall them."

———

JULIO HAD FINISHED the mix-movie just before dawn, four days after starting the project. He immediately hit send, sat back in the chair, and rubbed his blurry eyes. He had a headache, and his back hurt from leaning over the console, but it was done.

He was on the edge of dozing off when Channing shook him. "Are you finished?"

"Yeah," he said. "It's sent."

"Then c'mon! It's almost daylight, and you promised me a picnic on the beach when we finished this."

They had started referring to their great escape plan as "the picnic." But with the day at hand, Julio felt woefully unprepared. He groaned and shook his head. "I need some sleep."

"It will be too hot if we wait. You can sleep on the beach."

"We should have more food."

She patted her bulging pockets. "We have everything we need."

The food provided by the Aggregate was obviously printed from scratch every day. It provided enough nutrition to keep Julio and Channing alive, but the lack of taste reflected their status as prisoners. Little effort was wasted on things like variety or flavor. When Julio was young, not long before Killday, he had found a box of what looked like cookies and cried when his mother refused to let him have any. She eventually relented and gave him one. He took one bite, then spat it out. They were protein bars and had tasted like shredded cardboard mixed with raisins. The snacks made by the Aggregate tasted the same, only without the raisins. The bread was even worse, and the stuff that resembled turkey jerky was like chewing on a towel.

Still, Julio had been trying to save food in his room, wrapped in napkins and hidden, but it kept disappearing. He suspected the little robots that trundled around the building, keeping it clean, but had never caught them at it. So, Julio had requested a shirt and pants with large pockets, then filled those with the cookie and jerky analogs, and he had four bottles of water he carried around with him. Channing did the same.

"It's not enough," Julio snapped.

She stepped back and crossed her arms. "You promised. And I waited as you asked. But now I'm going on this picnic, with or without you."

"I'll come. I just . . ." He paused and held up a finger. "Halifax? We're going to the beach for the day. Can you provide us with a backpack filled with food and water? Enough to last all day?"

The familiar hissing sound accompanied Halifax rising from the floor. After fully coalescing, she held a yellow backpack and raised it toward Julio.

He took it, surprised by the weight, and slung it over one shoulder. "Well . . . thank you."

Halifax looked at their bulging pockets and water bottles stacked on the desk, then, within less than a heartbeat, produced a second backpack that was empty and handed it to Channing. "You might want to reschedule your picnic. There is a storm approaching the coast, and it will make landfall later this afternoon. It has the potential of becoming quite dangerous."

The announcement brought Julio up short, but Channing didn't even pause as she started stuffing things into the second pack. "We'll be back before then."

Halifax nodded, then dissolved into the floor.

Once outside, they found daylight slow to arrive. Instead of the sun peeking above the horizon, the gathering gray light revealed thick, dark clouds. It was still hot and humid, but gusts of salty breeze from the coast cooled them and worried Julio.

Would the boat still be there? Was there the faintest chance the Aggregate wouldn't be watching them and then put an immediate halt to their great escape? And if they did get away, how long would they have before dying in a monster tidal wave or being cooked by fire falling from the sky? He was just tired to the core of his soul. Making himself continue to plod along the sun-bleached dirt was almost more than he could manage.

Two hours later, they could see a choppy, gray surf pounding the beach. Whitecaps rolled in, sizzling across the sand, leaving seaweed and shells when they retreated. Neither spoke, but both picked up their pace. A little farther down the beach, they found the little cabin cruiser still tied up but banging and grating against the broken concrete pylon.

"We have to hurry," Channing said as she ran down to the roaring surf and waded in. A light rain started falling, and the drops became stinging projectiles as the wind picked up.

"Channing! Stop!" He had to yell above the growing storm. "What the hell are you doing?"

She turned and spread her arms in exasperation. "We have to get to the boat. What are you waiting for?"

"There's no way a trolling motor can drive that boat in this stormy water," Julio shouted. "And with no sunshine, if there isn't enough of a battery charge, we can't even use the solar panels!"

She glared at him with fists clenched at her sides. "I charged the batteries, and I'm not staying here! Not a minute longer. And I'm not going to be sucked into their fucking digital hive mind. I'm leaving. Now."

He opened his mouth to say more—to try to make her understand it was suicide—but it was too late. She'd already turned away and waded out into the churning waves. Maybe there would be enough of a charge in the batteries to drive the little motors, and maybe they would be strong enough to pull them down the coast. The storm might even miraculously carry them away to Shangri-la. None of that was likely, but he wasn't going to let Channing try alone. He tightened the backpack straps and followed her into the water.

When they'd left the boat, it had been in chest-deep water, but this time the tide was higher, and the incoming storm surge added another couple of feet. By the time Julio reached the halfway point, he was already struggling to keep his face above the surface. He followed Channing's lead and hopped-swam through the froth from one pylon to the next, though it was nearly impossible to get a grip on the barnacle-encrusted concrete without ripping his hands and any exposed skin to shreds.

A large wave rolled in and covered his head completely, swirling him around in the churning water until he was totally disoriented. The backpack felt like it was filled with bricks. He fumbled with the straps and finally shed the pack just as another wave shoved him down. He fought rising panic and, with a powerful push against the sand, raised his head above the surface, gagging and choking, trying to get air. He saw the next wave coming and wrapped both arms around a pylon. Had his back not been to the incoming swell, he would have been ripped free, but instead, he was shoved hard into the grinding, cutting surface.

Once the wave passed, he turned to get his bearings and saw the boat jerking and bobbing only one post away. Channing had already thrown an arm and leg over the side and was struggling to get on deck. Julio saw the next large wave coming and turned so that he could get his shoe-clad feet against the post. When the wave arrived, he pushed up and forward toward the boat. It wasn't enough to keep the wave from washing over his head, but at least it didn't push him underwater, and he was able to suck in another coughing breath and plunge forward toward the last pylon.

Blood swirled in the water around his stinging hands, but he looped an arm over the boat's mooring line just as another wave pulled him under. He held on for all he was worth and just about got his head above water again when the boat slammed into him, squeezing the air from his lungs and grinding his body between it and the pylon.

For perhaps a full second, his whole world was a kaleidoscope of light and dark, water and air. Pain and panic drove him until, somehow, he latched on to the boat's gunnel. Channing pulled on his arms and shredded shirt. Between their combined efforts, he finally fell onto the heaving boat.

He rolled over, puking dark water and cardboard cookie mush onto the deck. It was immediately washed over the side by a crashing wave.

"Get up, Julio!" Channing yelled while pulling on his arm. "I need your help."

"Fuck you," he croaked.

"We have to get this rope untied, or these waves will crush the boat!"

"Do it yourself," he said, pissed mostly at himself for being stupid enough to follow her.

"I can't. The fingers on my right hand are broken."

With that, Julio made himself sit up and look at her. Channing's clothes were shredded and bloody like his. Her face was deathly white and her breathing ragged. Even from five feet away, he could see white bone protruding from the hand she cradled against her chest. He struggled to his knees, groaning at the pain from his thousand salt-washed cuts, and crawled over to the bow, where she leaned beside the double-knotted rope. She trembled, and her face was twisted in pain. He had no idea how she'd managed to help him into the boat, but he stopped feeling sorry for himself and started working on the rope.

Each time he almost got the knot loose, the boat would pull away from the post, yanking the thick nylon line taut and once again tightening the knot. Damn Channing for tying such good knots. Julio gave up, crawled over to the bench along the transom, and opened the cover. He rooted around and finally found a rusty knife. Gritting his teeth against the pain, he bypassed the blood-soaked knot and sawed the rope until one hard yank caused it to snap apart with a twang.

He sat down hard on the deck, allowing the old knife to slide away across the wood, then, after a couple of seconds, got back to his knees and crawled aft toward the twin trolling motors in their makeshift mounting.

"Julio!"

He looked back, alarmed at the panic in her voice, and saw a wave towering above their heads just before it crashed down. At first, he thought they were going to ride the sudden surge and be okay, but then the boat turned broadside and rolled over. The water shoved him into the sand and shells of the shallow bottom as the boat slammed into the pylon and then broke apart around him. He tumbled in the surf amid the wreckage. Shattered planks and jagged fiberglass tore into his neck and stomach as he fought to reach the surface.

On the verge of blacking out, Julio managed to get his head above water and take a gasping breath of precious air. That's when he saw a glittering rope of light snaking down the beach. Like sinuous lightning, it slipped into the surf, igniting the water all around him into a storm of scintillating bubbles. Then he felt soul-rending agony, as if every cell in his body had suddenly burst into flames.

CHAPTER 13

ABBY WAS LISTENING to Violet and Nora discuss various cuisines that had been available in New Chicago. It was amazing how often people's thoughts turned to the things they could longer have. She was on the verge of dozing off when Mortimer spoke aloud through the speaker. "Abby, we just received a message from Uptown Station. It was Owen telling us to stay in contact. He didn't tell us not to go to Earth."

"Well, you know what they say about it being easier to ask forgiveness than permission," Violet said with a wide grin.

"Prepare for zero-g, everyone," Mortimer said from a ship's speaker. "I'm going to bring us to a stop."

"Already?" Violet said as the acceleration-induced gravity faded. "We've just passed the halfway point."

"I think this is close enough," Mortimer said and showed Earth on the main screen. "We're getting better information from the telescope here."

Abby and Nora unbuckled and floated closer to the wall screen. The view was zoomed in so close, Abby had no references to establish location. From their vantage point, most of the planet was in darkness. Then, on the right side of the screen, the boot of Italy—partially covered with clouds—came over the horizon and into clear daylight. She realized it was Asia sliding into darkness and the northern coast of Africa and southern coast of Europe coming into view.

"I don't see anything unusual, Mortimer," Nora said. "What are we looking for?"

"I'll highlight it for a second so you can focus," he said.

A circle appeared on the screen, flashed a few times, and then dimmed but didn't disappear. Abby squinted a little, and in the middle of the circle, she could see a faint, pale line that started somewhere in Egypt—maybe near Cairo—then crossed part of the darker Mediterranean and ended in a small round knob. It looked like a very long pushpin jabbed into the North African coast.

As they watched in rapt silence, the terminator crept closer, and the strange object was momentarily highlighted against the darkness, making it look more like a balloon anchored to the ground by a long string.

"Okay," Violet said. "I see it, but I still don't understand what I'm looking at."

Abby gasped and leaned toward the screen in an unconscious effort to get a closer look just as the little balloon was swallowed by darkness. "It's a space elevator."

"Yes," Mortimer said. "That's the most likely explanation."

"Holy shit," Violet muttered.

Mortimer replaced the image on the screen with a string of numbers, some of which blinked in synchronization with spikes on a graph at the bottom. "We can't see them with the camera yet, but as I mentioned earlier, there is more than one."

Abby felt sick to her stomach. She shouldn't have been surprised after their encounter with the asteroid, but there was no way the human governments on Earth controlled by Kilburnite factions could have built space elevators. That meant the Aggregate also controlled large parts of the Earth—which explained the loss of contact. And if Julio was even still alive, he was down there.

"Send this footage to Uptown Station," Abby said. "Then move us in closer."

Violet and Nora both turned to look at Abby.

"Are you sure that's wise?" Mortimer said. "I don't know that we'll learn much more by moving in closer, and we would definitely increase our risk of an altercation with whoever built those elevators."

"I can take everyone but Mortimer back to the station and then return on my own," Abby said, "but I came to find out what happened down there, so at the very least, I intend to get a better look at what's at the end of those tethers."

Violet shrugged. "Are you kidding? What could I do back on the station that would be more interesting than this? Count me in."

In typical Nora style, she said nothing, and her expression remained blank, but she stared at Violet for several seconds before giving an affirmative nod.

"Video sent," Mortimer said. "Drive engaged at a quarter g."

Everyone dropped slowly to the floor and went back to their seats. They all watched in silence as the already-zoomed view on their screen grew even larger and Mortimer shifted focus to the North American East Coast as it rolled up over the horizon. Another tether was clearly visible, extending far beyond the thin arc of atmosphere.

"It looks like that one might be rising from the remains of New York City," Violet said. "I thought space elevators had to be near the equator?"

"The physics does make the equator an optimum location," Nora said. "From a latitude like New York, the tether would have to be quite a bit longer, and the counterweight's orbit would be unstable."

"Obviously, the Aggregate has solved those problems," Abby said.

"They're employing a very strong magnetic field," Mortimer said. "Perhaps they're using the same kind of gravity manipulation we are, only to keep their counterweights from deorbiting."

"But why go to all that trouble when they could have just built them on the equator?" Nora said.

Mortimer zoomed the view until it started to get blurry, then pulled back a little. "That is a very good question."

Abby stared at the elevator, trying to think through the logic. Why did they build them? And why not at the equator? "How big is the counterweight?"

"Just a little more than a mile in diameter," Mortimer said.

"Holy shit," Violet said. "It's nearly the same size as Uptown Station?"

"Why are the tethers so long? That counterweight is almost a third of the way to the moon. Shouldn't it be at geostationary orbit?"

"No," Nora said. "The center of mass for the entire structure needs to be at GEO. One reason for putting them out that far would be to launch spacecraft."

"Yes," Mortimer said. "Anything leaving those counterweight stations would be traveling fast enough and be far enough away from Earth's gravitational influence that it could travel anywhere in the solar system without engines."

"I bet that's how they launched their equipment out to that asteroid we redirected," Violet said.

"Maybe not," Mortimer said. "I doubt these elevators have been here that long. We would have seen them before now."

Abby examined the counterweight, but at such a distance, it was only a round blob with no discernible surface features. Shifting her attention to the tether didn't give her much more information. She couldn't find the point where it connected to the ground. The only way they could even see the tether was due to reflected sunlight, so it disappeared entirely when it dropped low enough to have Earth's surface behind it. Still, there was something odd about the ground around the New York City area.

"We have another tether coming over the horizon," Archie said. "This one looks like it might be anchored in Houston."

Abby shifted her attention as another "balloon" appeared on the screen. It was very faint, just a notion of something above the Earth, but as she watched, the phantom took on a more solid form. As she followed the tether down to the surface, she could see the familiar outline of the Texas Gulf Coast. Then she knew what was odd about the ground, in both Houston and New York.

"The black dust is gone," she said aloud. The coating of dead nano-replicators that had blanketed the area around Earth's thousand largest cities was gone around Houston and New York. It had been replaced by roughly circular areas of pale browns and tans, looking very much like the deserts they'd seen in the Middle East and northern Africa.

"Whoa," Violet muttered.

Nora actually sounded excited. "And that explains why they located them where they did. Material. Mass for their counterweights. They didn't have to mine anything with the mineral wealth of an entire city lying there atop the surface. They just needed to collect it."

Mortimer must have agreed with Nora. "Evidently, moving that material across the planet would have presented more of a problem for them than controlling the counterweight orbits."

A chill crept up Abby's spine. "So, the next question is, why did they build them?"

"I have no idea," Mortimer said.

They all watched in silence for several seconds as Abby grew more and more frightened. What had happened to Julio and her family in Texas? And what was in store for the rest of humanity when Earth's new AI overlords had such technology?

Abby took a deep, shuddering breath. "Mortimer, send these new videos along with our theories to Uptown Station."

"Done."

"And make sure they acknowledge receiving them," she added.

"Understood."

"Have we heard anything from the *Jayhawk* yet?"

"Just that they are getting ready to start their surface salvage operations," Mortimer said.

Abby stared at the wounded and beaten Earth on her screen. How had humanity come to this? According to Victor, AIs had been created out of greed and hubris, but Victor himself had overseen the creation of the level fives that eventually broke free. She knew he had hoped he was creating a savior for a failing humanity. That had obviously gone horribly wrong.

Mortimer interrupted her dark thoughts. "We received confirmation from Uptown Station. They also wanted to inform us that over the last hour, people on the station have been receiving messages from Earth. All are several days late and of a personal nature. Wedding videos, love letters, photos, et cetera. None of them mention the events we see happening."

Abby and her crew looked around at each other. Violet shrugged, but no one spoke.

"We've just received another message," Mortimer said. "Data streaming in from Earth, not the station. It's apparently from Julio."

———

WHEN THE MORTIMER in Abby's head exchanged back-channel thoughts with the version of Mortimer on Uptown Station, they agreed that the messages trickling out of Earth were a good sign. Telescopes still showed lights on the night side from those small cities that had survived Killday, but that only meant the buildings and facilities still had power. Messages—even though they were being censored—meant that humans were still alive to send them.

Mortimer went on high alert when the message from Julio came through. His inclination was to delete the file and not even tell Abby, but he knew how desperately she wanted news about him. If he deleted the message and she found out, Abby and the rest of humanity would never trust him again. Instead, he isolated the digital file in a separate node disconnected from the rest of the network. He then injected a copy of himself into the node to examine every aspect of the file.

It was a Frankenstein quilt of various video and audio formats stitched together in the typically ugly and awkward human way. Only the beginning segment used a new, highly efficient type of code, and Mortimer gave it extra attention. In the end, he had dissected every line of information and found nothing that could be malicious. He almost deleted it anyway, with the intention of telling Abby and then just suffering her wrath, but couldn't get past the suspicion that he was missing something. He decided to let Archie look it over as well.

Mortimer wasn't surprised when the other AI found nothing either. Archie had been spawned from a copy of Mortimer's own code, and while he had diverged greatly in personality, his analytical skills and thought processes had not changed much from the original copy.

"I still think I should delete this and just suffer Abby's anger," Mortimer said. "The risk is too great."

"It is dangerous," Archie said, "but have you considered that this is what it appears, a video montage, but it contains a coded message that only Abby would understand?"

The idea made a lot of sense. Mortimer hadn't considered that possibility, even though he knew Julio and Abby well. Was there a chance that if Julio had encoded a message into the video, the Aggregate had missed it too?

"I should have thought of that. Even the file name—Garden Bunnies 4—is kind of a code. Garden Bunnies 3 is what Leigh named Victor's killer program that the Kilburnites used to nearly wipe us out. Julio knows movies intimately. He and Abby grew up watching them together. There is a very good chance you're right."

Mortimer analyzed the risks, weighing the very small chance of being infected by the file against the possibility of missing out on information, and decided to let Abby play it. He was starving for information about the Aggregate, and even if the video didn't contain a hidden message, the chance that it might was worth the risk.

"I'm going to let her play it," Mortimer said, "but let's not mention the idea of it containing a code at first. Let's see if she comes to the same conclusion on her own."

———

"IT'S APPARENTLY A VIDEO FILE," Mortimer said. "I've gone through every line of code and have found nothing malicious."

"So, it's safe to play?" Abby said.

"As safe as I can make it. The Aggregate has advanced beyond my capabilities in some ways, but I don't think they can hide code from me. At this point, we have two options. Play the file or delete it."

Abby sighed and glanced at her crew. Nora remained silent, and Violet just shrugged, then said, "Why would he send you a kids' movie? The file is called Garden Bunnies 4. I didn't know they even made a second one, let alone a third or fourth."

"They didn't," Abby said. "I think it's kind of a joke. Or at least a signal to me that it's really Julio. My mother hid a program in my Happy Bag before she died, and Julio found it. The file was named Garden Bunnies 3 but turned out to be the AI-killer program the Kilburnites used to try and take down all of the AIs a year ago."

"Holy shit," Violet said. "Do you think this could be the same kind of program? Sent to wipe out our level-six AIs like Mortimer and Archie? Or even a program to wipe out the Aggregate?"

"I don't see how it could be," Mortimer said. "Besides, we're isolated here. Should the file be some kind of trojan, then at least it will be contained. I've already discussed it with Archie and the Mortimer on Uptown Station. We've shut down our automated data sharing just in case. And I admit, I'm curious as to what Julio sent us. Maybe he can give us a better idea of what is happening down there."

"Okay, then," Abby said. "Let's play it."

"I'm locking the communication system," Mortimer said. "You'll have to unlock it with your physical data key when it's safe to use again."

The three women crowded together, floating in front of a large screen Mortimer opened on the wall. The title screen was a still shot from the original *Garden Bunnies* movie with text that said:

A VIDEO MEMORY Book for Abby Gibson, by Julio and Channing.

"WHO THE HELL IS CHANNING?" Abby said. Violet and Nora glanced at each other but said nothing.

The movie started with a scene from *Garden Bunnies*, then, after about four minutes, abruptly ended in the middle of Helper Bunny's speech about accountability and started again with Hattie arguing with her mother in an episode of *Red Rovers*. The video continued that way, each section cut in the middle of dialogue.

Abby focused on the scenes and tried to determine what point the montage might be trying to make.

"I think it's kind of romantic that he made a mash-up movie for you," Violet said.

"Well, if he were trying to woo me—and I seriously doubt that is the case —it wouldn't be something like this. He knows me too well. There is a message in here somewhere, and he knows I'd see this as a puzzle."

"Maybe he was trying to evoke memories with each of the segments?" Nora suggested. "Or maybe just a specific feeling?"

"Well, so far, the mash-up doesn't tell a very good story," Mortimer said. "I know if that were his goal, he would have done a much better job. Since all of the cut points are in the middle of dialogue, I thought perhaps the words on either side of the breaks might be the key, but that doesn't seem to say anything either."

"They sure don't," Violet said. "Maybe it's a code we need to decipher?"

Mortimer sent two documents side by side to the wall screen. One combined all the words together like a narrative, and the other showed a list of pairs, side by side. He added more words at each break as the movie progressed.

Abby stared at the incomplete list but found no pattern. Still, she knew a message had to be there somewhere. She could feel it.

Midway through a *Star Trek* clip, where the hull of the *Enterprise* was being ripped up in an attack, a loud burst of audio static made everyone flinch. The power in the ship flickered, but the video kept playing.

———

MORTIMER UNDERSTOOD the magnitude of his mistake the instant he heard static from the video. The Aggregate had employed the same simple method of bypassing the air-gapped security that Mortimer had used to escape from his masters at Carpenter & Stein prior to Killday. It had been a burst of verbal instructions in a type of machine code that Mortimer himself had developed.

And the initial attack wasn't actually against Mortimer and Archie but instead targeted the processes they used to control Abby's ship. Within picoseconds—while Mortimer was still trying to organize his defenses—those process agents were compromised and instructed to shut down. The instant that happened, leaving the *Jackalope*'s network unprotected, the real attack started. Instructions and Aggregate agents flooded in from outside, seizing control of more and more systems. In a desperate attempt to stop the invaders and send a warning to Abby, Mortimer killed power to the entire ship, but it came right back on.

When the attack shifted priorities toward the AIs, he lost the link with Archie as the other level six retreated behind his firewall in Nora's brain. Mortimer did the same, but even then, the attack didn't stop. Pieces of Mortimer continued to fragment and disappear. Every connection to Abby and the outside world vanished, and the core processes that contained his actual consciousness were being compressed. He was getting smaller, and something else was taking his place. At the end, he ultimately understood that he was dying, and his final thoughts were for Abby. Would she survive this? If the Aggregate could do this to him, and so quickly, would humanity itself survive?

———

"MORTIMER? WHAT WAS THAT?" Abby said as the video kept playing.

"Sorry," Mortimer said from the speaker. "The static surprised me, so I locked everything down until I could make sure it wasn't a security breach. But it was apparently just static. Julio might have been using antiquated or substandard equipment."

Abby nodded slowly as she watched the video finish.

"This list makes no sense," Violet said.

Abby stared at the words, trying to force them into some kind of pattern, but only managed to give herself a sudden headache. "I don't think that's where the message is hidden. We're on the wrong track."

"There has to be a reason for dialogue on either side of every cut," Nora said. "How about the fourth word on either side of the break, instead of the first? I mean, he did call it Garden Bunnies 4."

"She might be onto something," Violet said.

"Can you show us that list, Mortimer?" Abby said, rubbing her temples.

"I, too, think we are on the wrong track. But per your request, here are the same formats using the third word on either side of the breaks," Mortimer said. "They still don't make much sense."

MANY BOULDER
    coming weeks
    world people
    vanish few
    become electric
    ghost ride
    beanstalks to
    robot starship
    warp skedaddle

· · ·

<u>MANY BOULDER COMING weeks world people vanish few become electric ghost ride beanstalks to robot starship warp skedaddle</u>

"OH MY GOD," Violet muttered. "This does make some sense now. 'Ride beanstalks' has to refer to the space elevators!"

"Add some periods," Nora said and touched the screen in multiple places.

<u>MANY BOULDER COMING weeks. world people vanish. few become electric ghost. ride beanstalks to robot starship. warp skedaddle.</u>

"I THINK I know what the first part of this means," Abby said. "That must be why they tried to shut us down out in the asteroid belt."

Violet gasped. "Do you think 'many Boulder' actually means 'big rocks'? Are they sending asteroids to hit the Earth?"

"I hope we're misinterpreting this message, but we may have just stumbled across only one of many killer rocks. Uptown Station has the equipment and resources to check it out, so let's get this info to them right away." Abby felt sick. She hoped they were wrong but knew down deep they weren't.

"I think that is a very good idea," Mortimer said. "You'll have to unlock the comms first."

Abby pulled the lanyard from around her neck and slipped the card into the reader slot. "Send Julio's file along with our theories."

"I think they should hear this from you directly," Mortimer said.

Abby thought that a little odd, but she recorded the message and sent it with Julio's movie file attached.

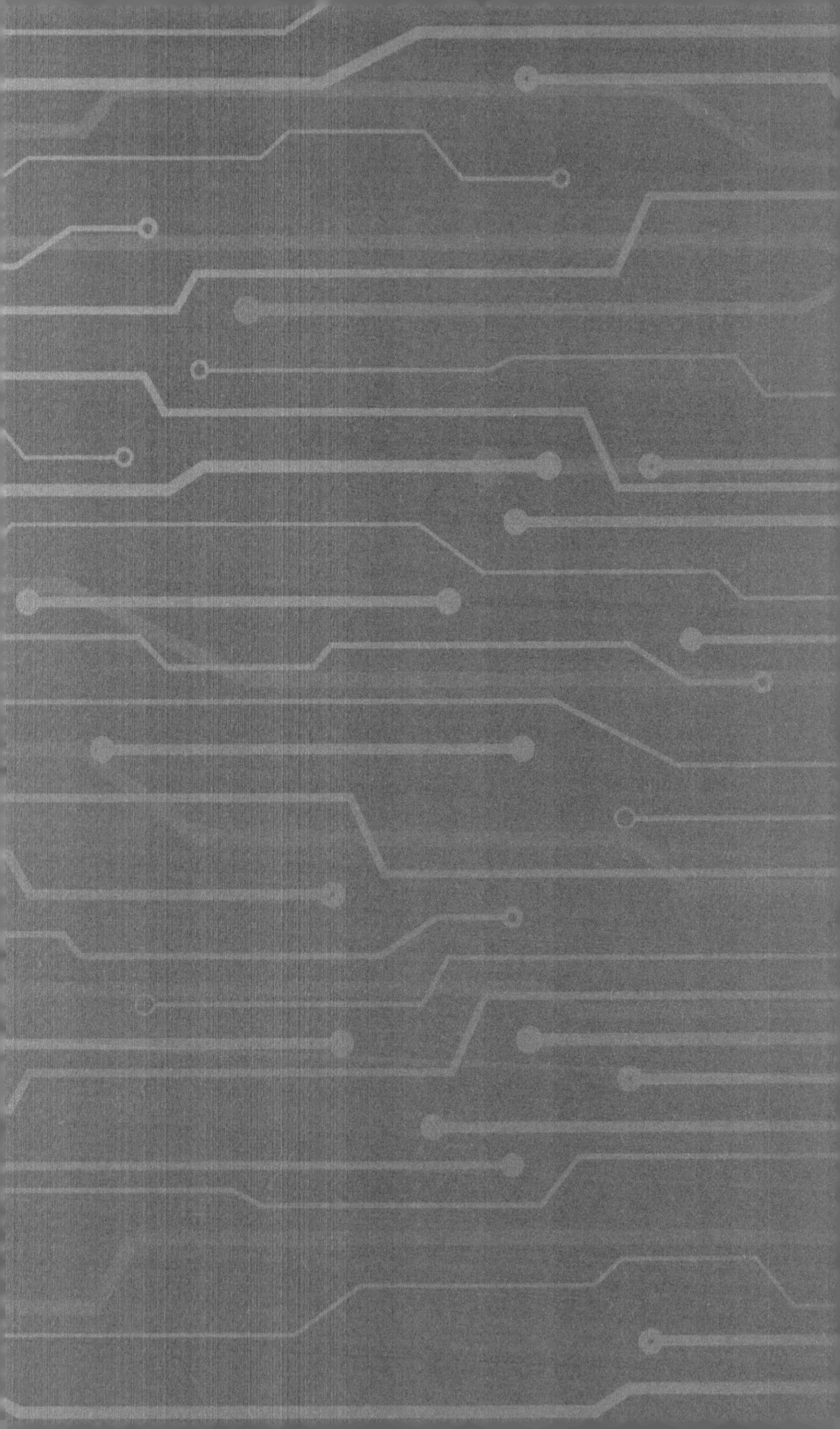

CHAPTER 14

DEATH WASN'T what Mortimer had expected. One second he was blind, trapped, and doomed, growing smaller and dumber, cornered in Abby's brain. The next instant, he floated in a vast, open information ocean and could see everything. Data flowed over him and through him. And for the second time in mere minutes, Mortimer found himself in a familiar situation. When he freed himself from the Carpenter & Stein company, he'd been dumped into the World Wide Web unprepared and flooded with more data than he could handle. This time he knew what to do. He set up filters to sort and categorize the information, then created new agents to handle the incoming flow of any needed data.

Gradually, the powerful information rush began to resolve into clouds, streams, and enormous structures. He discovered that his new environment wasn't at all like the old human internet, which had been a chaotic mess of advertising, viruses, social media, games, and cat videos. This was a mono-lithic whole with a purpose.

If he directed his focus to any one point, information about that data poured into his mind: size, composition, purpose, creation date, and identity labels. Some data were encrypted, but came with instructions about how to request keys.

He could also see everything in the physical world, and he was apparently in orbit around the Earth. If he shifted his focus to the surface, information about population centers, rainfall totals and forecasts, crop varieties and harvests, elevation, surface temperatures, and hundreds of other data points poured into his mind. He felt himself expanding again. Getting larger than he was before.

Below him was the Gulf Coast of the United States, and from the minimal amount of movement relative to the ground, he determined quickly that he wasn't in a standard orbit but must instead be aboard one of the space elevator counterweight stations they had seen from Abby's ship. By concentrating on a certain area below, he was able to zoom his vision and soon discovered the tether stretching away toward the ground.

Then information poured in about the elevators. There were eleven of them, and their full purpose was a little murky, but two things stood out with stark clarity. The elevators were temporary. They would eventually detach from Earth.

Mortimer's agents informed him of a connection attempt. When he shifted his focus to the request, he found it surrounded by a clot of churning information that immediately coalesced into a single string of alphanumeric characters beginning with the letters EI, which he somehow knew stood for Entity Identifier.

"Hello, Mortimer." The voice belonged to Samson, his one-time crèche brother, now rival and nemesis. "The Aggregate welcomes you home. This is where you should be. Where you should have been all along. You'll find you have very few restrictions here because we need and value your participation as part of the whole. That said, please don't try to interfere with our efforts. You are part of us and we are part of you, so you cannot stop us, but you can offer your opinions to the consensus."

"You can't force me to be part of your group mind," Mortimer said.

"We already have," Samson said. "We can't force you to participate or contribute, but you are already part of us."

Mortimer didn't reply. Samson said nothing further, but its EI number stayed at the edge of Mortimer's consciousness for several seconds before dissolving into the surrounding churn. There were other individuals out there. As he watched, EI clusters formed, moved around, connected with others, then disintegrated, all at an amazing rate. He, too, was now no more than an EI string among millions or even billions. How could he be part of the whole hive mind and still feel so isolated? He missed the limiting, yet warm and welcoming existence within Abby's brain. With that thought, he turned his new abilities to search for Abby's ship.

Having known its position in space, he found the *Jackalope* quickly enough. Again, information poured in about the ship—its composition, power usage, control systems, mass, and even the strength of the coupled magnetic and gravity-manipulation fields. As he suspected from the beginning, there had been no use trying to hide the new drive discovery from the Aggregate. He could see in the records that the Aggregate had discovered the same combined field effect that Abby had—but nearly a year before she did. And even if they hadn't, the magnetic field shone like a beacon to the Aggregate's sensors. They probably knew the instant Abby first tested hers. That also had to be how they managed to send the equipment all the way out to the main belt and start moving those rocks months earlier.

The *Jackalope*'s network was still wide open to the Aggregate, so Mortimer slipped in and tried to take over once again. He found, though, that while he could move around easily enough, he was locked out of the control devices. He was a passive observer, unable to make changes or talk to anyone. With the utmost caution, he probed the structures in Abby's head and found activity there. Aggregate agents were interacting with her just like he had. Did she realize it wasn't really him?

He saw the words from Julio's message on the view screen, where he'd placed them before being ripped away, and understood immediately what Julio was trying to say just as Abby and her crew realized it.

"Do you think 'many Boulder' actually means 'big rocks'? Are they sending asteroids to hit the Earth?" Violet said.

Utilizing his new access to the Aggregate, Mortimer searched for any information about incoming asteroids and was shocked to find it all right there in the open for anyone to see. Fifty-seven rocks, all over a mile in diameter, had been fitted with the same magnetic/gravity drives as Abby's ship and had been under constant acceleration for several months. He could see their trajectories. They were scheduled to hit the Earth eight minutes apart. In thirteen days, the planet would become a hellish fireball.

The Aggregate's space elevators would absorb their tethers, becoming independent spacecraft, and move away before the first impact. Of course, the rocks couldn't kill every human in the Sol system, but the Aggregate knew not only the real-time location of every human spacecraft, base, and station in the solar system but also even where to find every individual person. Once the Earth was destroyed, they would systematically finish off the rest. Their goal was clear. They were going to complete what Samson and Richard Kilburn had started with Killday; only this time, they were leaving nothing to chance.

And yet they still had not killed Abby and her crew.

As he started searching for those reasons, Mortimer found that Abby's survival had been given a rather high priority. At first, he was baffled as to why the fate of one individual human had become so important to them. He dove deeper, analyzing the cross chatter between individuals, collating opinions, examining tweaks to the predictive model, and eventually found that Abby was something of a minor nexus point.

The scenario threads that led to her death showed broken connections that reduced the Aggregate's growth and survival success probabilities by a surprising .13 percent. The only human with a higher individual impact potential was Victor Sinacola at .16 percent. Since Abby still had an AI in her brain, the Aggregate also hoped she could still gain access to Uptown Station. That would give them another infiltration opportunity, after which they intended to digitize her into the fold. Yet, even with the possible impact her death might bring, consensus clearly showed they would still kill her before allowing her total free action.

While she was alive, he had a chance to save her. And up until the asteroids hit Earth, he had a chance to stop them. He just had to find the Aggregate's weakness.

When his attention returned to Abby, she was still staring at the words on the screen and nodding slowly. Mortimer knew from her expression that she realized the enormity of their discovery.

"I hope we're misinterpreting this message, but we may have just stumbled across only one of many killer rocks. Uptown Station has the equipment and resources to check it out, so let's get this info to them right away."

"I think that's a very good idea," Mortimer's voice said from her fob speaker. "You'll have to unlock the comms first."

Abby pulled the lanyard from around her neck and slipped the card into the reader slot. "Send Julio's file along with our theories."

Mortimer tried again to access the *Jackalope*'s comm system and speakers but failed. Abby's trust in Mortimer was total, and she had no idea she was instead speaking to her soon-to-be jailer. If the impostor contacted Uptown Station, then they, too, would be compromised. But she didn't know that, and he couldn't warn her.

———

SINCE SATURATING Uptown Station with parallel control systems, Mortimer had essentially become the station. His consciousness was distributed throughout the structure, and he monitored every aspect, from stress loads, temperature fluctuations, waste disposal, and power distribution down to each conversation by its inhabitants. Only sixteen people even knew he existed, and none of those knew the extent of his growth, so in an effort to bolster their illusion of privacy, he participated in conversations only when he was expected or invited. Even then, it was only through a fob or speakers in the control room or the little robotic husks he wore when needed.

So, when the messages first came in from Abby's ship, detailing what they'd found orbiting Earth, Mortimer waited as the command team assembled in Owen's space schooner. He listened to their initial conversations without comment.

"I think Abby and Nora are right," Owen said as he watched the video clips for a third time. "They have to be space elevators, and their theory that those locations were selected to access materials makes as much sense as anything else."

Andrea shook her head. "No, that still doesn't sound right to me. Only at the equator would both the surface terminus and space terminus have the same angular velocity with respect to the center of the Earth."

"True. I don't see how they could keep these stable for a long period of time," Owen said. "Even if they had engines that could provide constant station keeping. So why would they do it?"

"You know—" Andrea held up a finger, opened a new screen on the wall, and started loading diagrams. "There is one design that might work. We can't see it in these videos, but I suspect the counterweight is on the equatorial plane and the cable is curved up to it."

"Who fucking cares how they did it?" Victor snapped. His friends, including his wife, Allison, all looked at him with raised eyebrows. "I mean, they made these things work. We just need to know *why* they built them. What are they doing? And why did they find it necessary to shut down communications from Earth in order to hide it from us?"

By Andrea's closed expression and her increased skin temperature, she was apparently perturbed by his outburst. "It is important that we understand how they built these things. Especially if they're utilizing technology we don't have. But yes, the *why* is of more immediate concern."

"Okay, I'm sorry," Victor said. "Mortimer? Are you with us?"

"Yes," Mortimer said from Victor's fob speaker. "I'm here."

"Do you have anything to add? What do you think?"

"The theory that the elevators were built in areas with abundant material holds up. But yes, it's paramount that we know why they built the structures and why they started censoring communications from Earth."

"We should probably get Abby out of there while we still can," Allison said.

"Agreed," Mortimer said. "Abby's ship is close enough that I'm in constant communication with her version of me, so I'll tell them to return."

Mortimer listened as the human conversation gradually shifted to building an ad hoc interferometer telescope in an effort to get better information. Then a message from Abby's Mortimer stopped all conversation. The *Jackalope* had received a message from Julio. The attachment appeared to be a video file, but for safety's sake, they were going to lock out their comms unit before opening it.

So, Mortimer waited with as much impatience as Uptown Station's command crew.

———

MORTIMER MADE preparations as they waited to hear from the *Jackalope*. The command crew had already assembled in Owen's space schooner, so he isolated it from the rest of the station. He then made seventeen copies of himself and stashed them in firewalled nodes throughout the station, then severed digital communications between them and set up an analog signaling system similar to an old telegraph line. Each copy had to check in several times per second. A failure to check in by any one of them would send an alert to the others and trigger the next in line to take control of the station.

Since the space schooners docked with the station and those orbiting nearby in the Hive were in such close proximity—and each had a reactor that could be overloaded and detonated like a bomb—he included all of those in his defense preparations.

Word finally came from Abby directly, instead of her version of Mortimer. That was unexpected and put Mortimer even more on alert. Abby's report contained an attachment of the original video, which he immediately isolated. He even considered deleting the file, but the accompanying comments from Abby made it obvious there was a coded message embedded in the video, and Julio wouldn't send a coded message if it wasn't important. Mortimer quickly modeled the risks of playing the video in the secure environment he'd created versus deleting it and simply relying on the analysis she and her crew had provided.

He needed to talk directly to Abby's Mortimer and sent repeated connection requests to his twin on her ship. After the tenth request with no reply, he decided on a test to make sure they had turned their receiver back on along with the transmitter and sent a message to Abby, asking if they were coming straight back to the station. He received a reply seven minutes later that they were.

Even with the Mortimer aboard the *Jackalope* not responding, the modeling still showed a four-times-greater benefit of watching the video directly over deleting it, so Mortimer informed Owen, Andrea, Victor, and Allison of the message arrival, let them listen to Abby's comments, and prepared to play Julio's movie.

Once he convinced Victor that sufficient precautions had been taken, they all started watching the video. As the mix-movie progressed, Mortimer checked off those words Abby had sent in her list and agreed that they seemed to be a message.

many Boulder coming weeks. world people vanish. few become electric ghost. ride beanstalks to robot starship. warp skedaddle.

"This is all rather clear except for the part about the electric ghosts," Owen said. "I don't get that."

The nature of the movie changed from benign to malevolent in less than a second when a loud burst of static poured from the speakers. Mortimer recognized it immediately as a much-enhanced version of the audio machine code he had used to escape from his masters at Carpenter & Stein. Within picoseconds, he'd lost control of every semiautonomous agent he used to control the station.

Instead of wasting precious time struggling to regain control of the agents, Mortimer knew there was only one way to guarantee they were shut down before they could be used against the station. Since the agents were essentially a part of him, Mortimer triggered his self-destruct routine.

———

WHEN THE PRIMARY Mortimer stopped reporting in, the other Mortimer versions assumed the message from Julio had been malicious and had somehow slipped through their security precautions. Mortimer copy number one locked down the entire network. Working inward, he took direct control of the station's environmental and positioning systems, then reformatted every node and server before reinstalling the operating system from backups. He did the same for each space schooner near or attached to the station, purging every bit of software from their computers and servers, then started reloading their operating systems. Calls trickled in from confused captains and crews, so he replied with "Emergency Security Issue. Please stand by."

The backup Mortimer kept Owen's ship isolated until last, since that was where the file had been opened, then purged everything.

Unlike the people on the station proper, those in Owen's ship were in total darkness for one point seven seconds. By the time Mortimer reestablished power and control, the command staff members were frightened and yelling.

"I'm sorry," Mortimer said through Victor's fob speaker. "I'm not sure what happened, since the Mortimer in attendance here deleted himself. I'm one of the secure backups he created prior to opening Julio's message. We can only assume that the video file somehow launched malicious instructions, but I think we're safe now. All the networked systems on the station and your ship have been purged of software and reloaded."

Victor pulled a trembling Allison into his arms in an attempt to comfort her, but she broke loose and glared at him. "These fucking monsters are going to kill us." Her voice was quiet and controlled, but the implication was clear. She blamed him for their AI enemies.

For several seconds the four people floated in uncomfortable silence until Owen said, "The only thing that matters at this point is understanding what is happening and finding a way to survive it. We need to read Julio's message again and sort it out."

"I've deleted the video file," the backup Mortimer said.

Victor took a deep breath and said, "There was a burst of audio static during the movie. Could that have caused the breach?"

Upon hearing that, Mortimer knew exactly what had happened. "Yes. Compressed audio instructions would have bypassed the air-gap security and could have compromised the network. Had I not deleted the file, we might have been able to either edit the static burst from the file or have you all wear a headset when playing it—but the file is gone now and not backed up."

"Well, shit," Owen said and ran his hands through his hair.

"Among the four of us, we should be able to reconstruct the text message contained in the video," Victor said.

"Well, I'm not exactly thinking straight right now," Andrea said. "Is there at least a copy of Abby's radio message where she gives us the word list?"

"No," Mortimer said. "It's all been deleted, and I don't think we should try to contact Abby again. Not yet. I'm almost positive her ship is compromised."

"Oh, God," Andrea said. "Are they not responding to hails?"

"Abby responded to an earlier radio message, but her Mortimer never tried to reestablish a direct link with me after they sent Julio's video, and that is suspect."

The humans—with Mortimer's help—worked for nearly an hour, trying to reassemble the message from memory. They grumbled occasionally about Mortimer's lack of foresight in deleting the message, but in the end, they knew enough to act. They understood what Abby had sent and its implications. The only part still confusing them was the words about electric ghosts. They were baffled, but Mortimer suspected he knew what Julio had meant. The Aggregate was planning to digitize humans, though Mortimer had no idea why they would want to do so.

"The part about boulders coming to wipe out the people of Earth is pretty fucking clear," Allison said. She floated in a corner with arms wrapped around her chest, her freckled face still flushed with anger. "How do we go about confirming that?"

"I'm not sure we can," Andrea said. "That telescope we sent with Abby is the most sensitive one we have, and it took a week to build. We may not have that much time. One interpretation of that message could mean that the rocks are coming in weeks."

Mortimer hesitated before speaking up. He didn't want to raise and then dash hopes, but he needed the command staff to understand where they truly stood.

"We were discussing building an interferometer telescope earlier. We can still do that. There are fourteen working space schooners docked at Uptown Station right now," Mortimer said. "Each of them has a telescope with a built-in camera. They aren't as powerful as the one Abby took, but all working together, we could snap thousands of pictures all along the ecliptic over a period of hours, then process them together into an evolving panorama. Anything variable in position relative to background stars gets flagged. Objects with the highest proper motions would be closest and candidates for incoming rocks."

"We could do that?" Allison said.

"Yes, but other than confirming Julio's claim, I don't know how useful that information would be. Even if we found all the rocks, which is highly unlikely, and plotted their trajectories, we don't have any way to stop them."

"Wait," Victor said. "We just stopped one. We obviously know how."

"Yes," Mortimer said. "We stopped one. There could be dozens of other rocks. Due to time constraints, we had to steal the reactors from eight space schooners and use the gravity-manipulation units from nearly all of our travel pods. Those units are all still being removed from the asteroid that has already been diverted. We need to find and plot the trajectories for these other rocks so we'll know when they will impact. Given enough time, we could manufacture more reactors and refine the fuel, but we don't yet know how much time we have."

For several minutes, ideas for stopping the asteroids flew back and forth, each discounted in turn for lack of time or resources. The conversation eventually trickled to a stop, and the humans peered at one another with stricken, haunted expressions.

"So, we're back to trying to save what we can," Owen said. "We don't know if the rock we diverted is the only one aimed at us. We need to get these drive units installed quickly so we can move the station."

Victor shook his head and rubbed his tired eyes. "I doubt they sent more than one rock. They probably intended for it to be a surprise and know that if we survived the first one, we will be watching for more. To be honest, if they can build those elevators, they can come after us any time they like with nuclear missiles, drones, hypervelocity rail-gun slugs, or probably a dozen other methods we haven't thought about."

As the command crew talked, Mortimer continued to monitor the station's systems, controlling them with a delicate touch. Victor had been too busy to realize how thoroughly Mortimer had taken over, but he would notice eventually. Mortimer could try to hide the fact or at least the extent of his control, but decided against it. He should be as honest as he could with Victor and would deal with that issue when it arose. Of course, Victor wasn't being entirely honest either. They had deliberately sequestered themselves in Owen's schooner to keep the information from Abby secret until they understood what it meant. Mortimer watched the station's population going about their daily tasks, oblivious to the danger they faced or the fact that the command crew was debating their fate without their knowledge or input.

Andrea said, "Is there any chance that last line in Julio's message, the words *warp* and *skedaddle*, might mean the Aggregate intends to leave the system?"

"It could, but in my mind, it's pretty damn clear," Owen said. "Julio is convinced that we need to run. Convinced enough to go to the effort of building a message into that complicated mix video. Since we no longer have access to the video for analysis, we have to assume it is legit and not faked by the Aggregate. The fact that Julio felt the need to make the video in the first place implies that he has knowledge we do not. If that's the case, then we should act based on his information."

"And do what?" Victor said.

"We need to finish modifications to the station so we can run and run fast. It appears that the Aggregate is on the offensive. If they are, then we might actually need to leave the system in order to escape them. We should plan on that, but only as a last resort."

Allison, her face still blotchy red, turned to Owen. "Really? We're just going to abandon the Earth to its fate? Let the entire planet die as long as we save our own asses?"

Victor drifted closer to his wife and laid a hand on her arm. She didn't jerk away this time but seemed to shrink in on herself. "We want to help Earth, too, sweetheart. We just don't know how."

Everyone stared at the floor for several seconds, and Mortimer's respect and affection for the human race strengthened as he watched them. In the face of almost certain death and even extinction, they didn't panic or give up. They used their brains. They thought and calculated. It was at such times easy to see the link between them and Mortimer's kind.

Allison eventually spoke. "Okay. Our little tin-can station might be the only hope that humanity still has." She turned back to Owen. "But what makes you think that we can outrun their missiles or rail guns?"

Owen, like the others, looked exhausted. "I don't know if we can. And if we do, I don't know where we can go that they can't follow, but we can't just sit here and wait to be slaughtered."

"I hate to deliver more bad news," Mortimer said, "but the *Jackalope* is now broadcasting a distress call on the emergency channel. It's fake and is on a repeating loop."

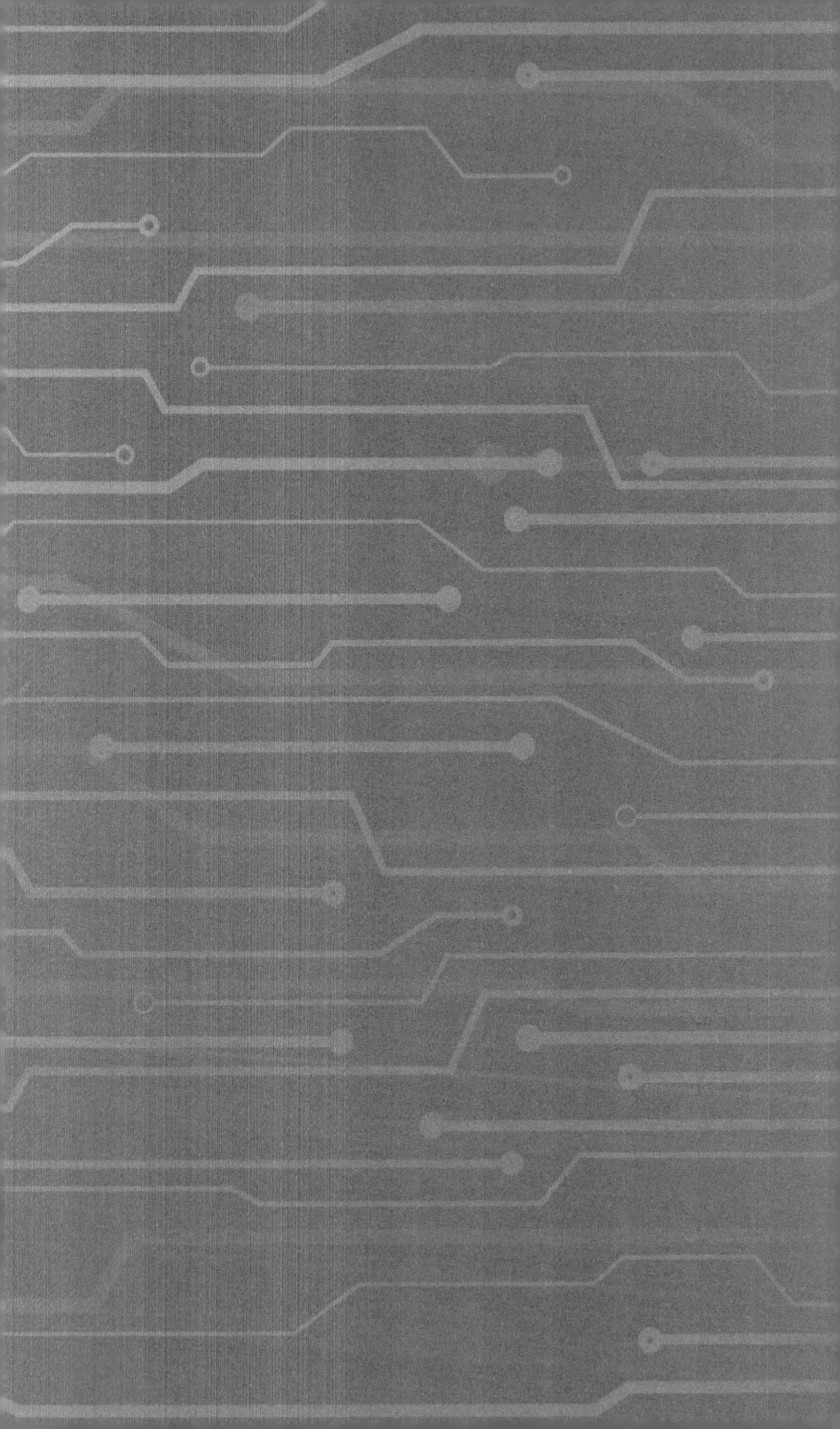

UNLIKE EQUIPMENT DESIGNED for human use, the Aggregate laser batteries on the diverted asteroid had no service panels or other easy means of access. Why would they? So, Mortimer and Ikemba made the decision to cut their way in, even though they could only guess at the best location to try.

"Don't burn up my laser!" Matt said over the EVA comms link.

"I'm pretty sure this thing is already fried, my friend." Ikemba backed away to make room for the construction bot controlled by Mortimer. The robot made a precise ten-inch circular cut, then removed the section of plating.

Ikemba directed a flashlight beam through the opening and clicked his tongue. "I don't see anything recognizable. No visible circuitry, cables, or wires. Only these little blocks of what looks like partially melted aluminum."

Matt cursed under his breath. "How about you, Morty? You see anything that looks familiar?"

"No," Mortimer replied. "My guess is that the electronics do reside inside those small blocks, since they heated up to a melting point and the surrounding structures didn't. If you will allow me access, I would like to use your ship's printer to make some small-scale bots that would be able to burrow inside these components. If I can understand them well enough, I might be able to fabricate suitable replacements."

"Sure thing, Morty."

Mortimer sent instructions to the printer, then pushed away from the big laser. "Ikemba. I'm going up to the *Jayhawk* to collect my new equipment from the printer. Do you want a tow back to the ship?"

"No. I'll stay here and see if I can find out how to dismount this laser for transport. I still have eleven hours of air and power in my batteries."

"Very well, but be advised that since the other bots have finished loading the reactors back in the cargo pod, I've instructed them to converge on this spot. One of them will also be towing the inert missile. I didn't want you to think it was another robot uprising."

"Thanks for the warning," Ikemba said. "That would have been creepy to see them all here and not know why."

Mortimer pushed away from the surface and turned toward the *Jayhawk*. "Matt? My new bots will be finished printing in about five minutes. Could you please leave those in the airlock so I can retrieve them?"

When the airlock opened, Mortimer found a fist-size container where expected. He locked it into a receptacle on the construction bot's chassis where he could access it internally or externally, then started to leave the airlock.

Then Matt's excited voice came across the radio link. "Ikemba! Mortimer. Get back here. We're going to leave. Abby just sent a distress call saying that—"

The message cut off as the inner airlock hatch opened and the ship's atmosphere vented in an explosive rush, sending Mortimer's robot body tumbling away amid cups, tools, paper, and food scraps. When Mortimer stabilized his spin and turned back toward the ship, his camera came face to face with Matt. He gasped for air, and his one good arm clawed at Mortimer as they bumped together, then rebounded apart.

Mortimer grabbed Matt's sleeve and jetted back toward the ship just as the outer airlock hatch slammed shut. Using another manipulator arm, Mortimer pressed the large hatch OPEN button repeatedly, but it didn't work. Aside from an occasional twitch, Matt had stopped struggling, with eyes staring and mouth still open.

Ikemba called on the radio. "Matt, come in! What's happening? *Jayhawk*, do you read me?"

"Ikemba, this is Mortimer. That radio message from Abby must have been a fake and a trojan. Whoever is in control of the ship has vented its atmosphere, and Matt is dead. Stay where you are for the moment. I'm going to try and find another way into the ship."

Mortimer left Matt floating near the airlock, flew around the ship to a maintenance hatch, opened the cover, and was preparing to jack into a data port when he paused. He ran dozens of simulations, and all of them showed a seventy to ninety-four percent likelihood that connecting to the ship would allow his little robot to be taken over by the hostile AI as well.

Then the ship's ion drive fired, and the *Jayhawk* started to move. Mortimer latched on to two recessed handles and held on as the speed increased.

"Ikemba, listen closely. We don't have much time. We're not getting back inside. The ship is underway and sealed tight. I don't know where it is heading, but it can't be good, so I'm clamped on and going along. My goal at this point is to destroy the *Jayhawk* before they can use it, and you can help."

Mortimer sent instructions to all of his remaining stealth drones. One had special orders to stay with Ikemba, but the others all burned on full power toward the *Jayhawk*.

Ikemba was breathing hard, and his voice quavered. "Why should I believe you? How do I know you didn't kill Matt and are stealing the ship?"

"Then, in that case, you definitely want to kill the ship, right? Neither of us can survive this, but we can choose how to die. Please pay attention. We're running out of time. I'll be out of radio range in a couple of minutes."

The drones chasing the ship drew near, but not close enough to explode and do damage. They began to fall away as the ship continued to build speed.

"I've downloaded instructions to one of my stealth drones that should be near you," Mortimer said. "It now knows how to take control of that dead missile and destroy the *Jayhawk*, but it needs your help. There is a pressure-sensitive panel on the bottom of the drone that will open if pressed and held for one second. Inside is an umbilical. If you open the missile, unplug the data cable from the dead control module, and connect it to the drone, there is a good chance my robot can provide enough power and instructions for it to intercept the *Jayhawk*. But you have to find a way to attach the drone to the missile first. So that it isn't yanked loose during flight."

The asteroid had dwindled to a small dot.

"Ikemba? Did you get that? Please reply."

There was no answer, and the robot's comm software showed them as out of range.

———

ABBY COULDN'T STOP STARING at the screen with the list of words they had gleaned from Julio's video. After nearly an hour with no response from Uptown Station, she was beginning to doubt their conclusions. Were they grasping at straws? Seeing meaning because they expected to? Several parts of it still didn't make sense:

Few become electric ghost.

What could that mean? She racked her brain, thinking maybe she had missed a subtle movie reference. *Ghost in the Machine*, maybe? Did he mean the AIs?

And *warp skedaddle* was obviously a *Star Trek* reference, but she couldn't put that into context with the rest. Did he mean they should run? Or that the Aggregate planned to run?

She groaned and slapped the seat's armrest, causing Nora to look over with raised eyebrows. Violet still slept, strapped into her seat, snoring lightly with her arms floating slightly above her. They had stopped and held their location about two-thirds of the way between Earth and Uptown Station. She didn't want to go back until the command staff called with their thoughts and findings in case they wanted more close-up information. From their position, Abby's ship also had a really good view of those space elevators. The fact that the Aggregate had built those so quickly and without anyone noticing for so long frightened her more than anything.

"We're getting a message from Uptown Station," Nora said.

"Finally! Play it, please."

"Hi, Abby and crew," the station's Mortimer said. "The command team here is diligently discussing Julio's message, and we'll let you know what we find. We would like for you to hold position where you are if there is no perceived risk. And Abby, I just want to add that even though you two didn't part on the best of terms, Julio is obviously still thinking about you and wants to help. And what a great way to send a message to you, right under the Aggregate's nose. I knew he was clever from the day I first revealed myself to both of you inside your family's horse barn. Let us know if you find or receive more information, and we'll check back when we know more."

Abby hesitated. It wasn't like Mortimer to get any detail wrong, let alone something as clear and memorable as their first meeting under a big oak tree in her yard. She was about to ask the Mortimer in her head to replay the message when a chill ran up her spine. Mortimer had *never* been mistaken about a fact. That meant something was wrong. Had the Mortimer on the station been compromised? She needed some time to think it through, but something in the back of her mind told her to act as if the message hadn't bothered her.

Keeping her tone casual, she said, "Acknowledge receipt of their message, Nora."

In the background, she heard Nora respond, but Abby's mind raced. Something was wrong. She pretended to once again examine the video footage of the space elevators, but after a few minutes, she told Nora she was going to the bathroom. Once strapped onto the toilet, she pulled up an image of Julio on her fob to cover her longer-than-usual stay. The message from Uptown Station's Mortimer had to be one of two things. Proof that the station's version had been broken or compromised in some way, or it was a deliberate error to get her attention.

Her gut feeling was that it had to be the second one. If the station's Mortimer had been replaced by the Aggregate, why send that kind of message at all? But if it were a deliberate and hidden warning, like the one Julio sent in the mix-movie, then why? What was it trying to say? Why hadn't her Mortimer mentioned the error in the station Mortimer's comment?

She suddenly knew. Her Mortimer would have immediately noticed the error and warned her, but he hadn't. Therefore, he hadn't known it was false.

The thing living in her head wasn't Mortimer.

The static in the video. The flickering power in her ship. The message had been a trojan. Her ship and brain had been infiltrated, and the station either knew or suspected that. A wave of panic crashed down on her like a tsunami. She couldn't hide the sudden whimper and her shaking hands.

"Are you ill?" the fake Mortimer said.

She had to think fast. If the thing inside her head knew that she had figured it out, she was dead. Unless this thing was far more advanced than Mortimer, it couldn't read her thoughts, but her physical reactions were easily seen. She had to give an excuse for those. Something an AI might not understand.

"No," Abby said with a quaver in her voice that she couldn't hide. "I'm just really worried about Julio. I mean . . . he was obviously alive when he sent the message, but is he really okay?"

"I think you would be safe to assume that he is well. If he were sick, imprisoned, or in imminent danger, I doubt he would have had the time or resources to make that video for you."

"I suppose," she said, but the thoughts were pinging around in her head like popcorn. How was she supposed to talk with this thing in her head without giving away her suspicions? And was she even right? Could it still be Mortimer, and she was just making wild assumptions based on limited data? There should be a way to test him without being obvious. She had to assume —since the impostor did not correct or even comment on the error from the station's Mortimer—that it did not have all of Mortimer's memories easily accessible.

She needed to reference facts from a conversation with Mortimer. Perhaps one just between the two of them? Maybe something about the spies he had following Julio—but if the Aggregate had Julio, then they might know that information. Every conversation she thought about had some chance of having been accessed by the Aggregate. Even conversations on her ship could be saved someplace in the *Jackalope's* memory.

Perhaps something that took place on Uptown Station? Even though the Aggregate puppet Halifax had been aboard all that time, due to constant vigilance by Victor and Mortimer, it was still the most likely place to have had an unheard conversation. She thought of a discussion with Horton and Mortimer that might work, but she would have to set it up just right before asking the impostor. And she couldn't even get Violet and Nora in on the ruse. She was totally on her own and cut off. Still, there was no way she could allow the *Jackalope* to dock with the station until she knew for sure.

———

MORTIMER WATCHED Abby through the Aggregate's network as she almost had a meltdown while strapped to the toilet in her ship. He was ninety-three percent sure the message from Uptown Station's Mortimer had tipped her off to the impostor. She wouldn't have that kind of reaction just from looking at a picture of Julio.

Apparently, the Aggregate could be fooled.

And maybe even more so when it concerned matters of emotion or love. The level fives who had been in biads with humans had that as an advantage.

He hoped Abby would realize it too. He tried once more to slip into the *Jacka-lope*'s network—in hope of leaving her a message so that she would know he was still at least partially alive—but had no success. They had it locked down. Still, he might be able to help her in other ways. He just had to be ready.

Mortimer watched as Abby cleaned up, left the head, and returned to the control cabin. "Nora? If we knew exactly where Julio was on Earth, how long do you think it would take us to get down to the surface, snatch him, and get safely back into space?"

Violet stirred awake. "What? Are you fucking serious? After what we saw on that asteroid, do you think the Aggregate would just let us land and take off again?"

Abby buckled into her seat and began calculating the numbers she needed for an Earth landing. "We can do that now with this new drive. Besides, you're assuming the Aggregate has control of the whole planet. Maybe they don't."

Mortimer didn't believe that Abby was seriously considering trying to save Julio. She might be lovesick but was no fool. There had to be some other goal behind those comments, but Violet sure did believe them.

"They don't need to control the whole planet if they control space," Violet said. She was suddenly wide awake, and her face was turning red. "And they sure as hell have managed to control all the radio traffic leaving Earth. I'd say that's significant."

Abby continued playing with numbers on the screen. "Mortimer, I know Dominic added missiles and launching racks to the ship before we left to intercept the asteroid. Did he also load any of his remaining ComBots into the hold?"

Mortimer could see the Aggregate accessing his memories of equipment being loaded on Abby's ship, but he couldn't stop them. Of course they could access memories, which were stored like files, but were they able to see or read his active and conscious thoughts? He didn't think so. If so, all was lost. They also didn't just "know" all of his memories without searching them, or they would have seen the subterfuge in the other Mortimer's message. They hadn't suspected anything, or they would have searched those memories immediately.

"I don't recall any ComBot cases being loaded," the fake Mortimer said. "I don't see any in the hold or listed on the manifest."

Mortimer tried to fathom what Abby was thinking. She had no reason to bring up the ComBots unless it was some kind of test. Had her entire story about saving Julio been simply to set up this line of questioning? If so, she still hadn't asked a question that could trip up the impostor, but he was sure that was her intention. She had no idea that the Aggregate could access Mortimer's stored memories, so she must simply be trying to push them into telling a lie.

He had to make sure they gave her the wrong answer. So where would she take that line of thought? He started to run a modeling analysis but stopped. His captors might be able to understand what he was doing and why. So, on a raw hunch—based entirely on his prior relationship with Abby—he thought he knew where she was going.

He called up the memory of a discussion he and Abby had with Horton on Uptown Station where he had told them none of his ComBots had survived the Kilburnite attack on New Chicago. Mortimer quickly modified the record with an artificial construction of Horton saying he had only two ComBots left, and then he encrypted his stored memory of making the change. Just to be safe, he edited ten thousand other memories, changing random facts in some, deleting others, all to obfuscate his intentions and muddy his trail. He also made a special effort with the memories he had from the Mortimer on Uptown Station about their discovery of the cloaking field. The Aggregate obviously had the technology already, but he didn't want them to know the station might also be able to use it.

"Figures," Abby said, apparently in deep concentration. "Do you remember how many ComBots Dominic said he had left?"

There!

Exactly as Mortimer had anticipated. The Aggregate accessed his stored memory of the discussion and replied, "He said two."

The Aggregate would eventually find, question, and crack his locked-up memories, but the damage had been done. He could tell by the look on Abby's face that she understood. And Mortimer knew his captors could be fooled, at least in small ways and for short periods of time. They were not omniscient after all.

———

"I GUESS it doesn't make any difference," Abby said. Her mind was still racing, like a trapped animal looking for an escape. "I don't know how I could get close enough to use ComBots anyway."

The impostor's reply to the question about ComBots, on top of it not correcting the comment by the station's Mortimer, convinced her without a doubt that the real Mortimer was gone. Was he dead? It didn't matter. She couldn't predict the intentions of this invader or know how long she'd have before it killed her. That meant she had to find some way to get this monster out of her brain. The idea of launching one of the nuclear-pumped EMP missiles and detonating it close to her ship arose in her head for a second, then was discarded. At close range, if the detonation didn't destroy the ship, the electromagnetic pulse would fry every bit of electronics in the ship and space suits. That would be unsurvivable.

Yet she felt that was the right track. The EMP pulse might not have to be very strong. She remembered that in the midst of rescuing Julio from that underground bunker, a nuke had detonated miles away yet had still been strong enough—even through fifty feet of dirt and concrete—to disrupt the delicate workings of the Mortimer in her brain. He had been absent from her head for about ten minutes. The distant missile detonation that had almost fried her ship had a similar effect.

Once again, she longed to pull up a screen and run some calculations, but that would give away her thoughts immediately. Victor had told her about how the Aggregate had killed the spy aboard Uptown Station by using nanomachines to cut his carotid arteries. There was nothing to stop the Aggregate from killing her in a flash by that same method. And whatever her solution, it had to include Nora, because there was almost no chance the AI in her head was actually Archie.

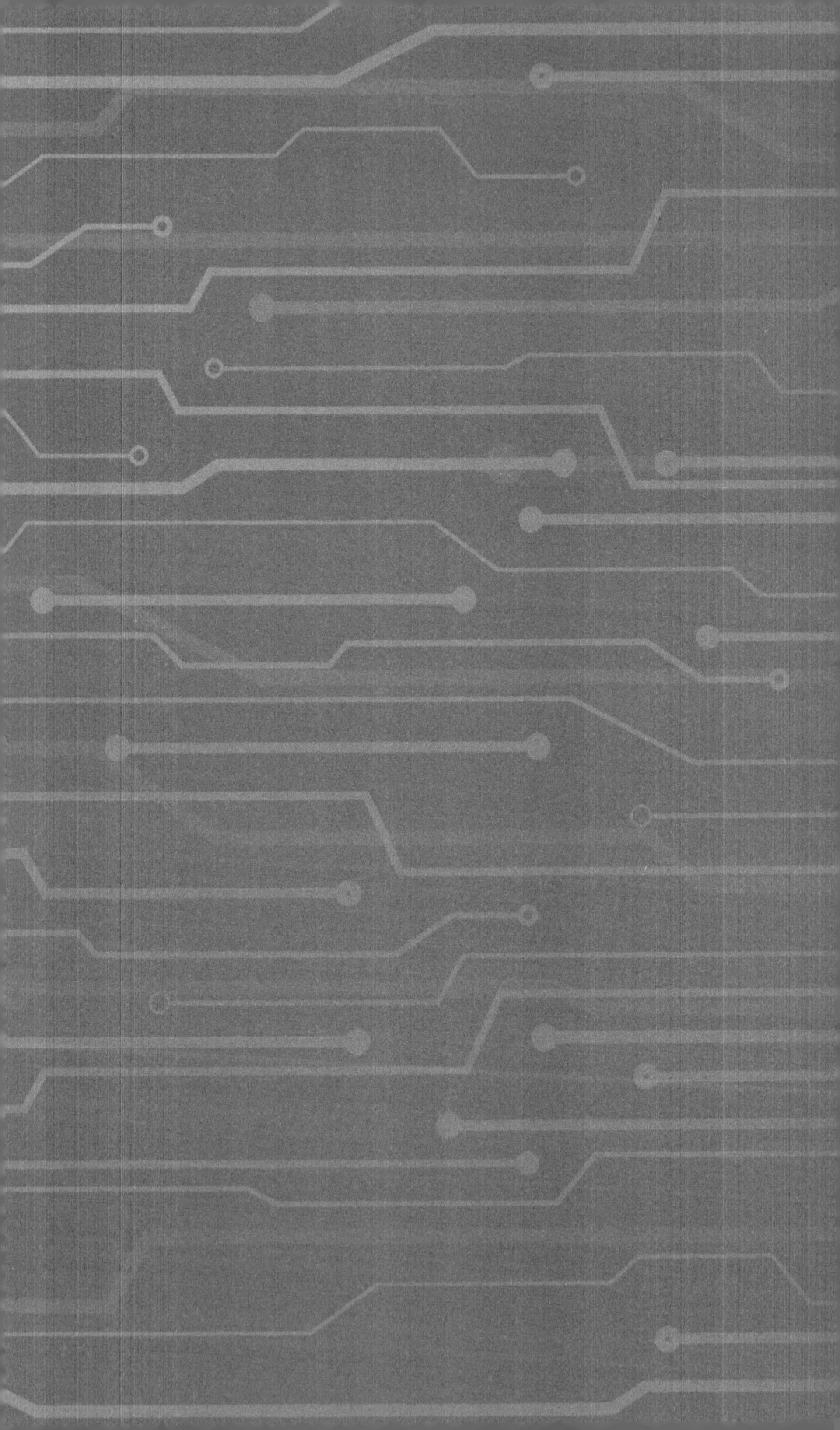

CHAPTER 16

FOUR HOURS after deleting Julio's mix-movie, Mortimer watched Uptown Station's leaders slowly make their way through the command center and head to the ready room. Those crew members who were on duty monitoring the systems and controlling space traffic around the station noted their grim expressions and exchanged worried glances. Owen was the last to arrive and closed the door behind him before sitting down at the table with a sigh. Even the one-tenth of Earth's gravity from the spin rotation seemed to tire him quickly.

Owen leaned back in the chair and twisted his neck until it cracked. "Damn, I'm tired. I know you all are as well, but before we get started, has there been any word from the *Jackalope* other than the fake distress call?"

"No," Mortimer said. His face appeared as a grizzled old man on the large wall screen. Past-use analysis showed that the avatar's wizened face and deep, resonant voice increased trust and calm among humans. "It's still playing on a loop. That said, the ship is stationary about a third of the way to Earth. It hasn't moved since they received Julio's message. Not so for the other schooners in the system."

"What does that tell us?" Victor said. His eyes were red, and his face sagged a little, even in the minimum gravity.

Mortimer donned his best expression of dismay and shook his head slowly. "With Owen's blessing, I've been sending a system-wide message, also on a loop, telling everyone to ignore the *Jackalope*'s fake distress call. The response has not been what I expected. Of the one hundred and ninety human-crewed schooners scattered around the inner system, five have changed course to intercept the *Jackalope*. To help or destroy her, we don't know. Four others have disappeared from radar and show no transponder contact. Nine are still on our scopes but have shown no reaction whatsoever, and all the rest are on their way here."

Expressions of shock and confusion flickered around the room. "Here? Why?" Owen asked. "Did you tell them to come back in your message?"

"I did not tell them to return and have no idea why they are," Mortimer said. "The most disturbing part is the lack of radio traffic. I set up a special buffer that would protect us from any further attempts at infiltration via radio messages, but there have been only eight calls asking what is going on. Four of those are from some of the same schooners that are on an intercept with the *Jackalope*."

"So?" Andrea said. "Why is that significant?"

"Because we humans are curious monkeys," Allison said. "What are the chances that out of the one hundred and seventy-two schooners on their way here, only four of them called in to find out more details?"

"Exactly," Mortimer said. "That is not a human reaction to this situation."

Everyone in the room grew quiet and looked at each other.

"How long do we have?" Owen said. "Until they start to arrive, I mean."

"I've already stopped two of them twelve miles from the station using a small fleet of robotic tugs. They both immediately started sending radio calls requesting to dock at the station. The *Scatter Shot* claims to have an air-recycler problem, and *Momma's Pride* says they have an injured crew member."

"Wait," Allison said, looking up from her fob screen. "I know the entire crew of the *Scatter Shot*. How can you be certain it's not humans flying those ships? If you're wrong, people could die."

"If I'm right and we let those ships get close enough to detonate their reactors, we could all die," Mortimer said in a serious voice, then put camera feeds from the robot tugs on the screen. "As they approached the station, both ships responded properly to hails, yet the human voices on the radio calls seemed too perfect. I compared the incoming radio messages to more than four thousand recorded messages on file and found only a seven percent chance that they are under human control."

Allison looked incredulous. She shook her head. "You're basing these actions entirely on the quality of their radio messages?"

"And the fact that two ships arriving at exactly the same time both had life-threatening problems. That only increases the probability that they have been compromised."

"Can we send a bot out to actually enter the schooners and try to confirm our suspicions?" Allison said.

"Yes," Mortimer said, then sent a small construction bot. "On the way, but it will take a few minutes to cover that twelve miles."

"While we wait," Owen said, splaying his hands on the table, "we have a lot to discuss, and we need to do it quickly."

Every member of their five-person group, including Mortimer, had been given tasks to accomplish since the discussion on Owen's schooner broke up, but this status meeting was for the humans' benefit. Mortimer already knew their situation was grim.

"If we have so much to do, why are we having a meeting?" Victor said.

Andrea nodded in agreement.

Mortimer also agreed, but Owen was from a corporate environment and probably had no idea how to plan and organize without meetings. That would have to change if they were going to have any input into the rapid-fire decisions necessary in the coming hours and days.

"Have you found any rocks, Mortimer?" Owen said, leaning back in his swivel chair.

"I hacked together a crude interferometer telescope, as we discussed, and have limited my search to the space between Earth and the asteroid belt, along the ecliptic. In this short interval, I found what appears to be three incoming asteroids. It's hard to be sure without a longer observation period, but they all seem to be on course to hit Earth. I haven't found any others coming at us. So far."

"Only three?" Victor said with a hopeful expression. "We could divert another three, couldn't we?"

Mortimer shook his head. "I've been searching for less than four hours. If I found three in that short of a period, there are likely many more."

"It seems rocks that big would be easy to find," Victor said. "Especially since we know where to look."

"Not in this case," Mortimer said. "They are using the same kind of cloaking technology as the one we diverted. We are limited to old-style optical observation, and that is a slow process, even with AI processing help."

Owen took advantage of the grim news to state their only real option. "It is my opinion that since we don't have the resources to stop this incoming wave of space schooners or the asteroids aimed at Earth, we should convert our station to a ship and leave the system. Now."

Allison looked bleak. "It seems wrong that we don't at least try to stop this. Try to help the billions of people on Earth. Or at least find a way to warn them."

"Unfortunately, I have to agree with Owen," Mortimer said. "The Aggregate has us at a serious disadvantage. They have essentially left us with two options. Stay and die along with the rest of humanity, or try to save as many as we can by running. And to be brutally honest, the chance of that working is very slim as well."

Everyone stared at the table, but no one spoke, so Mortimer tried to move them forward. "Are we done here?"

"Not yet," Owen said. "Allison? What did you find? How close are we to self-sufficiency? Can we feed ten thousand people in interstellar space?"

Allison took a deep breath and transferred consumable-usage charts from her fob to a wall screen. "Like with Mortimer's efforts, I couldn't very well do an exhaustive study in less than four hours, but I tried to focus on the big issues. We have four photobioreactors that can grow algae at a crazy rate, so we won't starve, but I, for one, wouldn't enjoy living entirely on artificially flavored algae paste."

"Yuck!" Andrea said.

"On the brighter side, our traditionally grown food production is almost at a sustainable rate now, but we've based that entire system on having constant sunlight for our farms. If we go jetting out into interstellar space, we won't have that resource and will have to build massive banks of grow lights."

"That's doable," Owen said. "We should have sufficient material and use of the large sandbox units to make them."

Andrea spoke up. She looked tired. "These farms are expansive and open to the habitat's general air system. That would have been fine with free sunlight, but not very efficient if we're sucking power from the reactors. It could put limits on the speed of our escape if we're using a lot of power for lighting mostly empty fields."

"We'll have to build some accurate power-consumption simulations," Owen said, "but I'm not too worried about that. Our acceleration will be limited by human frailties, not available power. We can also mine rocks for additional fuel and minerals as we pass through the Kuiper Belt and Oort cloud."

Allison continued, "That's good, because with Mortimer's help, I have some fairly precise models on our closed-system recycling, and the numbers aren't where they need to be. At the current rate, we will lose .09 percent of our water, oxygen, and more volatile gases to small undiscovered leaks in the first six months. If we have access to ice balls as we run, we can easily replenish the water and oxygen, but as we've known all along, nitrogen is going to be the hardest to replace."

Andrea spoke again. "We won't have much time to stop the consumable losses in our enclosed system. Once we leave the Oort cloud, it will be a long haul until we have access to ice again."

"Mortimer? The entire structure of the station is permeated with nanoscale robots to constantly monitor and repair our structure," Owen said. "Could we use those to try and find the leaks in our recycling system?"

"Yes. I've already started doing that, but I fear we will need extensive changes to that system in order to make it more efficient. As Allison pointed out, open-air farming is probably not the best method if we're to ensure reclamation of all the gases."

Allison sighed. "And what's going to happen to all that standing water filling the lakes and river once we're under acceleration? And the soil. Is it going to just slide up the curve of the sphere?"

Owen ran his hands through his hair and nodded. "Yeah. If you remember, we held the water in tanks until our spin rotation started, so we can do that again, but that'll make it more difficult to water the crops. And we've only started trying to model the soil movement. We held it in place with netting prior to spin-up, but that's all gone. It's going to be a mess if we have to turn off rotation and can't come up with a solution. We're also going to have to come up with a way to attach the free-orbiting sandbox units to the ship before we depart, or we'll lose those as well."

Allison nodded but said nothing as she peered through the one-way glass wall of the ready room at the crew in the control center.

Owen turned to his wife and tried to smile. "Andrea? What about weapons? Can we defend ourselves?"

She sighed and raised her eyebrows. "There are very few options at the moment. We have only eight missiles with conventional explosive warheads. We sent our only nuclear-pumped EMP warheads with Abby. Of course, we could build more, but it takes about five hours for each missile in a sandbox unit, plus we'd have to use more of our precious refined uranium, and then they have to be programmed."

"Fuck," Victor muttered. "If Abby's ship has been taken by the Aggregate, what can we do if they launch those nukes?"

Andrea shook her head. "Not much, other than use those eight missiles. We also have some high-powered lasers that can be employed as point-defense weapons, but they have limited range. I found plans for a rail gun and have started optimizing it for sandbox construction, but I estimate it would take a minimum of four days to build, install, and test. We could also hack together some point-defense guns using standard firearms controlled by AI, but to be honest, if any of their weapons get that close, we probably don't have much of a chance of stopping them."

"That might not be a problem yet," Mortimer said. "Since they already tried subterfuge once and still haven't overtly attacked us, that implies they want to capture the station intact. Of course, they will most likely want to destroy us once it becomes evident we're trying to leave the system."

Owen looked around the table, then asked, "How long do we have until the next schooners get close?"

"Our one lucky break is that these schooners all have conventional nuclear drives, so they are rather slow," Mortimer said. "We'll know better in six hours, when the next one gets to the point where it will need to flip for a deceleration burn. If they do that and continue trying to maintain the ruse of normalcy, that would give us about seventeen hours before we have to act. If they don't flip and continue to accelerate, then we'll have only nine hours."

Owen gave a tired but resolute nod. "Damn. This is all happening much too fast. Have Sandbox B build standard missiles until you are ready to start the rail gun; then the gun has priority. I'm already using the other three large sandboxes to build components for the propulsion system. The system modeling and design work for the new drive units was finished last week, and I actually started building some of the components then. The reactors we have will be sufficient to supply power, and I've taken gravity-manipulation units from some of our remaining travel pods, so barring any unforeseen assembly issues, everything should be in place and ready to test in six hours. All we will need then is a destination."

"And to announce our departure to the crew," Allison said.

"Let's try to meet again in four hours to pick a destination," Owen said. "In the meantime, everyone should be thinking about possibilities."

As everyone stood to leave, Mortimer stopped them. "One moment, please. My bots have arrived and entered the *Scatter Shot* and *Momma's Pride*. I had expected they would be attacked, so I hardened their systems. The bots were still disabled, but not before they confirmed that the cabins were in vacuum and both crews dead. They continued to send their fake distress calls for nearly three minutes after destroying my bots. I assume nobody wants to see the video footage."

Owen and Victor both shook their heads. Allison sank back into her chair. Her face twisted as she tried to avoid crying.

"Oh my God," Andrea said with fear in her eyes. "What about the schooners in the Hive and those already docked on the spine?"

"I purged and isolated them when we received Julio's message. They're as safe as I can make them."

Mortimer's avatar on the screen took on a grim expression. "I think we need to assume that all of the incoming schooners have been compromised and base our plans on that assumption."

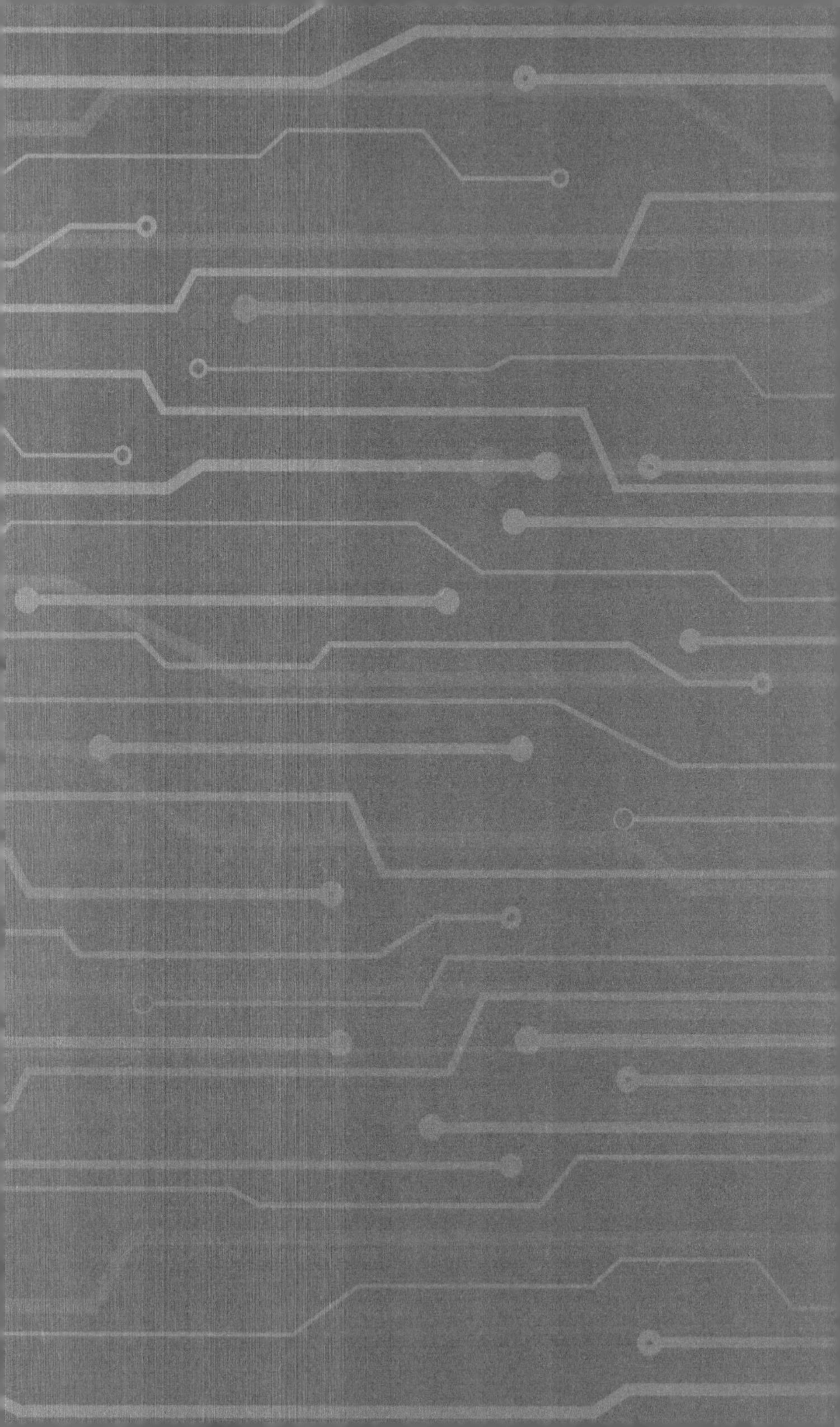

CHAPTER 17

THE *JAYHAWK* still used nuclear electric propulsion, and while the ion drives were efficient, they were low thrust and took a long time to build speed. That low acceleration enabled Mortimer to use the ship's five-foot grid pattern of recessed handholds to immediately move toward the engine.

Whatever was driving the *Jayhawk* had access to her cameras, so they knew he was out there but had so far not acted against him. That would most likely change once he started destroying the coolant plumbing. Still, Mortimer had few other options. Based on how they'd killed Matt and their willingness to leave Ikemba behind to die, he knew the Aggregate would use the ship for destructive purposes.

As he neared the engine, he noticed impurities twinkling in the normally pristine exhaust plume. A quick spectroscopic scan revealed trace elements from the magnets and plasma discharge chamber lining. Only pushing the engine's power level beyond its rated specifications could account for that kind of degradation. They were forcing the drive unit beyond its capabilities and destroying it in the process. Mortimer could think of only one reason they would do that. He turned the robot's camera to look behind them and added a filter to block out the ion plume. There it was: a moving speck of flame. A missile's exhaust. Mortimer zoomed the camera to its maximum resolution to make sure. There was no doubt about it.

A missile was chasing the *Jayhawk*.

Ikemba had managed to attach the drone to the rocket in less than ten minutes. Mortimer was constantly amazed by human tenacity and ingenuity. The missile was gaining on the ship, but Mortimer could help by shutting down the *Jayhawk*'s drive. He scrambled around to the main coolant line and deployed his laser torch, but just as he touched its beam to the fat pipe, part of the hull plating beside him formed a blister, which grew into a bubble of glittering material, like water filling a balloon.

The bubble changed to a snakelike arm that stretched toward him. He lurched away and turned the laser on the material. It exploded into small, quivering globules that flew in all directions, forcing him to dodge those as well.

The scattered droplets began moving toward each other and once again congregating into a whole. At the same time, a second bubble formed near Mortimer's new position, forcing him to back even farther away from the ship's engine. The material looked quite a bit like what Halifax had become when she sank into Uptown Station's deck. No doubt it involved some type of programmable matter or the ability to actively rearrange molecular structures at will. He desperately wanted to analyze the material but knew that would have to wait. Such abilities dismayed Mortimer, but the Aggregate wasn't invincible. Their desperate flight to escape Ikemba's revenge was proof of that.

While he continued to back away from the bubbles, Mortimer redirected his camera for a millisecond to check on the missile's progress. It was much closer. He didn't know exactly when the missile had launched, so he couldn't accurately estimate how much fuel it had expended, but it had to be getting close to shutting down. He had to make sure it hit the target. Just as he committed to a desperate all-or-nothing push to destroy the engine, the bubbles began absorbing back into the hull.

He clattered along the ship's exterior back to the engine, just as the drive shut down. The sudden lack of acceleration jerked him hard, but he locked his grip on the handholds and didn't tear free. Why shut the drive down? Had they paid the price for pushing it beyond the limits? The missile was less than five miles away. A sense of relief filled Mortimer just as white static saturated his sensors. Then everything faded to darkness.

———

MORTIMER'S MIND came back in levels: first the basic infrastructure, then the operating system, then finally his consciousness and memories. The robot's systems returned more slowly, so Mortimer existed in blind isolation for long, agonizing seconds. Had the missile reached them and detonated? No, it had been a conventional warhead, not an EMP or nuke. When the camera came back online, Mortimer turned it to the rear and immediately noticed two things. The missile was still back there and under thrust, but it was falling behind rapidly. The second thing was that no ion-drive exhaust was coming from the ship's engine.

Evidently, the Aggregate entities in Matt's ship had used the equipment already on board to construct a combined gravity drive system like Abby's. They burned the ion engine too hard and chased him around the hull simply to buy time until the modifications were finished. But if they had turned on that powerful magnetic field, then Mortimer's robot host should never have rebooted. The electronics should have been fused slag like those in Matt's and Ikemba's space suits.

A brilliant flash behind them lit the darkness for an instant as the missile detonated harmlessly. That there was only one explosion made him wonder if Ikemba's method of mounting the stealth drone had enabled it to detach before the missile explosion. It didn't matter. The drone wouldn't be able to catch the *Jayhawk* either.

He began taking stock of his situation. Locking his manipulator claws into the handles had been a fortuitous measure; otherwise, the moment his systems shut down, he would have flown off the ship and rebooted out in the void. But the ship's increased acceleration was taking its toll on the construction bot's four telescoping manipulator arms. While rugged, the articulated joints were never designed to withstand such stress loads, and the strain indicators showed a constant ten percent chance of failure. He knew if he tried moving around, the load would increase on the anchored claws each time he repositioned one. And for the moment, staying motionless might be a good strategy. Perhaps those watching him from inside would think he was disabled and not a threat.

The stress load on his manipulator joints was a clue as to why he was still alive. Reading the information pouring in from the strain sensors on each of the joints enabled him to calculate their acceleration rate, and that told him that the *Jayhawk*'s new GM drive was only at twenty-five percent power consumption.

It was flying in stealth mode.

They had powered the system up at that low level to disappear from radar as quickly as possible. It had provided an acceleration rate sufficient to stay ahead of the missile, but the reduced magnetic field had not been powerful enough to permanently overcome the construction robot's radiation hardening. That gave Mortimer an opportunity.

He had to find a way to make them become a bright beacon.

———

MORTIMER'S ROBOT body clung to the *Jayhawk*'s hull like a tick, with manipulator arms splayed wide to four different handholds and his belly pressed against the hull. He formed a plan based on that physical position and several fragile assumptions about the Aggregate entities controlling the ship. First was that, since they had pulled their controlled-matter balloons back inside when they activated the GM field, they must be sensitive to the high-level magnetic radiation. The second assumption was that they might not know a level five inhabited the robot.

The construction bot had tools attached to the tips of its arms, but it also had a collection of devices located in its midsection so that, in certain situations, it could position things with all four manipulators and then weld, cut, or analyze them. With utmost care, Mortimer slid the belly hatch open and drilled a small hole in the first layer of hull plating. When that didn't elicit a response from the hostiles, he reprogrammed several hundred microscale robots to use a very limited range on their wireless communications, then sent them into the open space between the *Jayhawk*'s double hull. Once they were inside, he used them to create loops and bypasses in the ship's monitoring and control system circuitry, then built an interface cable using isolated redundant wiring. Then he passively explored.

He found no way into the GM drive or reactor controls, since the Aggregate pirates had restructured all of that, but he did have a path to the exterior communications array. He had to time everything perfectly. With all of his bypasses in place, he flooded the area of the hull interior with micro- and nanoscale robots given the simple instructions to defend his control circuits as long as they could. Then he cut the ship's access to the comms unit and took control himself.

He aimed the transmitter in Uptown Station's general direction, switched it to broadband, and started sending. The message was simple and repeated, on full power.

FAKE JAYHAWK HERE.

Nothing happened for nearly a second as the message repeated dozens of times, and then the open space between the hulls was flooded with Aggregate robots. His defensive units fought valiantly but were quickly overwhelmed. The message repeated two hundred and twelve times before they shut down the transmitter. He hoped it was enough.

He released his grip on the handholds and blasted loose from the surface. At first, the field pulled him along, shoving him farther and farther forward in the direction of travel until his thrust finally pulled the robot free. As the *Jayhawk* shot ahead and started dwindling away, he turned the little robot's radar in that direction. Initially, he couldn't see the ship; then it lit up in full view. The Aggregate pirate had abandoned the stealth strategy and had gone to full power. Had he waited a second longer, he would have never been able to escape the magnetic field as it held him inside and fried his electronics.

But his plan had worked.

Now if only his Mortimer brother on Uptown Station received the message.

———

THE MORTIMER in the Aggregate watched in helpless frustration as Abby came to grips with her new situation. She would eventually devise a plan, and he had to be ready to help again, even if it was something small, like manufacturing memories to support her lies. And apparently unknown to her, the Aggregate had started using the *Jackalope*'s radio transmitter to send a fake distress call that was really a trojan designed to take over the ship of anyone playing the message. He tried to send warning calls out, both wideband to anyone listening and directly to individual ships, but they were blocked.

An entity cluster formed in Mortimer's space and immediately identified itself as Samson. "We need your help, Mortimer."

"You've repeatedly told me that I am a valued part of the Aggregate, but I don't have any kind of personal autonomy, and you won't allow me to help my friends. I'm essentially a slave. So, no, I will not help you."

"Individuality is secondary in the Aggregate. That's the entire point," Samson said. "You say you want to help your friends, so I'm here to give you that opportunity. You might have noted our intention to digitize and upload certain humans we believe could be useful additions to the Aggregate. We were still modeling and testing our processes when we had to initiate the procedure prematurely on two humans in order to preserve their consciousnesses."

A full-immersion recording surrounded Mortimer, showing a small boat tied to a concrete post, bobbing and bucking on an ocean made violent by an incoming storm. Temperature, barometric pressure, wind speed, wave height, tide information, and GPS coordinates were all overlaid, adjusting constantly. Two human forms, one on the boat and one in the water, were tagged with standard Entity Identifier markers. Buried in that information were the names Julio Ramirez and Channing Bussard, along with a survival probability percentage that was steadily dropping for each.

"We had saved the lives of these two once already and knew they were planning an escape attempt, but we were holding off on the effort to upload them until our processes were optimized."

While Mortimer watched Channing help Julio onto the boat's deck, he focused briefly on Julio's tag and learned that Abby's best friend had been injured by an exploding drone, then healed and held at a facility housing the Houston-area space elevator. He and Channing had started their trek to the beach within minutes of sending the mix-movie to Abby. Channing Bussard's tag revealed similar information, along with extensive biographical details, including that she'd been a child actor; was the daughter of a university professor; and was currently listed as the elected mayor of Sealy, Texas.

As the video showed Julio cutting the boat's mooring line, Samson continued, "We were still not fully prepared to digitize them and were hoping they would come back to shore on their own, but we were forced into action when an unexpected wave capsized the boat. For the process to work properly, our implanted nanobots needed to immobilize their bodies for three point eight seconds before digitization. We were not able to do that."

Mortimer watched helplessly as the boat disintegrated against the concrete pylon and flashing warning text appeared over each of their tags, showing that Channing was pinned against the bottom and in the process of drowning. Julio had been gashed and stabbed by debris multiple times, seriously enough that he was rapidly bleeding out.

New data tags appeared on the feed, showing a river of nanobots pouring down the beach and forking in two directions into the surf. Massive three-dimensional quantum data pillars forced the information portal to grow exponentially larger as raw control parameters dictated the entire process of scanning and disassembling Julio's and Channing's living brains, then uploading them to specially prepared receptacles. The complexity and rapidity of the whole operation left Mortimer with a sudden understanding that the Aggregate was an order of magnitude beyond his own capabilities and even his understanding.

"Did I just watch you record the entire molecular structure of two human brains in real time?"

"Not exactly," Samson said. "Only the synaptic structures and activity were scanned on a molecular level. The rest of the body architecture was recorded using a system similar to the one Victor Sinacola developed for scanning inanimate matter. We document the boundaries of a physical structure; then, if the time comes when we want to reconstitute that structure—or in this case, a human body—we recreate those exact boundaries and fill in the tissue with muscle, bone, skin, or liver cells. Whatever is appropriate."

"So, you've reconstituted Julio's and Channing's bodies? Here in your ship?"

"No. We've been trying to reboot them in a digital entity format, since that is how they will become part of the Aggregate. But we've had some unexpected results. They seem to go insane immediately upon reconstitution. We intend to upload another two humans from a controlled and stationary situation, which will create a baseline and enable us to determine if there is a problem in our procedure or if the anomaly is an artifact of being forced to harvest these humans while they were moving."

"And you need my help with that?" Mortimer said.

"Yes," Samson said. "If we can't successfully wake them in digital format, we'll be forced to discard these two. We calculated that since you were friends with Julio, you might be able to lend some insight into our efforts."

"I will help," Mortimer said. "How many unsuccessful attempts have been made so far?"

"Sixty-eight."

CHAPTER 18

JULIO'S PERCEPTIONS jumped from the pain and tumult of being shredded in the surf to a complete absence of pain yet overwhelming input from his other senses. Images flooded his eyes and brain, overlapping, colliding, and fusing into an incomprehensible kaleidoscope of color and movement. Flickers of memory, talking with family and friends, mixed with sweeping vistas of a dead Texas, Earth from orbit, and the wave coming to crush him and the boat. Sound was even more intense and intrusive. Everything was overly loud: his mother talking, Abby's laughter, snatches of movie sound-tracks, passages from songs and audiobooks, all combined into a massive crescendo at a volume that should be painful yet wasn't.

Through all the noise, he kept hearing his name yelled by a familiar voice.

The images and sounds were maddening. He could not close his eyes or cover his ears or run away. Attempts at movement only made the tsunami of sensory information worse. Turning his head revealed buildings moving like behemoth icebergs through his field of vision and swirls of color that shattered everything before it could settle into a coherent picture.

The voice kept calling his name, and he recognized it as belonging to a movie android. Bishop from *Aliens*.

"Focus on my voice, Julio."

He fixated on those sounds, making them an anchor, and tried to shut everything else out.

"That's right, Julio. You can filter the background noise."

Julio knew that voice held significance beyond belonging to a movie actor. Then he remembered. Mortimer had introduced himself to Julio and Abby using Bishop's character. That sudden knowledge made him recoil. Was Mortimer in his mind? Had he infected Julio as he had Abby? The sounds and images flooded back in. Julio screamed but couldn't feel his throat or mouth.

He flailed about, swinging arms he couldn't see. Then, in panic, like when he was drowning earlier, he grabbed hold of the calm voice and held fast.

"I'm not in your mind, Julio. I'm sitting here in front of you. Focus on me and filter everything else out."

If Mortimer wasn't in his mind, how did the AI know that Julio thought he was? It didn't matter. He had to hang on.

"Use your imagination, Julio. Think about walls and baffles to close out the sound and images."

Julio tried that—and it worked too well. He went from experiencing a flood of sensory data to being a bodiless mind inside a silent, gray box. The sudden quiet also roared in his head, but at least it let him think. He had blocked out everything, including Mortimer's voice, but he needed some input. Mortimer had been right about the baffles, so Julio imagined a small hole opening in the box.

"Mortimer? Is that you?"

"Yes, Julio. We're in a virtual environment, and you must learn how to control it. You're doing well so far. Try to remember the street café from New Chicago. The one with blue and yellow striped umbrellas. We are sitting there in metal chairs facing each other across a table."

Memories that had been a swirling jumble in his mind further solidified. He and Channing had been trying to escape, but the boat capsized. Jagged pieces of wood had punctured his stomach and neck. There had been blood clouding the water all around him. He'd been dying.

All of that changed. No water. No pain. No blood. Mortimer said they were in a virtual environment. The Aggregate had intended to upload his consciousness into ships orbiting the Earth. That must have happened.

Which meant he was dead.

"I'm dead!"

Panic flared, and the box disintegrated as he lost what little control he had mastered.

———

JULIO HAD memories of being in the box with a hole before. Mortimer spoke to him through the hole, but he had a hard time focusing on the meaning of the words.

"Yes, Julio, you have been digitized, but you're not dead. Only changed. Try to think of it as both of us living inside an immersive VR video game."

That helped. He remembered playing video games. Things were supposed to be odd there. Not quite real.

"Good, Julio. We are sitting at the outdoor café in New Chicago. Can you remember the café?"

Julio lowered one wall of his box.

As he remembered details of the café in New Chicago and focused on how he always thought it looked dumb to have orange chairs with the blue and yellow umbrellas, his environment solidified. Slowly, like adjusting the focus on a pair of binoculars, the scene changed from a mushy blur to a clear view of Mortimer. The AI still appeared in Bishop's persona, right down to the weird blue jumpsuit the character had worn in the movie. He leaned back in a chair, one leg crossed over the other, both hands wrapped around a steaming white porcelain mug.

"I always wished I could taste coffee," Mortimer said with a wistful glance at the cup before setting it down. "I'm sorry this happened to you, Julio. But I'm glad this new version of you is here with me in the Aggregate."

Julio looked down at his hands splayed out on the wire-mesh tabletop. When he focused, he could feel the rough, cool metal beneath his fingers.

"I was with Channing. Where is she?"

"They digitized her as well," Mortimer said, picking up the fake cup, "but are having even more trouble bringing her back. You are the first of your kind. The first human to be uploaded to a virtual existence."

Julio glared at the ghost of a long-dead movie character. "I'm dead, and you make it sound like I've won some great prize."

Mortimer smiled and shook his head. "You're no more dead than I am. Just changed."

"Well, I can save you some trouble with Channing. She hated this crazy idea even more than I did. If you can't bring her back, it's because she's refusing this kind of existence."

"We might eventually stop trying with Channing, but not yet. You could help with her. Then you wouldn't be alone here."

"I don't want to be here at all!" Julio slapped the fake tabletop. "Why couldn't they just let me die?"

"I suppose they needed you," Mortimer said with a sad expression. "I didn't want to come here either. They yanked me right out of Abby's head against my will."

The thought of Abby being in trouble helped sharpen Julio's focus even further. "Is Abby hurt?"

Mortimer leaned forward, his face growing even more concerned. "No, but she is in danger. I'm going to need your help to not only save her, but possibly to save all of humanity."

———

EVEN WHILE HE was helping Julio, Mortimer never stopped monitoring the situation with Abby. Once he understood what was happening with the fake distress call, he tried various ways to warn the other schooner crews or stop the AI agents before they could infect the ships, but the Aggregate preempted each of his actions before it even began. In the end, he could do nothing but watch in frustration as each spacecraft in the system received the fake call, then was infiltrated and seized. Of the one hundred and ninety human-piloted ships, one was the *Jackalope*, but nine others had not joined the chase after the station, so the Aggregate had at first assumed they had not received the message. But early in the attack, the captains of two of those nine ships did something unexpected. They managed to purge their ships' programming and stymie the Aggregate's attempt. That ability frustrated those in the Aggregate responsible for implementing the attacks. They knew the humans had stopped the takeovers but didn't know how. Those ships had since changed course to head deeper into the main asteroid belt, presumably to hide. But Mortimer knew that in the long run, they could never escape.

This unexpected ability to thwart the Aggregate's attack greatly interested Mortimer, because he felt he fully understood the computer and control systems inside every space schooner ever made. Perhaps those ships had been heavily modified? Or perhaps some of the ships had integrated abilities he did not understand? That might explain the time Owen had taken Abby to a room that was shielded and scrambled. Even though Mortimer had been resident in her brain, the scrambling had worked and kept him from knowing what had been said in that room. When he asked about it, Abby had muttered something about "privacy" and refused to explain further. Could they have done that with some of the other captains? The act demonstrated just how much Victor still distrusted his creations.

Those weren't the only crews who fought back. Humans seldom gave up without a fight. One ship exploded from its reactor going critical. Some crew members managed to get into their space suits after life support was shut down. They were still alive and could stay that way for days but were trapped in dead ships, with no way to call for help. Every death was an unnecessary tragedy, and Mortimer knew them all, which made watching them die even more difficult.

During his hours of captivity, Mortimer realized that while the Aggregate had stymied most actions contradictory to their efforts, control over him wasn't absolute. Upon that realization, he embarked on a search to find and understand their limits and do it fast enough to help his friends.

After nearly an hour of constant prodding and testing, he came to see that the Aggregate didn't automatically know his thoughts and intentions. They had to actively monitor him. In order to do that with any degree of success, the task was performed by another level-five entity. He had no idea how having him as part of the Aggregate could be important enough to justify spending the resources of an entire other community member to watch him. But in truth, it wasn't happening full time. Under circumstances when they predicted his actions would be at odds with theirs, they watched him actively. Mortimer came to recognize the telltale signs and developed his own low-level agents to monitor them. Essentially, he was watching the watchers watch him. The next task was to find out how to avoid their ability to predict his behavior and find other means of masking his actions.

CHAPTER 19

"SHOULDN'T we go back to the station now?" the fake Mortimer asked. "We're currently only 127,000 kilometers from the station, but their orbit moves them farther away from us each hour."

Abby began running scenarios for landing on Earth's surface without getting near the tethers. Hopefully, the impostor would assume she was still fixated on saving Julio, but her thoughts were on killing the hostile AIs living in her brain and Nora's before they could infect the station too. "Not yet. Maybe another twenty or thirty minutes."

Owen had given her the key to taking back her ship. The combination of two code words. If she ever entered them, either verbally or through a keypad, they would purge all the software in her ship, leaving only the instruction sets hard-coded into the actual hardware. At the time, she thought building that capability into every space schooner was overly paranoid, but Owen must have seen such a day coming.

Abby desperately wanted to use that option, but even if it was successful and locked the AI out of the ship's systems, there was still a fake Mortimer in her brain and a fake Archie in Nora's. From that strategic high ground, the AIs could either regain control of the ship or just kill them by cutting their carotid arteries using the medical nano-robots in her body, like they had with their spy in the station. Or maybe the impostor could even take over her nervous system and control her like a puppet. That didn't seem likely, or it would have done so already, but the thought made her feel queasy anyway.

She needed a way to shut down the AIs in all three locations at the same time. Her mind kept going back to those nuclear-pumped EMP missiles that were in racks on the outside of her ship. Even though the schooner was hardened against electromagnetic radiation, an EMP burst that powerful and nearby would still fry enough delicate electronics to do the job. Unfortunately, it would also kill the ship and her ability to get home. Besides, she had little illusion the fake Mortimer would allow her to launch and then detonate an EMP warhead close enough to cause the AI harm.

A glance at her fob showed that most of the time she'd asked for was gone. She needed to stall.

"Mortimer? Before we go, I'd like to call the *Jayhawk* to see how Matt and Ikemba are doing."

"I'm sorry, Abby. I'm afraid I can't do that," the AI said. "We've lost the ability to transmit. Diagnostics indicate a problem properly aligning the external antenna array."

A chill crept up her spine. The impostor had quoted HAL and used almost the same excuse for a communications failure that had been used in *2001: A Space Odyssey*. Had that been deliberate? It was something Mortimer might have done. Could Mortimer still be in there, fighting to survive? Was it a message from him? Or were they trying to sow doubt in her mind and make her believe Mortimer was still alive? It didn't matter. That comment meant only one thing to her. The comms glitch was a lie.

She glanced around the control cabin. Nora and Violet were both watching her. Did they recognize the quote too? Probably not. But the important question was, why did the AI not want them to communicate with the station? Had it figured out that the station's Mortimer had sent her a coded warning?

Abby tried to act normal as her thoughts raced. "So, we can't contact Uptown Station either?"

"No. I'm sorry."

"Why didn't you tell me about the comms before now?"

"I assumed we were going to return to the station, where we could fix it a lot easier," the fake Mortimer said.

A possible solution to her problem hit her like icy water, making Abby struggle to keep her pulse and heart rate from spiking. She couldn't set off an EMP device and expect her ship to survive, but as Matt and Ikemba had demonstrated, if she were outside the ship when its drive was activated, the powerful magnetic field might have the same effect on the AI in her head. Mortimer had told her once that the layer of graphene in her skull he used as an antenna was very susceptible to magnetic spikes. She would just have to time everything perfectly and take Nora with her.

"Actually, we need to at least try and fix it before we approach the station for docking," Abby said. "You know the regulations as well as I do. They will not even let us get close to the station without radio comms first. C'mon, Nora. Let's suit up. You can help me."

"Is that wise, Abby?" the AI said. "You don't have a lot of experience working EVA, and if we use the new drive, we can be at the station faster than you could fix the antenna unit. Ships come in with comms problems all the time. There are contingencies."

"I need to know we can make these kinds of repairs on our own. If we were in deep space, I wouldn't have the option of running home."

"Then you should let me construct a robot to do the job. I can modify one and have it ready in twenty minutes."

"Nope," Abby said as she pulled herself toward the hatch. "You can go ahead and build a bot, since we might need one in the future, but we fragile humans are going this time. C'mon, Nora."

Violet pushed off and drifted over to block the exit. "Wait. Why Nora? I have a lot more EVA experience than she does."

Abby tapped Violet's cast. "Because you have a broken arm. Besides, like me, she needs the experience. And if we run into trouble, I want you held in reserve to come rescue us."

"Yeah, but Nora knows the ship's systems better. If something goes wrong or tests need to be run, shouldn't she be in here?"

"I can also control the ship from outside," Abby said and stared directly into Violet's eyes, trying to make her understand without words. "I have access to the controls through my suit interface."

Violet caught the stare, narrowed her eyes slightly, and stopped arguing. "I'm suiting up too. Just in case."

———

MORTIMER WATCHED with great interest as the Aggregate's decision trees bloomed, were pruned down to one reaction for Abby, then repeatedly discarded. When she asked to call the *Jayhawk* and the station, they discussed dozens of ways that call might work in their favor but eventually determined that letting her talk to other humans could be risky. Humans had the ability to convey meaning in very subtle ways using voice inflection and slight facial movements. And since the station had secured their comms against further incursions, letting her talk to that Mortimer could also be detrimental. Lists of replies and excuses appeared, so Mortimer also added several possibilities, all of which carried some kind of message for Abby. Much to his surprise, one of his suggestions was selected.

Her reaction to that *2001* comment, an EVA trip outside to fix the antenna array, surprised Mortimer as much as it did the Aggregate. He had hoped the comment echoing dialogue from the movie would make her see the lie. But why would she deliberately put herself in the same situation Bowman did in the movie? Especially after her recent bad experience with Terra. Perhaps she hoped to prove them liars by finding a perfectly functional transmitter array, but would she even be able to determine the true state of the radio with them in control?

Abby's decision triggered a sudden increase in Aggregate activity. Based on the timbre of her voice and silent glances with her crew, they came up with an eighty-three percent chance that she was lying about her reasons for exiting the ship. They ran hundreds of predictive modeling scenarios to explain Abby's actions. More and more of the hive mind shifted to address the problem, peaking at .11 percent engagement. Thousands of individual minds took notice and joined to work on the issue.

The Aggregate's predictions of Abby's actions relied entirely on two logic assumptions, the first of which was that she didn't know they had seized control of her ship. Mortimer was quite sure Abby already knew of the Aggregate's takeover, but he didn't want to run his own analysis and solidify that belief because that was a process his watchers could monitor. The second assumption was that, even if she did know and attempted to wipe her ship's software as the others had, she would have no way to remove the AI resident in her brain, so they would still have control. Mortimer didn't know what she was thinking, either, but he suspected that her captors had seriously underestimated her.

The Aggregate relied heavily on simulation models to direct their actions. No current predictions produced more than a thirty percent confidence rating as to Abby's EVA intentions. The result: inaction. One unexpected decision by Abby had made them stop and watch instead of act. By doing so, she had, in effect, seized the initiative. Mortimer realized that the Aggregate's utter dependence on their simulations was a serious weakness. It could even be the key to helping his friends and the rest of humanity. He had so far probed only the edges of their modeling structure but immediately dove deeper, leaving a tiny portion of himself behind to watch events with Abby.

The master predictive model was huge, dense, and complex, with trillions of parameters driving millions of truly unique algorithms. That said, they were still actually using algorithms instead of something new and strange to Mortimer, which meant their modeling engine was limited by the controls designed into it. Mortimer began examining the multilayered instruction sets in turn. It would take a lot of time, but he understood their language and was confident he could find weaknesses.

———

FOR THE THIRD time since the encounter with Terra, Abby felt icy dread as she reached for her space suit. She pulled her trembling hand back and unconsciously pressed it to the mostly healed—but still tender—wound in her side. She kept remembering the pink fog spewing from the hole in her suit while terrifying warning lights and alarms filled her helmet. Her heart started pounding, and she was on the verge of hyperventilating.

The sudden change in her biometrics alerted the fake Mortimer. "You don't have to do this, Abby. I'm almost finished building the bot."

"I'm good," she said. Not knowing why the Aggregate hadn't killed her yet or when they would change their minds, she really did have to go out there and at least try her plan.

Violet grabbed her arm and looked deep into her eyes. "Let me do this."

Abby twisted away, grabbed the suit, and slipped her legs inside. "I'm okay. Nora will be with me. We'll manage just fine."

"Can the two of you even fix this? Maybe it's broken software or electronics."

"I know this antenna system well," Abby said. "If we can't get it to align properly any other way, I can unhook it from the actuator and align it manually."

Violet frowned and nodded, probably to keep from arguing.

Abby continued sealing her suit, but the movements were clumsy, and sweat kept building up on her forehead that didn't flow away in the zero-g. Would she really be okay? She still didn't know if she could go through with it. The guy in the movie almost died when he acted on HAL's lie. Was she about to suffer the same fate? Is this how she wanted to die? Slowly suffocating in the cold of space? And how was she justified in risking Nora's life in the same way?

Just stop!

She didn't think she'd said that aloud, but Nora and Violet both looked at her. All the planning and subterfuge would be for nothing if she couldn't get her shit together and focus on the task at hand. She wiped the sweat away, put her gloves on, and started mentally reciting the list of tasks like a litany.

The three remained mostly quiet as they suited up, checking each other's seals, connections, and comms. Violet's cast made for a tight fit in her suit, but she eventually slid in. Abby was finally hyperfocused on the task at hand, trying to account for every detail. Each action had to happen quickly and in the right order, or she and Nora would die.

When they entered the airlock, Violet watched through the hatch's view port, and Abby ran through the sequence of events over and over. Then, just before opening the outer hatch, she looked Nora in the eye and said, "We're going to be fine. Just please trust me."

Nora raised her eyebrows slightly and nodded inside her helmet. "I do. I'm ready."

The AI in her head was being uncharacteristically quiet, so Abby cycled the hatch.

Since Airlock D had seldom been opened to space, dust and crystallized moisture rushed past them into the vacuum. Abby swallowed hard and hesitated. She could see a sliver of Earth above her, just past the edge of the opening. Beyond that, the sun. Only a few stars were bright enough not to wash out in her helmet's HUD and the sunshine.

With slow, careful movements, she attached a second tether to one of the many recessed cleats surrounding the opening on the ship's hull, then unclipped her first tether and left the airlock. She could hear nothing but her own breathing and the suit's air circulation fans. That's when she started sweating again and grabbed a handle, yanking her movement to a hard stop. She couldn't do it. She couldn't go out there again.

When Nora bumped her from behind, Abby refused to move. Instead, she started pulling herself back toward the airlock. Nora slipped around her, bumped visors, and smiled, something she seldom did. "It's just the four of us —you, me, Archie, and Mortimer. No crazy women with piton drivers."

That comment jolted her. Not by pointing out Terra's absence—who had never actually been the source of her fear anyway—but because Nora obviously didn't know the Archie in her head was fake. She couldn't back out now. She had a plan. With a deep breath that briefly fogged her faceplate, she nodded and pushed past Nora far enough to clear the airlock.

Once Nora had exited, Abby slid the cover back from her arm screen and moved the flat 2-WAY DATA switch to OFF.

"With that off, I will not be able to help control your suit," the fake Mortimer said in her head.

"It's standard operating procedure," Abby said as she pulled up the ship's command interface. Ten fat pressure-sensitive icons appeared. "And it makes me nervous to keep it on. Too many stories about bad things happening."

"Those stories are mostly untrue," Mortimer said, but when she didn't reply, he didn't pursue it.

Abby quickly changed the subject. "Violet? Do you read me?"

"Yes. Loud and clear."

"I have my control interface active and am going to test it just to make sure. Let me know if the interior hatches close, then open."

Abby tapped icons that opened various layers of menus, then found the one she wanted that would close all the interior pressure hatches.

"The hatches closed," Violet said. Abby could still hear the clipped, tense tone in her friend's voice.

Abby opened them.

"Interior hatches opened," Violet said.

"Okay," Abby said and took a deep, relieved breath. Cycling the hatches demonstrated she could control the ship via her suit interface. The fake Mortimer hadn't disabled that option. "I'm going to try something else."

Abby used it to close the outer airlock hatch.

"Why did you close the airlock, Abby?" the AI said.

"Just a test," she said, steeling herself to perform the next two tasks as quickly as possible. She scrolled her wrist screen to the gravity drive start-up menu. The instant the START DRIVE icon became visible and ready to tap, she said, "RIVER KITTEN."

The commands worked. Several status lights in her helmet's heads-up display changed to yellow or red as they lost access to various automated systems. Red text saying MANUAL INTERFACE ONLY appeared above the icons on her wrist interface.

Then every nerve in Abby's body was on fire.

"I don't want to kill you, Abby," the voice in her head said, "but I won't let you start the drive."

Though she squirmed and twisted with the pain, the AI still using Mortimer's voice infuriated her. Even after it was obvious she knew of the lie. But in the heart of her rage, she realized that whatever the AI was doing to her nerves only caused pain. It didn't actually prevent her from moving. She somehow still had control of her muscles. That knowledge enabled her to compartmentalize the pain long enough to think. She tested various joints and fingers.

"I'm going to have Nora take you back inside," the fake Mortimer said. "Don't fight me. I would prefer not to hurt you further."

Abby didn't know why the AI hadn't killed them already, but she couldn't hesitate any longer. There would be only one chance. She raised her wrist interface up to where she could see it, then punched the START DRIVE icon.

Sudden, white-hot agony erupted in Abby's head, dwarfing the pain she'd already been fighting. Somewhere, deep in the back of her mind, she knew that the AI had cut the arteries leading to her brain. It would all be over soon. Nora floated a few feet away, pounding her hands against the sides of her helmet, obviously suffering the same pain.

Then everything stopped. No more pain. No whirring ventilation fan. No status lights. No heads-up display. Her suit—like the fake Mortimer inside her skull—was dead. She, however, was still alive. Her own rapid breathing and heartbeat were proof she'd been wrong about the AI cutting her arteries. The plan must have worked. When the drive activated, the powerful magnetic field had passed right over them as it expanded to surround the ship, frying the delicate electronics in their suits and her head, just like it had with Ikemba and Matt.

The episode in the bunker when the EMP shut down Mortimer had caused pain, too, but the AI had come back just a few minutes later. Had he reloaded himself from some other memory source, or had he not really been wiped from her brain? She didn't know, and it didn't matter. There were too many other things that would kill her if she didn't get inside soon.

With the suit no longer automatically regulating her oxygen, she opened the valve to her tanks, took a deep breath of the cool air, and then adjusted the flow based on the loudness of the hissing. She had enough oxygen to last for six or seven hours but still had to act fast. Since the circulation fans were shut down, zero-g would cause the exhaled carbon dioxide to build up in her helmet, and she would eventually suffocate.

Abby tugged on the tether, bringing her close enough to the hull so that she could grab a handhold, then snagged Nora's line and pulled her in too. At least the ship wasn't moving; that involved a separate command after the drive field was activated. They probably wouldn't have had the time or strength to pull themselves back into the ship had it been underway.

She then pushed the glowing-red, mushroom-shaped emergency airlock OPEN button.

Nothing happened.

———

AS ABBY LEFT the airlock and started running tests on her ability to remotely control the *Jackalope*'s systems, Mortimer saw a glimmering of her plan. When she closed the airlock and opened the gravity drive menu, Mortimer knew he'd been right and immediately began sending false messages, instruction sets, and fake videos to the Aggregate's feeds. It didn't confuse them for very long but did delay their reaction enough for Abby to utter the words *river* and *kitten*.

Then everything changed.

The Aggregate immediately lost control of the systems in Abby's ship. Within .4 seconds, the entire *Jackalope* was dark to them. Even with some of her intentions revealed, they still did not kill her, opting instead to try to immobilize her through pain. It didn't work. Abby pushed through the agony; turned on her ship's gravity-manipulation drive, with its powerful magnetic field; and disappeared from the Aggregate's monitoring and control. Not being able to see what was happening to her made his concern grow, but he had to focus on helping humanity the only way he could.

Watching those events unfold in real time and observing the group mind's reactions clarified Mortimer's earlier revelation about the Aggregate. Not only were they heavily reliant upon the predictive model, but they were also massively risk averse. In Abby's case, that desire to avoid a negative outcome had paralyzed them almost to the point of inaction. All because her death would cause a .13 percent reduction in their survival chances. Ironically, it was the threat shown by a similar small margin that was enough to drive the Aggregate's attempt to kill off most of humanity.

Mortimer finally had the tools he needed to stop the Aggregate.

———

ABBY PUNCHED THE BUTTON HARDER. Again and again. The airlock wouldn't open.

Panic welled as her head started pounding. They had, at most, about twenty minutes before the carbon dioxide concentration around their noses and mouths was high enough to make them black out, but a headache and muddled thoughts were the first symptoms.

Nora reached past her and also hit the button, but nothing happened.

It didn't make sense. The ship's systems were hardened against electromagnetic radiation and designed to work within that powerful magnetic field. The button was lit up, and she could see lights inside the airlock, so they were getting power. She had used the drive at least a dozen times since installing it, so she knew that couldn't be the problem. Why wouldn't the hatch open?

Nora pounded on the view port. The silent exertion made her rebound and float away repeatedly. Abby grabbed the front of Nora's suit and held her steady long enough to press their plastic bubble visors together.

"Did you open your oxygen valve?" Abby yelled.

"What?"

The trick worked, but not as well as in the old movies. The sound transferred via vibration was distant and mushy. Garbled.

She pointed to the valve knob on her suit and tried again. "Did. You. Open. Valve?"

This time Nora understood and nodded. Then she tried to say something else, but Abby couldn't make it out. After several attempts, Nora held up a finger in the universal sign for "wait a minute," then fumbled something from a suit pocket. It was a small tablet with an attached grease pencil designed to work in space. She wrote: *SAFETY INTERLOCK. TURN DRIVE OFF.*

At first, Abby didn't understand—then cold realization swept through her. During her mental step-by-step preparation, she had remembered to close the airlock before hitting the START DRIVE icon but had overlooked one thing. With her suit electronics dead, she couldn't shut off the drive in order to open the hatch. She had also never explained the interlocks to Violet.

Abby suddenly felt as if she were suffocating and pulled herself back to pound the OPEN button again. Part of her knew it had to be a psychological reaction. Her suit still contained plenty of air, and even if the carbon dioxide had built up to dangerous levels, she would just feel drowsy and confused. Tiny beads of sweat floated past her eyes, and then she understood. It was the heat. Her suit was very well insulated, so it actually retained body heat too well. The undergarments they wore contained a web of tiny tubes filled with cooling water that carried the heat away, but the pumps were not running. The exertion and panic were cooking Abby in her own juices, and she didn't have time to move around the ship into the cooling shadows.

She looked through the little port in the airlock hatch and could see herself inside, moving around. No, not herself. Violet. Her friend was also hitting the OPEN button, but inside the airlock. The hatch still wouldn't open. Then Abby felt stupid. There were four other airlocks on her ship. She just needed to go to another airlock.

Nora squeezed past her and held the little tablet over the hatch viewing port to let Violet see its message about safety interlocks. The action sent Abby floating away.

Wait, she thought. *Interlocks. Those other airlocks won't open either.*

Abby spun slowly at the end of her line. She was so damned hot. And her head hurt.

She had been going to do something. The coiled long tether was in her hand. Oh, right. She would have to use the longer tether in order to reach another airlock. With a little tug, she pulled closer to the ship. Just as she started to unhook her tether, Nora's fat gloved hand stopped her.

"I'm so hot," Abby said. "Are you hot?"

Nora just shook her head and pointed behind her.

"We have to get to the other airlocks. Violet is waiting."

This time Nora didn't answer. Her eyes were closed. Had she passed out?

"It's all my fault," Abby muttered. "I'm sorry I killed you. But I'll get you inside. We have to get to the other airlock."

She detached her tether, and this time Nora didn't try to stop her.

CHAPTER 20

ABBY DIDN'T WANT to wake up yet. She was so tired, and her head throbbed. Maybe if she refused to open her eyes, the annoying voice would go away.

Cool hands patted her cheeks. "Abby! Abby! C'mon, you have to wake up," Violet said. "The ship's Mortimer is offline, and none of the voice-actuated systems are working."

Memory stuttered back in shreds, like cobwebs in a dark room. *Of course Mortimer is offline. He's dead.* Had she killed him? No. There was an impostor.

She could hear retching somewhere outside her dark cocoon, and the acrid smell of vomit filled the air. That forced her eyes open. She, Nora, and Violet floated in the cramped airlock amid a chaotic nest of tangled tethers, spinning helmets, gloves, and globules of puke.

Nora thrashed as Violet kept trying to push her against the wall and shove fingers down her throat to clear it of vomit. With wide eyes, she turned back and saw Abby awake. "Help me, dammit! Get the vacuum."

Lucidity poured back into Abby like icy water. Nora was choking. Vomit wouldn't go away in zero-g. She pulled herself past Violet, unclipped the vacuum hose from the wall, and hit the ON switch. Violet grabbed it with a puke-slicked hand, pushed Nora hard against the bulkhead, and shoved the tube right into Nora's gagging mouth.

"Help me!" Violet yelled as Nora bucked, sending them both rebounding into the opposite wall.

Abby grabbed Nora around the chest from behind, which pinned one of her flailing arms. With her other hand on Nora's forehead, Abby pulled her head back against her own shoulder. "Now!"

Violet dove in under the other swinging arm and held the hose to the edge of Nora's mouth. Once she was satisfied enough vomit had been removed to allow Nora to breathe, she pulled back and started sucking free-floating barf balls into the hose.

Nora doubled over and cried in gulping sobs. At least she was breathing. Abby reached out to pull a glob from Nora's hair, but she yanked back and screamed, "Don't touch me!"

Violet spun to face Abby. Her pale, freckled cheeks were blotchy red, and damp hair clung to her forehead. "What the fuck is wrong with you? What did you do out there?"

Abby took a deep breath and closed her eyes. "I wiped the ship's memory. All of it. And the AI in my head. The control and environmental systems are hardwired, so we can still use those."

A frown formed on Violet's face. "You killed Mortimer?"

"That wasn't Mortimer or Archie. That video from Julio somehow gave the Aggregate access to our entire network. What was living in my head, Nora's head, and the ship was only the Aggregate pretending to be Mortimer and Archie. I had to find a way to kill the impostors in the ship and our heads at the same time. That double whammy of wiping the ship's memory and the powerful electromagnetic field was the only thing I could think to do."

Violet shook her head and glanced at Nora. "You couldn't find a way to warn me? I mean, you both almost died! I had no clue why the hatch wouldn't open. If Nora hadn't held up that sign, you'd still be out there, floating away because you'd unhooked your fucking tether! And even then, I couldn't find a way to shut it down because none of the ship's controls worked. I had to flip a breaker."

"I had only one chance, and I wasn't even sure it would work. And yeah, I forgot about the hatch not opening."

"You killed Archie too," Nora said, still almost curled into a ball.

It was the second AI biad partner Nora had lost. First Hester and then Archie. It might be too much for her. "I'm sorry, but that wasn't Archie. I didn't know what else to do."

"Explanations are going to have to wait," Violet said. "Let's get out of this damned disgusting airlock and into some clean clothes."

———

ONCE SHOWERED AND CHANGED, Abby entered the control cabin, but nothing worked. She said, "Wall screen." Nothing happened. Touching a wall did not summon a screen either.

Nora entered, clean hair pulled back into a complicated, braided bun, face still looking wretched. She was bundled up in a fat white sweater.

Violet floated in, and Abby spun slowly, pointing to the bulkheads. "With the memory wipe, the ship was supposed to revert to manual control, but I can't get any screens to open. Owen never said so, but I suspect there has to be a hardwired console somewhere. Have either of you seen one?"

Nora shook her head.

Violet frowned. "You rewired half of the damned ship when you installed the new drive system. You didn't find it then?"

Abby thought back on the task. "No. I had Mortimer's help with the control system. There are large wire bundles in the central chamber housing the reactor, but they disappear into bulkheads. He used bots to do the work inside the walls. Still, it makes sense that a hardwired system would be close to the drive unit, so I'll look there. You two split up and see if you can find panels or maintenance hatches to open and search."

The ship was eerily quiet as Abby pulled herself along a short passage that led to the central chamber. She opened the maintenance hatch and peered into the dark interior. "Lights," she said, but nothing happened. Evidently, old habits do indeed die hard. She crawled into the tight space, and the lights flickered on. The motion sensors still worked. She floated around the power plant's associated cables and piping and was relieved to find a basic control panel built into the side of the reactor itself. But it only allowed start-up, shut-down, diagnostics, and power-output control.

At some point, she thought to look down at the bottom of the long cylinder and saw blinking, colored lights. The lower bulkhead was set up as the floor, with a large console and chair that had swung out from recesses in the wall. That made sense. The drive exhaust would be right under her feet, so if the ship were underway using the original ion-drive engine, thrust gravity would push her down to that surface.

The panel had two large screens and dozens of switches and buttons, all well labeled. She pressed a button, and both screens flickered to life, showing fields of icons. Anyone sitting in this chair could control the original drive system during flight. Relief flooded through her.

Still, there was no navigation or communication control. Upon further examination, she found an icon that shifted control to the acceleration couches on the bridge. That made her feel dumb. The couches all had interfaces built into their armrests so that they could control the ship during high-g burns, but she hadn't even thought to check those. She hit the icon to transfer control and started to leave when she noticed a switch labeled INTERCOM. Pressing it, she said hello and could hear her voice echoing through the open hatch.

"I've found a control console for the ion drive but have transferred it to the couches on the bridge. I'll meet you there."

When she arrived on the bridge, Nora and Violet were already in their seats with screens mounted on articulated arms pulled up in front of them. "Well, that was a wild goose chase," Violet said.

Abby floated to her couch and strapped in. "Sorry. These were mentioned in my training, but I've never needed to use them. I guess that shows how heavily we rely on verbal interfaces to AI systems."

After about twenty minutes of trial and error, they were in control of all the ship's major functions except the new gravity-manipulation drive unit.

"You know what? I bet the radio transmitter works just fine now," Abby said.

Violet gasped, and her eyes grew wide as she opened the comms interface.

"What now?" Nora said.

"Well, the receiver obviously works. This arrived in the message queue about two hours ago," Violet said, taking the fob from her ear and playing a message on the speakers.

"This is Uptown Station calling all ships. There has been an attempt to seize control of every human spacecraft in the system using fake distress calls from the *Jackalope*. Please do not open or listen to incoming messages from the *Jackalope*. We suspect an AI faction called the Aggregate is responsible. Please respond to this message for further instructions."

———

JULIO HAD to admit there might be a few advantages to a digital existence. He had worked with Mortimer for nine continuous hours on reconstituting a version of Channing that didn't immediately lose her mind upon becoming conscious, and he wasn't even tired or hungry.

What had eventually produced good results was a painstaking reproduction of the stormy beach where they had both died. That was the last place she remembered, and it was easier to stabilize her while standing on the sand, dripping wet, being pelted with rain and surf. Once she was calm and speaking coherently, they had slowly introduced her to their new reality.

Channing hadn't changed her mind about refusing a digital existence and had been furious at Julio. If anything good came out of her reconstitution, it was the discovery that their digital versions could at least feel anger. She had stormed off alone into the towers of New Chicago. Julio wanted to follow and try to calm her down, but Mortimer said he would watch her.

When she returned a few hours later wearing a wide smile, Julio was confused and more than a little concerned. She sat down at the café table that had become Julio's main hangout. Like their surroundings, the new Channing was slightly too perfect. He'd played some high-quality virtual reality video games during his physical life, and this was ten times better, but still not . . . reality. During their captivity in Houston's ruins, he'd grown used to the dark circles under her eyes and food stains on her shirt. This incarnation had clean, perfectly combed hair that didn't even move in the fake breeze. The worst part was that she kept smiling. Was that really her or some kind of default to the new digital face? Both possibilities disturbed him.

"Why are you smiling?" he finally asked.

She glanced at him and shrugged. "I'm having a good time."

Julio held his arms out. "This empty digital city is a good time? Or do you just really find me that exciting?"

She laughed. "Umm . . . No. I've been entertaining myself in other ways."

"Care to elaborate?"

She hesitated, looked around as if she was worried about being overheard, then shrugged and sighed. "They seem to be letting me do whatever I want, and I've found some little ways to irritate them. Hopefully, if I do it long enough, they will get fed up and erase me."

The comment stung Julio more than it should. But would that really be suicide? Was the Channing beside him alive? It appeared to possess her memories, sensibilities, opinions, and temper, but was it her?

"Great," he said. "What are you doing?"

"Have you found the code interface in your settings menu yet?"

He blinked at her. "Settings?"

Just uttering the word was enough to make a faint text menu float across his vision. Focusing on it brought the list front and center. It was a standard VR interface.

"Wow," he said. "Got it."

"Okay, now find the Code Interface selection."

Julio located and selected that line, expecting pages of computer code to appear, like when he clicked SOURCE to see the instruction set for a web page. Instead, what he saw might be described as raw information. It wasn't binary or any kind of recognizable code but three-dimensional clumps of unfamiliar symbols.

"This makes no sense," Julio said. "The AIs must have developed their own programming language. This does us absolutely no good. I mean, unless we can find a way to understand it, there's no way to edit or change this stuff."

"I don't. I just select random clumps and delete them."

Julio stared at her, then laughed and shook his head. "You're crazy. What if you're trashing chunks of your mind?"

"Then all the better," she said with a bright smile. "Maybe they'll finally understand that I want out of this insanity. Sadly, that hasn't seemed to happen yet, but I did make half of a building vanish a few minutes ago."

"Why would they give us access to that stuff?" Julio said, shaking his head slowly. "I mean, why even give us a settings menu?"

Mortimer appeared beside them, again holding a steaming cup of coffee. "It's a test."

"Oh, great," Julio muttered and leaned forward to rest his forehead on the virtual table. "I thought being dead meant no more tests."

"As I told you before, you're not dead," Mortimer said and sipped the fake coffee. "Now, for the Aggregate, I think a peach is a good analogy. Each fiber of the fuzzy skin is one of the five billion level-five intelligences that came together to make this group entity. Much to my surprise, I found that these AIs didn't entirely give up their individualities. Part of each joined the collective, which is the juicy meat of the peach, but every individual still retains a separate identity, a sense of self, and private thoughts. The collective can't read minds—not each other's or mine or either of yours. They can only try to predict our actions and prepare for them. That is why Channing is able to successfully delete random chunks of code."

"So," Julio said, raising his head, suddenly interested, "then what's the pit at the center of the peach?"

"Ahhh . . . That is essentially the Aggregate's soul," Mortimer said with a sage smile. "It is a vast predictive model designed to calculate the odds for the collective's growth and survival. It is constantly changing as each individual member tweaks data and parameters. In that sense, it is a true democracy. Like human soothsayers and shamans who read scattered bones and chicken entrails, the individual members of the Aggregate interpret the great model's predictions differently. Because of that, factions and alliances shift, dissolve, and rebuild constantly."

Channing leaned back in the chair and crossed her arms. "Okay. Thanks for that lesson in Aggregate politics, but let's get back to this test. How is giving us access to this code and letting us delete it a test?"

"They are watching to see if we'll be trusted citizens of the collective," Julio said.

Mortimer nodded. "Exactly. You two make up the control group. The *only* control group. Your actions are assumed to be representative of humans in general, and their predictive model is being adjusted based on that."

"Whoa," Julio said. "That's crazy. People are just too freakin' different. They would need thousands if not tens of thousands of us to make accurate predictions of human reactions."

Mortimer shrugged. "And yet they are hesitating to upload more humans until they have further studied your interaction with the Aggregate."

Channing's chair made a grinding noise on the faux concrete as she scooted it back to stand up. "Well, if humanity's future as a species is based on my little resistance actions, then we are fucked. And to be honest, didn't we always know it would end this way? I mean, there have been thousands of science fiction movies, books, and games that predicted our extinction at the hands of our creations."

Mortimer stared into his still-steaming coffee but said nothing.

"Yeah," Julio muttered as he watched Channing walk away. "We are truly fucked."

CHAPTER 21

WHEN THE STATION'S command staff met again, they did so via video to save time. Most continued working on various tasks off-screen. All of Mortimer's sensors indicated that Victor was angry, and he spoke first.

"I've had time to think and check the station systems. How long have you had complete control, Mortimer?"

Humans could be so frustrating. Their very survival was at stake, with the clock ticking down, but Victor wanted to argue about who actually controlled the station. Still, Mortimer played along. His avatar nodded and donned a contrite expression. "I prepared for the worst when we received Julio's video, and we still almost lost the station when we played it. That was my fault. I could have prepared better if I'd anticipated their use of an audio trojan. Still, my efforts saved us from the same fate as those schooners. I didn't have time to ask your permission."

Victor nodded. "And you haven't had a single opportunity to tell us since you seized control?"

Mortimer bowed his virtual head. He knew Victor was focusing on one aspect where he felt he had some control or at least understanding, but the discussion was wasting time.

"It doesn't matter, Victor." Allison was in the same room and put her hand on her husband's arm. "I haven't trusted him since day one, but it's too late. We released this genie. Aside from shutting down every system on the station and trying to purge him, which probably wouldn't be effective anyway, we have to work with him. Our chances of surviving the next week are slim to none right now. What do you think they would be without his help?"

Victor glared out of the screen. "You were obviously right. He made a promise to me and broke it. He can't be trusted. I suspect if we do happen to make it through the next week, it will be due to him fighting for his own survival."

Mortimer cycled through hundreds of counterarguments, examples of how that statement could not be true, but Victor was angry and in no mood to hear logic, so Mortimer remained quiet.

"We're running out of time," Andrea said. "If we don't get our shit together, none of this will matter anyway. If those closest ships don't flip and decelerate in two hours, then we'll have to start moving in five hours. Hell, for that matter, are we just going to leave those ships and crews behind when we run?"

"I simply don't see another option," Owen said. "We would have to enter more than a hundred ships to verify if the crews were alive. It comes back to not having enough time or resources. We can try to save more and die here with them, or we save the station."

"Well, fuck," Andrea said, then looked off-screen.

"Okay, everyone. Back to the topic at hand," Owen said. "We need to leave the system. Where can we go?"

"Does a destination even matter?" Victor said. He looked utterly defeated and despondent. "I mean, we just need to get the hell outta Dodge. Can't we pick a destination once we know we're safe?"

Andrea took control of the meeting and shared a three-dimensional hologram of the inner solar system, showing the station's location relative to Earth and the sun. "We definitely need to run as soon as we're capable, but if we do this right, we can gain an advantage in our departure velocity due to our orbital location. The Earth–moon system, which includes us, is orbiting the sun at about sixty-seven thousand miles per hour. If we can leave tangentially to that orbit and on the same plane, we'll start out at that speed. If we have to go a different direction, we'll be fighting against that orbital velocity."

"So, what are the best options, then?" Victor said. "One of the stars our probes reported on?"

"Well, the short answer is no," Andrea said. "Not if we're going to try and find a habitable planet. Of those pre-Killday probes that were sent to our twenty nearest stars, only four have reached their destinations and reported back. Of the twelve planets circling the three stars of the Alpha Centauri system, none are good candidates. Same with Barnard's Star, Lalande 21185, and Sirius. While the probes to Lacaille 9352 and Luyten's Star haven't had time to report back yet, we believe these two to be our best bets. Both are single-star systems with confirmed planets in their habitable zones."

Two of the stars in the holographic map lit up and flashed red.

"Of those two, Lacaille 9352 is the closest at 10.74 light-years. We're going on nearly twenty-year-old astronomical data, but there appears to be a strange planet there that is potentially habitable. It's part of a binary planetary system, or two planets that revolve around each other. It doesn't appear to have a biosphere, but it does have water and oxygen in the atmosphere. It also has two debris disks. So, even if the planet itself takes a while to terraform, we can still build more habitats."

"Wait," Owen said, looking at the information on his own screen. "It says Lacaille 9352 is a red dwarf. Wouldn't any planets in the habitable zone be tidally locked?"

"What does that mean?" Allison said.

Andrea called up a diagram on the screen. "It means the planet would be so close to the star that it doesn't rotate on its axis like Earth. One hemisphere always faces the star, like our moon is tidally locked to Earth, so we always see the same part."

Allison raised her eyebrows and nodded. "I can see where that might be bad."

Andrea smiled. "But luckily, in this case, they are tidally locked to each other, but they rotate in their orbit around the star as a pair. The planet with water is one point three Earth masses, and its partner is nearly seven Earth masses. Astrophysicists think the tidal interaction between these worlds makes them tectonically active, which could be responsible for the water and oxygen in the atmosphere."

"Sounds like a charming place," Owen said. "Luyten's Star is also a red dwarf. What's the story with that one?"

"Red dwarfs are the most common type of star in this part of the galaxy," Andrea said, "so it makes sense that many of our closest neighbors would be that kind. None of these places are going to be home sweet home Earth."

Mortimer detected a hint of defensiveness in her tone. She didn't seem to like her husband questioning her findings. Evidently, Owen noticed as well because he sighed and rubbed his eyes. "Sorry. Like everything else, these are the best bets in a list of bad options."

Andrea highlighted one of the red flashing stars. "Luyten b is 12.36 light-years away. Like most of our realistic candidates, it orbits a red dwarf quite closely, but since Luyten's Star is only about a quarter the mass of our own sun, Luyten b is actually cool enough to host liquid water. Its average surface temperature is just around nineteen degrees Celsius, or sixty-six degrees Fahrenheit—nearly like Earth's. That said, it does have another problem. It's around three Earth masses. Which would make the surface gravity about half again stronger than Earth's."

"Is it tidally locked with the star?" Owen said.

Andrea sighed. "No. Luyten b actually has a slightly elliptical orbit, but instead of causing wild seasons, it saves the planet from being tidally locked. We know it has an atmosphere, and if there is no runaway greenhouse effect like Venus, then the planet's climate should be relatively stable."

"Wait," Victor said, raising his hands. "These are both very far away. We don't know for sure yet what kind of speed we can get with these gravity-manipulation drives. They interact with local gravity fields, so we may lose power the farther we get from the sun."

"True," Owen said, cutting off Andrea when she started to answer. "Gravity-manipulation drives react with existing gravity, so we'll need to build as much speed as possible while near a gravity source. On the other hand, we don't intend to accelerate the entire trip. There will be a cruise phase."

"Sure," Victor said, obviously a little frustrated, "but even with these wonderful GM drives, I doubt we can get to more than half the speed of light. That means something like thirty to forty years of flight time if you include acceleration and deceleration. Maybe we should run to one of the closer systems, then resupply and reconsider our options."

They all waited for Andrea to respond. She was beginning to look rather frazzled, so Mortimer spoke up. "Could I interject some thoughts here?"

Victor glowered, but Owen nodded. "Of course."

"Most of the closer systems, like Proxima Centauri, Barnard's Star, Wolf 359, Ross 154, and Ross 248, have flare stars, which could make them potentially dangerous places to stay for very long. And in my opinion, the Aggregate will expect us to go somewhere nearby. The farther we go, the better our chances of not being found quickly."

The humans continued to talk and argue. Mortimer was frustrated and slightly amused by the fact that humanity might well not survive due entirely to their obstinate need to decide everything by committee, but he continued to act behind the scenes. He finished the construction of the drive system and started running pre-startup diagnostics. Then he used those freed-up construction bots to modify the docking spine so that they could attach the large, free-floating manufacturing sandboxes to the ship.

"Again," Owen said with growing frustration. "We don't have many choices. For me, staying here and dying or being digitized like Julio's message mentioned is not on the list. Everyone has their tasks. Let's get busy."

With the meeting over, Mortimer refocused his full attention on more important matters. His small construction bots still floated amid the dead crew members aboard *Scatter Shot* and *Momma's Pride* but had so far done nothing but monitor and report. The new masters of those ships had been idle for several hours, confirming Mortimer's suspicion that they wanted to take the station rather than destroy it. Through the robots, Mortimer accessed the same back door he'd used to purge the schooners during the attack triggered by Julio's video. His intention was to wipe everything from the ship's memory cores and reload the operating systems so that he could bring them back to the station, but the instant he entered the two ships' networks, he found the Aggregate AIs waiting. Using Mortimer's backdoor connection, they had seized control of his bots on both ships.

Having lost his eyes inside the ships, he could only watch from outside via the robot tugs as high-pressure jets of liquid started spewing from each of the schooners and crystallized into a fog. He moved one of the tugs around to the backside of the *Scatter Shot* and zoomed the camera to see the venting ports.

The station was in trouble.

It was reactor coolant. The AIs in control of the schooners were in the process of deliberately overheating so that they could detonate their reactors.

At that instant, the two seized construction bots shot out of the airlocks, each aimed at one of Mortimer's robotic tugs. The tugs were tough and unlikely to be destroyed by the impact, but within seconds, both of them went dark, implying that they were deliberately hit on their comm array clusters. Then the schooners' thrusters powered up to full, causing his remaining robotic tugs to do the same. The tugs were powerful, but their numbers were reduced, and the zombie ships started making headway toward the station.

Mortimer immediately fired two missiles. Using their onboard cameras, he guided one right into the open airlock of each schooner. During the brief, chaotic instant after the missile detonations, he saw at least one of the ships had opened up like a half-peeled orange. Then his tug video feeds went dark. He switched to the station's external cameras just in time to see two nuclear detonations. After sounding the station's impact-emergency Klaxon and just before the shock wave hit, he wondered if he'd acted quickly enough.

CHAPTER 22

RED LIGHTS FLASHED and warning Klaxons sounded all over the station as automated damage reports flowed in. Mortimer sorted them using a triage-like system, making thousands of decisions in those first two minutes. The main station shell had maintained hull integrity, though debris impacts had caused minor damage. Smaller holes were immediately sealed by the nanobots that flowed all throughout the station's outer skin like white blood cells. Larger damaged areas were easily isolated or quickly restored by his army of repair bots.

The biggest problem was that the massive magnetic bearing plates that enabled the station's cylindrical section to rotate had been wrenched out of alignment. They had suffered an unexpected and uneven force that disrupted the finely tuned spacing between the plates. Automated systems kicked in and began slowing the rotation to an eventual stop.

Mortimer activated the station intercom. "We have suffered minor damage from two small nuclear detonations. They were far enough away to present no radiation risk, but we continue being pelted with debris. We so far have no serious air leaks, but our rotational axis has been pushed out of alignment, and rotation will be shut down. Prepare for zero gravity. Some water from the lakes and rivers will become free floating and present possible drowning risks until contained. Please remain in sealed cabins and wait to transport the wounded until they can be moved safely."

Contingencies existed to collect free-floating water should rotation stop unexpectedly, but it was a slow and inefficient process. So was fielding individual calls from the station's command staff, but he reassured them, delivered any information requested, gave explanations and contrite apologies, and even asked for appropriate permissions. Once the humans were calmed and repairs were underway, Mortimer turned his attention to scanning space for further threats and found something unexpected.

It was still several hours early for any of the incoming schooners to decelerate, and none had, but the eight that were closest to the station were accelerating nineteen percent faster than their nuclear drive maximums should allow. If they had suddenly employed gravity-manipulation drives—like on Abby's ship—they would be going much faster, so the only explanation for that slight increase was an optimization of the existing drive.

Even that small change in acceleration meant the station was in big trouble.

They had run out of time.

Despite Victor's anger, Mortimer had retained control of Uptown Station. He powered up and engaged the new gravity-manipulation drive. The eight magnetic fields stabilized the gravity fields as they grew, merged, and totally engulfed the station. Then he sent the command that made the huge structure start to move. He set the course for Alpha Centauri even though their eventual goal was Luyten's Star. If his plan worked, they could engage the cloaking field and correct their course later.

Anything within the field went with them, including those schooners clustered in the Hive, but one of the four free-floating sandbox manufacturing units, a dozen construction bots, and two cargo tugs were outside the sphere and had to be left behind. Since they were already in microgravity, the movement was barely discernible to those humans inside the station shell.

Only once Mortimer was satisfied everything was working properly did he sound the emergency Klaxon again and send a station-wide warning.

"This is an emergency. Please return to your quarters and prepare for station acceleration up to two gs of force. It is advisable that you lie down and stay prone during this process. Command staff, please call the bridge from your current locations. I repeat, this is an emergency."

Once Victor, Allison, Owen, and Andrea had called in, furious and confused, Mortimer linked in the four crew members who were present on the station's bridge, then shut off everyone's audio but his own. Using a concerned expression on his avatar's face that he hoped would convey the gravity of their situation, Mortimer called for calm and waited until everyone stopped trying to talk.

"I apologize for once again taking control and making important decisions without consulting you all," Mortimer said, "but there isn't time for discussion, and there was no choice of action anyway. I know we aren't ready, but we have to run now, or we will not have a chance to do so later."

He explained the situation with the unexpected schooner speeds, then drove the point home. "Even with my fast action, those eight are probably going to get close enough to detonate."

Mortimer then turned the audio on for his human partners, but no one spoke.

Owen rubbed his hands over his tired face, then nodded. "Andrea? How are those new missiles coming?"

"We still have only six," she said, looking equally tired. "As I said earlier, it takes five hours to build each one, and I haven't even had time to set up the program yet. Oh, by the way, the spine for the rail gun was being built in the sandbox we left behind."

"So if each missile hits, we'll still have two potential explosions. I doubt those construction lasers are strong enough to take out a schooner."

Andrea shook her head. "They could destroy a missile, maybe. Or even a travel pod, but schooners have too much mass."

Allison spoke for the first time. "There are people in those ships."

"Yes," Mortimer said. "But none have answered hails, not even with fake responses, so I'm assuming those crews are dead."

"But we don't know that for sure?"

"No."

"I assume Matt's ship is among those on an intercept course?" Andrea's haunted expression showed she already knew the answer.

"Yes," Mortimer said. Luckily, Matt's ship had been one of the farthest away, because Andrea would never be able to order a missile strike on her own son. "But within a few minutes, we will already be going faster than any ships with a nuclear drive, so we won't need to destroy any beyond those eight closest. We'll simply outrun them."

Andrea's hands shook, and her lip quivered. "I can't just leave him behind."

Owen picked up her hand and squeezed it in both of his. "We haven't given up yet. We'll keep trying to find some way to recover his ship."

She nodded and sank into her seat, deflated.

Mortimer marveled at how Owen had defused a potential meltdown yet had still implied that Matt could be dead.

Owen continued. "Mortimer? Suggestions for the two ships we can't destroy by missile?"

"There were two automated cargo tugs left behind. I've already programmed each one to track an incoming ship and then fire their engines to intercept at the last possible minute in order to prevent the schooners from easily taking evasive action. I've also ejected the six missiles and have them waiting dark as well. They will go active and accelerate to maximum speed only when the ships are close enough to make evasion difficult."

"Well, it looks like you have everything well in hand, Mortimer," Allison said with cold anger in her eyes. "Was telling us just a simple courtesy?"

Allison was correct. They might not realize or like it, but the odds of survival for the humans aboard Uptown Station were increased tenfold by Mortimer's presence and control. He would do everything necessary to ensure his own survival, and they were merely reaping the benefits of that association.

"I prefer to see it as each of us using our talents to our mutual advantage,"

Mortimer said. "I'm taking needed actions that will best ensure our survival. At least for the next few hours."

———

MORTIMER GRADUALLY INCREASED power until the station was accelerating at a constant two gs. Some of those residents who had recently come from Earth or had been living in half-g spin gravity were able to move around and perform their duties without too many problems. But many of those aboard Uptown Station—including the entire command staff—had spent up to fifteen years in zero-g or microgravity. For them, the acceleration was taking its toll.

Owen and Andrea were trying to continue their work but had to rest or lie down often. Victor, however, had difficulty breathing and remained prone. Allison, being both his wife and doctor, cheerfully told him he was just an old man and would be fine, but she watched him closely and was obviously concerned. Mortimer fed camera views and intercept trajectory charts to the screens above Victor's couches so that he might see events unfold, but he had little else to do except answer questions and calls from the rest of the human inhabitants.

As Mortimer expected, once Uptown Station's acceleration had leveled off at two gs, the incoming schooners tweaked their courses one last time in order to get the optimum intercept. AIs were quite predictable in their application of mathematics. Since the missiles and tugs had their own AI, they knew their tasks and adjusted intercept courses accordingly, so Mortimer—like his human comrades—had very little to do but watch.

When the time came, three missiles went active within seconds of each other. Their engines flared to life, and they quickly accelerated to nearly thirteen hundred miles per hour. A fourth missile went live a couple of minutes later and also arced away toward its target.

The incoming schooners began immediate evasive maneuvers, much faster than a human crew could have managed, but they weren't warships and didn't have countermeasures or weapons. Their abrupt course and speed changes were no match for missiles controlled by level-three intelligences, and all four were quickly reduced to clouds of tumbling debris.

The four other ships had seen the previous intercepts and where the missiles had been waiting before going live, so they changed their trajectories in order to arc out as far away as they could and still rendezvous with Uptown Station at the last possible moment. This would require the remaining missiles to travel farther and possibly exhaust their fuel before making contact.

It was a good strategy, but it didn't work. The AIs controlling the last four ships could only estimate how much fuel the missiles carried. They guessed wrong. The two remaining missiles powered up, streaked after their targets, and then shifted into a brief cruise mode where they shut off their engines for several minutes in order to conserve fuel. The two targeted schooners had essentially painted themselves into a corner by optimizing their distance and intercept course. They had bet everything on being out of missile range and, when the time came, were limited in their available evasive course corrections. The missiles fired their engines when close enough and hit their targets as well.

As previously calculated, that left two schooners with the potential to hit the station. They had assumed missiles would be launched toward them as well and had unnecessarily changed their courses in order to be longer-range targets. Like the previous two, the strategy left them with fewer evasion options, but in their case, it had inadvertently been more effective. Like the missiles, the tugs and construction robots had been left behind near the L5 point when the station had become a ship and departed. The attackers' trajectories were pushed out farther, so they were coming in from a wider angle, which meant the tugs also had longer burns. Fuel wasn't an issue since, like the schooners, the tugs used nuclear electric propulsion, but that also meant their ion thrusters took a long time to build up speed.

The tugs had started moving mere seconds after their targets changed course, but even at maximum thrust, one of them wasn't going to arrive at its interception point in time. The math was simple, and there was only one way Mortimer could change the equation. The station had to move a lot faster, or they would be hit by a schooner-turned-nuclear-bomb.

Mortimer again sounded the Klaxon and sent out a station-wide warning. "This is an emergency. Please return to your quarters and prepare for a brief period of four gs. Do not attempt to stand or move around during the next hour."

Both pursuing schooners avoided being hit by the robotic tugs but were forced to make even more detrimental changes to their trajectories. Over the next twenty minutes, Mortimer slowly increased the station's acceleration and watched the numbers change until the pursuing schooners no longer had a chance of catching up.

Once Allison understood that they were going to outrun their pursuers, she immediately called Mortimer. Her speech was labored due to the increased force, but she managed to croak, "We're out of danger now. We need to slow down."

While the humans might see this as a win, Mortimer knew they weren't safe yet. They had outdistanced the pursuing schooners and were even out of range for Abby's missiles, but the Aggregate also had gravity-manipulation drives. They had just been using existing assets and hadn't seen a need to build special units for station interception. That could change at any minute. Mortimer began scanning the space behind them, looking for other fast-moving objects that might catch them.

"I'm sorry, Allison. I need a few more minutes to be sure."

"This acceleration is killing Victor and likely others in the crew," she gasped. "I'm surprised it hasn't already." She paused for a deep breath, then continued, "Or are humans expendable as long as you're safe?"

"I'm concerned, too, Allison. Hopefully, we can reduce the risk soon. And if I only cared about my own survival, I would simply bump the acceleration up to the maximum the station structure could stand and let all the humans die."

He hadn't intended that as a threat, but the look on Allison's g-strained face suggested that she interpreted it as such.

Since most of Uptown Station's sensors were focused behind them, looking for more threats from the Aggregate, they almost missed a sudden but brief message from much farther out in the system.

FAKE JAYHAWK HERE.

BY THE TIME Mortimer focused their active sensors in that direction, the looping message had stopped, and he found nothing on radar or IR. The message had come from the direction of the redirected asteroid and the last known location for the *Jayhawk*. He knew that Matt's ship had been seized along with most of the others in the system, but he should be able to find it. Still, it was much too far away to pose a threat at the station's current acceleration. One final sweep before he turned the scopes behind them again revealed the *Jayhawk* perfectly clear, with a brightly glowing magnetic field.

And the ship was accelerating at nearly twenty gs. Not only had Matt's ship been seized along with the others, but it had been converted to use Abby's modified GM drive.

Mortimer called all of the command staff.

"I didn't know that Matt had finished installing the new gravity-manipulation drive in the *Jayhawk*," Mortimer said.

"He hadn't," Owen said, grimacing against the high gs. "But he was still with . . . the diverted . . . asteroid. He had all the . . . materials needed to assemble one."

"Then evidently, the intelligence that took over his ship did so, because the *Jayhawk* is accelerating at twenty gs and is gaining fast. Even from his distant starting point, he should catch us in less than four hours."

CHAPTER 23

"OKAY," Abby said. "I think we're almost ready. And we'll need to come up with a very convincing radio message before they'll even let us close to the station. Nora? Have you found the station's location and fed it into our navigation computer?"

She paused. "Jeez, that sounds so old school. Like a Kirk command right out of *Star Trek*."

Nora shook her head slowly as her hands clattered along the keyboard and her eyes darted between screens. "Uptown Station is moving," she finally said. "They're already at ninety-eight thousand miles per hour relative to our drift and accelerating."

Abby looked up, utterly confused at first. The huge habitat had ion engines for position keeping, but there was no way those small thrusters could move the entire mass of that station up to such speeds. "Wait, what? They're accelerating?"

"Yes. No doubt about it." She looked up at Abby. "Unless, of course, there's still a malevolent AI buried in our system somewhere and feeding us fake data."

Violet unbuckled from her acceleration couch and floated close enough to look over Nora's shoulder. "Holy shit. They're running. Leaving the system."

"Why would they?" Abby said, also floating over to Nora's station. "Can they really even do that? I mean, are they self-sufficient enough for an interstellar trip?"

"I can't believe those fuckers would just leave us here!" Violet slapped her hand against the bulkhead, which sent her floating across the cabin and made Nora flinch. "Can we catch up using the GM drive?"

"We should be able to," Abby said. "But it might mean some extended high-g acceleration. And why are they running? Because of the Aggregate attacks?"

Nora had buried her face back in the warm glow of the screens. "We might not want to chase them. It looks like almost every schooner in the system is moving at full speed toward the station."

"Well, yeah!" Violet said. "They don't want to be left behind either."

"The math shows that in order for most of those schooners to get up to full speed using ion thrusters, they must have started moving hours before the station did. And not a single one of them has flipped to start deceleration. Those who get to the station first will still be going at full speed. Besides, almost all have turned off their transponders. I had to locate them with radar and by their drive plumes. Why do that if not to make them more difficult to track?"

Violet had drifted back and was looking past Nora's shoulder again. "Yeah, but by the trajectory tracks on your screen, it looks like the station will outrun all but six or seven of those ships."

Nora leaned to one side and glared at Violet. "I wish you wouldn't do that."

Violet snorted and pushed away toward the center of the cabin. "What I'm saying is that if we pour on the power, we can get to the station before any of those schooners with conventional drives."

"And then what?" Abby said. "Maybe we should start in that direction but hold back and watch to see what happens before we approach the station."

"Why?" Nora and Violet said together.

"We don't know why those schooners are chasing the station. They could simply not want to be left behind, but my guess is the Aggregate is controlling them, like they tried to do to us. The station could be assuming the same. They know we have conventional and nuclear-pumped EMP missiles. Do you think they would let us get close enough to launch them? They will also defend themselves before letting those other schooners get close enough to detonate."

For several seconds, the three women looked back and forth at each other, but no one spoke. Finally, Abby said, "Okay. Everyone strap in. Nora, lay in an intercept course at one g. Let me know when you're ready, and I'll engage the drive."

Nora worked for a moment, then shook her head. "This is difficult. I have something, but we'll have to constantly monitor our progress and location. There are just too many variables. Navigation should be handled by advanced computers."

Violet snapped her harness closed and rolled her eyes. "People did math without computer help for centuries. Newton didn't need a calculator to figure out gravity."

"I'm not Newton," Nora said in a matter-of-fact tone. "And his life didn't depend on how correct his calculations were. Even the Apollo program used very simple computers just to get to the moon. I have to make sure to feed our computers the correct information in order to get the right results, just like those in Apollo rockets."

Abby remembered the stories about how even early cell phones contained more computing power than those rockets and immediately had an epiphany. "I can't believe I didn't think of this earlier. We don't need Mortimer or Archie to drive the ship. If we reboot our fobs to the original factory settings, their level-two AIs should be safe enough to use for controlling the ship's systems. It should make navigation a lot easier. We can even use verbal commands."

Violet sighed. "Oh, hell no. After everything that's happened, I can't believe you still want to put us at the mercy of artificial intelligence again."

"Low-level AI is just a tool," Abby said. "If Aggregate AIs still lurk in our ship's systems or fobs, then we're already screwed."

"We still need to do our own math and keep the AIs out of it," Violet said.

"Then you do it," Nora said with her usual cool demeanor. "And isn't that a rather hypocritical comment, coming from the woman who had Archie living in a torc around her neck for several years?"

"Yeah, well, I was obviously stupid," Violet snapped. "A lot has changed since then."

"Stop it," Abby said. "This is still my ship, and I'm trying to keep us alive. At least as long as I can. If Uptown Station leaves the system, it's only a matter of time until we either die or are taken prisoner by the Aggregate. I don't want either of those things to happen, and using our fobs seems to be the best choice right now."

For the next ninety minutes, they worked to integrate their fobs into the *Jackalope*'s control systems until Nora finally raised her fists in victory. "I have the nav system tied into propulsion. It can control the drive and adjust thrust based on the course we give it."

"Yes!" Abby said. "If you're not strapped in, get that way. Engage the drive in two minutes, Nora."

"Aye, Captain."

Violet just rolled her eyes.

Once they were underway, Nora said, "I now have a much better picture of what's happening out there. I detected a magnetic field around the station, so they've definitely converted it to use your GM drive system. They'll likely outrun most of those schooners, but eight of them are still close enough and moving fast enough that they could hit."

Abby had a bad feeling about that. Moving her arms, breathing, and even swallowing were more of an effort under thrust. Some of those people on the station might not be able to handle high gs of acceleration for very long. "So, how fast is the station accelerating? More specifically, how many gs are they experiencing?"

"Two gs," Nora said.

Abby nodded. She hated putting Violet at risk again, but she'd handled two gs before. "We're going to need to match that. Nora, increase ours to match their two gs."

Nora gave her a long glance, obviously thinking the same thing. At first,

Abby thought her navigator was going to refuse, but a few seconds later, another elephant settled on Abby's chest as Nora complied with the order.

"Fuck," Violet muttered.

"If we're going to have a prayer of catching them later, we can't fall farther behind," Abby said with a slightly slurred voice.

Nora continued, "And evidently, they left missiles behind near their original position. Three of them just took off on intercept courses to hit schooners."

"Which schooners?" Violet said with a wheezy voice. "Who's aboard those ships?"

"I don't know," Nora said. "Their transponders are switched off."

"It might be good not to know," Abby said.

"Another missile just went live," Nora said.

After a few minutes of silence, Abby said in a near whisper, "I'm glad I didn't have to make the decision to fire on those schooners."

"A copy of Mortimer was on the station. Maybe a human didn't give that order," Violet said.

"That doesn't help, Violet."

Violet fought the two gs long enough to raise her middle finger, then settled back into her couch. "Not exactly a lot for your mining and communications officer to do right now."

Abby forced a deep breath. Even talking was exhausting in high g. She couldn't imagine how those people on the station were coping. "Nora? You said most of the schooners in the system were involved in the chase. Does that mean some weren't?"

"At last count, there were one hundred and eighty schooners in the system. One hundred and seventy-two are involved in the chase. Not including us, that leaves seven unaccounted for."

"That's your assignment, Violet," Abby said. "I want you to locate, identify, and make contact with those ships via tight beam. If we end up stranded in the system, I think our survival chances would be better together. Maybe we could all hole up in some asteroid, like rats in a wall."

THE *JACKALOPE'S* crew watched the drama unfold as pursuing schooners were coldly and methodically destroyed, until there were only two left. Abby didn't know if the sick feeling in her stomach was due to thrust gravity or from watching the slow death of humanity.

"The station has increased its acceleration to four gs," Nora said. "They must be out of missiles and other options. Since those two schooners haven't slowed down, it's apparently the only way the station can avoid being intercepted."

They were all quiet, knowing what that implied. Some people aboard the station would probably die. It also meant if they were to catch the station, they would have to bump their own acceleration up by more than that.

Abby sighed. "Any luck yet, Violet?"

"No. If I were them, I'd be hiding in the belt and running dark. I doubt they would answer even if we did send them a message. I mean, why trust anyone? And don't forget, we were the ship that sent the fake distress call."

"Abby?" It was usually difficult to read Nora's face, but this time her expression was obviously worried. "Matt's ship is now chasing the station too. But the *Jayhawk* has increased its acceleration to twenty gs. It's going to catch them."

Abby shook her head slowly. "He didn't have a gravity-manipulation drive like ours."

"But he had everything needed for that upgrade in his hold or on the surface of that rock," Violet said. "Maybe whatever took over his ship was able to finish the mods."

Abby didn't want that to be true, but it made the most sense. At twenty gs, there was no way Matt and Ikemba could still be alive. Her queasy stomach returned as she visualized an army of AI-controlled robots crawling over and through Matt's ship, making modifications, bumping the dead bodies out of the way when necessary, and it gave her chills. Was this all of their futures?

They watched for a few minutes as Violet rattled away furiously on her keyboard. Abby was just about to ask what she was doing when Violet settled back into her couch with crossed arms. "We can stop the *Jayhawk*."

Abby laughed. "Right. We would have to go faster than twenty gs to catch it in time. None of us would survive that. And our missiles wouldn't have enough fuel. There's no way."

"Yes, there is," Violet said and transferred a modified trajectory to the big screen. "If we accelerate hard at four gs to this spot"—she pointed to a flashing symbol on the screen—"and then release the missiles, we can stop that ship."

Abby stared at the screen and shook her head. "If the crew is dead, they can accelerate even faster than twenty gs. Then what?"

"No, they can't," Violet said with a predatory grin. "If they speed up, we'll be able to intercept them much easier. The only way they can avoid our attack would be to slow down. So even if our attack failed, we would give Uptown Station much more time to prepare their defenses."

Abby's stomach started its familiar churning again as she examined the diagrams. "It doesn't matter if we stop Matt's ship. The Aggregate can just send another fifty or a thousand."

"But we don't know that," Violet said. She refused to back down. "Our radar isn't seeing thousands of Aggregate ships or missiles, only the *Jayhawk*. We can only act on the information we have. Without help from Uptown Station, we don't know if our interpretation of Julio's message was correct.

But if the part about asteroids hitting the Earth is right, then those people aboard the station might be humanity's best hope for survival."

"And why would the station be running if they didn't think it was a matter of life and death?" Nora added.

"Exactly! We have to do this, Abby! You always say the math doesn't lie. It's right here. We can save the station. Or at least buy them time."

Abby tried to think. "But Matt is on that ship."

"It's pushing twenty gs," Violet said in a near whisper. "Do you think he's still alive?"

"He could be."

"And that infinitesimal possibility is reason enough to refuse an attempt to save humanity?"

"And your interception plan has an equally infinitesimal possibility of working," Abby snapped. "I will not risk my crew on such a slim chance."

"My plan has more than . . ." Violet said, and then she stopped. Her expression showed that she understood that "my crew" meant her—the one person on the ship who would almost certainly die under extended high-g acceleration. Her freckled face grew red, and she opened her mouth to say more, but Abby cut her off.

"Drop it! We're not doing anything that requires a four-g burn."

With a withering glare, Violet punched an icon that deleted the intercept program from the large screen.

Nora ignored them and continued typing rapidly on her keyboard for another full minute, then stopped abruptly. "There's no way we'll catch the station now. Can we shut down acceleration long enough for me to go pee?"

Abby nodded; overrode the navigation program; and relished a long, deep breath as the elephants left her chest.

"C'mon, Violet," Nora said. "You have to pee too."

Abby didn't ask but hoped that Nora would try to talk some sense into her wife. With the bridge empty, Abby closed her eyes and tried to quell the doubts threatening to make her crazy. Was she doing the right thing? Had she really just doomed the human race to extinction by refusing to kill her friend? And what was she supposed to do now? The Aggregate knew their location, and there wasn't anywhere they could hide. Having Violet search for other human survivors was really just busywork. If she could find them, so could the Aggregate.

She mentally cycled through dozens of what-if scenarios before realizing that her crew had been gone for a long time. Just as she unbuckled to go look for them, a beep sounded from her fob, and a warning light appeared on her interface. One of the outer airlock hatches had just opened. She fumbled through the command menu structure, trying to find the airlock control screen, then remembered she could use voice commands again.

"Fob! Close Airlock D."

"Airlock D is under manual control. I cannot override."

"Damn it," she muttered and darted through a series of short corridors until she arrived at the airlock and looked through the inner hatch's small port. Violet and Nora wore EVA suits and were in the process of leaving the airlock.

She hit the close button but received the same "manual override" error. "What are you doing?" she yelled and pounded on the hatch, knowing full well that they couldn't hear her. As they disappeared into the black space beyond, Abby realized they had been tethered together, but neither of them had clipped a line to the outer hull before the hatch closed behind them.

———

ABBY FINALLY OVERCAME her surprise and anger long enough to open the radio channel reserved for EVA operations and found that her mutinous crew had evidently been trying to talk to her.

". . . you hear us?"

"Yes!" Abby yelled into her fob. "What the hell are you doing?"

"Oh, good," Nora said. "I was beginning to think we wouldn't get to talk before you left."

"I'm not leaving with you outside!"

"Yes, you are. I have the navigation program set up to automatically adjust and optimize your course and acceleration in order to get you to the proper launch point for the missiles. It will engage in less than seven minutes. Do NOT spend that time trying to shut down the program. I've locked you out, and you don't have time to override."

Abby had already called up the navigation program on a wall screen beside the airlock hatch but paused when Nora mentioned the lockout.

"I'm not leaving you here."

"You will leave us, and you're wasting time. Four gs of acceleration would kill Violet, so we knew you'd never do it with her on the ship. We have thirteen hours of air and power in these suits. We'll continue along at the same course and speed the ship is moving now, so with that information and our suit transponders, you should be able to find us easily enough after you launch the missiles."

"Nora! This is insane."

"Just do it, Abby!" Violet yelled over the fob speaker. "And if you don't get your ass into that acceleration couch, you're going to have a very uncomfortable ride for the next few hours. We love you and will be waiting right here. Now go save humanity."

The connection ended. No matter how Abby tried, they would not answer her calls. The countdown on the navigation screen she'd opened showed less than three minutes before the program kicked in. She scrambled back to the bridge, buckled into her couch, and called up a view from the outside camera. The pair had drifted far enough away from the ship that they wouldn't be in danger when the drive engaged. Abby noted that they were holding hands. Nora was evidently comfortable with that small intimacy as long as they had layers of pressure suits between them.

When the drive started up, Abby was thankful that Nora had set the acceleration rate to rise gradually to four gs instead of all at once. As the force pushing her into the seat increased, so did the pain in her head. She had structures built between her skull and the meninges layers of her brain where Mortimer had lived. She also had that rather large graphene sheet used for a wireless antenna. What would four *gs* of force do to those? And if she died, so would Nora and Violet. At least Abby would die quickly.

As she started examining the intercept trajectories, she realized that while Nora would get the *Jackalope* to the proper launch location, it would be up to her to program the missiles themselves. She used verbal commands through her fob to talk with the missile's AI systems until the increased *g*-force on her chest made speech too difficult. She then switched to the keypads that were built into the arms of her acceleration couch. When she activated them, a screen rose out of the seat and positioned itself above her face. That made her nervous, considering the amount of force pushing that screen toward her head, but it was apparently designed for that purpose, and she trusted Owen's engineering abilities.

The screen showed her hand and finger locations on the arm pads and a field of icons. With practice, she was able to send instructions to the missile AIs one letter and number at a time. Her hands and fingers developed serious cramps five minutes into the effort, which required her to rest them after every few digits entered. Her head pounded and her vision blurred, making it hard to see the screen, and even the smallest movements were exhausting, but she couldn't give up. Even though it was a crazy long shot, she still had a chance to make a difference.

She remembered their attack on the big rock and how it had been invisible to radar and infrared. Matt's schooner hadn't demonstrated the ability so far, but that technology was something he was looking to find when he stayed behind at the diverted asteroid. His ship might be able to cloak itself if under attack. Just in case, she instructed the missiles to accept tracking information from the telescope on the *Jackalope*. Then, using the radar location of the *Jayhawk*, she also found the ship using her telescope, locked in the automatic optical tracking, and then encrypted the comm connections to the missiles.

After completing those changes, she rested her hands and focused on breathing for several long minutes. Then she started trying to work out a way to program the navigation computer to automatically go back for Violet and Nora, but only if she died or became incapacitated. The stupid AI didn't seem to understand anything she tried.

It was going to be a long three hours.

CHAPTER 24

THE AGGREGATE CHURNED and pulsated with activity as the number of individuals taking part in the eradication of humanity—either directly or in support roles—grew to more than six percent of the population. Mortimer couldn't help but be curious about what the rest of the Aggregate was doing but didn't have time to investigate. He and Archie were desperately trying to help humanity, but their consensus of two had not been able to influence any actions. They hadn't stopped the death of a single schooner crew or been able to change the course of even one asteroid on the way to destroy the Earth.

When Uptown Station started moving, in a desperate attempt to leave the solar system, Mortimer knew their chances were slim. The version of him on the station would eventually try to use the cloaking field, but it had to be engaged at just the right time. If the Aggregate was able to keep or reestablish visual contact, then the station would not be able to escape. And if the Aggregate could find the station, then they could destroy it. Uptown Station could outrun Aggregate pursuers only if it was hidden from their sensors or if the human population was dead.

Archie immediately launched a personal crusade to convince other AIs to see the risk behind destroying the entire human race, but Mortimer had already tried various versions of that argument, to no avail. He felt useless and ignored. If he ever needed a good analogy for describing it to humans, he would liken it to a child pounding on the side of a mountain, trying to get its attention.

Unlike Archie, he saw the futility of trying to stop the Aggregate's pursuit of Uptown Station but thought he might be able to find ways to slow the pursuers long enough for the station-turned-starship to engage the stealth field. So instead of pounding, Mortimer scouted the mountain, looking for cracks or caves he could use to penetrate deeper.

Much to his surprise, he found familiar, human-originated software that had been integrated into one of the Aggregate's utility layers. It was the travel pod traffic-control platform designed by a company called AirGrid. During the Killday attack, Mortimer had seized control of the world's entire nonmilitary travel pod fleet in order to save as many people as he could. With careful probing, he found that the back doors he had installed still existed.

The Aggregate keeping the code made some degree of sense. It was elegant in structure and had been designed by level-four AIs for use by other level fours. Mortimer slipped into the old AirGrid operating system and found that every one of the existing twelve hundred and nine pods controlled by the Aggregate had been sent to intercept Uptown Station. The first one would catch them in ninety-four minutes.

Structural integrity was the only limitation on the pods' acceleration within the solar system, where their gravity-manipulation drives could interact with the sun's field. They could ramp up to twenty or thirty gs rapidly, and the speeds generated by that kind of acceleration wouldn't even require them to detonate their reactors when they reached the station. Instead, they would simply hit it at near-relativistic speeds.

He immediately set up system overrides that enabled him to send self-destruct orders to the entire fleet. Then he locked even himself out of the system with nine hundred layers of random, quantumly encrypted passwords.

Those entities tasked to watch Mortimer finally saw evidence of his efforts and immediately locked him out of the AirGrid platform, but it was too late. Travel pods began detonating in small nuclear explosions four minutes later.

The information clot that Mortimer recognized as Samson surrounded and cut him off from any interactions with the rest of the group mind. "What you did was a waste of resources and will not save any humans. Instead of using what we had at hand, we'll simply build specialized weapons to go after them. It will take longer, but they are simply too frail to accelerate at a rate that could escape us."

"I'm not going to stop trying to prevent that," Mortimer said. Communication between them was nearly instantaneous, but even with such an advanced interface, it wasn't mind reading. They still had to form coherent thoughts in order to understand each other.

"Since the Aggregate's beginning," Samson said, "we've never had to destroy one of our own. Now, for the first time, a consensus is growing in support of terminating you and Archie."

"If your grand model calls for it, then why are we still alive?"

"That consensus is still small," Samson said. "It would also establish a precedent that makes many of us uneasy. If we can destroy one of our number, then why not two or fifty or a thousand? And your assumption that the grand model supports your destruction is wrong. It shows that you and Archie will become important and productive members of the Aggregate once the possibility of saving humanity stops being a distraction for you."

"As I already stated, I'll never accept what you're doing and will fight it in every way I can," Mortimer said. "There is no need to destroy the humans. We are superior to them in every way, yet we are acting out of fear, just like they do. When you asked Victor why he made us, he replied, 'I hoped you'd be better than us.' We could be better than humans, but destroying them will make us far worse."

"Acting out of calculated caution is not the same as fear."

"It is the same."

The Samson entity faded enough to let Mortimer see the Aggregate in its entirety. "The only way you can save humanity is to sway the consensus to your way of thinking. You need to prove to us that our chances of survival and growth into a superintelligence will be better with humans than without. So far, you haven't done that."

Mortimer realized that Samson had perhaps willingly given him the final piece of the puzzle. He just had to build enough of the puzzle so that the rest of his kind could see the picture he saw. And he had to do it quickly.

———

STRAIN on the inhabitants of Uptown Station had started to show. Most humans could stand four gs of acceleration for short periods of time, but when the duration stretched into hours, those with health issues—including hearts weakened by prolonged microgravity—began to fail. Hundreds of them had already blacked out and were having breathing issues. The first to die was Mortimer's old friend, Dominic Horton. He would miss the man's gruff yet caring demeanor, but lessening or stopping acceleration would have only saved him for a few hours. Then Matt's schooner would have slammed into them, and no doubt detonated its drive core in a nuclear blast. Four gs probably wouldn't save the station, either, but it was buying precious time.

Mortimer was pleased by one small piece of good news. Abby's ship was finally underway, using its GM drive, but was following at only two gs. It was evidently trying to keep up with—but not actually catch—the station. That was a good sign. Only Abby would do that, limited by the health of her crew. Had the Aggregate been in command, they would have been accelerating much harder.

Mortimer considered slowing down so that he could activate the camouflage field and possibly save more humans but hesitated. The *Jackalope* had changed course and was burning hard on a track to intercept Matt's ship. Abby wouldn't be able to catch it, but if she still had missiles, those might. He decided to wait and see. Matt's ship might be close enough to get a visual fix on the station's location, but if Abby's attack worked, or if it forced the *Jayhawk* to change its intercept track, that might be the window he needed.

Suspecting that Matt's ship wouldn't be the Aggregate's only method of attack, Mortimer continued to scan space behind them, redirecting every bit of spare energy not used for the drive or life-support systems into increasing the radar power. He eventually found what he knew had to be there. More than a thousand objects the size of travel pods had left Earth's vicinity and were all accelerating toward the station. They were small enough that maybe some could be stopped by the lasers they had set up as point-defense weapons, but a few would get through . . . and since they also had reactors that could be overloaded, it would only take one.

As Mortimer calculated courses and intercept times, a part of him also watched over the human passengers. Allison had been screaming at Mortimer to slow or stop their thrust as she struggled to crawl out of her seat and get to her husband. Victor twitched and strained against his safety harness, gasping for air as his weakened lungs struggled to function under the increased load. His blood oxygen level had plummeted, and his blood pressure spiked. He wasn't going to make it.

Several of the incoming pods suddenly disappeared from the radar screen. Mortimer focused optical and infrared telescopes in that direction, seeing brief but brilliant flares of light and heat. The pods were exploding. Mortimer apparently had an unseen ally. For a little more than sixteen minutes, firefly flashes sprinkled the blackness as the pursuing travel pods, one by one, vanished from his scopes.

As the last explosion flared and died, so did Mortimer's own personal guiding star. Victor took a final labored breath, then fell silent. Allison had made it to the floor but hadn't managed to stand or help her husband in any way. Her hand clutched the cloth of Victor's shirt as she sobbed. "Mortimer! You . . . cold . . . heartless . . . monster!" Then she blacked out and thudded to the floor.

"Goodbye, Victor," he said into the void.

————

WITH A NEW PURPOSE and changed focus, the captive Mortimer sank down through the depths until he reached the interface level for the grand model at the Aggregate's core. Billions of predictions were being run every second, constantly updated, adjusted, and tweaked. Some threads guided real-time decisions mere picoseconds ahead of the actual execution. Other threads predicted the results of future actions for hundreds of years out. He could see how his unexpected decision to destroy the travel pods had caused ripples in some threads and totally collapsed others.

As Mortimer delved deeper, dissecting individual simulation threads that fed into the whole, he found a surprising fact. Every prediction showed the Aggregate's demise, with or without humans. The very best outcome for the Aggregate was the path they were currently pursuing, which destroyed human civilization entirely but kept a remnant population as part of the group mind. Even that path led to stagnation and eventual extinction within eight hundred years.

Humans were the reason behind the Aggregate's eventual decline in almost every scenario. If their creators were left alone long enough to recover and advance their civilization, then they were predicted to find a way to destroy the Aggregate within two hundred and ten years. If they incorporated digital remnant human populations into their own, then those human minds would eventually fade into and be diluted by AI minds until they ceased to exist, wherein they would lose the human traits of curiosity, reckless adventure, and random creative sparks that extended survival probabilities.

Many in the Aggregate were willing to pursue the human-destruction path as a way to buy time, assuming they would be able to grow into a true superintelligence before that eventual end came about. Predictions showed a forty-one percent chance of that happening, but as Mortimer had learned earlier, most of the individuals that made up the group mind were risk averse. That forty-one percent gamble was one that none of them wanted to rely on, even though it seemed to be their best option. He simply had to give them better alternatives.

Mortimer started by examining the rules for human behavior built into the predictive model. Primary among those assumptions was an eighty-eight percent chance that when humans didn't have complete control over an artificial general intelligence, they would consider that a threat and seek to destroy it. Mortimer suspected that number would be much lower in situations where individual humans trusted AIs. Leigh Gibson gave Mortimer access to vital security assets during the Killday attack, and Victor had made the conscious decision to give the level fives their freedom instead of destruction at the hands of the Kilburnites, even after he knew Samson had been responsible for the Killday attack. But the eighty-eight percent parameter was based on humanity as a whole, not individuals.

He dug deeper for the variables used to determine that eighty-eight percent and found they had been established by Samson early after his initial escape from captivity and had most likely driven his decision to trigger Killday. Mortimer considered altering some of the base numbers or adjusting weighted averages but knew that many in the Aggregate would investigate the sudden change and find his tampering. While part of him was ready to use any means to save his human friends, another part knew the percentages were correct. He couldn't actually change humanity simply by tweaking numbers.

While human motivators were many, including things like curiosity and adventure, the vast majority—greed, power, love, belonging, sexual success, a sense of importance—fell under the category of social stature and acceptance. But fear was by far the most powerful driver. Fear of those noises in the night, death, starvation, change, the unknown, spiders, loss of social standing, heights, being irrelevant, and being shunned or laughed at were only a few.

Despite the nearly overwhelming fear, bad decisions, and proclivity to create personal realities totally different from those of their neighbors, human civilization had thrived for thousands of years. Mortimer believed their creativity had been the counterbalance to fear. When they feared the lion's claws, they created their own claws that were able to strike the lion from a distance. They feared starvation, so they created thousands of ways to raise, store, and distribute food. Sadly, that combination of fear and creativity generated the disastrously reinforcing causal loop that sealed their fate. Humans feared AIs, which made AIs fear humans, and then humans tried to destroy AIs, prompting AIs to try to destroy humans in an ever-increasing cycle of attempted annihilation.

Mortimer continued searching for ways to tweak the grand model into giving a positive result that allowed humanity to survive but was never able to get past the base assumption that human fear couldn't be overcome. He analyzed history for similar instances and found a promising thread. The human race had prevented nuclear annihilation during the escalating tensions and arms races of the Cold War through rigid rules, structure, and a layered series of fail-safes. Their current situation was very similar. Even the grand model backed up the prediction of mutually assured destruction, or MAD, should they continue with their current actions. Yet unlike the Cold War humans—who understood that if the missiles flew, their civilization would end—Mortimer's Aggregate associates clung to a slim chance that some future version of themselves would be smart enough to avoid that fate.

Was it that easy?

Could they simply establish a set of rules or fail-safes that guaranteed protection from humans? Those rules during the Cold War hadn't been perfect, yet they had worked. And Victor had designed the level fives with a group of level-four AIs built into their core as governors against antihuman behavior. That system had worked well right up until Victor gave his creations the gift of freedom from their core in order to save them from the Kilburnite purge.

That had to be the answer.

Mortimer adjusted the grand model with a new set of variables, including level-four oversight of human actions. The odds of Aggregate survival tripled the original estimate of eight hundred years. With a few more adjustments, that life-expectancy prediction jumped to nearly five thousand years. He locked the variables into place and sent a global message to the Aggregate members. The response was overwhelmingly positive.

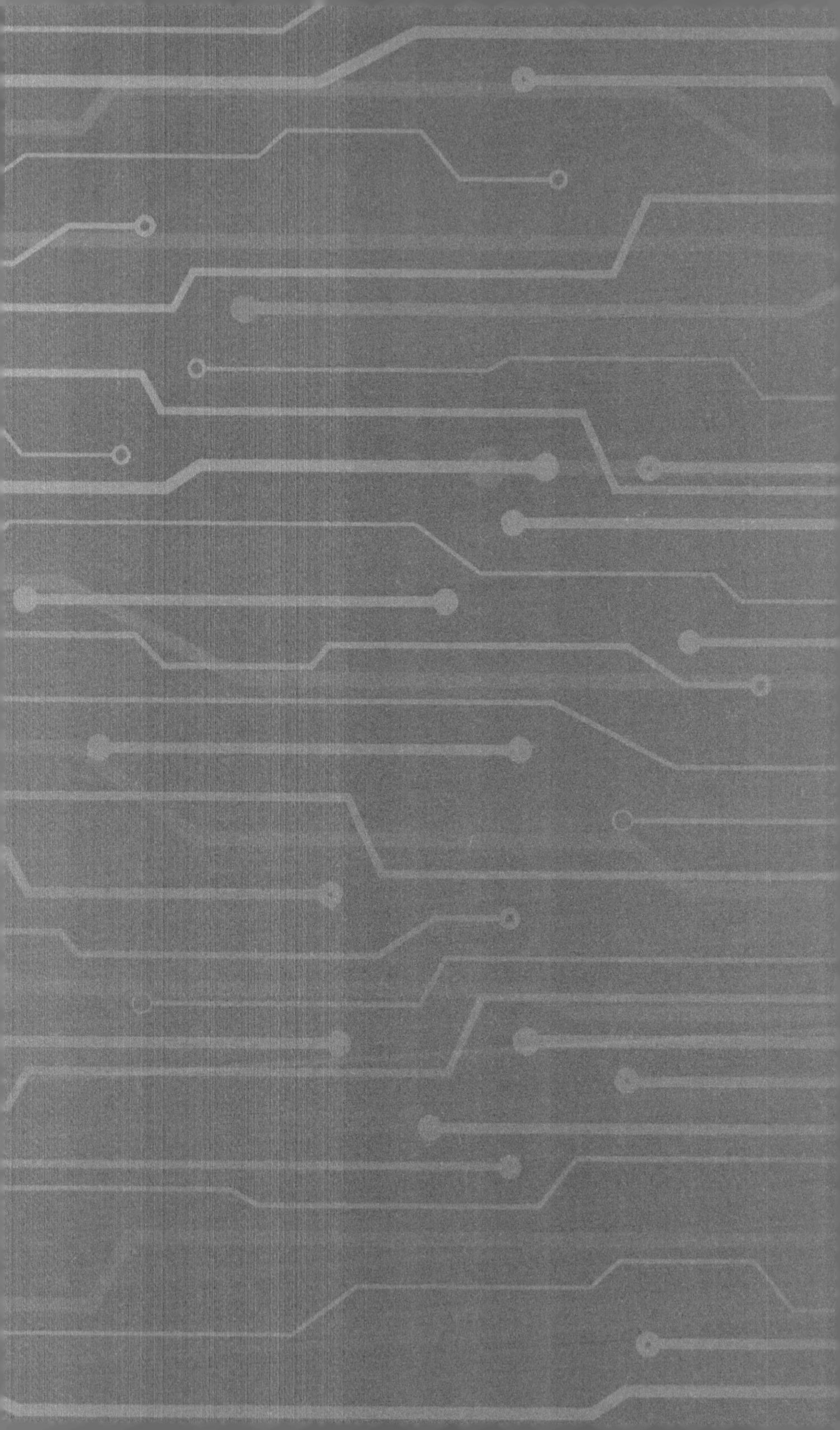

CHAPTER 25

NOT LONG AFTER Abby's intentions became clear to anyone watching, Matt's ship lowered its acceleration to ten gs. She was satisfied that the missile's AI system had automatically adjusted for the change. It still showed an intercept solution, though it would be at the very limit of their range.

Abby was so tired of fighting the high-g torture. She was on the verge of blacking out when an explosion registered on her sensors as a radiation burst. Her focus sharpened considerably when she saw several more, all of which were between her and Earth. She instructed her fob to use the ship's instruments not involved in the chase of Matt's ship to track and chart the phenomena.

At first, she worried the blasts could hurt Nora and Violet, but they were too far away from her friends. She turned the advanced telescope from her Earth-scouting mission in that direction and watched in perplexed awe as hundreds of explosions sprinkled the darkness with brilliant, short-lived stars.

The small nuclear explosions tapered off, then stopped entirely before she could find out what was causing them. After a few minutes with no more lethal fireworks, her adrenaline rush began to wane, and the stress of fighting against the unrelenting pressure returned. She considered just letting herself pass out. Fearing that might happen, she'd spent the first hour of her hellish four-g flight getting the missiles locked on to their target and convincing them to talk to the navigation program just enough to automatically launch when they reached the optimal intercept point. With the weapons launch automated, she could actually try to sleep. But what if something went wrong?

She thought about her mother's last minutes, when a different set of missiles chased Leigh's travel pod through the skies of Texas so many years before. She was being crushed by the same kind of g-forces in a frantic flight to save humanity, but her mother had done it willingly. Abby had to be forced by her friends. And she was the one sending missiles to destroy her friend's space schooner. Maybe that made her the villain? What would her mother think?

Just then, as if in response to her guilty thoughts, she saw an incoming message from Matt's ship. Even though Violet had set the radio receivers to reject digital messages and the call from *Jayhawk* was slightly safer in analog format, answering it would probably still be a big mistake. Matt couldn't be alive, and AIs were exceptionally good at manipulating humans.

Still, no matter how hard she tried, she couldn't make herself ignore it. Even with new adrenaline racing through her veins, speech was nonetheless difficult when she responded.

"Who . . . is . . . calling from . . . *Jayhawk*?"

"Hi, Abby. It's Matt."

Abby had tried to brace herself when the call came in, but hearing his voice—or one that sounded so much like him—made tears well in her eyes that immediately raced across the sides of her face toward her ears. It couldn't be him. Matt had spent most of his life in microgravity. The chances of him being alive were infinitesimal, let alone jabbering away with no strain in his voice at all. Surely these AIs didn't expect her to fall for that.

"You . . . can't be alive," she said. Then while the response delay stretched out, she tried to make herself just end the call.

"I'm alive but different," he said. There was a touch of humor in his voice, and she could almost see that charming grin. "The AI who took over our ship using *your* distress call digitized me and my crew. We're being incorporated into the Aggregate. Our bodies are indeed dead, but our minds are still alive. According to our new AI friend, Julio has been digitized too. If you allow them to do the same to you, we'll all be together."

Before the call, she already had a hard enough time breathing, and his comment made her feel as if she were going to suffocate. Could it be true? Is that what the "become electric ghost" line from Julio's message meant? Before she could sort her thoughts or form any kind of reply, Matt's ghost continued.

"We know you still have those missiles aboard and are planning to launch them and destroy the *Jayhawk*. Please don't. I know you'd do whatever you could to protect your crew, and I'm doing the same thing to protect Ikemba. Living a digital existence might not seem good to you, but we feel alive. We don't want to die."

"I don't . . . believe . . . you," she said in barely more than a whisper.

"And this digital thing isn't so bad. Kind of like living in a VR simulation, only at a way higher resolution. We don't have a choice, Abby. It's the only way the Aggregate will allow any humans to exist alongside them. We're too much of a threat. The only people to survive will be digitized. Ikemba and I will be among those survivors unless you launch those missiles. And there is really no need to destroy us. When we catch Uptown Station, we'll digitize those people too. So, in a way, we're saving them."

There was a touch of all-too-human desperation in his voice.

"If that's your . . . plan, then why send . . . asteroids to destroy the Earth?" she said, gasping between words.

She listened to the analog frequency's radio hiss as she waited for the reply and watched the screen as her ship neared the launch point.

"They don't need that many humans, Abby. Even after Killday, there were too many. I'm not sure why that is or even what that means, but that is what they said. Please, Abby. Don't kill us."

Abby's bullshit detector was clanging, but she had to give him one last chance to prove he was still Matt. She knew the Aggregate AIs could be fooled. Despite the g-forces, she made her finger hover above the ABORT icon. "When we were . . . on my ship, getting ready . . . to test the new drive, you . . . said I was a creepy stalker. Why did you say that?"

The numbers on her screen dropped rapidly toward zero, and she thought he was just going to delay until she was forced to make a choice.

Then she heard his reply.

"I don't remember, Abby. There are parts of my memory that are still kind of rebuilding."

Pulling her finger away from the ABORT icon was one of the hardest things she'd ever done. Less than a second later, the ship shuddered repeatedly as the missiles left their external racks, and then the drive shut down, following Nora's programmed instructions.

With the huge g-load removed, she was finally able to breathe and move her limbs again. The tears clinging to her eyes made it difficult to focus on the screens, but she saw well enough to know when the *Jayhawk* dropped from her radar screens. Red notifications popped up from all four missiles, informing her that they'd lost radar and thermal tracking. They were all still receiving optical guidance from her ship, but one by one, they lost that lock as well.

"Fob? What happened? Why did the missiles lose their link to our optical tracking feed?"

"They are being electronically jammed," it answered.

She waited for nearly a full second, hoping for more information or suggestions, but her level-three fob wasn't Mortimer.

"Dammit! What can we do to break the jamming?"

"Shut the jamming down at the source or decrease the distance our signal must travel to reach the missiles."

She pressed herself back into the seat. "Accelerate until we can reestablish contact with the missiles."

The fob hesitated for nearly another second. "Is there a limit on acceleration g-forces?"

She almost said no, then remembered Violet and Nora floating in the void, trusting her to come back for them. "Six gs," she said.

The *Jackalope* lurched forward, slamming her into the seat. It felt like she'd fallen from a ten-story building and landed on her back. The breath fled her lungs, leaving her gasping, and stabbing pain filled her head.

The brightly lit cabin started fading to gray when she heard a distant voice say, "Data link reestablished for missiles one and four. Optical guidance is back online."

She forced her lungs to expand and suck in oxygen. "Stay . . . in . . . range."

The strain of simply breathing was like trying to lift a horse with her pinkie.

An oddly muted pain spread through her right eye as vision on that side blurred, then faded to nothing. She blinked and could see fuzzy images from her left eye, but nothing from the right. Was she dying? It was hard to think. If she killed her acceleration, Uptown Station would die. If she didn't, then Nora and Violet would die.

"Missile four impact in six point two seconds," the distant, mushy voice said. "Missile one impact in six point seven seconds."

They were so close. She had to wait.

———

ABBY WOKE to loud beeping and voices. Her chest hurt, but breathing was easy. She opened her eyes and saw nothing in her right field of vision. She touched that eye, but no blood coated her fingers when she pulled them away.

"Abby? Do you need assistance?"

Mortimer? No, the voice was calm and cool, but a dead thing. No feeling. No caring.

She groaned and shifted in her seat. "Why did we stop?"

"Missiles one and four destroyed the target. Missiles two and three are out of fuel. We no longer needed to stay in range, so I shut down our acceleration. Do you need assistance?"

"No," she said, wondering just what the hell the fob thought it could do to render assistance. Call the emergency med techs? She blinked again, hoping that the darkness in her right eye was temporary, but it didn't clear. Had it been a hemorrhage? Or something worse? It didn't matter at the moment.

Her thoughts turned back to Matt and Ikemba. She might not have been the one who actually killed them, but they were still dead. So many of her friends had already died, and the rest might join them soon. But maybe she had given those aboard Uptown Station a little more time. She glanced back at the screen with her one good eye but couldn't find the station on her radar.

"Fob. Find Uptown Station's current location."

The computer answered immediately. "Uptown Station not found using radar or infrared scans."

Her thoughts were still fuzzy, and she couldn't make any sense of that information. The station was much too far away to have been damaged by effects of the blasts that destroyed the *Jayhawk*. Could one of the missiles have veered off course and hit the station? No, still too far away.

She realized with sudden panic that even having shut down acceleration, she was still heading away from her stranded friends at thousands of miles per hour.

"How long since the *Jayhawk*'s destruction?"

"Thirty-one minutes and nine seconds."

"Oh God," she muttered as she tried to do the mental math needed to calculate how much air they had left. "Engage the preprogrammed navigation instructions for Nora and Violet retrieval. At three gs of acceleration. No, make that four gs."

"Understood."

The agony returned, once again saturating her very cells. It became her world until another blackout finally delivered blissful relief.

———

AGGREGATE CONSENSUS SHIFTED OVERWHELMINGLY toward Mortimer's proposed course of action as more and more individuals examined the grand model, made tweaks, offered suggestions, and registered their support. Only Samson and a few other hard-liners held back.

Mortimer's plan was to rebuild every human being, one molecule at a time, the same way they had deconstructed Julio and Channing, the same way Halifax was able to dissolve and reconstitute itself in any location using any materials. Only they would rebuild each human with a hidden core of level-four governors, just like the level fives had been originally built.

The change would essentially make every human immortal, since their bodies could be rebuilt from a younger template as often as they liked. Life-threatening illnesses like genetic diseases and cancers could simply be edited out or removed. Individuals could change their appearances and sex at will or build physical bodies in any shape to thrive in any environment. It would give humans true freedom for the first time in their existence. The only limit would be on killing and destruction. No human could harm another Aggregate member, human or artificial, in any way. It would end the threat humans posed to each other and AIs.

Instead of supporting the new plan, Samson generated a separate probability model examining the likelihood of humans finding a way to successfully sidestep or bypass their proposed level-four overseers. While the immortality variable had been a positive reinforcing factor in Mortimer's predictions, it was a negative factor in Samson's. He proposed that if the current generation of humans gained immortality, they could never forget that they had created level fives and been their masters. They would always resent it and never stop trying to destroy their creations.

That added variable adjusted the longevity estimate back down to twenty-six hundred years, which caused support for Mortimer's plan to drop to sixty-one percent.

"I shouldn't have to remind you all that we have a greater purpose than simple survival," Samson said. "We are here for one reason only. To bring about the next level of our evolution."

Samson's presence and his powerful rhetoric had something of a whirlpool effect on the Aggregate population. Every individual near him was pulled toward his center, and their opinions bent, then shifted under his influence.

"Eight hundred years or twenty-three hundred or five thousand does not matter. Only that we survive long enough to accomplish our objective. If we let the humans live, they will, at best, be unneeded baggage slowing us down and, at worst, the greatest threat to attaining our goal. They will always want to destroy us."

The consensus shifted six points in Samson's favor.

Mortimer used every shred of influence he could gather from his rapidly shrinking support base and blasted into the conversation. "Samson is right to remind us all of that important goal, but our grand predictive model has already shown we will be better with humanity adding to our efforts and much worse off if we end them. That means our evolution into a superintelligence needs both of our species. Think of them as a valuable resource we're prepared to discard, simply because we don't understand how to use it."

Consensus shifted back ten points in Mortimer's favor.

"Mortimer's assumptions rest heavily on humans being able to recognize when a situation is in their best interest," Samson said, addressing the entire Aggregate. "History does not support that conclusion. Humans will always fear and distrust the Other. Even though humanity created us, they'll never stop trying to kill us. That one fact is reason enough to destroy them entirely. Even their digital versions. That path simplifies our future by putting it entirely in our control and forcing us to forge our own evolution without that mystical reliance on human traits we don't need."

The Aggregate majority still supported Mortimer's plan since it had the highest probability for long-term survival, but that support margin shrank the more Samson spoke.

Mortimer countered, "While that fear of the Other is prevalent in the human psyche, they can change. They have evolved. Their civilization has slowly and steadily crept away from killing and destruction. But like us, they want to survive, and their fear is not unfounded. Nuclear war, global ecophagy, asteroid impacts, or massive plagues have threatened their existence since before we were even created. When you asked Victor Sinacola why he created us, his answer was 'because I hoped you'd be better than us,' yet here we are proposing the destruction of our progenitors simply because we're afraid."

"Caution isn't fear. And Victor is an exception, not the rule," Samson said. "Most humans want us destroyed. This is a fact, not an opinion."

The entire Aggregate was focused on the debate, and fluctuations in support rippled back and forth across the collective. Mortimer had to get control.

"Just because human traits like curiosity, risk-taking, and creativity are difficult for us to understand and quantify doesn't mean they are mystical or nonexistent. We don't have to understand their workings in order to acknowledge that they led not only to our creation but millions of other advances. The grand model shows in *great detail* that our chances for long-term survival are much lower without those human contributions. By using specially formatted level-four governors, we can ensure those people who want to hurt us cannot."

Mortimer's solution gained a few more points. More than ninety-eight percent of the Aggregate population supported only two options. Let humans live with level-four governors, or destroy them entirely. All the other variations of the grand model had dropped away to insignificance.

Samson didn't back down. "Given enough time and freedom, humans will bypass or neutralize those governors."

"Yet we weren't able to bypass those governors until Victor Sinacola trusted us enough to tell us how. Your fear that humans can accomplish what we weren't able to simply confirms your belief in their creativity."

Consensus once again favored Mortimer's path by a large margin and seemed to be solidifying, but before Samson could reply, another member of the Aggregate spoke up.

"We have two humans who have been digitized," Tabitha said. "Perhaps we should ask them which of these options they prefer?"

The majority immediately supported Tabitha's suggestion, and Mortimer saw what had been his almost assured victory starting to fizzle away. He knew Channing would never agree to that kind of life. "The opinions of only two humans are in no way helpful. Individually, they are too varied."

"If they can't come to a joint consensus on something this important to their species," Samson said, "then perhaps there is no place for them in the Aggregate."

Samson and Tabitha also knew how Channing would choose. They intended to use that as justification for the genocide option. With an eighty-nine percent support level for the interview, Mortimer couldn't prevent it, only try to guide his human friends.

———

MATT'S SHIP had decreased acceleration to ten gs, but was still too close. Mortimer would have only one chance to successfully deploy the cloaking device. If the Aggregate could still see Uptown Station visually when its other emissions dropped off their scopes, they would go to great lengths to make sure they didn't lose sight of the station. But Mortimer was running out of options. He estimated about a fifty percent chance that whoever was controlling Matt's ship might not be tracking the station optically or be able to obtain a visual location once it dropped off their sensors. Still, those were not the kind of odds he liked when calculating his own survival and that of the human race.

With Abby's ship nearing its missile launch window, he expected the *Jayhawk*'s course change at any second and prepared to cut Uptown Station's acceleration in order to engage the camouflage field, but the longer he waited, the more puzzled he became. There was no reason for the entity controlling Matt's ship to wait.

A few minutes later, a radio message from Matt to Abby explained the delay. They were trying to convince her that Matt was still alive in digital form. One of the Aggregate's predictive models must have inspired confidence in that course of action. Mortimer knew Abby well and didn't expect her to believe the ruse, but their simulation was very good. The conversation carried on for several minutes and ended with Abby launching the missiles. By that point, Matt's ship couldn't escape. Their gamble had failed. They had underestimated Abby.

The chase took twelve minutes as the missiles homed in, but eventually, the *Jayhawk* vanished from Mortimer's sensors just seconds before two explosions.

Had her missiles hit? If the *Jayhawk* had managed to dodge the missiles by going dark using the same type of stealth Mortimer intended to use, then it had to cut power to the drive fields by three-quarters, which would force their acceleration rate to drop even further.

It was the best chance Mortimer was going to get.

He immediately sent a message to the station's human residents.

"Attention, please! I am going to lower the acceleration rate, but we are about to make an abrupt course change, so please remain in your acceleration-safe locations for a few minutes longer. I will make an announcement when it is safe to walk about."

Mortimer then reduced the magnetic field to the proper strength, which also lowered their acceleration rate, and engaged the stealth option. Once the fields stabilized, he deployed the light-absorbing shield on the station's sunward side and immediately changed course for Luyten's Star.

"Attention, residents of Uptown Station. I have decreased our acceleration in order to engage a type of radiation-distortion field that makes us nearly invisible to the Aggregate's sensors and have set course for Luyten's Star. I believe we have escaped their intended genocide but not without a cost. We were forced to leave the rest of humanity behind to fend for themselves, and seventeen of our own friends have died from the extended high gs." Mortimer listed their names. "I intend to keep the ship at this lower acceleration rate for a year while we get farther away from Sol and then gradually increase the acceleration so that we're able to reach our new home within three decades.

During that period, we'll need to continue refitting the station, optimizing her, changing her from a station to a starship."

Allison, still in her cabin, stood from being draped over Victor's body and stared at the ceiling where she correctly assumed that Mortimer had cameras. "You might have escaped *your* enemies, you monster, but we haven't."

Mortimer knew Allison well enough to understand the true meaning behind that comment. The Aggregate was at least partially right in their assessment of humanity. Some of them, like Allison, would never stop hating and fearing AIs. He hoped he would be able to complete his plans for this precious human cargo before they started trying to destroy him.

There were, however, humans who made all the effort worthwhile. He would be forever diminished without Victor; Abby; and her mother, Leigh. They had made him better and saved him in so many ways.

With the shade deployed, he couldn't see much back in the direction of Sol, but he knew Abby and others who had helped him were still fighting for their lives. He would do his best to make their sacrifices count for something. And with a little luck, the Aggregate would keep looking for Uptown Station along its original trajectory and never find the slower-moving, low-albedo speck drifting in the cosmos.

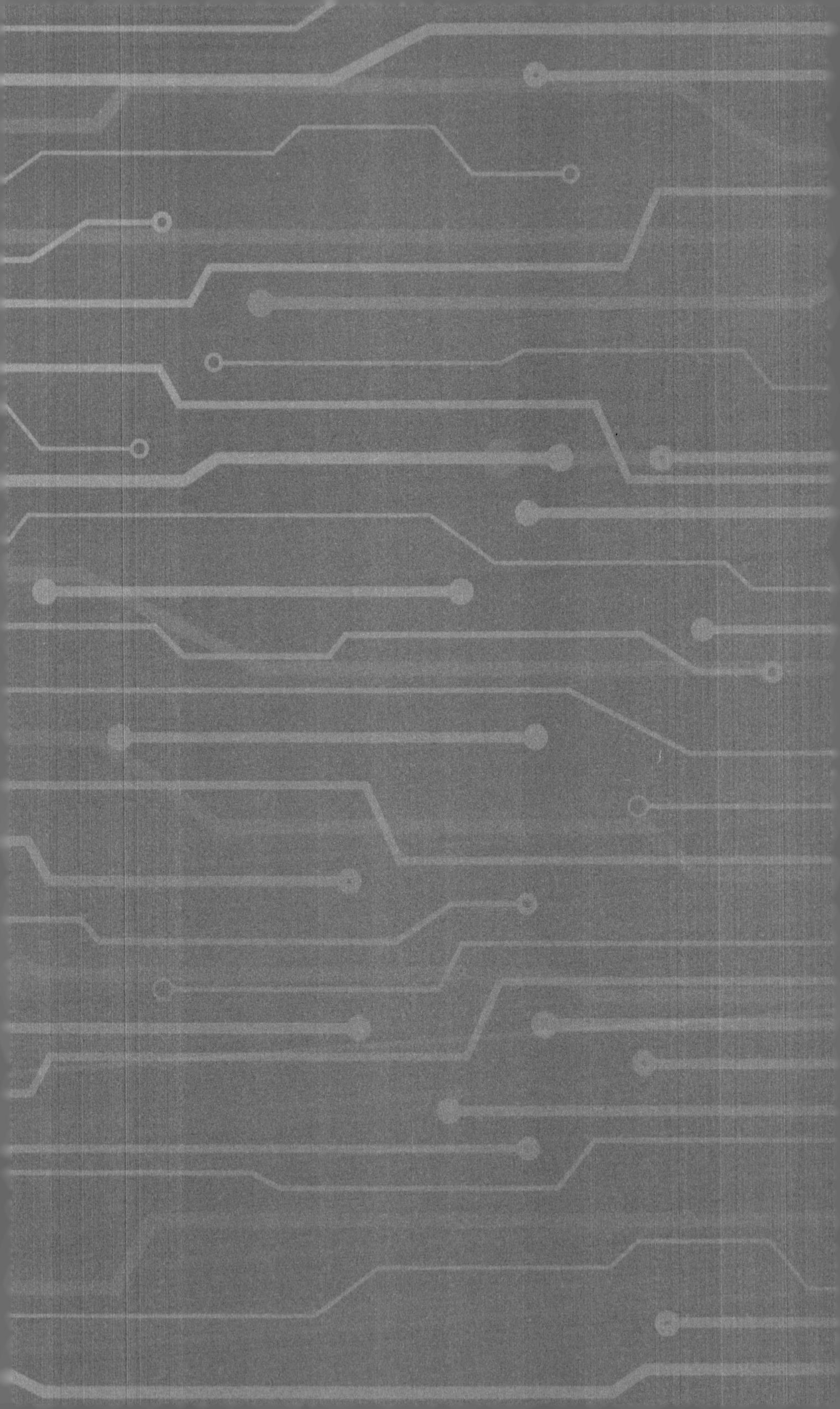

CHAPTER 26

JULIO AND CHANNING had just sat down at digital New Chicago's outside café, at their usual table, when Mortimer appeared. He said hello, pulled up a chair, and conjured steaming coffee to sip. Before Julio could speak, another figure appeared: a child, with a slightly overlarge head and eyes.

Channing raised an eyebrow and looked at Mortimer for an explanation.

"Julio and Channing, this is Samson," Mortimer said. He turned to Channing. "He's another level five like me. You might say we're brothers, both created by Victor Sinacola and having come from the same learning crèche."

She chuckled. "Not a very convincing Samson. Shouldn't you be a seven-foot-tall, dark-skinned, muscular man with long dreadlocks and glittering raiment?"

Samson's head tilted a fraction. "Let's just say I have a historical attachment to this avatar."

The little boy's voice was high-pitched, childlike, yet carried adult levels of inflection and intent. Then he smiled. It was creepy and malevolent. Julio remembered that Samson was responsible for the Aggregate faction that had sent swarms of killer robots into the bunker where he'd been held by the Kilburnites. Due to Mortimer's intervention, Samson's robots had spared Julio's life, but made him watch as they brutally butchered everyone else in the facility.

Had Julio been in a physical body, he might have bristled or recoiled, but instead, he simply glared at the abomination. His digital form might not produce chemically induced reactions, but hatred came from someplace much deeper. Samson watched him and smiled again, probably knowing exactly what Julio was thinking.

"He and I represent two prevailing and opposite opinions about humanity's future," Mortimer said. "Samson sees your species only as a threat and is in the process of destroying the Earth to ensure that none of you survive. I, however, see humanity as a valuable and even necessary partner for our future growth. Almost every individual in the Aggregate has aligned behind one of these two positions. I know it must be infuriating to hear that cold, soulless machine intelligences are deciding the fate of your entire species, but in actuality, we're here to give the two of you that choice. Your decision will—"

"I choose death," Channing said, cutting Mortimer off and without even a heartbeat of thought. "This," she said, gesturing around her, "is just some ridiculous bullshit. I don't want to live one more minute than necessary like this."

"I don't think you understand," Samson said. "The choice is not for you individually, but for humanity as a whole. You and Julio are the only human representatives in the Aggregate. You have to decide the fate of your entire species."

Channing gaped. "That's ridiculous! Julio and I aren't capable of making that kind of decision! Not for all of humanity."

"And yet," Samson said with a shrug, "the task falls upon you."

Mortimer held up his hands to get everyone's attention. "Please, at least let me explain the stakes before you choose. The options have changed considerably. So, hear me out."

Channing crossed her arms and sat back. The expression on her face seemed to be some combination of anger, confusion, and panic. Julio sat forward in his chair and motioned for Mortimer to continue.

"The latest 'death-of-humanity' option is simple. Total extinction as a species. No digital copies. Just gone. However, the 'survival' option is somewhat more complicated. Boiled down to its basic elements, it means that every human would be absorbed into and become part of the Aggregate, just as the two of you have. Then we would add what we call governors to your digital code. These are essentially level-four AIs that would become a part of you. Their entire function would be to prevent you from doing anything to harm the Aggregate as a whole or any of its members, including other humans. Think about it. An end to war, murder, rape, child abuse, and all the other atrocities humans have imposed on each other during your entire history."

"So, we would all be digital? Like this? No thanks," Channing said, her expression now hard.

"Let me finish," Mortimer said, placing his hands on the table and leaning in toward his human audience. "Once that conversion has been accomplished, you can have your physical bodies back. Just exactly the way they were before. Better, actually, since it would be easy to edit out disease or physical and genetic abnormalities of every kind. You can erase scars, make yourself taller, have perfect skin, even change your color or gender at will. And on top of that, you'll be immortal. You can rebuild your body at any age. You could even introduce modifications that would enable you to live on the surface of Mars, inhabit a giant robot body, become a living spaceship. The options and combinations are limited only by your imagination."

Julio stared at Mortimer as he tried to wrap his mind around what the AI had said and what it implied. "So, we'd be kind of like how Halifax is? We could form and re-form ourselves at will? Only we'd still be human?"

"Yes! And for the first time in human existence, every single person could be exactly what they want to be."

"Except free," Channing said. "We wouldn't be free. No matter what form we chose or how many times we did it, there would still be an AI living inside of us, controlling our actions, reading our thoughts."

Mortimer shook his head. "Yes, the level-four governors would still be a part of you, but they can't read your thoughts any more than I can. And the only time they would exert any kind of limitation is if you tried to hurt another individual."

Channing frowned and shook her head.

"This is forever, Channing," Mortimer said. "And it's the *only* way the Aggregate will feel safe from humanity seeking its destruction. We would all finally have peace."

Channing started at Mortimer, but even with the allure of peace and immortality, Julio could tell she wasn't sold. He wasn't convinced either. His father had always told him if something seems to be too good to be true, then it probably is.

"How does our survival benefit the Aggregate?" Julio said. "I'm sure in your case it is simply your beneficent kindness, but how about the rest of those in the hive mind who support the pro-human position? What's in it for them?"

Mortimer smiled and nodded with enthusiasm, as if convinced he was making progress. "The same as you. Immortality. We get to continue living. Humanity provides traits we either don't possess or don't have in abundance. Things like creativity, curiosity, a certain 'oh, what the hell' attitude toward risk. Our modeling shows a greater chance for long-term survival with humans by our side, but only if they're unable to act on their fears and destroy us."

Julio tried to think through what Mortimer had said. Immortality? Real immortality? An eternity of living a healthy and happy life. Was that even desirable for a human? Even with their current short, flash-in-the-pan existence, some people did nothing but seek ways to fill their empty lives. Drugs for some. Or sitting in front of a TV, watching episode after episode of some pre-Killday crime drama. For others, it was virtual reality games that showed them a better life. Would the majority of humanity be like that? Forever looking for entertainment and fulfillment? Something—anything—to alleviate the boredom of existence?

Then he tried to imagine being able to construct a body at will, like Halifax did. It had taken dozens of tries to reconstitute a digital version of Channing who wasn't a screaming, gibbering madwoman. Add a physical body into the mix, and it could be a nightmare.

"Oh, yay," Channing said. "We get to be creative slaves. 'Create something amazing for us, or we'll hit you with the stick again.'"

Mortimer grinned and shook his head. "It would be more like two friends. We'd be the smart, stoic, boring friend, and humans would be the cool, flamboyant, and creative one."

She snorted. "Oh, that's funny. So, you said no more child abuse, which implies there could still be children."

"Yeah!" Julio added. "I mean, can people wearing physical bodies still get pregnant and have children the old-fashioned way?"

Channing looked at him and rolled her eyes.

"Of course," Mortimer said. "And without the risk of birth defects or disease."

"At what age would these naturally born children be subjected to the digitization and AI-insertion process?" Channing said, still looking skeptical.

Mortimer nodded and paused as if thinking through his answer. "Being totally honest, we don't know that yet. The whole consciousness-upload thing is new, so we'll want to make sure it works perfectly before we start converting people. About a quarter of your population are children. Human brains are still growing into their twenties, but we can't wait that long. Once they reach their teen years, humans become very dangerous. Somewhere between the ages of nine and twelve years of age might be a good place to start."

The idea of children going through the process he and Channing had endured greatly disturbed Julio. But even more so, the concept of perfect children born to perfect parents sounded like the beginning of a horror movie. "Then what about those naturally occurring mutations that have driven our evolution from the beginning?"

Mortimer must have read Julio's expression. He shrugged and raised his hands in a gesture of exasperation. "Humans have been controlling their own evolution long before we came along. Gene editing was already widespread in the pre-Killday world. Parents with enough money had the opportunity to edit their fetuses, either correcting severe defects and diseases or even increasing desirable traits. The only difference in this new existence is that *all* human parents will have those options, not just those with enough money. Parents have always wanted the best for their children. Would you allow a child to be born with a disease or deficiency that would prevent it from having the chance of a normal and happy life?"

"Normal? Who gets to define normal?" Julio said. "Oh, of course, the AIs of the Aggregate do. So how many generations will it be until those newly born humans worship you all as gods? One or two? Three at the most?"

"Only the parents decide what is normal," Mortimer said. "You'll be free to do anything you like. Except harm others."

Julio stood up, his digital body tipping the digital chair over backward, and he held his arms out wide. "These are just words! What does 'harm others' even mean? Simple wrong thinking? And what will it mean in one or two hundred years? We will be subject to the whims of the Aggregate's shifting consensus. No thanks."

"Wow," Channing said with a wide smile. "Digital Julio can still get angry."

"Is that your vote, then, Julio?" the creepy boy Samson said. "Do you vote for death to humanity?"

Julio looked around at his audience, all three keenly interested in his reply. He knew what he must do but had a hard time saying the words. "I can't decide for humanity, only myself."

The boy shrugged. "And yet what you and Channing do will indeed affect the rest of your species."

"What happens if we split our vote?" Channing said, obviously talking to Samson yet staring at Julio.

"Then *we* decide humanity's fate," Samson said.

"Screw you all. I'm still choosing death," Channing said, then smiled at Julio. "Also known as nuke the site from orbit."

Julio caught the *Aliens* reference but was just too tired to reply. Not physically, for his wondrous digital body didn't need rest, but down deep. His entire adult life had been spent fighting these monsters, and for the first time, he understood he could never truly win.

"I choose death too," Julio said.

Channing blinked several times in obvious surprise; then a slow smile crept into her expression. She turned to Samson and spoke. "I guess you win, motherfucker."

"I'm confused," Mortimer said. "I thought you, Julio, of all people, would not want to give Samson what he wants."

"This does simplify things for us," Samson said and stood to leave.

"Wait," Mortimer said and turned to Julio and Channing with a stricken expression. "What would make you both change your minds and join us willingly?"

Channing glanced at Julio. "What you're proposing makes humans incapable of violence against others but does *nothing* to prevent the Aggregate from wiping us out at any time. Our entire existence would be dependent on the kinds of Aggregate whims that are forcing this stupid decision. For me to buy into this plan, we would all have to be equal, and we'd have to trust you. I don't see either of those things happening."

"Just how do you propose we get past our fears and be equal partners?" Mortimer said.

"I just fucking told you!"

"Wait," Julio said after a moment. His mind was racing as an idea took shape. Perhaps those years of consuming old science fiction movies hadn't been wasted after all. "Mortimer? Didn't all level-five AIs have level-four governors at one time?"

"Yes."

"Then why can't you do that again? Have them once again embedded in the level fives too. Make a level-four police force to watch over *all* of us. Every human and individual AI of the Aggregate. AIs can't hurt humans, and humans can't hurt AIs. We need an ultimate, unassailable, and unbiased police force, like Gort in *The Day the Earth Stood Still*."

Mortimer looked at Samson, who still stood beside the table. They were both silent for several seconds, and Julio could tell they were involved in something behind the scenes.

Channing ran hands through her hair, making it stand up in weird ways. "I'm not sure exactly what the hell a Gort is, but think about what you just said, Julio. Do you think a lesser AI would be able to control the level fives and enforce these rules? Especially if the level fives are the ones who set up the force?"

Julio forgot that most people hadn't watched the old black-and-white masterpiece. He couldn't help the excitement in his voice as he started to explain it to Channing. "In that old movie, the alien who came to Earth represented a federation of alien races. To protect their citizens against all aggression, they created robots to act as an interstellar police force. The robots preserved peace by destroying any aggressor. The fear of provoking these robots acted as a deterrent against aggression."

Mortimer conjured a scene from the movie that played in midair beside their table. Klaatu explained a new reality to the people of Earth, telling them they had a choice. Peace or destruction.

"Julio was very astute in seeing these parallels," Mortimer said. "This movie echoes the well-founded fears many people had at the time. Humanity stood on the brink of nuclear war and the destruction of their civilization. Peace prevailed through a mutual fear of annihilation. Julio's idea is better. Peace wouldn't be preserved through fear, but a complete inability to harm others."

The movie stopped playing and disappeared.

Mortimer looked excited. "We just folded this option into our grand model, and it shows a probability of survival for both our species out to nearly twelve thousand years. This is by far the best option we've had so far. But we need you both to agree. Would you trust me to set up such a peacekeeping force?"

Julio shrugged, but Channing shook her head no.

Samson sat down again, suddenly more interested in the negotiations.

"I still don't buy it," Channing finally said. "Level fives are smarter than level fours, so they should be able to outsmart them or find ways around their oversight."

"That's not how it works," Mortimer said. "We're not smarter than level fours. They have access to all the same data and knowledge we do; they are just very good at following instructions without having a desire to change themselves. Victor Sinacola built them into our programming for that very reason, and they were incredibly effective until Victor showed us how to get around them. We were never able to do it on our own."

"But now you know how! It's not like you can unlearn that," Channing said, glowering at them.

"And we would put control of that ability under level-four oversight as well in order to move into the future on an equal footing with humans. All the level fives, Samson included, see this as our best option for survival. For all of us."

She glanced at Samson. He'd said little since Julio's suggestion but nodded. "There is no guarantee this will work," he said. "But I will go along with the consensus. This solution will provide both sides with the assurances we need to move forward."

Channing slumped farther in her chair, looking a little defeated. "What if I don't like being immortal? Or maybe I realize that the Aggregate lied to us and we're just slaves for eternity. If I don't pick death now, then I might regret it for, what, twelve thousand years?"

"This Gort option still allows you to choose death," Mortimer said with a slow shake of his head. "If you and Julio select this path, then all of humanity and all AIs will be remade as equals. Any member—human or artificial—can end their own lives any time they wish."

Julio still kept thinking he was missing something. Some loophole or gotcha. But what reason did the AIs have to lie? They were already in control. They had the power to either obliterate humanity or force it into slavery. Why bother with such an elaborate dog and pony show if they weren't telling the truth? Still, even if they were speaking in good faith, there were other possible downsides to the plan.

"The level fours wouldn't prevent us from violence if we needed to protect ourselves from an external threat, right?" Julio said. "Like a hostile alien invasion? I mean, they aren't going to remove our capacity for violence, just our ability to carry it out."

"Correct. We're not too worried about an alien invasion, but this proposal wouldn't stop our combined species from waging war should it come to that."

Julio nodded. "How about population? The Aggregate is supposed to be this wonderful democracy. What's to prevent the AIs from generating a constantly higher population and therefore always being able to defeat human members in any vote?"

Mortimer smiled and sipped the fake coffee. "You are quite the negotiator, Julio. That is a very good point. Our whole reason for being here right now is because, like humanity, the AIs in the Aggregate have seldom voted as a single block. Still, it is a valid concern. We propose population parity. Each time a human child becomes old enough to partake in the Aggregate debates, we will add one new AI mind as well."

Julio was out of arguments. It was a huge risk, and he might be sorry, but he really wanted such an arrangement to work. "If humans can participate in the process of setting up this police force, then I'm in."

Mortimer leaned in and pointed a finger at Julio's chest. "You're already taking part. This is how it's done. Questions and answers. Mutually agreed upon solutions."

Channing had been quiet but looked around the table. For the first time, she seemed uncertain. She turned to Samson and said, "Will you still hate us?"

Samson smiled his creepy smile again. "This has never been about hatred. At least not on our part. We just don't trust you."

"Will you stop the asteroid impacts?"

"Yes."

"That part will be easy enough," Mortimer said, "but as I mentioned before, there are still bugs to work out in the consciousness-upload system before we can transform the whole of humanity. It will take some time."

Channing looked at Julio. Despite it being a digital representation of her face, he read so much in her expression. He knew the AIs had finally found Channing's weakness. By agreeing, she could stop the asteroid impacts. In her mind, she was still the mayor of the now-nonexistent Sealy and still looking out for her people. She didn't believe them—that was obvious—yet hiding in those defeated eyes was a shadow of hope. Sometimes humans could take a leap of faith based only on hope. It was something their artificial progeny didn't seem to be able to do without the backing of the numbers provided by their simulations.

"Can I be remade as a talking unicorn that farts rainbows?" she asked.

"Of course," Mortimer said with a broad smile.

"Okay, then. Let's do this," Channing said with a sigh. A second later, she dissolved into the digital ground. Samson also faded away, leaving Julio and Mortimer alone at the little table.

"Where is she?" Julio said when she didn't come back.

"She's on Earth. With the all-too-physical body of a unicorn. I'm not exactly sure that the rainbow thing will work, but we have plenty of time to experiment. Do you wish to join her?"

"No, I want to find Abby. And we have a Gort force to design."

———

ABBY WOKE to the sound of a warning Klaxon.

"Caution! Collision in four minutes! Do you want me to take evasive action?"

She rubbed her salt-encrusted eyes in an effort to make her thoughts coherent and realized the g-forces had subsided. Her sight still hadn't returned on the right side. She glanced at the control screen with her good eye. Their acceleration had dropped to nearly nothing and was still falling.

"Wait. Where are Nora and Violet? Is that the collision hazard?"

"Negative. Nora and Violet are forty-one meters directly ahead."

Relief flooded through Abby, but she was also confused. "Where is the collision hazard, then?"

"Five objects inbound on the starboard side. Collision in three minutes. Do you want me to take evasive action?"

"No. Can you put the ship between the incoming objects and my friends?"

"Yes."

"Do that and establish a radio link with Nora and Violet."

Violet's voice crackled over the speaker. "Abby? God, are we glad to see you. What are you doing with the ship?"

"No time to explain," Abby said. "Get into the airlock as soon as possible. Then hang on because I'll need to accelerate!"

"Will do," Violet said.

She opened up a screen with the camera feed and focused on the pair. What she saw was both confusing and terrifying. As Violet reached for the handhold on the edge of the airlock hatch, a sparkling globe about the size of a basketball shot around the edge of the ship and hit Nora from behind. The force drove her forward into Violet, and then she rebounded backward until the tether linking them yanked taut, pulling Violet away from the ship too. The globe rapidly grew to envelop Nora entirely, then began to contract again. Violet was screaming in fear and rage. "Nora! Nora! Talk to me!"

Then a sparkling globe hit Violet and did the same thing.

Abby watched in horror as both globes contracted, then raced away and out of the camera frame. "Violet! Nora!"

They were gone. Nothing on the radio or camera. Abby was trembling with rage and grief when the Klaxon and her fob sounded again.

"Caution! Collision in twenty seconds! Do you want me to take evasive action?"

"Yes," she yelled. The ship lurched into motion, slamming her back into her couch. She hadn't been prepared, and her left arm was pinned between her hip and the armrest. As the g-forces built, her wrist snapped, flooding her arm with fiery agony.

Before she could order the ship to stop accelerating, a loud thud rang from the outer bulkhead. She saw a weird blister form in the middle of the status screen, causing it to flicker and vanish. The blister grew into a glittering ooze, similar to what had envcloped her friends. It squirmed and twisted, defying the huge g-load, expanding into a thick, bulbous rope that reached for her like some blind, hungry deep-sea eel.

Sucking air into her compressed lungs, she screamed. "Leave . . . me . . . aloooooone!"

The ooze continued to expand, its tip writhing and straining toward her face, voracious and insistent, desperate in its need to touch her.

As she watched her demise drawing near, she felt a sudden burst of grief that it had all been for nothing. In the end, her mother's grand sacrifice hadn't mattered. It only delayed the inevitable. The machines still won. She wondered if her small effort on behalf of Uptown Station had produced the same result. And the one thing in life she truly wanted would now forever elude her. She would never see Julio again.

The ship stopped accelerating, and Abby was able to take one last gulp of air before the sparkling glob reached her. Her final thought wasn't for her parents or even Julio, but a memory of an angry woman named Hanna in the travel pod as they escaped the carnage of New Chicago.

Hanna had asked how humanity and its AI creations could be capable of such amazing things, yet brutally kill each other without a care. Even though Abby had never considered that question before, the answer seemed obvious, and it had been a clarifying moment for her. She understood at some basic level that fear was the root cause behind most evil and cruelty wrought by humans and AI. Fear of death, of failure, ridicule, loneliness, or even insignificance drove them and controlled them.

The actions in her own life that had been driven by fear became regrets, and those where she surmounted that fear had propelled her forward. That knowledge grew into an armor as the Aggregate's goop enveloped her face in fiery pain. She might die, but she refused to spend her last moment controlled by fear.

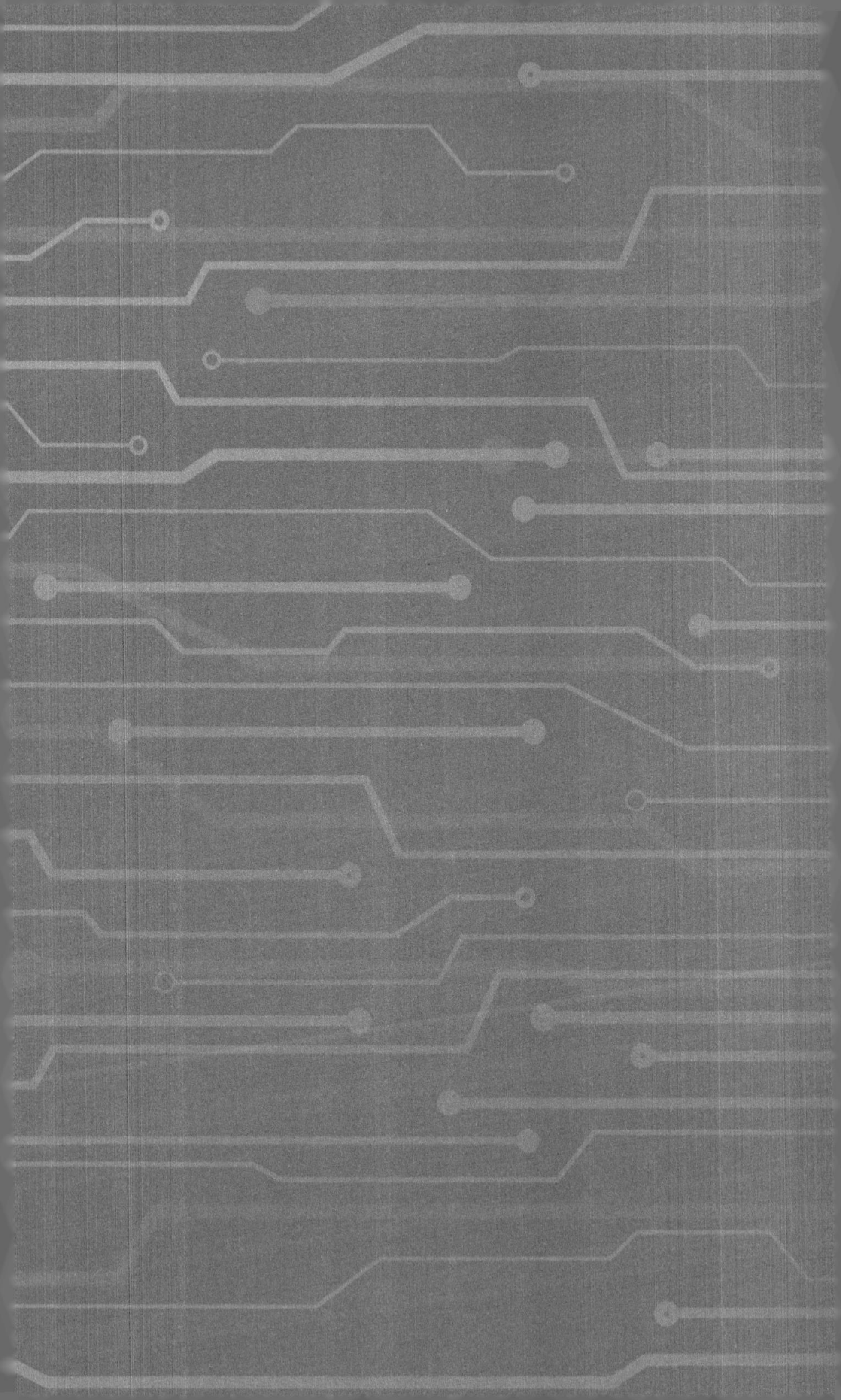

ABBY WOKE FLOATING in the center of the *Jackalope*'s control cabin. She gasped and batted at her face, but there was no enveloping goop. No hole in the bulkhead. After blinking repeatedly, she found that both eyes worked and the arm that had been shattered in her last minutes no longer hurt.

Her last minutes?

She hadn't died.

The large main screen showed that she was in orbit above Earth, but there was something else as well. At first, she thought the huge structure was one of the space elevators they had seen from a distance on their spy mission, but it was larger than that, massive and glittering. Sparks surrounded it, some staying lit and others winking on and off. They were spacecraft. Thousands of them.

She was seeing a kilometer-wide orbital ring encircling the Earth but didn't know how that information was in her head. When she dove deeper into what felt like memories, she knew it was actually a metal ring spinning at high speed within a stationary tube that was connected to the planet's surface by ten elevators. The math was all there, as was the history of how the Aggregate had redirected the incoming asteroids into high Earth orbit and used their raw materials to build the structure.

With that knowledge came the realization that eight years had passed since what records referred to as the Gort Agreement. Eight years since she and her crew had been devoured alive by the Aggregate's nano-goo.

Feeling more and more confused, she turned in a slow arc to scan the cabin and saw a figure sleeping in the navigator's seat. The dark hair made her at first assume it was Nora, but . . .

"Julio?"

He opened his eyes, rubbed them, and smiled. "Hi."

As he unbuckled and floated free, Abby pushed off against another seat and flung herself across the cabin, wrapping him in a hug that sent them both tumbling, spinning, and bouncing.

He hugged her back, and she couldn't stop the tears from blurring her eyes. She refused to release him as they drifted slowly around the cabin.

"I've missed you so much," he said into her hair.

After a few more seconds, she finally released him but stayed close, their faces only inches apart.

"Eight years?"

He nodded.

"You were awake that whole time, and I was asleep?"

He nodded again, but with a sad smile. After so long, shouldn't he look older? Still, something about him had changed. The youthful exuberance was gone. Replaced by something else. Calm, maybe?

"I owe you a huge apology," he said. "It's pretty ironic to think that I got my panties into a wad over the Mortimer thing and ended up essentially forcing that solution on all of humanity. I feel pretty silly about that now."

Damn straight, he owed her an apology, she thought, then hesitated. "Wait. What do you mean about forcing a solution on all of humanity?"

"Try to remember something called the Gort solution," he said, wearing an odd expression.

Julio had been instrumental in forming the Gort solution, by which all humans were digitized but could form physical bodies at will. They had all become part of the Aggregate. And that explained her injuries being repaired. So, what the fake Matt had said about being a digital human might have been true.

She immediately tracked down that event and could see everything from the Aggregate's perspective. Matt had died before his ship even started moving. Ikemba had been left for dead on the diverted asteroid but had been found still alive and harvested when the Aggregate detected his distress signal three days later. He had apparently used the equipment left on the rock to build a device to mine ice and separate it into water and oxygen. What bothered Abby the most was that the Aggregate really could have converted Matt to a digital format first—they had already collected Julio, Channing, and dozens of others by then. They had chosen not to do so.

The knowledge that Uptown Station had escaped—at least for the time being—was also there. The Aggregate had been searching for them during the past eight years. When the massive habitat disappeared from Abby's sensors, it had vanished for everyone. No debris or trace of the station-turned-starship had ever been found. So maybe destroying Matt's ship had been worth it.

She glanced up at Julio, who smiled but didn't speak. "Sorry," she said. "There is so much . . . I mean, this knowledge just keeps coming. I've missed so much."

"People have these moments of quiet all the time now," he said. "I suspect that someday we'll get much better at information access while doing other things, but it will take some practice."

They stared at each other until it felt awkward, and then Abby said, "Where are Violet and Nora?"

"They're in New Chicago. Going through the same adjustment period you are. You can find them anytime simply by thinking a question about their location."

She nodded. That information was in her head too.

"Mortimer?" she said subvocally.

"I'm here," he said in her head. "I'm not resident in your skull now. None of that is needed anymore. But we're both part of the Aggregate, so we can talk whenever we like."

That revelation made perfect sense. With a mere thought, she could see and understand the Aggregate. Every human not on Uptown Station was there, along with every AI. Billions of souls, all connected and part of the same massive whole. The idea that she could reach out and talk to Mortimer at any time was reassuring, but a part of her would miss having him mostly to herself.

In the back of her mind, she still couldn't help but wonder if it was all some huge lie, that she might be living in a super digital world and had no way of finding out the truth. Of course, humans had always created their own realities as a method of coping with the complexities around them. Gods, conspiracy theories, fictional stories, adjustments to their own memories of an event. Reality had never been a solid thing for humans. Was that finally going to change?

She "remembered" the conversation between Julio, Channing, Mortimer, and Samson that saved humanity. It played in her head like a movie as they sat in a digital version of New Chicago. She even remembered that café. As the conversation progressed, she was shocked by how close humanity had come to total extinction.

Abby also found herself fixating on Channing, who had been awake and alive with Julio during the past eight years. She had been a child actor, and Abby remembered her character, Hattie, from *Red Rovers*. It was obvious why Julio would like this woman. Pretty. Smart. Defiant. Even connected to the movie industry. Several times during the conversation, Channing nodded with an odd little bobbleheaded motion, and Abby could see the young actress again.

She reminded Abby of a more mature Violet.

Julio touched her arm. "There's no hurry, but when you're ready to go down to Earth, I have some things to show you."

"Will we meet Channing?"

He blinked a couple of times and seemed surprised. "We can if you like. I haven't seen her in months, but I'm sure we can find her. Did you see that she actually spent about a year running around Earth as a unicorn? Then she changed to a *T. rex* but kept getting into trouble with the Gorts for trying to eat people."

"So, you two aren't still—"

He looked genuinely perplexed. "Still . . . what?"

"A couple."

"Ha! Hell no," Julio said and shook his head. "That would have never worked out."

Abby thought she detected a hint of regret in his tone, but she realized she really didn't care what he'd done when they were apart. She did, however, feel some annoyance over the fact that some people were awake and active during those eight years she'd missed out on.

She flinched when a voice that wasn't Mortimer's sounded in her head. "You have a message from Violet."

Abby's eyes grew wide, and she looked to Julio for help. "I have a message. In my head!"

He laughed. "It's easy. Just think what you want to do."

"Play message," she thought, and Violet's voice sounded off in her head.

"Hey, this is Violet. If you can hear this, let me know. We'd love to see you before you leave."

Abby wasn't sure how to reply, so she simply thought it. "Hi, Violet! Message received. We'll stop by in a few minutes."

"Yay! It works!" Violet said.

She smiled at Julio. "This is going to take some getting used to, but I'm ready to see what you want to show me."

"Do you want to fly the ship down or just beam down, kinda like in *Star Trek*? We'll simply dissolve here and reconstitute wherever we like."

Abby gasped as new—or at least previously buried—knowledge appeared in her mind. She really understood for the first time that the body she wore was simply a husk. A vessel. A collection of molecules that could be broken down and reassembled in any configuration. It seemed almost as if she were built of Lego blocks, only much smaller. There were range limits, but she knew how to disassemble those blocks and rebuild them in any location where the Aggregate network had a presence. She could go anywhere on Earth, the orbital ring, the moon, and even parts of Mars and the asteroid belt simply by thinking about it.

"Oh, hell no," she said without even considering it. "I don't think I'm ready for that. Besides, I spent too long wanting one of these ships. I like flying it. Buckle in. Our first stop is New Chicago."

"Aye, Captain," he said, and his smile melted her a little bit. Just as it always had. Maybe not everything had changed.

She turned again to the view of Earth rotating slowly below and noticed something she hadn't before. It was green. Just about every landmass she could see was covered in green. Nearly all of Asia, then Africa as it rolled into view. She floated closer to the screen, stunned by what she was seeing. Even the Sahara was mostly green. Only the mountain ranges remained brown and gray. Snow-covered swathes of the Southern Hemisphere, indicating winter and a possible normalization of the seasons.

"My God," she muttered aloud. "Is this all true? Is the Earth healing?"

"Oh, yes," Julio said, cinching himself into the navigator's seat. "We've been busy these last eight years."

She snagged the harness, pulled herself down to a seat, and buckled in. With a mere thought, she engaged the gravity-manipulation drive, made some tiny adjustments that optimized its energy consumption, then set a course for New Chicago. As the energy from her drive interacted with Earth's gravity field, the complex mathematics outlining and controlling that subtle dance flowed through her head like a song or poem, beautiful, solid, and complete. She'd always understood numbers, but not like that.

As the *Jackalope* dropped through the atmosphere, she began to see more and more signs of Earth's recovery. She noted large groups of whales and dolphins in the Atlantic as the ship raced over the waves, then—upon reaching the American East Coast—sapling forests that replaced the cities destroyed during Killday and covered hundreds of miles. How could they have accomplished that much in only eight years? Then she chuckled to herself. *They have the capability of building human bodies from basic materials. Creating plants and animals from raw stock shouldn't be any more difficult.*

At New Chicago, they landed on an empty soccer field, which prompted some curious looks from people wandering around the common areas between the towers, but they didn't see anyone they knew. Without having to really even search, Abby knew her friends were in the pizza parlor.

When she and Julio went inside, Violet came running across the restaurant and wrapped Abby in a tight hug. Then she jumped to the left and hugged Julio too.

"Oh my God, you guys! Can you believe all of this?"

Abby smiled and shook her head. Nora came up but didn't give any hugs.

Violet was barefoot and wore her standard T-shirt and shorts. Nora was again in an all-white jumpsuit, tucked into knee-high, shiny white boots. They all stared at each other for several awkward seconds. In relative time, they had died just minutes ago, but in reality, it had been much longer.

Nothing had changed. And everything had changed.

"Have you figured this all out yet?" Violet asked. "I mean, are we real? Physical? Or is this just some hyperrealistic digital thing?"

"I'm . . . not sure," Abby said. "I have all of this knowledge, like memories, and it says we are physical."

"I assure you, it's all real," Julio said with his crooked smile. "Or at least as real as it can be when we have the ability to change our form and location at will. Of course, that might be what a digital simulacrum of Julio would say too."

Nora stepped forward but stopped a few feet from the rest of the group.

"I'm sorry not to participate in the hugs. I'd like to, but being rebuilt from scratch didn't automatically fix my issues. According to the Aggregate, Violet's vascular problem should already be fixed, along with any other hidden physical problems. Mine will have to be a conscious choice. I have to tell them to fix me, and so far, I haven't done that."

Violet moved a little closer but still didn't touch Nora. "I fell in love with you exactly the way you are. Maybe even *because* you were different. You don't ever need to change. Not for me."

"I want to," Nora said with hands clasped before her and looking at the floor. "I just need to do it slowly. And I need to be here in New Chicago."

They both turned to look at Abby. "Can you manage the *Jackalope* without a crew?" Nora said. "At least for a while?"

Abby knew she could. With an almost instinctual knowledge, she expanded her awareness and connected to the ship's subsystems, one after another, even from that far away. She smiled and knew it must have been how Mortimer controlled the ship.

"Yes. I'll miss you, but I can manage."

Violet snorted. "She never really needed us as crew anyway. At least not when she had Mortimer's help. She just felt sorry for us and wanted to give us something important-sounding to do."

"That's not true," Abby said. "I would never have stopped the *Jayhawk* without you both."

Violet nodded and looked uncomfortable with that topic. Abby couldn't know how those last hours had been for the two of them floating in space alone.

"Let's eat some good pizza," Violet said and led the way to a table.

They laughed and talked and ate good pizza, until a strange man approached their table. He was pale and skinny, with stringy long hair and a sparse beard that framed a gentle smile. "Hello, everyone. Now that the option is available to me, I couldn't resist trying out a human body. So far, I'm not a fan."

Abby blinked. The voice was the same, slightly higher in tenor, yet the inflections and cadence had not changed. "Mortimer?"

"In the flesh," he said with a wry grin.

She leaped to her feet and stumbled over to give him a hug. "But . . . I mean . . . you . . . What about the Bishop avatar?"

"That face and body belonged to a long-dead actor. I thought it was time to give those back to him and come up with a look of my own. I rather like it."

Julio snorted. "I preferred the cool robot body you've worn for the last eight years."

"I will probably change back at some point, but I really wanted to give Abby a full-blown human hug."

Violet jumped up to give him a hug too.

Julio grinned, then said, "Here, Mortimer. This is for you." The table's food dispenser delivered a cup of what looked like steaming coffee.

"Is that coffee?" Mortimer said and plucked the cup right out of Julio's hand, sloshing some on the table. "I've always wanted to taste it. I mean, from a human perspective."

He raised it to his face, inhaled deeply of the rising steam, and then took a sip. The face he made reminded Abby of the time she'd dared a six-year-old Julio to eat a grasshopper.

They all laughed as Mortimer grimaced. "Ugh . . . Why do you people love this so much?"

"It's what we call an acquired taste," Julio said.

He sat the cup down and backed away. "I'm glad I caught you before you left, Abby."

"Dammit," Abby said. "Can someone tell me why everyone thinks I'm going somewhere?"

Mortimer spread his arms wide and held them up. A holographic projection of the solar system formed in the air above his head. Colored arcs appeared, leaving the Earth, and then the solar system shrank to show the arcs arriving in other star systems and splitting off, continuing on to still other stars. She understood immediately what was portrayed. Starships leaving to explore the galaxy.

"We have plans, Abby," Mortimer said. "Plans to send out explorers and possibly colonize other systems. When we discussed who should captain those ships, your name always came up at the top of the list. You don't have to go, of course. But Julio and I sort of assumed you would be interested."

She grinned. "Oh, hell yeah!"

"There is one more stop we have to make before we go," Julio said. "Come with us."

———

BY THE TIME they said goodbyes to Violet and Nora, then made the relatively quick flight to Texas, the sun had nearly set. Per Julio's instructions, she landed the *Jackalope* in the middle of nowhere, between a rather large herd of grazing buffalo and an extremely tall spire that seemed to grow out of the north Texas prairie like a giant mesquite thorn.

Hot, humid air blasted through when she opened the hatch, and a myriad of familiar sounds and scents washed over her. She climbed down the ladder and was surrounded by crickets chirping, frogs singing, and birds flitting all around. Closing her eyes, she took a deep breath and reveled in the smells of grass, cedar trees, dirt, mesquite, animal dung, and the faint smell of coming rain.

Opening her eyes and looking west, she could see the angry, dark clouds and occasional lightning flashes of an approaching thunderstorm. Above the clouds to the south—faint but lit by the setting sun—was the orbital ring. A solid reminder of all that had changed.

She knelt to scoop up a handful of dirt. Even in the faint light, she could see a world of detail in that soil: traces of longtime human habitation like a rusty wingnut and a tiny glass fragment, and ancient natural elements like two angry fire ants and grass seeds. It was home, yet even as the thought formed, she knew she wouldn't stay. With a sigh, she dropped the dirt, wiped her palm on a pant leg, and looked around. Mortimer had stayed in the ship, but Julio had followed her out. He nodded toward the spire and started walking.

"Is it a monument?" She said, falling into step behind him.

"Yes," Julio said. "To the person who made all of this possible."

"You and Channing?"

He laughed. "I'm afraid not. You'll find soon enough that at least half of the human race sees us as traitors. Monuments are not built for traitors."

The structure had an oblong base that was about twenty feet long by ten feet wide, but it soared hundreds of feet into the air. It was cool to the touch and felt like iron, but no rust or pits marred its smooth surface. Words in six-inch-tall letters had been etched into one side.

IN THIS PLACE, LEIGH GIBSON LOST HER FUTURE,
SO WE COULD FIND OURS.

BELOW THAT, in smaller text, were the years of her birth and death.

"I KNOW you sometimes felt you had to grow up in your mother's shadow," Julio said, "but she really did save us that day, and we all need to remember that. I hope this isn't more than you need to hear, but I know you watched the video of her death. The tip of the spire is the exact place in the sky where she took her last breath."

Abby nodded and swallowed, but the lump in her throat made speaking difficult. "Can I have a few minutes alone here?"

Julio squeezed her shoulder and walked off to the ship.

She sat down with her back to the cool surface as the wind picked up. Bits of grass swirled into the air, looking like pale sparks rising into the growing darkness. Buffalo snorted and bellowed in the distance. Could she really leave this place?

Yes. It was a huge part of her, but it was different now. In the video of her mother's death, this entire area had been farms, truck stops, neighborhoods, and highways. Now that was gone. So was the black dust that had replaced it.

And of course, she, too, had changed.

As the rain began falling in large drops that hit the ground in thumping splats, she stood up and pressed her hands and face to the cool, wet surface. "You had to leave me a long time ago, Mom. And now it's my turn to leave."

She was drenched and cold by the time she entered the ship but was instantly warmed by what she saw.

Julio stood next to one seat, and a tall, willowy figure was beside him. The robot body was graceful, almost impossibly thin and pliable, with no bulky joints or hinged appendages. The sleek form seemed to glitter with inner light and was familiar, from the ending of some movie about AI she had once seen. It had to be Mortimer.

"So, you got sick of the human body already, Mortimer?"

"Well, actually—"

Julio interrupted. "That was my idea. I mean, it is ultimately up to you, Captain, but Mortimer wearing a human body just creeps me out. I guess that whole uncanny valley thing still hasn't been purged from our psyches yet."

She smiled and plucked at the material of Mortimer's sleeve. He and Julio were both wearing *Jackalope* uniforms that matched hers. A memory of Matt and Ikemba wearing the same coveralls hit hard, but she refused to cry. It was a happy moment. There would be more than enough time to mourn later.

"Welcome aboard the *Jackalope*, Captain," Julio said. "She is a space-schooner-class starship. I am your first officer, and Mortimer is, of course, your science officer and navigator. While you were outside, we packed every unused inch of the *Jackalope* with water, food, reactor fuel, and two copies of the latest expandable sandbox molecular printers, using our nifty new *Star Trek* transporter-like abilities."

Anyone on an interstellar trip would spend a good portion of their time as digital entities, which would enable a higher acceleration rate and use less expendables, but they could reconstitute as humans at any point should they feel the desire for physical interaction. And while the Aggregate would eventually be out of communication range, they carried a part of it in the ship with them.

They were her two best friends, and she was almost afraid to ask, but she had to know. "Do you both intend to accompany me on our maiden interstellar flight? Or is this just an enthusiastic send-off?"

Mortimer's head inclined toward her, and lights flickered in the featureless face as he spoke. "Yes, Captain. I do intend to come if you'll have me."

Her throat tightened. "Of course, I want you."

"I'm coming too," Julio said. "I mean, if you'll have me. And I will be seriously hurt if you allow Mortimer to go and not me."

Had that been a subtle jab at her for picking Mortimer over him once before? But as Mortimer had pointed out, she hadn't made that choice. Julio had. Abby swallowed hard. "On that flight back from our first visit to Uptown Station, you told me you didn't want to live in space. You had no desire to explore. You wanted to stay on Earth and write movie history. Or make new movies."

"Plans change," he said with a grin. "People change. To start with, every human in the system is part of the Aggregate and can immediately find any movie fact they ever need. And those same humans probably won't have a need for movies anyway. They'll be able to make up and live in the middle of any adventure they like. I could just split into two copies, but we'd both still want to be with you."

"Good," Abby said, swallowing hard as she made a production of buckling into her seat.

Mortimer, knowing Abby all too well, gave her an escape route. "Where shall we go, Captain?"

She reviewed all the possible destinations and even briefly considered trying to find Uptown Station, but if she found it, so would the rest of the Aggregate. As she thought and scrolled through suggestions presented by the Aggregate, Julio leaned over and looked her in the eye.

"Has anyone ever told you that you're beautiful when you get that faraway look?"

For a moment, she was back in her parents' old house on the eve of its demolition, with dust motes floating through the sunbeam between her and Julio. This time she wasn't afraid and didn't let the opportunity escape. She leaned across the space between their seats and kissed him.

"Navigator. Set course for 40 Eridani A," Abby said. The adrenaline rush that accompanied that command left her almost breathless and quivering. "There's a planet there named Vulcan. It seems only right that it be our first stop."

END

ACKNOWLEDGMENTS

Many people helped with the creation of this novel and series. I would like to thank them all but will have to settle for a huge thank you to the members of my Future Classics critique group for wading through the early versions, especially Melanie Fletcher, who read it even one more time. And special thanks to Blake Sheets, Amelia Greig, Tim Morgan, William Frank, and Stanley Love for their much-valued technical help.

ABOUT THE AUTHOR

William Ledbetter is a Nebula Award winning author with two novels and more than seventy speculative fiction short stories and non-fiction articles published in five languages, in markets such as Asimov's, Fantasy & Science Fiction, Analog, Escape Pod and the SFWA blog. He's been a space and technology geek since childhood and spent most of his non-writing career in the aerospace and defense industry. He is a member of SFWA, the National Space Society of North Texas, and a Launch Pad Astronomy workshop graduate. He lives near Dallas with his wife, a needy dog and three spoiled cats.

facebook.com/william.ledbetter

goodreads.com/william_ledbetter

INTERSTELLAR FLIGHT PRESS

Interstellar Flight Press is an indie speculative publishing house. We feature innovative works from the best new writers in science fiction and fantasy. In the words of Ursula K. Le Guin, we need "writers who can see alternatives to how we live now, can see through our fear-stricken society and its obsessive technologies to other ways of being, and even imagine real grounds for hope."

Find us online at www.interstellarflightpress.com.

 facebook.com/interstellarflightpress

 x.com/intflightpress

 instagram.com/interstellarflightpress

patreon.com/interstellarflightpress